reSet

T0150985

I DON'T
WANT TO KNOW
ANYONE TOO WELL

I Don't Want to Know Anyone Too Well

NORMAN LEVINE

FOREWORD AND AFTERWORD
BY JOHN METCALF

BIBLIOASIS
WINDSOR, ONTARIO

Library and Archives Canada Cataloguing in Publication

Levine, Norman, 1923–
[Short stories]
      I don't want to know anyone too well / Norman Levine.

(reSet books)
Collected short stories.
Issued in print and electronic formats.
ISBN 978-1-77196-088-5 (paperback).—ISBN 978-1-77196-089-2 (ebook)

      I. Title.   II. Title: Short stories

PS8523.E87 2016   C813'.54   C2016-901178-X
C2016-901179-8

Readied for the press by Daniel Wells
Copy-edited by Emily Donaldson
Cover and text design by Gordon Robertson

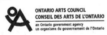

Published with the generous assistance of the Canada Council for the Arts, which last year invested $153 million to bring the arts to Canadians throughout the country and the financial support of the Government of Canada. Biblioasis also acknowledges the support of the Ontario Arts Council (OAC), an agency of the Government of Ontario, which last year funded 1,709 individual artists and 1,078 organizations in 204 communities across Ontario, for a total of $52.1 million, and the contribution of the Government of Ontario through the Ontario Book Publishing Tax Credit and the Ontario Media Development Corporation.

PRINTED AND BOUND IN CANADA

MIX
Paper from
responsible sources
FSC® C004071

CONTENTS

FOREWORD

NORMAN LEVINE'S stories stand at the very centre of achievement in Canadian short story writing. His masterful stories are already a familiar part of our mental and emotional furniture. Everyone has their own favourites, but I could not imagine Canadian literature without such stories as "By the Richelieu," "A Small Piece of Blue," "We all Begin in a Little Magazine," and "Champagne Barn."

The stories may be familiar—but they are decidedly not comfortable. In them Levine conveys various forms of displacement, of discontent, of alienation, of loss. Like Alexander Marsden, the roundabout maker in "A Canadian Upbringing," Levine left Canada "because he [felt] the need to accept a wider view of life." Levine stands aside, observing life's to and fro; he elected to be a permanent outsider as immigrant, as resident alien, as writer, as Jew.

The Cambridge Guide to Literature in English says of Levine's work: "Written in a tight, economic prose style, his stories evoke places vividly and frequently focus on social outsiders, the problems of the writer's life and his Jewish-Canadian upbringing." *The Oxford Companion to Twentieth Century*

Literature in English says: "Levine's spare, understated prose style is seen at its best in his short stories. Predominantly first-person narratives, they exhibit a keen eye for external details, but their prime concern is with the subjective experience of the outsider."

While Levine's writing always *seems* clear and simple, the stories themselves are far more complicated than the simplicity of language suggests. One might say that his work is as simple or as subtle as the people reading it. The stories usually function as an accretion of images—all of which contribute to the story's emotional current, adding tiny detail to what will be the finished shape. Levine refuses to explain or interpret his scenes for us, requiring us, in a sense, to *compose* the story for ourselves. It is that act of composition that turns these stories into such powerful emotional experiences.

Consider "Champagne Barn," for instance. We are treated to a range of scenes and images: the Senior Citizens' Home where one of the residents, Mr. Tessier, has watched 68 corpses carried out over the years; the mindless chatter of the narrator's mother; a restaurant meal with the narrator's spinster cousin who is in her forties and still a virgin; a meeting with a childhood friend who has become a butcher; a tour of the decaying neighbourhood of the narrator's childhood. The story ends with the hack, hack, hack of the butchers' choppers in Reinhardt Foods. The last line: "I would carry that sound with me long after I left."

As we will carry this story with us. Levine has created a world in this marvellous story—a world deftly suggested and then nailed with telling detail. He forces us to compose meaning from the seemingly random encounters and events in five days of the narrator's life. Through the vividness of his detail (steely master that he is) he moves us to brood on the narrator's life, a brooding which overflows the story's bounds and compels us to confront our own direction and mortality.

This way of writing is essentially poetic and it is no surprise that Norman Levine's first two books were collections of poetry: *Myssium* (1948) and *The Tight-Rope Walker* (1950).

> The beat and the still
> And the beat, caught, lift,
> Of the rook and the gull
> Over sea, roof, hill
> Disturb this place from sleep.

Of these lines he wrote: "It was the first line—describing the way the bird flew—that made me realize that the leaner the language the more ambiguous it becomes, and the more suggestive . . . The more you tell—the more you are keeping the reader out from bringing his or her experience in. So if you can reduce a thing to a minimum like 'The beat and the still'—then the reader brings his or her associations to that. So contrary to what people think: the more cryptic you are the more resonance there is." (Metcalf, J., and J.R. Tim Struthers, eds. *How Stories Mean*. Erin, ON: The Porcupine's Quill, 1993.)

Levine's work has resonated with readers in England and Europe for many years. Canada has been slower to respond. *The Times* said that Norman Levine's work was marked by "timeless elegance." *Encounter* said: "Norman Levine is one of the most outstanding short-story writers working in English today." *Le Monde*, a paper not given to rhapsody, simply compared him with Chekhov.

* * *

Norman and I remained in fairly close contact. I have long admired the integrity and courage of his artistic life. I once said to him that we had both left our countries of origin and that I thought he had made the right decision and that I had probably made the wrong one. He replied that we had both made decisions that suited our personalities.

After a brief stint in London, Norman moved to St. Ives— "silence, exile, cunning"—and began forging his style, the main preoccupation of most modernist writers. Norman's mature work is marked by its fragmentation, unorthodox grammar, and denial of cadence. We can imagine the effect upon his youthful work of daily contact with such blossoming abstract painters as Peter Lanyon, Terry Frost, Patrick Heron, Roger Hilton, and Bryan Wynter all with their own preoccupation with technical innovation.

Norman wrote:

If it hadn't been for St. Ives, and especially the painters I grew up with, I wouldn't be the writer I am.

Another thing I got from the painters was the need for immediacy. When they finished a painting they wanted me to see it in their studio. And there it was. At a glance. Through the eyes. Onto the nervous system. I remember thinking: how could I get this immediacy in writing? And I remember Peter Lanyon telling me, in his studio, that all that mattered was the work. 'You take something from life. Make something from it. Then you give it back to life.'

In an interview with Cary Fagan in *Descant* 40 (Spring 1983), Levine said:

. . . the visual is very strong for me. I believe a writer, or anyone, should have a good pair of eyes. If I can see something and describe it in very plain language that's about as much as anybody can do. The straitjacket of language deadens any kind of emotion, any kind of excitement. You're always working within a deadening effect which language has on the feelings which you've experienced through your eyes. So you've got to somehow get this excitement from the feeling that helps you select the kind of words in the order that will give you some of that excitement when you read them. That sounds complicated but it isn't. It's very simple.

In a special Levine issue of *Canadian Notes and Queries* Cynthia Flood wrote brilliantly on the evolution of Levine's style.

Like a painter himself, Levine lays down colour, line, mass, dimension, angle.

'All vegetation was killed by the sulphur that the wind carried from the Sinter Plant. You could see the direction of the wind. It was like a scar in the landscape. In the distance, on either side, I could see more hills with the blue-black outline of growing trees on them. But here everything was dead. The rocks the colour of ashes and the burned-out remnants of trees sticking up like a field of gibbets.'

That was 1958. An older Levine would peel out 'You could see,' 'It was like,' 'I could see, on them' and 'sticking up like a field of gibbets' (he is not a simile fan), but the simple diction and spatial clarity continue.

'She had kept everything neat and clean. Now a thin layer of dust was on the furniture and on the wooden floor, and on the leaves of the plants in the front room. The earth was dry. I watered the plants. Looked in the fridge. A few potatoes were sprouting. The pears were bruised…'

That's 1991…

We must see the images singly, if we're to read Levine.

'Past Bytown Museum that always seemed shut. Past the jail with its high, smallgreystone walls. Up Laurier Bridge. The horse straining.'

So precise. To reach this plainness, Levine abandons plain sentences.

'The glare from the snow. Washing hanging out. The long winter underwear. Then by an open crossing with the red arm flashing in and out like a heartbeat, the cars waiting on either side. Why can't I settle for this?'

To strip out all that plugs up prose: that is Levine's aim. Articles, linking verbs, clause-breeding relative pronouns, wordy modifiers—dangerous. They draw attention to themselves. Worse, they smother energy. Readers, rolling along the shiny habitual rails of subject and predicate, enter the familiar sentence-tunnel knowing when the verb will arrive and the terminal light appear. We read to reach an expected end. That habit Levine wants to break. We are to *look*. Outside the train.

The following passage from the late story "Soap Opera" describes the narrator's mother's apartment. The narrator is staying in the apartment while visiting his mother who is in hospital and thought to be nearing her end.

I opened the door of her apartment. In the half-light I could see the three small rooms. Brought the suitcase in, quickly drew the curtains, and opened the windows. All the clocks had stopped.

The place looked as if it had been left in a hurry. In the kitchen, dishes on the draining-board were upside down. In the bedroom the large bed was not made. A dress was on the back of the rocking-chair. Two-tone, beige and brown shoes were under the bed. The calendar had not been changed in two months.

She had kept everything neat and clean. Now a thin layer of dust was on the furniture and on the wooden floor. And on the leaves of the plants in the front room. The earth was dry. I watered the plants. Looked in the fridge. A few potatoes were sprouting. The pears were bruised and had started to go rotten. I couldn't understand why Sarah hadn't tidied up. There was some half-used cottage cheese, a bottle of apple juice, a tin of *Ensure*. The cupboard, by the sink, was packed with tins as if for a siege. I made a cup of coffee, brought it into the front room, sat by the table and started to relax.

I had not been here on my own before. How small and still. And full of light. The chesterfield set, from the house, was too large. She brightened the settee with crocheted covers—bands of red, yellow, green—that kept slipping down. And cushions with embroidered leaves of all kinds. The same was on the chair, by the side of the window, overlooking the street and the small park. (The Lombardy poplars are gone. But the gazebo is there. And the kids throwing a ball around.) On the other side of the window, against the wall, a large black and white television was on the floor. No longer working. Its use, to support the plants on its top. Beside it: the glass-enclosed wooden cabinet with her best dishes, best cups, saucers, the Chinese plate that goes back to my childhood, the Bernard Leach mugs and bowl that I brought back on visits from St. Ives. On top of the cabinet a family tree. Small, round, black and white photographs in metal frames hung from metal branches. Father and mother, in the park by the river, some fifty years ago. Sara and I . . . when we were around ten and eight . . . the people we married . . . our children . . . with their husbands . . . their children . . .

The first things to remark on about this passage are its simplicity, its fidelity to detail, its seemingly documentary quality. What *he* sees is what *you* get, narrator as camera. But is this, in fact, what Levine is up to? For though I would insist absolutely that each detail is itself absolutely—the stopped clocks are stopped clocks, the dust is dust, the bruised pears are bruised pears—the slow (plodding, say the insensitive) accumulation of physical detail, because of the context, (the old woman lying in the hospital, death possibly approaching), the accumulation of physical detail begins to turn into an emotional "atmosphere," each detail, while always itself, becomes something larger than itself. *Not* a symbol, God save us! But a tremor in the near-invisible web Levine is spinning.

Given the context of the possibility of the mother's death, can we persist in reading these paragraphs as flat documentary?

"In the half-light."

"All the clocks had stopped."

"left in a hurry"

"the calendar ... had not been changed in two months."

"now a thin layer of dust was on the furniture"

"and on the leaves of the plants."

"The earth was dry."

"The pears were bruised and had started to go rotten."

"packed with tins as if for a siege."

"crocheted covers that kept slipping down."

"with embroidered leaves"

"The Lombardy poplars are gone."

Television "No longer working."

"On top of the cabinet a family tree. Small, round, black and white photographs in metal frames hung from metal branches. Father and mother, in the park by the river, some fifty years ago. Sara and I ... when we were around ten and eight ... the people we married ... our children ... with their husbands ... their children ..."

Things broken, slipping, abandoned, bruised, stopped ...

Flat documentary?

Or something much closer, perhaps, to ... poetry?

*   *   *

Norman Levine died in 2005. I wrote the following obituary for *The Independent* at the request of his daughter, Carrie.

It was written in great sorrow and as an act of homage.

Norman Albert Levine, writer: born Rakow, Poland, 22 October 1923; married 1951 Margaret Payne (died 1978; three daughters), 1983 Anne Sarginson (marriage dissolved); died Darlington, Durham, 14 June 2005.

In the late forties, after having served as a pilot and bomb-aimer with the RCAF, flying Lancasters out of Leeming, North Yorkshire, Norman Levine decided to leave Canada's cultural desert and return to an England he had come to admire. What had attracted him, he wrote was "seeing paintings, hearing concerts, reading new books and *New Writing*. And, especially, seeing how the English lived and behaved in wartime."

In those early days he was introduced in a Thames-side pub to poet George Barker who said to him: "Sorry, chum, nothing personal. But coming from Canada, you haven't got a chance."

Levine who died at the age of 81 on June 14, 2005 spent many years of his life in St. Ives, Cornwall, proving George Barker profoundly wrong. Like all modernists, he spent his life forging and honing a signature style. His was fragmentary and imagistic, prose stripped to the bone, conventional expectations of rhythm denied forcing the reader into a new, intimate, and uneasy relationship with the word on the page. His most important story collections were *Champagne Barn*, *Something Happened Here*, *By a Frozen River*, and *The Ability to Forget*.

Canada has never recognized Levine's amazing talent and achievement. Canada's cultural nationalists have never forgiven Levine for his 1958 autobiographical travel book *Canada Made Me*. The book closed with the words, "I wondered why I felt so bitter about Canada. It was foolish to believe that you can take the throwouts, the rejects, the human kickabouts from Europe and tell them: Here is your second chance. Here you can start a new life. But no one ever mentioned the price you had to pay, and how much of yourself you have to betray."

Written at the beginning of a boosterish period, this rather sour look at Canada's underbelly closed for Levine the possibility of Canadian publication. It was to be 17 years before another Levine title appeared in Canada.

Levine was always by temperament and choice an outsider. As a Jew, as a resident alien, as an immigrant, he was always on the margins observing with an unsentimental eye. His stories usually have an elegiac quality and typically explore loss, impermanence, and the fragility of human hopes. He wrote in the story "Soap Opera": "...whenever I go to a new place and walk around to get to know it, I inevitably end up in a cemetery."

The son of an impoverished fruit-peddler who plied his trade with a horse and cart, Levine at 18 volunteered for officer training and was sent on a course to take what he used to call "gentleman lessons." These he duly learned but he belonged to no class or cause. If he believed in anything it might have been Chekhov.

If Levine was ignored in Canada, his reputation in England and Europe was high. The *Times Literary Supplement* described his work as "masterly." *The Times* talked of his "Timeless elegance..." and *Encounter* wrote: "Norman Levine is one of the most outstanding short story writers working in English today."

In Europe his German translator was Nobel laureate Heinrich Böll and in recent years his work has been translated in Holland, Switzerland, and France.

Younger writers in Canada now are slowly discovering his work and some have been directly influenced by his stylistic experiments. Michael Winter, a young writer directly influenced, said of him: "His style is not one that appeals to a lot of people, but a lot of writers marvel at his talent . . . His economy of so little saying so much—when you try to write like that, you realize how hard it is to capture things accurately and truthfully with very few words. He was a writer's writer."

* * *

Dave Godfrey, founder of presses, spokesperson, *animateur* of nationalist *brouhaha*, won the Governor General's Award for his 1970 novel *The New Ancestors*, a tome the *Oxford Companion to Canadian Literature* describes admiringly as "an Einsteinian vision of relative values." The indefatigable Professor John Moss of the University of Ottawa judged the book "as monumental an achievement as our literature has yet produced."

In the same year, Norman Levine published *From a Seaside Town*.

The New Ancestors drifts down towards history's footnotes while Norman Levine, who never won anything and ended his life on a stipend from a charity for indigent writers, stands more and more clearly revealed as at the centre of our literature, one of its most radiant figures.

Unheralded as he is, he is my daily companion.

John Metcalf
Ottawa, 2017

A FATHER

THERE IS A PICTURE of my father that is still around the
house in Ottawa. It shows a youngish, handsome man with
a magnificent moustache, waxed ends; a fine head with
black wavy hair, and eyes that I know to be brown. That picture was taken in Warsaw. And to it belong the anecdotes: "Man
about Town," "Friend of writers and painters," ("Yes, I knew
writers. I used to buy them meals.") "Owner of a shoe concern,"
("You can always tell if the leather's good by the way it creases,").
And "Smuggler"—I'd like to think it was of diamonds.

I never knew that man.

The person I got to know in Ottawa was in his early forties,
a fruit peddler. Slightly built, bald, with a sardonic face. And
very emotional.

He was five foot four, yet he had the highest wagon of all
the Ottawa peddlers. It was painted a bright red. And it had,
on its sides, wooden steps and iron rungs to help him get up
to the driver's seat and to the wooden boxes where he kept the
fruit and vegetables. Over the years the red wagon was pulled
by a succession of second-hand horses—discards from the
local bakeries and dairies. Yet even these nags could place him
in difficulties. The one that was around the longest was called

Jim. A heavy white horse with nicotine-coloured tufts, and a delicate slow walk. My father jerked the reins. He said, "Gid-yup." He shouted, "C'mon Jim." He even used the whip. But the horse ignored them all, until it was time to go home. Then he would gallop—the wagon swayed as it went through red lights, took corners flat out: Father pulling back on the reins, standing up, fists against his chest, red in the face—until he turned into Murray Street.

Mother watching on the veranda took this running as a sign that the wagon was empty and Father had a good day.

Saturday was a fruit peddler's busiest day. And being twelve, and not having to go to school, I'd go peddling with my father. I'd walk along Murray Street (our lunch in brown paper bags that Mother made up), past the houses of sleeping friends. Up King Edward Boulevard. Between the large elms where I skated and skied in winter. Crossed the streetcar tracks at Dalhousie. Hung around the Français, looked at all the stills. By the time I arrived in the Market the clock in the Peace Tower showed after eight. And my father had bought the load and loaded it on the wagon himself. He had left the yard, behind the house, in the dark, before five.

When we came back that night he put the horse in the stable, gave him oats, hay, water. And by the time he had unloaded, washed, eaten, counted his takings, it was nearly eleven. Then he joined the others outside. A whole street sat on the wooden verandas, in rocking-chairs, on the veranda steps, in the shade of the hanging morning glory.

In winter, Saturday nights were spent in the kitchen around the linoleum-covered table playing cards. The play-ers came from different parts of Ottawa. How much of these sessions was due to gambling fever, I don't know. But some of it, I'm sure, was just to get together with their own kind. They played from Saturday night right through Sunday and usually Sunday night as well.

The games they played were twenty-one and poker. And for holding the game in our house Mother collected ten cents from each pot.

I'd watch. Standing behind the players' chairs, so I could see their hole cards. If they were winning they wanted me to stay behind them. They said I gave them good luck. If they lost, they said I was making them nervous, and I moved on.

Around ten I'd be sent to bed—school tomorrow. Upstairs, in the dark, I listened to the sounds of the game that came through the floor-boards and wondered when we would be raided by the police.

Nearly all the players were born in Europe and had come to Ottawa just before or after the First World War. There was Shalevsky—he used to deliver bread for a Lower Town bakery (he gave me rides on his sleigh) before he went into real estate. There was Joe—the youngest player (he was born in Ottawa)—he drove for the same bakery after Shalevsky left, then worked as a porter at the Lord Elgin and told me marvellous stories of what went on in the hotel. He was killed delivering a new car from Toronto. There was Harry, our silent roomer, who worked for his cousin in a paper factory—he sorted the rags the rag peddlers brought in. He died of lung cancer. There was Mr. Nadolny, and Soloway, also fruit peddlers. And Sam Shainbaum, who had a fruit store uptown, then went into real estate. And I hear he's made a bit of money too. The only woman among the men was my mother. She won fairly consistently. My father always lost.

He made costly mistakes. He thought the ace of clubs was the ace of spades—in a flush hand. He mistook numbers. He took twice as long as anyone else to decide whether to call, pass, or make a bet. They always had to wait for him. And when he ran out of money he reached over for a couple of dollars from my mother's winnings—a habit she didn't like. After a while of his inept card-playing, Sam Shainbaum said,

"Why don't you give up, Moyshe?"

"You're spoiling the game," Soloway said.

"Why do you have to think so long when you've got nothing?" my mother said.

"Just one more hand," he pleaded with her, having gone through five dollars of her winnings.

"You'll only lose it."

"Just Nadolny's deal."

He tried this time. He had a pair of tens showing, but he didn't raise. When the five cards were dealt my father passed to Soloway, who had four hearts showing. Soloway bet a dollar, and my father, who didn't have a dollar to call, folded up his cards.

Soloway began to rake in the money.

"I wasn't bluffing, Moyshe," he said. "I've got the flush."

He turned up his hole card—a seven of hearts.

No one spoke.

"I didn't have to show it to him," Soloway said angrily to the others.

On the next deal they missed him out. He watched the cards go to either side of him for a couple more deals. Then he got up and stood behind my mother. After that he didn't play any more.

Instead, he went on errands for the players. He went to Dain's on the corner and came back with a brown paper bag of soft drinks. He opened up the bottles, handed them around. In below zero he walked to the Smoke Bar on Rideau Street and came back with corn beef, smoked meat, rye bread, that he made into untidy sandwiches; gave them to the players, and to me as well. And apart from a quiet game of casino during the weekdays with his cronies who dropped in for a social call, no one played cards seriously with him any more.

In February 1944, I was on the last day of embarkation leave. I was sitting in the living room with my parents, in a brand new pilot officer's uniform, waiting for a taxi to come to take me to the Union Station. Mother had cried earlier. She was sure I wouldn't come back. And as we waited she sat in the chesterfield chair staring in my direction. Her anxiety unnerved me as well and I remained in the chair not knowing what to do or say.

"You know this town called Chelm," Father said. "A town of halfwits?"

I nodded, wondering what he was getting at.

"They were having trouble with a cat. They decided to get rid of it." He got up from the chair and stood in front of Mother and me. "They went to the beadle and convinced him that it would be a blessing for him if he put the cat in a sack and went with the sack to the bottom of the river."

My father paused.

"The beadle drowned. The cat managed to get out and scrambled ashore."

My father came over and touched me on the shoulder. "The wise men had another council. They decided to tell the people to bring pieces of furniture. And the people of Chelm came back with brooms, tables, beds, chairs. Piled the stuff in a heap in the shul. Put the cat inside. Set fire to the wood. Locked the doors."

My father grinned.

"The shul burned down. The cat, feeling the heat, leapt through the window ... Then the wise men had another meeting. They decided to approach their hero, Abrasha—he killed twenty Cossacks in one pogrom. They told Abrasha to take the cat up their highest building, the old people's home, and jump." My father was speaking with eloquent gestures.

"Abrasha said a weeping goodbye to his wife and children. He took the cat in his arms. All of Chelm came to watch. He climbed to the top of the old people's home. The band played the national anthem. When they finished, Abrasha jumped. Abrasha was killed. The cat, on the way down, wriggled loose and landed safe."

My father was laughing. And I laughed because he was. And we both glanced to where Mother sat. And though she didn't join us she had visibly relaxed. And suddenly I felt immensely proud of my father—who cared about those cards.

"Two liars met in the street," my father said with growing confidence. "And one liar said to the other: *Guess what I saw today—?*"

But the doorbell went. It was the taxi. We embraced and kissed and said goodbye.

I was riding away to war in a taxi. Along the streets I had walked and played as a child. Murray Street looked drab, empty, frozen. Solemn boxes with wooden verandas. Brown double doors and double windows. Not a soul was outside. On King Edward the snow heaped in the centre had a frozen crust. It glittered underneath the street lights. And the houses, on either side, in shadow, appeared even more boarded up, as if you would have to go through several layers before you found something living.

IN QUEBEC CITY

I N THE WINTER of 1944 when I was twenty and in the RCAF I was stationed for seven weeks in Quebec City. Fifty newly commissioned pilot officers were billeted in an old building right opposite a cigarette factory. It used to be a children's school. The wooden steps were wide and worn in the middle but they rose only a few inches at a time.

We were sent here to kill time and to learn how to behave like officers. Some of the earlier Canadian Air Force officers who were sent to England lacked the social graces. So they had us play games. We took turns pretending we were orderly officers, putting men on charge; being entertainment officers, providing the escort for a military funeral. We were instructed how to use knives and forks. How to make a toast. How to eat and drink properly. It was like going to a finishing school.

To keep fit we were taken on early morning route marches. We walked and ran through frozen side streets, then across a bridge to Lévis. And came back tired but with rosy cheeks. Evenings and weekends were free. We would get into taxis and drive to the top restaurants, have a steak and french fries, see a movie. On Sunday we behaved like tourists. Took pictures of Champlain, Bishop Laval, The Golden Dog, the Château

Frontenac, the wall around the city, the steps to Lower Town. There was not much else to do.

On the Monday of the second week Gordie Greenway, who was make-believe orderly officer for the day, came up to me during lunch.

"Someone rang asking for you."

"Who?" I asked. I didn't know anyone in Quebec.

"They didn't give their name," he said and continued his tour of inspection.

Next morning I received this letter.

Quebec, 15 January.

Dear Pilot Officer Jimmy Ross,

We would be honoured if you could come to dinner this Friday. It would give me and my wife much pleasure to meet you. If I don't hear from you I'll take it that we'll see you on Friday at eight.

Yours sincerely,
Mendel Rubin

Out of curiosity, I decided to go. The taxi driver drove to the most expensive part, just off Grande Allée, and stopped at the base of a horseshoe drive in front of a square stone building with large windows set in the stone.

I rang the bell.

A maid in black and white uniform opened the door. She said with a French accent, "Come in, sir." I came inside. A short man in a grey suit came quickly up to me, hand outstretched. He wore rimless glasses and had neat waves in his dark hair.

"I'm so glad you could come," he said smiling. "My name is Mendel Rubin. Let me have your coat and hat. You didn't have any trouble getting here?"

"No," I said.

He led me into the living room. And introduced his wife, Frieda. She was taller than he was, an attractive dark-haired woman. Then their daughter, Constance. She was around seventeen or eighteen, like her mother, but not as pretty.

"It's nice of you to ask me over," I said.

"Our pleasure," Mendel said. "Now, what will you drink. Gin? Scotch? Sherry?"

"Gin is fine," I said.

He went to a cupboard at the far end of the room.

"Where are you from?" Frieda asked.

"Ottawa."

"I've been there a few times," she said. "But I don't know it well. Mendel knows it better."

He came back with drinks on a tray.

"Do you know the Raports?" he asked. "The Coopers? The Sugarmans?"

"I went to school with some of the kids," I said.

"Where do you live?"

"On Chapel Street—in Sandy Hill."

"It's a part of Ottawa I don't know too well," he said. "What does your father do?"

"He's a teacher."

The maid came in to announce that dinner was ready. And we walked towards the dining room.

"I bet it's a while since you have had a Jewish meal," he said.

"Yes," I said, "it is."

"Every time a new draft comes in I find out if there are any Jewish officers. Then we have them up. It's nice to be with your own kind—you can take certain things for granted. Come, sit down here." And he put me in a chair opposite Constance.

While Mendel talked I had a chance to glance around the room. The walls were covered with some kind of creeper. The green leaves, like ivy leaves, clung to the walls on trelliswork and to the frames of oil paintings. The paintings looked amateurish, as if they had been painted by numbers.

"Do you like the pictures?" Mendel asked. "My wife painted them."

"They're very good," I said.

Mendel did most of the talking during the meal. He said they were a tiny community. They had to get their rye bread, their kosher meat, flown in from Montreal.

"We're so few that the butcher is only a butcher in the back of the shop. In the front he sells antiques."

After the meal we returned to the other room. It was dimly lit. The chandelier looked pretty but did not give much light and there were small lights underneath more of Frieda's pictures on the walls. The far wall was one large slab of glass. It had now become a mirror. And I could see our selves in this room, in the dark glass, as something remote.

Mendel went to a cupboard and brought back vodka, brandy, whisky, liqueurs. He gave me a large cigar.

"You know what I feel like after a meal like that? How about we all go to the theatre?"

"But it's half past nine," Constance said.

"How time goes when you're enjoying yourself," Mendel said. Then he glanced at his wrist. "I think we'll still catch it."

He walked to the far cupboard and turned on a radio. A Strauss waltz was being played. It stopped, and a commercial came on. A sepulchral voice boomed, "*Rubin's*." And then "*bins . . . bins . . .*" echoed down long corridors. Then another voice spoke rapidly in French. And again, "*Rubin's*" and the echoing *bins . . .*

He switched the radio off.

"I have a store in Lower Town. We carry quality goods and some cheap lines. Sometime I'll show you around, Jimmy. But what can we do *now*?"

"Mummy can play the piano," Constance said. "She plays very well."

"I don't," Frieda protested.

"Play us something," Mendel said.

Frieda went to the piano and played "Für Elise" and some Chopin, while we drank brandy and coffee and smoked cigars.

At eleven he was driving me back to the children's school.

"Do you know the one about the two Anglican ministers?"

"No," I said.

"There were these two Anglican ministers," Mendel said. "One had seven children. The other had none. The one with the seven children asked the other, 'How do you do it?'"

"'I use the safe period,' the other minister said.

"'What is that?'

"'When *you* go out of the house—*I* come in. It's safe then.'"

And Mendel laughed.

"Here's another one. There was this Jewish tailor. He had an audience with the Pope. When he got back to Montreal they asked him—'How was the Pope?'

"'A nice-looking man,' the Jewish tailor said. 'Thirty-six chest, 32 waist, 28 inside leg...'

"Are you taking out Constance tomorrow night?"

"Yes," I said.

I took her to a movie. We got on fine. On Sunday we went out in the country to ski. We skied for miles. We both seemed to have so much energy. We came to a hill. I went down first. She followed and fell at the bottom. I picked her up and we kissed.

"My father is worried that I'll be an old maid," she said, laughing.

I didn't think he needed to have any worries about that.

"He only lets me go out with Jewish boys."

We kissed again.

"Am I going to have a baby?"

"You don't have babies that way," I said.

"I know. But I have a girlfriend in Montreal. She told me that if you let a boy kiss you like that you can become pregnant."

Although I was being thrown together with Constance (we went out often for meals; saw movies; had romantic night rides in a sleigh, wrapped in fur skins, behind the swaying rump of a horse) and Mendel took me to several hockey games, it was

Frieda who interested me. But so far I didn't have a chance to be alone with her. If Mendel was there, he didn't let anyone else talk. If Constance was there, I was expected to be with her.

I managed to get away from the children's school early one Wednesday and drove up to the house to find that Mendel and Constance had driven to his branch store in Three Rivers.

"I was just reading," Frieda said when I came into the living room.

She got me a drink. We stood by the glass wall looking out. It's a nice time, in winter, just before it gets dark. When the snow on the ground has some blue in it, so has the sky. She told me she came from Saint John, New Brunswick. Her father was a doctor. At seventeen her parents sent her to Montreal. "Just the way we worry about Constance." She met Mendel. He was working for his father, who founded Rubin's Department Store in Quebec. She was eighteen when they married and Constance came along when she was nineteen.

"After she grew up I found I had nothing to do with my time. And when I tried things—I found that I can't do anything well. That's my trouble."

"You had Constance," I said.

"Anybody can do that," she said contemptuously.

"I tried to paint—I have all these nice pictures in my head—but look how they come out. I tried writing—but it was the same. Sometimes when I'm walking through the streets or in a restaurant I see something. It excites me. But what can I do with it? There's no one I can even tell it to. I hardly go out of the house now. I feel trapped."

"Can't you leave Quebec City," I asked, "for a short—"

"I don't mean by this place," she interrupted. "I mean by life."

This conversation was out of my depth. I didn't know what she wanted. But her presence excited me far more than did Constance's.

"I taught myself French," she said, "so I could read Colette in the original. And I have my flowers. Do you like flowers?"

"Yes," I said. "I like the colours."

She led me to her conservatory. It was full of orchids: yellows, purples, oranges, pinks, browns. There were other exotic flowers. I didn't know their names. There were several creepers overhead. And a smell of jasmine from the one in a corner. But it was mostly orchids, and in different stages. Some were only beginning to grow. They seemed to be growing out of stuck-together clusters of grotesque gooseberries. While outside the glass of the conservatory, the thick snow had a frozen crust. It glittered underneath the street light.

She showed me a striped orchid on the table in the hall. Yellow with delicate brown stripes. It was open and curved in such a way that you could see deep inside the flower.

"Do you know how Colette describes an orchid?"

"No," I said.

"Like a female genital organ—I have shocked you," she said with a smile. "I would be promiscuous if I was a man. I know it. I wouldn't be like my husband. He's so old-fashioned—telling jokes. But I can't do anything like that here. If I step out of line—"

She broke off again. She would talk, follow a thought, then, unable to see it through, break into something else.

"Poor Mendel. He desperately gets in touch with every Jewish officer who comes to Quebec. Throws them together with Constance as much as he can. Then they go overseas. They promise to write. But they never do."

I heard a car drive up. Mendel and Constance came through the door.

"Hello Jimmy," he said. "Boy, it's a cold night."

The other officers complained about the deadness of the place. They thought I was lucky. Some met girls through a church dance or YMCA do. A few could speak French. Most tried to pick something up.

Tucker and Fleming got into trouble, accused of raping a waitress. But nothing came of the charge, except they were confined for three days to a make-believe cell in the children's school.

I tried to get Frieda alone again. The only time I did she was upset. The boiler for the conservatory had broken down.

"You must get a plumber," she appealed to me. "If I can't get a plumber the orchids will die."

I got a taxi into Lower Town. Half an hour later I came back with a French-Canadian plumber.

Our time was up. To see how we finally passed, the Air Force organized a ball at the Château Frontenac, and all the eligible debutantes from Quebec and district were invited to be escorted by the officers. I took Constance. She looked very nice in a long white gown. We danced, made small talk, ate, passed the carafe of wine around. The dance band played.

> *To you he might be just another guy*
> *To me he means a million other things.*
> *An ordinary fellow with his heart up in the sky,*
> *He wears a pair of silver wings.*

Air marshals made speeches calling us "Knights of the Air," "Captains of the Clouds."

At half past two we left the Château Frontenac. In the taxi, driving back, she pressed against my side.

"Don't you love me a bit, Jimmy?" she said softly.

"I'll be gone in a few days," I said.

She took my hand.

"Would you like to come up to my room? You'll have to be very quiet going up the stairs. I'll set the alarm for six. You'll have to be out by then."

I wondered how many times this had happened before.

"Is this the first time?" I asked.

"No," she said. "There have been other officers passing through." She squeezed my hand. "I didn't like them as much as you."

"How many others?"

"Four. This will be my fifth time."

She spoke too soon. After we went up the stairs, closed the door of her room, undressed, got into bed, turned out the light. I found I couldn't do a thing. And she didn't know how to help things along.

"Let's have a cigarette," I said, "and relax for a while."

I lit one for her and one for me. We lay on our backs, the cigarette ends glowing in the dark.

I was wondering what to do when I heard a door open. Then footsteps. Someone was walking in the corridor. The footsteps stopped by the door.

"Con, are you awake?"

It was Frieda on the other side.

We both stopped breathing. I was aware of Constance's body becoming tense with fear.

"Con—you awake?"

She was lying beside me, not moving, breathing deeply and rapidly.

I waited for the steps to go away, the sound of a far door closing. I put out our cigarettes. And took her easily.

"That was the best yet," she said softly. "Goodnight darling. Wake me before you go."

She lay on her side, away from me, asleep. And I lay on my back, wide awake. I listened to the ticking clock, her regular breathing, and thought of Frieda.

Just after five I got out of bed, dressed, disconnected the alarm, straightened the covers on Constance, and went out of the room, down the stairs, and out.

It was snowing. Everything was white and quiet. It felt marvellous walking, flakes slant, very fine. I didn't feel at all tired. I heard a church bell strike and somewhere further the sound of a train whistle, the two notes like the bass part of a mouth organ. The light changed to the dull grey of early morning and the darker shapes of a church, a convent, came in and out of the falling snow.

Next day we were confined to barracks and told to pack. That afternoon we boarded a train for Halifax. And at Halifax we walked from the train onto the waiting troopship. Two weeks later we docked at Liverpool.

Those first few months in England were exciting. I moved around a lot. A week in Bournemouth in the Majestic Hotel. Ten days' leave in London. Then a small station, in Scotland, for advanced flying on Ansons. Then operational training near Leamington on Wellingtons. Before I was posted to a Lancaster squadron in Yorkshire.

Perhaps it was this moving around? Perhaps it was being twenty, away from Canada for the first time, spring, meeting new people, new situations? The uniform was open sesame to all sorts of places. And there were plenty of girls around. I had forgotten about the Rubins except to send them a postcard from London.

In the middle of May I had an air-letter, redirected twice, from Constance.

> Dear Jimmy,
> I hope this will reach you soon. Probably you are having all kinds of exciting things happen to you … meeting new people … doing things … and you have long forgotten me and the time we had together. I hope not.
> Now my news. We're just getting over winter. It's been a long one, cold and lots of snow. The next lot of officers after you was a complete washout. But the one now has three Jewish officers. Shatsky and Dworkin from Montreal. And Lubell from Winnipeg. None of them are as

nice as you ... but I like Shatsky best ... he's fun.

Don't forget to write when you can and take care.

Mummy and Daddy send their regards. We all miss you.

Love,

Constance.

Two months later I received a carton of Macdonald cigarettes from Mendel. I bet he sent them to all the boys he had
up at the house.

When the war was over I went back to Ottawa and to the job
I had in the government with the construction department.
In my absence I was promoted. Now I'm assistant to the Head.

I have not married. Nor had I been to Quebec City, until
this winter when I had to go to New Brunswick to see about
a proposed dam that the federal government was thinking of
putting some money in. The plane stopped at Quebec longer
than the usual stop to let off and pick up passengers. A blizzard
was blowing. Flying was off. A limousine brought us from the
snow fields of the airport to the Château Frontenac. We were
told the next weather inspection would take place at three.

I took a taxi to Lower Town. Down St. Jean. Down the
slope. Past the cheap stores, the narrow pokey side streets,
horses pulling milk sleighs, the bargain clothes hung out, the
drab restaurants. An alligator of schoolgirls went by along the
sidewalk with two nuns behind. Even with the snow falling
men doffed their hats to priests.

I found Mendel standing in the furniture department. He
looked much older and fatter in the face, the skin under the
jaw sagged, and the small neat waves of hair were thin and grey.

"Hullo Mendel," I said.

He didn't recognize me.

"I'm Jimmy Ross," I said. "Remember during the war?"

"Of course," he said becoming animated. "When did you
get in?"

"Just now. The plane couldn't go on to Fredericton because of the snowstorm."

"Let's go and have some coffee next door," he said. "It's been snowing like this all morning."

We went to the Honey Dew and had coffee. The piped-in music played old tunes. And bundled-up people with faces down went by the plate-glass window.

"I wish Constance were here," he said. "I know she would be glad to see you."

"How is Constance?"

"She's living in Detroit. Married. He came over from Germany after the war. His name is Freddie. He's an accountant. They're doing well. They have four kids. And she's expecting another. How about you?"

I told him briefly what I had done.

"There were some good times during the war—" he said.

"How is Frieda?"

"She died a year and a half ago. I married again. Why don't you come up to the house and meet Dorothy."

"I'd like to," I said. "But I don't want to miss the plane."

"They won't take off in this weather," he said. "But here I am telling *you* about airplanes."

"That was twenty-two years ago," I said. "I couldn't fly the airplanes today."

We got into his black Cadillac with black leather seats. He drove through all-white streets, the windshield wipers going steadily, to the house.

Dorothy was the same size as Mendel, plump, a widow, very cheerful.

"This is Jimmy Ross," Mendel said. "He was a young Air Force officer here during the war. He used to be much handsomer." He went to the far cupboard to get some drinks.

The oil paintings, the creepers, the flowers were gone. A rubber plant stood by the plate-glass wall, its bottom leaves shrivelled and brown.

"Would you like some sponge cake?" Dorothy asked.

"She makes an excellent sponge," Mendel assured me.

"I had lunch on the plane," I said. "I can't stay very long."

It had almost stopped snowing. Only the wind in gusts blew the loose snow up from the ground and down from the roofs.

"Where are you from, Mr. Ross?" Dorothy asked.

"Ottawa," I said.

I felt awkward. It was a mistake to have come.

Mendel drove me to the Château Frontenac.

"Don't forget," he said. "Next time you're here let me know in advance. We'll have you up for dinner."

"You used to tell me jokes, Mendel," I said. "Where did they come from?"

"From the commercial travellers. They come to see me all the time. All of them have jokes. I had one in this morning. What is at the bottom of the sea and shakes?"

"I don't know," I said.

"A nervous wreck," he said and smiled. "Here is another. Why do cows wear bells around their necks?"

I said nothing.

"Because their horns don't work."

He stopped the car outside the entrance of the Château Frontenac.

"When I write to Constance I'll tell her I saw you—"

An hour later I was back in the Viscount taking off from a windswept runway.

A SMALL
PIECE OF BLUE

ON THURSDAY morning the train arrived at Sault Ste. Marie. Leaving my bag in the left luggage, I asked the way to the office of the Algoma Ore Properties. The man in the company's office was tall and wore a loose-fitting summer suit. He had the appearance of an athlete turned salesman. Straight blond hair combed back without a parting, a well-fed face. But there was something deceptive about the way he talked. For his mouth, when open, seemed unnatural in that position, as in those films where animals are made to speak like human beings. I showed him my letter from the mine manager. He read it, said I was lucky, for I would be able to get a train out tomorrow.

"There are only two trains that go up a week, Tuesdays and Fridays."

He walked to a large map on the wall. It hung there framed. The bottom had a large blue area marked "Lake Superior." Smaller pieces of blue were scattered all over the map.

"The only other way is by seaplane." He tapped a spot in the far right-hand corner. "There won't be a plane till Saturday, and if the weather's bad there won't be a plane."

He enjoyed what he had said, for he walked away from the map to his desk and offered me a cigarette.

"It'll cost you twenty more dollars to fly in."

It was the way he mentioned money that brought back those classes in salesmanship we had at high school where we had to stand in front of the class and pretend we were selling something while the teacher criticized our technique.

"Besides, it's a job," the tall man said, "finding the right lake. There are thousands like them. And the bush pilots are just as likely to put you down on the wrong one."

I said I would take the company's train.

Sault Ste. Marie was the kind of place that I had been in before. The quick stay in a small town where I knew that after a few years, I would remember very little of it, in this case a zoo. Away from the main street I walked in a residential area. The houses were set back from the sidewalk by lawns; grass, trees, but no flowers. One wooden house with a large veranda had a cardboard sign, *Room To Let*, nailed to a veranda post. Above the bell-button was a metal plate, *L. M. Kalma. Music Teacher. Qualified.* I rang the bell. I could hear the bell ringing inside. But the tall, grey door remained closed. I rang and knocked and waited. A window on the top opened but no one looked out. Then I heard steps.

The woman who opened the door was small. She had a dressing gown on over a nightdress. Her hair was grey, fuzzy, and held in place by a net. Though it was early afternoon the fact that she had obviously just come out of bed did not seem as startling as her face. The eyes were there. So was the mouth. But where her nose should have been there was a flat surface of scarred flesh with two small holes.

"You caught me undressed."

I told her I wanted a room for one night. She led me upstairs to a bedroom. A square room with a window and a large four-poster bed. "It's a feather bed," she said. "They are much better than spring or rubber. The feathers, they sleep with you like another person."

My first impulse was to make some excuse, leave, and find another place.

"The clever doctors, to them I ought to be dead."

She said this without sadness or humour. Then she showed me the bathroom, the light switch, asked me if I liked music, if $1.50 was not too much for the room, and placed on the kitchen table some cold chicken with sliced cucumber that she had taken from the ice-box. She insisted that I sit down and eat. I ate the food and she talked. She talked as if we had known each other for a long time. Like boat passengers who have been forced into each other's company only for a particular journey and are safe with the knowledge that no matter how much one says or does, there is no consequence to be faced. I now found a strong physical attraction to her face.

Later in the evening when I returned with my bag from the station, it was difficult to recognize her as the same woman who opened the door. She had on a dark dress instead of a dressing gown, but her face was different. She wore a false nose attached to a false piece of skin that stretched from one ear to the other and by wearing glasses held it in place. Face powder and rouge generously put on only helped to show the falseness. I preferred the scarred face with the two air holes to this manufactured monstrosity. In her attempt to look normal she looked ugly.

Next morning the train did not begin from the railway station but from a private siding by the Algoma Ore Properties' office. In the coach, besides myself, were four middle-aged Americans dressed in bright lumberjack shirts, with fishing gear piled around them. The only other person was the ticket collector who, I discovered later, was also our cook.

The coach was old and of a type I had not seen on either the Canadian National or the Canadian Pacific. The inside was like a worn-out billiard table with large patches eaten out of the green. The seats were hard and uncomfortable. Gas brackets hung from the ceiling. In the centre of the ceiling, a light bulb did not give much light. But we did not go through many tunnels. Travelling into the bush we continually crossed trestle bridges, curved by small lakes, and moved slowly through miles of pine and softwood. By noon the journey had gone on much too long. The total distance was less than a hundred miles north and we had travelled half of it when the ticket collector came and asked me if I wanted some grub. I followed him into his compartment at the head of the coach. One side had deep shelves from the ceiling to the floor and the shelves had tinned goods in them. The ticket collector took a tin from a shelf. He showed me the tin. *Grade A. Specially Selected Ready To Serve Chicken.* "Want this?" he asked. "Go to your seat and I'll call you when she's ready. Here. Have a funny. It's on the house." He went over to the loose papers on top of a bundle. "What do you want? Annie. Tarzan. The Katzenjammer Kids."

A dog barked. In the corner opposite to where we were, a cocker spaniel was kept in a large wicker cage.

"She's going the same place as you're going," he said.

I looked out from the small observation window. The train was going through a narrow valley. The earth was banked along the track. We were travelling so slow that it was possible to see the cracks in the soil. The ticket collector put down the chicken tin and filled a bowl with water from a kettle.

"You don't mind if I give her water. Trains give them this thirst."

He made a clucking noise with his tongue and walked over to the wicker basket and put the bowl down so that the dog could reach it.

"She belongs to an engineer at the mine. He sends her to the Soo whenever she's on heat."

He knelt to the dog and fell over as the coach jolted. Instead of getting up he lay sprawled on the floor and talked to the dog.

"Was it good girl? Eh, my beauty. C'mon tell me—"

I left the ticket collector talking to the dog and returned to my seat with the Katzenjammer Kids and looked out of the window. The first excitement of seeing so much green and trees had passed. The trees were monotonous and I wanted the journey to end. I wondered why I was going to the mine. Part of it was for the money and the experience. But I felt convinced that there was something else. Four years of lectures and campus enthusiasms had given me an overdose of books and words and examinations. I felt as if I was on a see-saw, stuck to the one side that was raised, where my head was the only part involved in "the goings on." Not that those four years were unpleasant. They only seem a waste of time, looking back.

I did not see the mine until sundown. From the train it looked like an old ruin on top of a hill where the hills around were without trees or grass. The station was at the bottom of the hill and we stopped by a long wooden platform. The train picked up water. Parcels and crates were moved from the train to the waiting trucks. Then the spaniel, free from the wicker cage, was given to someone in a car. A cream-coloured bus was also by the side of the platform. Some men were inside. I went to the bus. The driver sat like a sparrow over the wheel, a jockey cap on his head. He wore an orange sweater with a large *H* in green across the front.

"Your name Tree?"

When I said it was he said, "Hop in."

The men by the station were watching the reunion of the spaniel with her owner. There were some guttural jokes made at the spaniel's friskiness, for they knew where she had been. Then the bus backed, turned, and drove off.

We came to a lake with wooden houses on one side. The bus stopped by a general store. Several men with black lunch-pails climbed in. They called the driver "Jack" in various accents. He punched small cards that the men held up as they entered the bus. We drove around the lake and up a hill. Above us a steel cable carried large buckets of iron ore from the mine to the sinter plant. We stopped at the top of the hill, beside a wooden building. I asked the driver where the office was. He said to follow him. He carried a mail sack over his shoulder.

"Where you from?"

"Montreal."

"Play ball?"

"A bit."

"What position?"

"I pitch."

He remained silent as we went through a wooden gate and into a frame building partitioned off for several offices. The bus driver dropped the mail sack on the floor and a girl came out of one of the partitions.

"Hi, Glorie. Someone from Montreal." And he went out.

She came to the counter, unsmiling, and took some paper, spread it flat.

"When did you come?"

A skirt and sweater, and on her sweater at the neck she wore a black cross.

She took my name, age, and home address. Her eyes moved nervously. Her other features were coarse. When my card was filled out she told me to go to the cookhouse, a building some twenty yards away, and ask for the cook.

I crossed the bare, hard-packed ground and saw a man with glasses, stripped to the waist, holding a white apron. He stood by the cookhouse near several large barrels filled with garbage and looked towards the horizon. I asked him if he could tell me where I could find the cook.

"Where you from?" he said with a Scottish accent.

"Montreal."

"Montreal." He said the word slowly. "It's seven years since I've been there. How are the Canadiens doing?" Not waiting for a reply, he became excited and talked quickly. "The last time I was there I did a food crawl. I started at Pauze's with a dozen oysters, then I went to the Bucharest for a steak, Ben's for a smoked-meat sandwich, Chicken Charlie's on St. Catherine for spare-ribs, and ended with spaghetti and meatballs at FDR's, and before I caught the midnight train I took a taxi to a place called *Au Lutin qui Bouffe* where somebody blind played a piano while I had frogs' legs and my picture taken giving a baby's bottle of milk to a little pig." As spontaneously as he started, he stopped. To cover up his embarrassment he became silent, then formal, as he led me to his cookhouse office.

In his office he issued me a new black lunch-pail and I signed a slip for it. He told me to scratch my name on the lunch-pail with a nail and that supper was at seven thirty, so that I still had half an hour to get a place to sleep. We walked outside, through the dining hall. Unpainted large wooden tables. Benches on both sides. The first table near the door had chairs, and a sign, *Staff Only*.

He showed me a building about fifty yards down the hill.

"Go to room nine, laddie, and ask for Willie Hare."

The cable stretched over the cookhouse and I could hear it creak as the buckets kept passing overhead. Where the cable crossed between cookhouse and office a steel net was suspended above the ground.

I found number nine in a building smelling of paint. Outside the door a bundle of dirty laundry was tied together by a shirt. Some time passed between my knock and the door being opened. At first I thought he was a boy, then he switched the room light on and I could see that he was old, unshaven, and sleepy. He could not be much more than five feet, a thin frame covered by a dirty white shirt buttoned tight at the neck, collar crumpled, and grey trousers that were too small. He wore no shoes but heavy woollen socks. His fly-buttons were undone.

"My name is Tree. The cook told me that you would let me know where I sleep."

He hesitated, then turned back to the room leaving the door open. He went to a cupboard and pulled out a large piece of cardboard. Then he sat down on his bed and began to examine the large writing on one side of the board. I looked around the room. It stank of old age. Shelves covered an entire wall. In these shelves toothpaste, soap, razor blades, shoe laces, and chocolate bars were propped up in open boxes. Above his bed, pasted to the wall, was a map similar to the one hanging in the company's office in Sault Ste. Marie. Covering most of the map were pictures of boxers, hockey players, movie stars, old Christmas cards, pin-up girls, and an old calendar advertising life insurance.

"Yours will be number forty-two."

He spoke with difficulty, for he had no teeth. They were sunk in a glass of water on the floor by his bed. "You'll have another student in with you later. Tree." And he laughed. "That's an easy one to spell." He licked the end of the pencil and printed my name large on the cardboard. "You can get most things from me." He showed me the cupboard built into the wall where he returned the piece of cardboard. Inside sprawled hundreds of paper-backed books. "Mystery, cowboy, sex stories, no need to pay. It'll come off your cheque." He gave me the key to my room and returned to his bed, entering between the sheets fully dressed.

"By the way Tree, where you from?"

"Montreal."

I waited. There was no reply.

As I walked out he called back. "Shut the light."

Number forty-two was a square room freshly painted white, with one window directly opposite the door. Two beds. Two dressers. A naked light hung from the ceiling. I tried to raise the window but was able to move it only a few inches. I could see the side of a hill, the sky, and trees. The outside air tasted cold in my throat.

I unpacked and had put on a sweater and old flannels when I heard a bell tolling. There was nothing urgent about the sound. Silence. Then the sound again. I went out of the room and looked out of the window in the passage. Men were pressed tight to the door of the cookhouse. Others were running towards it. Suddenly the door opened and those that were there disappeared inside. By the time I reached the cookhouse the tables were crowded with men eating. Latecomers, like myself, were running from one table to the other until we found a place on a bench.

At my table they were speaking German. The only one not speaking was deformed. He sat opposite me. Stubbles for fingers on a wrist which was raw. A large red handkerchief, tied around his head, went underneath his chin. He used this handkerchief to hold his jaw together. To eat he would loosen the knot above his head and with one stubbled hand he would slide the food from the table to his mouth while the other worked the jaw up and down.

"You a Canadian?"

He had bad teeth.

"Yes," I said.

"Look at the monkeys eat."

As a platter of food was placed on the table, often before it reached the table, bodies pushed, hands snatched whatever they could get. In less than ten minutes it was all over.

Outside, the tramline continued to creak. The men stood waiting by the side of the cookhouse where, on to the main wall, a wooden booth was built. It stuck out like an ear. Steps without handrails led to a door. Someone shouted. "Here he comes." I saw Willie Hare coming from the office towards the cookhouse, his hands full of letters and newspapers. He gave the letters to the first man, then went up the ladder to the booth and threw the papers inside. "Shout them out." Another man took the envelopes away from the first man and began to call out names. Letters passed from hand to hand. After all the names had been read out several times the DP s went through them again.

I woke next morning to the sound of blasting followed later by the steady tolling bell. Breakfast was a repetition of the supper last night, except that different faces were at the table. After breakfast I walked over to the office. The manager had not yet arrived. Glorie suggested that I go and see the doctor as I had to have a medical before I could begin work.

The doctor's office (a wooden building, as were all the buildings on top of the hill) was a few minutes' walk from the cookhouse. His hours according to a sign were 10:00–12:00. I arrived after 10:00 and it was now 11:32 and still no one had arrived. A man with a crewcut, wearing white shorts and an open shirt approached. I asked him if he was the doctor.

"I'm not that lucky," he said, and walked on.

The doctor arrived at noon. He was the palest person I had so far seen at the mine. A long head on a tall thin body. His face reminded me of a goat. Straight black hair parted on the side. A thin mouth. It was difficult to guess his age. He could as easily have been in his thirties as in his forties. He opened the door and indicated that I enter.

"They said in the office to come and see you about a medical."

He remained silent, took off his jacket and flung it onto the leather couch that was near his desk. The room was small and stifling. All the windows were closed. Papers were on the floor. A file, like a broken accordion, lay on the floor with papers sticking out from the bellow pockets. A telephone was on the desk. Beside it, piled high on top of each other, were old telephone directories. On the desk, a dish had dried apples, overripe pears, and an onion sprouting. A green filing cabinet stood against the wall by the window. On top of it several parcels, tied crudely together, had holes in the brown paper as if the rats had been there. A picture of Mickey Mouse was the only bright spot in the room and it hung as a target on a piece of cardboard underneath the eye-chart. There were three chairs and a leather couch to sit on.

"You another student?"

I said I was.

He began to listen to my chest.

"Where you from?"

"McGill."

He looked up, surprised.

"And how is the dear place? Are they still after you asking to give money for some building or drive, writing you letters, telling you how important you are to them—"

"I just graduated," I said.

"You'll get them soon enough."

He did not bother to examine me further but went over to his filing cabinet, unlocked it, and from the back he brought out two large glasses and a half-full bottle of brandy.

"It's all right, Tree. I was there myself. Good time. Best time I ever had."

He poured the glasses nearly full and we drank.

"We must have a reunion. You know you are the first McGill man who has hit this God-forsaken hole. The others at the staff table are a bunch of hicks from all the hick colleges across the country." Then, as if he remembered something, he came and shook my hand.

"My name is Crepeau."

We continued drinking. I told him who on the faculty had died, who had left, and he appeared to be interested when I said a name he knew. The conversation jumped from the campus, to Montreal, to sport, to the different places we had seen. "Look at yourself," he suddenly interrupted. "You talk. You can talk like I can talk. We both can make talk. Talk on anything. They have seen to that. But what good does it do you, or anybody else? They've sandpapered all your rough edges, your instincts, your intuitions, then turned you out with a fake smartness like a car on the assembly line. You happen to be the 1950 model. I was the 1933. The funny thing is we like it."

He stood up.

So did I.

"You'd better sit. You're only here for this summer so you'd better listen. I was like yourself twenty years back, perhaps better. I had first class honours, won prizes, had an offer to continue research in a San Francisco hospital. But I said to hell with them—"

He opened his arms indicating the untidy room.

"—they don't make it easy for you to be a failure."

Suddenly he seemed to lose interest in what he was saying, for he walked to the filing cabinet and from behind it took out an air rifle and a candle. He lit the candle and stood it up on top of the filing cabinet, in front of the crudely wrapped parcels. He broke his rifle and inserted a slug.

"Let's see what kind of shot you are. Go against the far wall and put the flame out."

The distance was about ten yards. I aimed. I missed. He made me try again. This time I hit the candle, knocking it down, but the wick still burned. He tried. His first shot either went through the flame, or very near it, for it flickered. The next one put it out. He returned the rifle to its place and offered me a cigarette.

"I know I'm tight, but it does not matter. What does any one person matter? They come into your world for a while then leave it just as quickly as they entered."

He finished what was in his glass, poured more in, and drank it down.

"Don't expect the men to like you. When they find out that you've been to university and have come here it's like telling them that what they believe in is rotten. They work hard to save money so that their kids can go to university, get a degree, and not have to come to places like this. Then they see you here—"

The room was stuffy yet all the windows were shut. I was glad that he stopped talking, for I found the atmosphere in the room and the brandy had made me sleepy and I wondered how much longer he would go on before I could excuse myself and leave.

"Use your eyes and you can see a lot," he said. "Everyone else who is here has not come by choice. The DPs are counting the days, marking them off on their calendars until they can get away to Toronto, Montreal, or Winnipeg. Those who work underground stay as long as the bonus makes it worthwhile, then they drift to some other place. A few scarecrows like Willie Hare and Old Harold hang on because the company ruined them as human beings. For fun the men play crap, smuggle hootch, and pin black lace panties on their walls that they get from the Soo."

He stopped talking to drink and fill the glasses again.

"I suppose you'll return to Montreal." He burped and excused himself.

"I don't want any of that kind of civilization. I've contracted out from all of them. I drink, and I write poetry."

He tried to get more brandy out of the bottle but it was empty.

"Sometimes I go to the Soo. The last time, I took a case of Scotch, found myself a hotel room, locked the door, and I didn't get out of bed as long as the Scotch lasted."

He went over to his desk, unlocked a drawer, and brought out a leather folder. From it he took a piece of paper.

"I wrote this on my last blow."

All your experiences:
Those bits.
Those pieces you carried away with you.
How long will they last?

At the undertaker she showed me the coffin.
"Oak the best wooden one
Won't last you more than twenty-five years.
It falls away like paper."

Those bits and pieces you carried away.
How long will they?

He stopped. For some reason he looked embarrassed. He went to his desk and returned the piece of paper to the leather folder.

"I've got a couple of hundred poems. Some day I'll get them put into a nice book and send it to the dear old place with my compliments."

The effort of reading seemed to sober him up for he threw the empty bottle into a large sack by his desk that had something soft in it, for there was no sound of the bottle hitting. He picked up his jacket.

"There's no point staying in here."

We went out and walked along the slope of the hill. The bell began to toll for lunch. Grass was burnt, and scattered were small patches of blueberry bushes. We walked on a narrow path sunk in the hard ground following the contour of the hill. I could see the tramline going down but we were too far away to hear the buckets creak, although the sound of the bell still reached us. The doctor walked in front.

"Fly in?"

"No. I took the train."

"It only takes an hour to fly in."

"The manager at the Soo told me pilots can't find this lake easy."

"There's only one lake in the bush shaped like ours."

We walked on. The sun was still hot. The bell tolled behind us. And I could now see a gull flying alongside the hill and a small piece of blue locked in the surrounding earth and rock growing larger below. The slope of the land entered the water and split the top quarter in two.

"What does she look like to you?" the doctor said.

I stood on a flat rock looking at the lake that I had come by on the bus yesterday.

"To me it's more like a heart."

He said this without waiting to hear what I might say.

SOUTH OF MONTREAL

SEE HER NOW. In some kind of outer garment. Tugging at her lapels, as if it was falling off her shoulders. Her hair, a thin yellow-blond, piled on her head. She was short. A pale white skin. A largish nose. Talking elaborately, closing her eyes, exaggerating her gestures. She could have been an actress in some melodrama. Her name was Madame de Wyssmann. She was French Canadian, a widow, a Huguenot. She wanted her nephew Paul to be taught English so he could go to Loyola in the autumn. That's how I came to Ile Aux Noix. I was to tutor Paul and two of his school friends—Jose and Mario—Guatemalans.

I am writing about the summer of 1947. I had just finished third year at McGill when I went down to the placement bureau to get fixed up with a job for the summer months. Madame de Wyssmann's letter giving me detailed instructions on how to get to Ile Aux Noix was written in the largest copperplate I had seen.

On Saturday I left Montreal, by bus, over the light green bridge. And soon we were on a straight highway that led to the United States border. The countryside was uninteresting. Flat fields to the river that went parallel to the highway, with a few stilt cottages along the bank. The river had overflowed in the spring, and the receding water left reeds wrapped around the fence posts and around the trunks of the few trees.

I got off the bus by a telegraph pole that had a sign, *Riverside Hotel*, pointing down a dirt track to the river. Further along the highway was the white church steeple where the village began. Across the road, this fine row of poplars, a nice lawn, and a large stone house with white trimmings.

"You had no trouble getting here?"

"No Madame. Your instructions were exact."

"Would you like some coffee? This is *Madame.*"

She introduced me to a gentle old woman in a brown print dress. She had bow legs and a small moustache. She spoke a few sharp words of French to her.

"*Oui, Madame,*" the old woman said and went to the kitchen. It could have been the voice of a young child.

My room was the small room on the first floor. The staircase was wide and wooden and it went up to a large tapestry on the wall showing a battlefield. There were shelves of books, mostly Balzac, and old *National Geographic* magazines. It was a fine house, cool in the middle of the summer, high ceilings, with highly polished wooden floors. Downstairs, the dining room was filled with Japanese screens and other stage props.

"They were given to me by Tyrone Power Senior," Madame de Wyssmann said at lunch. "He and his wife had a cottage next to us by the river. I taught young Tyrone Power how to drive a car. We had fine times—but the interesting people who were here are gone."

Her nephew Paul wore glasses and had straight blond hair that he combed back. He was tall but flabby. The two Guatemalans were quite different. Jose had brownish skin, curly dark hair. Until he met me he thought everyone in the world was a Catholic. Mario was smaller, white skin, sharp features. He mispronounced ham and jam at the breakfast table. They both laughed and smiled a lot.

On the second day, after breakfast, when they had gone to the village to collect the mail, Madame de Wyssmann came up to me.

"Sir," she said. "Look what I have found in his bed."

She gave me a rubber doll. It was a miniature nude woman about seven inches long. "What am I to do?"

"Boys are boys," I said.

"It's all he thinks about. He's got this little DP in St. John's. A little prostitute." She closed her eyes and spat out the word. "He thinks of nothing else." Then she said something in French that I didn't understand. "I was married. But we slept in different rooms. He had to knock if he wanted to come in."

"Were you married long?"

"Six months," she said. "He was a lawyer. Much older. I came straight from the convent."

At the end of the first week I realized why I was here. It wasn't only to get her nephew into Loyola. Madame de Wyssmann believed that English meant refinement, and French Canadian was coarse and provincial. I was expected to help her nephew make the change.

Lessons meant reading from *Vanity Fair* (it was the only English book she had on her shelves) and giving them words from my *Pocket Oxford Dictionary*. We had spelling classes. We had reading classes. We talked in English. Sometimes it was on the grass around the stone house with the poplars overhead. And I would hear Madame de Wyssmann playing Chopin on the piano. More often I would go with the boys down the dirt path to the river, and there, from a garage, take out one of the three boats: the sailboat, the canoe, the dinghy. And we'd go up and down and across the Richelieu River while they read or spoke English.

I liked the river. There were red and black buoys in the middle to mark the channel. But weeds had claimed most of it. And sometimes the boat got so tangled in them that it came to a stop. Towards dusk, swallows would come over the water.

And the beeches, the mountain ash, looked very pretty along the shore.

One Saturday afternoon, when there were no lessons, Paul and Jose and Mario came back to the stone house with a large white bird. They said they found it in a field by the river. It couldn't fly. Paul carried it very gently in his arms. Outside the kitchen door he tied its long thin legs to a fence post with a leather strap, then pulled it by the neck until it stretched fully out, its whole length parallel to the ground, the wings hanging lifelessly by its sides. Jose came out of the kitchen with a knife and gave it to Paul, and Paul began to saw away at the neck. The wings began to beat the air. They were large wings. They made a swooshing sound and sent the dust on the ground moving. All the time he was fiddling away at the neck, the bird was stretched out as in flight, the wings beating powerfully, until he cut through.

At next day's lesson, in the sailboat, I had Paul alone. In the middle of reading Thackeray he said, "I am French. Why should I try to be like the English?"

"It doesn't hurt to know another language," I said, not very convincingly.

But it was the end of that lesson. After that, Paul went through the motions. He was too polite for any more outbursts. But with his aunt, even when I was there, he spoke French. When she said, "Paul. *Speak English*," he just smiled.

It had been the nicest summer I ever had in Canada. I had gone out fishing by myself, trolling for pike. I had gone out with old Lacosse (he did errands for Madame de Wyssmann). He taught me how to spear carp at night using a light. And I had gone with him in his old Ford when he collected the mail from the tin letter-boxes stuck crookedly to the wooden posts of the farms, and also on Saturday afternoons when he went for frogs. He had a sack and a stick. And he would knock the frogs and put them into the sack, then sell them to a Montreal restaurant. One afternoon, late in August, the frogs began to leave the fields by the river and move to the higher ground. But they had to get across the highway. The cars killed most of them. There were thousands of dead frogs lying on the highway for the next few days.

In the first week in September the trees had started to change colours. The swallows flew lower over the river. And splashes of red settled slowly on the reeds by the shore. The nights were cold. One day the radio said snow was expected. Jose and Mario were excited. They had never seen snow. They wanted to stay up all night. So we all did. The moon was large and orange. It was cold. But no snow fell.

Next day it was time to go away. I thanked Madame de Wyssmann. I said I enjoyed the summer. Old Madam brought me some coffee. Paul and Mario and Jose shook my hand. Then we went outside and stood by the spot where Paul had killed the bird waiting for the bus to come.

"What are you going to do?" Madame de Wyssmann asked.

I said I would finish university. Then go somewhere. Where, I didn't know.

"You are young," she said. "You still have your ambitions."

A CANADIAN
UPBRINGING

WHEN PEOPLE ASK ME why did I leave Canada and go over to England, the answer I give depends on the kind of person who is doing the asking.

If it is someone of my own generation, at some party, I tell them it was because of the attractive English girl who sat beside me at college and took the same courses as I did, and who was going back when she graduated. If it is someone like my bank manager, I say it was because of the five-thousand-dollar fellowship I got for postgraduate study. The only condition being that I had to do it at some British university. And if the question comes from an editor, I tell him that at that time I had just written a first novel and my Canadian publisher (to be), having read the manuscript, said that I would have to go to New York or London to get it published, then he would look after the Canadian market.

All of these have something of the truth about them. But what was behind them, and which I could not admit at the time, was the work of Alexander Marsden.

I had never heard of Marsden until I went to McGill. In my second year, Graham Pollack, one of the English professors—poor Graham, he's dead now. No one, apart from the handful of students who took his courses, gave him much credit for the range of his reading, nor understood the kind of humility he brought into the classroom. He lectured, in a weak voice, on utopias throughout the ages, on science fiction, and on comparative literature, wiping away with a large white handkerchief the sweat that broke out on his forehead.

His office, which he shared with an assistant professor, was swamped with his books. Not only were they around the walls, but in piles on the floor. And it was from one of these piles that he pulled out *A Canadian Upbringing* by Alexander Marsden.

"I think you might enjoy this," he said, blowing off the dust.

I began to read it late that night—in that large basement room on the corner of Guy and Sherbrooke that I rented from the Dean of Christ Church Cathedral. And when I finished the last page I was far too excited and disturbed to go to sleep.

It's a small book, 112 pages. It was published in England in 1939. The first half deals with Marsden's growing up in Montreal, the rest with a trip he made across the country in the early thirties: by riding freight cars, by bus, hitchhiking, and walking.

What first disturbed me was the shock that one gets when, without warning, you come across a new talent. But I was also disturbed by something else.

Although I was brought up in Ottawa—and Ottawa has, compared to Montreal, a small Jewish community—the kind of upbringing I had wasn't much different from the one Marsden describes in Montreal. He pinned down that warm, lively, ghetto atmosphere—the strong family and religious ties—as well as its prejudices and limitations. And when, at the end of the book, Marsden decides to leave Canada for England, not because he wants to deny his background but because he feels the need to accept a wider view of life, I knew that was the way I would go as well.

From Professor Pollack I found out what I could about Marsden, which was very little. Marsden had gone over to

England in the late thirties, and as far as Pollack knew he had never come back.

I graduated that summer and set out for London with my five-thousand-dollar fellowship, the English girl, the manuscript of my novel, and the well-marked copy of *A Canadian Upbringing*.

In London I soon discovered that I didn't care for the academic. And I dropped it. The attractive English girl went over to Paris and on the cross-Channel boat met an Englishman. And they married.

But I did get my novel accepted by an English publisher. And with this I decided to try and make, like Marsden, some kind of literary career over here.

I also tried to track down Marsden's whereabouts. But the publisher of *A Canadian Upbringing* was out of business, and it was only a chance remark by the librarian at Canada House that put me on his trail. She didn't know who he was, and had never heard of the book. But she remembered his name.

"I send him batches of Canadian papers," she said, and pulled out a card from a file that had "Alexander Marsden" on top, and below, a series of crossed-out addresses. The last one she had was: The Little Owls, Mousehole, near Penzance, Cornwall.

I copied it into my address book and there the matter rested.

Until this summer. One of my short stories was bought up for a film, and with the money from that I bought myself a small English car, rented a cottage in Mousehole, and took my wife and kids for our first holiday in Cornwall.

It was very pleasant. The weather was marvellous. The kids played along the rocks at low tide and found rock pools with sea anemones in them. Towards evening we drove down to Land's End, stopping off at the coves, the small coastal villages, on the way. Or over to Penzance, where my wife did some shopping and the kids played on the lawns of the Morrab Gardens.

On the sixth day I couldn't put it off any longer. I asked the postman where Marsden lived.

The small greystone cottage, without a front garden, was easy to find. Across the unpaved road, water flowed in the ditch. A few chickens were wandering about further up the road, from a field. And a black dog was stretched out in the sun.

I knocked.

The man who opened the door was about five foot ten, a little on the plump side. He had a sardonic, very pale face. And a short pointed blond beard. He reminded me of one of those engravings of Shakespeare.

"Mr. Marsden?"

"Yes," he said gently.

"I'm a Canadian, and since I was in Mousehole I thought I'd come over and tell you how much I've enjoyed *A Canadian Upbringing.*"

The pale face looked very vulnerable.

"Come in," he said quietly. "How is Canada?"

"Fine," I said.

"When were you last there?"

"Eight years ago."

"What part?"

"Ottawa."

I then told him my name, that I left for much the same reason as he did, and that since my college days I had carried around his book, like a Bible.

"Would you like some tea?" he said in that gentle, detached manner.

"Yes," I said. "Thank you."

"I'm sorry I haven't any spirits," he said, as he disappeared into the back.

It was a small tidy cottage, very simply furnished. An unvarnished wooden table in the middle. A couple of well-made wooden chairs. A fireplace with some coloured postcards on top.

Marsden returned with a tray that had a small teapot, two earthenware mugs, a loaf of bread, and a sliced lemon. Then he went back again.

"I've got a surprise," he said.

He came back with a large salami that had "Blooms" written across it, in white, several times.

"I get this sent to me once a month from a delicatessen in London. I tried to get some rye bread, but they won't send it."

He cut a thin slice of the salami and, spearing it with the knife, gave it to me.

"Delicious," I said.

He made me a salami sandwich and one for himself and we had tea and sandwiches sitting by the bare wooden table.

"That's what I miss most, the food," he said, and for the first time he sounded enthusiastic. "I tried to make *gefilte* fish. It turned out uneatable. I tried to make *putcha* and finally persuaded the local butcher to get me some calf's legs. But the thing looked like jellied dishwater, and I threw it away. Where are you staying?"

"In a cottage across from the Coastguards. We rented it for two weeks."

"Married?"

"Yes," I said. "I've got two kids."

"I never did," he said, and seemed to go off again on some private thought. But I wasn't going to let this meeting play itself out in small talk about food. I had rehearsed this occasion during too many sleepless nights. I wanted to talk about *A Canadian Upbringing*, and how he had made me aware of my background and why it was necessary to leave it.

"Go home," he said suddenly. "Go home while you are still young."

"But I thought you were critical of Canada?"

"Maybe. But I care less about England."

He cut some more salami, very carefully, and made another two neat sandwiches.

I decided to change the subject. "How is your work going?"

"Fine. I do that upstairs. Would you like to see my work-room?"

I said I would and felt somewhat flattered. Writers' work-rooms are usually private things.

I followed him up the stairs—I noticed he wore brown leather slippers—to a largish airy room that had planks of wood on the floor, some packing cases, an electric saw, several planes, several chisels, tins of glue and paint.

He led me to the far side where, in what looked like former bookcases, were standing brightly painted toys.

"I make roundabouts," he said, picking one up for me.

They were the gayest roundabouts I have seen. Bright blues, crimsons, oranges, yellows, green—with a barber-shop pole in the middle around which farmyard animals went to the tinkle of a small silver bell.

"I make these for various toy shops in London, and they go all over—" Marsden said.

He saw me look at the Canadian newspapers on the floor.

"I get those sent from Canada House. They're handy for packing."

He had a large mirror on one wall with various postcards stuck along the inside of the frame. They showed Piccadilly with the Guinness clock and several red buses; the midnight sun over a lake at Landego, Norway; a snow scene in Ober-gurgl, Austria; a bull elephant from Kenya; and the Peace Tower and the lawns in Ottawa. On the backs of the cards was written much the same sort of message.

I think your roundabouts are
wonderful. They have given my
children much pleasure. Thank you.

I told Marsden that I thought the roundabouts were splendid.

"Do you make any other kind of toy?"

"No," he said, "just this one model."

Downstairs. The tea was cold. He had put away the salami and we had smoked all my cigarettes. I stood up and shook hands and said I would see him again before we left. He opened the door for me.

"I'm very glad you called," he said, in that gentle, unemotional way of his.

For the next few days I didn't go and see Marsden but thought of little else. I have not had many heroes lately and as I grow older they get less. But Marsden had meant something personal to me, and I felt I had been cheated. Of what exactly I didn't know. But the man who wrote *A Canadian Upbringing* no longer existed as far as I was concerned, and I was quite prepared to leave Cornwall without seeing him again.

But on the morning we were to leave, and as we were packing things to take back in the car, he turned up, looking very elegant in light cream trousers, brown sandals, yellow socks, and a maroon shirt.

"I hope you don't mind," he said. "I thought your children might like these." And he gave each of the kids a roundabout.

Their reaction was immediate. They kissed him. They jumped around him. They gave little squeals of delight. And Marsden was enjoying it as well.

For my wife he had an enormous bunch of anemones— and my wife is a sitting duck when it comes to flowers.

He played with the children while I and my wife finished bringing the packed things from the cottage into the car. I was trying to close the back when Marsden came up.

"Can I help?"

"Thanks," I said, shutting it. "It's all finished."

"It was good of you to come and see me," he said. "You're the first author who has." He was, I think, going to say something else, but the kids came running around. So we shook hands, and we all got into the car.

"I'll send you some rye bread," I said, starting the engine.

"I don't want to put you to all that trouble, but if you could send me a couple of loaves, just once—"

And he waved.

And we were waving as I drove away. Around the first bend he disappeared from sight. The road went by some large blue rocks and by the briny sea that lay flat to the horizon. It made everything, suddenly, seem awfully silent.

I LIKE CHEKHOV

I T WAS a warm afternoon in July. And in the Yorkshire town the sheep were grazing on the grass of the school lawns that sloped to the river. Chester Conn Bell walked along the footpath under the avenue of heavy trees. He was twenty-nine, blond, and with a fine profile, he looked more like an actor than a schoolmaster. Beside him the river had little water in it. It was mainly mudbanks with beached rowboats and old bits of wood.

He turned off the footpath, as he had done five days of the week for the past nine months, and went through the small park with its scented gardens of lemon thyme for the blind.

It's over, thought Chester. And then a sudden light feeling of release. How marvellous to be free again.

Tomorrow he would leave this provincial backwater with its bad library and deadness at night. He didn't mind the teaching as much as he disliked being reminded that he was a teacher. When he walked through the streets the schoolboys were always there touching their caps with their hands.

"Good morning, sir."

"Afternoon, sir."

"Good evening, sir."

By the church with the slate spire he left the park and walked along the side street that brought him into a residential area. On both sides were pale yellow brick houses. Halfway down, on the left, lived Miss Fort, who was in her sixties. She taught music, and Chester rented her front room. As he opened the front door he heard the piano and a girl's thin voice singing "A Lover and His Lass."

He took off his navy blue blazer, loosened his dark blue tie, undid his collar button, sat down in the comfortable chair, lit a cigarette, and listened to the singing and the piano. And he began to think that no more would he be coming back to this room. Nor early mornings going out for coffee and toast, then through the park, by the cemetery, the mist hanging over the river in the winter. Nor going on the stage and singing solemnly the morning hymns. Then the roll-calls, detentions, telling them to stop talking. He had hated it all the time he was doing it. But now that was over.

The singing and the piano stopped. It was five thirty. He knew he would like to round off his teaching days and his stay in this town with some kind of gesture. And he was looking forward to seeing the Latin Master and the Geography Master later that evening in the Antelope.

It was the Latin Master's idea to go to the Antelope. He had told Chester about Sophie Jewtree, the proprietress, who served behind the bar. And Chester had also heard from the others in the staff room about Sophie and the Latin Master.

Sophie Jewtree was one of the attractive women in the town. When she was behind the bar there were, at various times in the evening, five or six married men who left their wives to be with Sophie. Her husband, a stocky, retired RAF officer, did not mind. (The men came regularly, talked quietly, stood together in a small group, like overgrown schoolboys.) He called them Sophie's admirers. And the most consistent of all the admirers was the Latin Master.

He was a lean, taut man with rimless glasses, a small neat moustache, and thin lips. He spoke quietly and precisely. But when he became angry with a pupil, his face would flush and leave him speechless.

Every Monday to Friday the Latin Master went to the Antelope to have a few drinks and to see Sophie. They talked quietly, and kept looking at each other. Then the Latin Master went back to his wife. It had gone on like this for three years.

The Geography Master was different. He looked like a corpulent schoolboy whose suits were always in need of a press. And he couldn't shake off the classroom. Away from it he continued, in his conversation, to explain the obvious. He was married with five small children. And while the Latin Master lived with his wife in a neat rented flat, the Geography Master inherited money and owned one of the finest houses in the town.

What held these two together was that they both went to Cambridge, while the rest were graduates of provincial universities. And Chester, being Canadian and socially unclassifiable, was accepted by both sides. He was invited to the Latin and Geography Masters' homes for dinner—a thing they had never done with the other masters. And when Chester went out to a pub with some of the masters from the provincial universities they told him how stuck-up the two Cambridge men were.

The Antelope was a combination pub and hotel. It had one long copper bar that stretched most of the width of the room and some wooden cubicles against the wall opposite the bay windows.

When Chester came in, the two were already there.

"What are you having?" the Geography Master asked.

"Whisky," Chester said. "*Teachers.*"

They laughed.

"This is Chester," the Latin Master said to the woman behind the bar.

"I heard a lot about you," she said.

She looked handsome but vulnerable. A tallish woman with brown loose hair that she kept pushing back from her eyes. There was something about attractive women that drew Chester to them. Unlike the other masters, Chester felt more comfortable in the presence of women than of men. And women soon realized this.

"You look different," the Geography Master said to Chester.

"All people look different when they are going away," Sophie said.

While she was serving at the other end of the bar, the Latin Master asked, somewhat proudly, "What do you think of Sophie?"

"Wish I'd come here before," Chester said, noticing how her belly pushed out against the tight stone-tweed skirt.

"—years from now we'll be saying," the Geography Master said, "'Remember the time Chester Conn Bell...'"

"Couldn't you teach, and write in your spare time?" Sophie said.

"I tried," Chester said, "but I didn't do any writing all the time I was here."

"Have you had things published?" she asked.

This was a sore point with Chester.

"I've had some stories, in a magazine, in Canada."

Sophie said her husband was born in New Zealand (he was away in London) and told them how they met in London in 1944 when she was a WAAF. And what a gay exciting time she had when she ran her own MG and met new people nearly every day.

"You must miss that—living here," Chester said.

"When I do I go to see my doctor," she said. "He tells me I have good legs."

"The thing I missed most in this town," Chester said, "was not being able to get a decent book. The library here is terrible."

"I've got books," said Sophie.

"What kind of books?"

"Chekhov—Tolstoy—"

"You have books like that?"

"Yes," she said. "I like the Russians. They're in the back. Would you like to see them?"

The Latin Master didn't like the way the conversation was going.

"You can see them tomorrow."

But there was no confidence in his voice.

"I'll be gone tomorrow," Chester said.

"We'll only be a minute," Sophie said to the Latin Master, and touched his hand as she went by.

She led Chester into an adjoining room. She put on a wall light that kept most of the room in shadows, then walked over to the bookcase. There weren't as many books there as Chester expected. He bent over to read the titles. There was a thin olive-green volume of Chekhov's short stories—books of poetry—Browning—some wartime anthologies—*Penguin New Writing*. She was bending over beside him, he could smell her scent. Their hips touched. He turned and they kissed gently on the mouth. Then they straightened out. And they kissed several times, not gently.

"I think we'd better go back," she said, after a while.

The light in the bar was hard on their eyes as they came in. The Latin Master looked annoyed and puzzled, the Geography Master as if he had been told a dirty joke and had just got the point.

"She's got some good books," Chester said to them. Then to Sophie, who was now behind the bar, "I like Chekhov. He understands people."

But the atmosphere had changed. And there was something noticeably uneasy among them now. They finished their last drinks in a series of silences and said goodbye to Sophie.

As soon as they were out on the gravel drive the Latin Master came up to Chester.

"What did you do in there?"

"We kissed," Chester said.

A flush appeared on the Latin Master's face. He looked at Chester but said nothing, then turned, walked over the gravel to his bicycle, and rode away.

"I'll drive you home," the Geography Master said quietly.

"Thanks," Chester said. "It's my last night. I think I'll walk."

"Don't forget us," the Geography Master suddenly called out from the car, as he drove away.

Chester began to walk down the slope. The moon was out and it shone on the water, on the stone bridge, on the small park and the town behind it. A breeze from the river. He turned the collar of his jacket up and put his hands in his trouser pockets and began to whistle. He felt very happy as he walked through the empty provincial streets and heard the echoing sound of his own footsteps. "It's nice to be on the move," he said to himself.

ENGLISH FOR FOREIGNERS

THE CLASSROOMS were above an optician, by a seedy restaurant, overlooking a large, bare cathedral. When I started, at the beginning of May, the season had not begun. I had eight pupils, the intermediates. If anyone could carry on a few sentences in broken English he left the beginners—which was crowded—and stayed in the intermediates until there was room for him in the senior class. Each class consisted of a small room with tables pushed together in the shape of a horseshoe. I sat behind a desk, at the open end of the horseshoe, by a portable blackboard. The windows had to be closed because of the traffic noise. On a warm or a rainy day, the room was stifling.

On the first day I wondered whether my Canadian accent would matter. "Ladies and gentlemen. I'm your new teacher. I'm a Canadian. And the kind of English I speak is not the kind that Englishmen speak. So if you have any trouble understanding what I say—" But I was interrupted by an Italian girl who beamed and said how clear my diction was. And they all said they understood me and complimented me on how clearly I spoke. I was getting to feel quite good. But I found out, on the second day, that the Englishman I replaced had a speech impediment. He left without saying goodbye. That was one of the occupational hazards. One was hired without references and left the same way.

Teaching consisted mainly in giving them new words, correcting their pronunciation, dictating to them small pieces of anything I happened to see while looking out of the window. And reading excerpts from Conrad. Or else we played games. I would borrow one of their watches with a sweep second-hand and say: "Miss Laroque. You are walking in Brighton from the Steine to the West Pier. Tell me, in one minute, all the words beginning with the letter "M" that you would see. *Now.*"

"Mouse . . . Mutton . . . Murder . . . Mister . . . Missus . . . Miss . . ."

"Sir. That's not fair."

"Six, Miss Laroque," I said. "Twenty-five seconds to go."

"Mimosa . . . Macaroni . . . Man . . ."

They were mainly young girls. Some were there for business reasons: to be a receptionist in their father's hotel; another was going to be an air-hostess; another to work in an export office. But the majority were there for a holiday.

I had been there three weeks when Mrs. Siemens came in. The age of the students didn't vary a great deal; they were in their teens or early twenties. But Mrs. Siemens, a handsome-looking woman, with grey hair combed neatly back in a bun, and very light-blue eyes, was in her seventies. The immediate reaction to her presence was to subdue everyone. And we got a lot more done. She sat halfway up the left of the horse-shoe, listening to what I was saying. Sometimes she took out a handkerchief and wiped her eyes. I took it that she had some allergy. When it was her turn to read, she read softly and very slow, and apologized at the end for not doing better.

At eleven we had a ten-minute break. The teachers would go into the office and have coffee. The students would either go to a small cafe nearby or stay in the room, open the windows, lean out, and smoke. One morning I came back early and a new student, a Mexican, offered me a cigarette.

"Sir. You like Turkish?"

I said I did.

Two weeks later, on a Friday, Mrs. Siemens came up to me.

"Thank you very much," she said graciously. "This morning was my last lesson. I enjoyed myself very much. I have a small present for you."

We shook hands. And I went down the stairs holding my books and this package carefully wrapped in white paper with a neat red ribbon.

In the office I unwrapped it. It was a large package of Turkish cigarettes. I was deeply touched. None of the others had bothered to say more than "goodbye." Perhaps, I thought, it's just old age that feels it has to pay for even the briefest encounter.

I asked the secretary in the office about Mrs. Siemens. She said that Mrs. Siemens was a widow. That she was part of *the* Siemens, in Germany. They were extremely wealthy. Her son had died and the doctors advised her to get away and do something to take her mind off things.

And as the secretary was talking I remembered that the words I introduced to the class during her stay—the passages I chose to read or dictate—for some reason kept harping on some aspect of death: on cemeteries, gravestones, funerals, coffins.

But this was Friday and there was little food in the house and I knew that I would have to walk back the three miles. If I had breakfast that morning, I didn't mind the walk. After Preston Circus it was very pleasant. There were the small gardens, each one with the name of an English city and with a single stalk of corn growing incongruously in their middles.

I went into a large tobacconist and told the girl behind the counter that I had bought this package of Turkish cigarettes for a friend as a gift, and I found out that he doesn't smoke.

The girl examined the box closely. Finally gave me fourteen shillings.

I went out and bought half a dozen eggs, a tin of luncheon meat, a loaf of bread, some sugar, tea, cheese, a newspaper, and took the bus back.

But that afternoon—though I watched my wife and children eat—I felt I had betrayed something.

RINGA RINGA ROSIE

THE BUCHANANS' fourteenth move in five years was to a
semi-detached brick cottage in Bogtown. The front faced
the main road. The back had long gardens, then a cricket
field which sloped down to brush and a river.

Moving had, by now, become an accepted but reluctant part
of their lives. Whenever they moved into a new address, no
serious attempt was made to change the place or impose on it
any sense of possession. All Sheila did was to take down a few of
the pictures from the walls and cover with cloths the tin trunks
and tea chests until they became part of the set furniture.

Bogtown was a row of labourers' cottages on one side of
the main Guildford-Horsham highway. At both ends were
filling stations and two pubs. One would have long gone out
of business had it not also been a rest point for the coaches
plying between London and the south coast. On Sundays the
village boys sat on their motorbikes in front of the filling stations and watched the cars go by. At night the place was lit up
by a yellow-glass *Shell* sign, above a garage. When the garage
closed the village was in darkness except for the sweeps made
by passing headlights and the glow from thrown-out cigarettes on the road.

The Buchanans came here, as they did in their previous moves, out of necessity. They were unsatisfactory tenants. They were always behind with the rent. The electricity never received payment until they were threatened with disconnection. And since most of the time they were just trying to make sure that there was enough for the day's food, there was little inclination or time left in seeing that the garden was looked after, or the place kept tidy. In any case the furnished accommodation which they could afford, by the time they had moved into it, had already become run down and seedy.

This time they had moved from a partly furnished semi-detached suburban house in East Finchley. At two-pounds-ten a week, the cottage was exactly half of the rent of the house. But even at that price they were being taken.

The rooms were damp. Patches of grey clotted the ceilings and the walls. The furniture was uncomfortable—a collection of junk that was picked up at various auction sales. And until the cold weather came, the place had fleas.

On their second day the Buchanans went on a tour of inspection. In the long back garden dead stalks mixed with new shoots. The grass was overgrown. The rhubarb was wild. There were weeds and two dead apple trees. The middle of the garden was a rubbish dump. And from the rubbish and from every other mound where previous tenants had emptied the lavatory bucket, giant nasturtiums with thick fleshy-white tubular stalks twisted magnificently up. The nasturtiums were enormous. The white of the stalks swamped the yellow orange brown of the petals. They crawled and twisted over the ground like a series of swollen blood vessels.

In the neighbouring gardens the grass was cut, the dividing hedges trimmed. There were small greenhouses and rose-bushes and apple, plum, and pear trees. There were cultivated blackberries, strawberries, and straight rows of vegetables.

"We always seem to move," Sheila said, watching three blue tits on the other side of the hedge—faces like Indians with war paint—picking at a piece of fat dangling from a wooden post, "into places where the gardens on either side are always neat and well looked after."

Whenever the wind dropped there was a smell of decomposition.

He was writing a new book. And she, besides housework and trying to make ends meet, also kept the children out of the cottage by taking them for long walks so he could work in quiet—and on the way filled the second-hand pram with bits of wood which she would hide with the raincover so that the neighbours wouldn't see—and wrote a weekly air-letter to her parents in Ottawa, which was a form of blackmail, for only on that basis did they send her ten dollars every week. Besides this, their only other income was the eighteen shillings family allowance.

George and Sheila had never lived in the country before. They had grown up in Kingston and had come over after graduating from Queens for their one trip abroad. But this was extended when Sheila became pregnant. They married. And George refused to return until he had a book published. So far their lives consisted of changing addresses, from one of the outskirts of London to the other, leaving small debts behind. But never had they allowed themselves to be cut off in the way they were now.

In the country when they couldn't pay the monthly newspaper bill, they had to go without newspapers. And likewise when the coal ran out. There was no alternate choice. The coalman lived five cottages away and when George promised that he would pay at the end of the week, and then couldn't, the coalman said, "I'm a man of principle," and refused to deliver any. George then took an old sack, went across the snow-covered cricket field, and into the drifts of the brush.

The wind blew the loose snow onto his face and against his eyes. In the fields across the river he could see horses. They swirled in and out of focus, manes blowing. It was, he thought, like a scene in a Russian film. He went to the river, which was frozen, and began to pull the dead branches from the trees. Breaking easily the very green, strong-smelling light wood with his foot and then throwing the pieces into the sack. And carrying the sack on his back, like the coalman, he went back through the gusts. He thought that this should make him hate this kind of life. That it ought to give him some incentive, to do something else. Instead, he looked at the drifting snow, the staring horses, the backs of the cottages, the blurring gardens, and thought it was fine. Someday he would write about it.

It was fine until he brought the sack inside the cottage. The two small children were there with running noses, and they had brought the cot down for the baby as this was the only room they could keep warm in winter. Nappies were around the fireplace, and drying clothes hung on a line from the ceiling across the room. But the wet wood only filled the room with smoke. They had been living in Bogtown five months. It was a Saturday morning, the middle of February, when she came upstairs and said, "There's no food for the weekend. You'll have to do something." He hitchhiked into Horsham and pawned his typewriter. That lasted them a week.

The following Saturday it was raining when she walked, without her usual knock, into his room. "The baker is outside. I'm not answering the door. We've no food for the weekend. And the milk lady isn't going to deliver any more unless we pay a pound tomorrow. You'll have to do something."

So he came down and fumbled with the broken kitchen-door handle. When he finally opened the door he made a joke about the broken handle. But the thin, dark man in white uniform did not find it amusing. He stood there. One hand held the wicker basket, the other his book. George took a plain white loaf. "We'll pay next week." The man didn't say anything. He closed his book. But when George put his hand out again to get another loaf, the man said, "I was told that all you could have was one bread."

George went back upstairs to his room, sat down in the chair, and looked out of the window. The garden was muddy and drab, the cricket field very green. He saw a large bird at the end of the field, by the river, gently flapping enormous wings. It had a small black body. Then he realized it was a man carrying a long plank of wood on his shoulders. And made a note of this in his notebook.

Downstairs he could hear Sheila becoming irritable with the children. And for his benefit she kept saying out loud, "It's all right. Daddy will do something."

He came down again.

"There's nothing I can do," he said quietly. "It's raining too hard. I've got nothing to sell."

"How about the printer?"

"He's away for the weekend. Gone to see his sister at Bognor."

He went over his list of what he could do. When there was nothing, he could usually borrow ten shillings from the printer down the road. Once, when they were hungry and living in Clapham, he did a song and dance for them, crossing his hands while he moved his knees together and apart. It made them laugh. And laughing they went to bed. But this time she was becoming hysterical.

"You gotta do something."

"But what can I do?"

The baby fell over a broken plastic flute and began to cry, then ran up to him and buried her head between his legs. The rain came down from the roof, and down the windows, and into the barrel by the drain. It overflowed onto the sogged earth, forming pools in the depressions.

"I don't care what. Long as you do something."

He went upstairs and looked through his room. Only a few used paperbacks were left on the bookshelves and an old copy of *Gulliver's Travels* that the secondhand bookseller in Horsham had refused to buy. He came down carrying a small green address book and began to telephone. Sheila and the children just stood and watched.

"Hello, Bill. This is George Buchanan. How are you? I bet you are. We're fine. Sheila and the kids. Look, Bill, the reason I rang. I'm hard pressed at the moment. Could you send me ten pounds? You'll have it back by the end of the month . . . I see. Sure, I understand. How's Tangier? No, just raining. I'll tell Sheila. Any time you come to England, drop in. I don't know. Maybe I'll go back home next year. Sure. Bye."

He hung up. Looked through his address book. Then he was talking again.

"May I speak to Paul de Secker-Remy? Hello, Duke. Guess who this is? No. George Buchanan. Bucky, the genius. Long time no see. I bet you are. Me too. Three, girls. We're living in England. I hear you've got yourself some hotel in the Laurentians. Paul, the reason I called. I'm in a spot at the moment. Could you telegraph a money order for fifty dollars? You'll have it back by the end of the month. Rose Cottage, Bogtown, near—Twenty-five will do. No . . . I didn't. I don't worry too much about income tax. Yeh, sure. Sounds like a nice car. I understand. Bye."

He continued to go through the pages of his address book, calling up people, and he was getting near the end when Kate, the three-year-old, said: "What Daddie doin'?"

"I'm doing something."

"What Daddie doin'?"

"Talking on the telephone."

"Don't be silly, Daddie, that's only the top-end of my toy iron," Cassie, the eldest, said—a blue-eyed girl of five with blond, curly hair.

"Daddie funny," Kate said. "Daddie pretendin'."

He had gone through to his last address when Kate ran to him and took his hand. For her that game was over. She began to pull him. "C'mon, Daddie, play inga-inga-osie."

Now Cassie took his other hand. And Sheila, standing by the stairs, began to weep. For a short while Cassie didn't know whether she should join her mother and cry as well. But Kate pulled him, then her, and then went over and held out her hand for Sheila. She took hold. And the four of them went around the room in a circle, singing loudly.

Ringa—ringa—rosie.
A pocketful of posie,
A tishoo. A tishoo.
We all fall down.

And they all did, laughing.

I'LL BRING YOU BACK
SOMETHING NICE

I

GORDON RIDEAU'S eyes were closed and he could hear
the trucks going by outside the window on the main
London-to-Guildford road, and in between the trucks,
the alarm clock on the floor. At his feet the hot water bottle
was cold. He shoved it to the edge of the bed. Then he opened
his eyes and saw the wallpaper: wide yellow bars separated by
thin black lines.

His wife, Coral, lay with several blankets over her so that
just her dark hair was sticking out. Between them a National
Health orange bottle was wrapped in a nappy to keep the milk
inside it warm in case the baby woke during the night.

He could hear Kate walking down the stairs. The hall light
was on. The brown curtains across the bedroom were drawn.
The room was cold. There was a pitcher standing in a large
basin—both had a red rose painted on the enamel—and a
large bedpan with an old copy of *Vogue* on top. A small trip-
tych of three angels stood on the mantel above the small fireplace which was stuffed with newspapers, cardboard, and bits
of coloured crepe paper. All this they had inherited from the

owner of the cottage. Their belongings: a steel trunk was open in a corner, in another corner two smaller trunks. Inside were clothes jumbled and spilling out.

Coral sat up quickly, turned back the cover, and looked closely down one leg. Near the ankle she picked off a flea and, carefully, crushed it between her fingers. Then she left the bed.

Gordon watched her. There is nothing graceful about her movements, he thought. She was wearing a grey sweater and put on a blue skirt. She took the nappy with the makeshift milk bottle and the alarm clock, and went downstairs.

Now he lay in bed in a sense of luxury. He was alone, staying in. He drew his knees up to keep warm. He heard the radio downstairs playing dance music. And lay there wondering whether she would bring him a cup of tea.

A door opened below and Kate called out,

"Breakfast is ready Daddy."

"Coming," he said.

And remained in bed knowing that in a few minutes she would open the door again and say, "Breakfast is ready Daddy."

And he would say, "I'm just getting my socks on."

But he had them on all night, and his shirt, and a heavy black sweater.

The child came lightly up the stairs. She had just turned four. A shy attractive child with blond straight hair and fine small features.

"OK," Gordon said as she came into the bedroom. "I'm coming."

"Post, Daddy."

She gave him a brown envelope.

He opened it. It was a letter from the electricity company saying that a man had come yesterday to disconnect the electricity but no one was in. He was going to come on Friday at eleven unless they could pay £12 5s. 2d.

It means a trip to London, Gordon thought. And that was enough to make him get up.

He dressed and went to the window and pulled back the brown curtain. The diagonal crack in the glass was like a scar. The fields, across the road, muddy and drab. The trees on the border of the field—misshapen by the ivy that was slowly killing them—looked very pretty. He watched a motorcycle accelerate as it went by splashing mud on either side and with a muddy wake. Then he closed the light in their bedroom and went down a narrow passage. By the children's open door: the smell of urine, the camp bed, the mug of water, the comics and books on top of an overturned orange case. He turned sharply. Down the narrow stairs. At the bottom he opened a door and immediately felt the warm air. It was the one room that was warm. A coal-fire was going in the fireplace. Beside it, in a corner, was a baby's cot.

Kate stood by the cot dressed in a jumper, a red sweater, which someone had given them when their own children had grown out of the clothes. She was talking to the baby. "Ah goo lie goo Rachel. Ah goo lie goo." The baby stood up in the cot, grasping the wooden struts, and gurgled back a couple of vowels. She looked like something caught in a cage.

"Good morning," Gordon said cheerfully to the children and went into the kitchen.

Coral was at the stove. "High keeps changing," she said. "I don't know if the hot plate is off or on."

"Use the master switch."

Then he decided it would be better to show her. "Off," he said and put the switch up. "On," he pulled it down.

"What do you want," she said. "There's a bit of cheese—I could make toast."

"Fine," he said and went into the other room. Kate was playing with some pieces of paper and a pencil. The baby was crawling on the floor to the coal bucket. She took pieces of coal and tried to put them in her mouth. Her lips were black. Gordon took the bucket away and put it by the side of the fireplace, behind a chair. The child crawled after it.

"What post did you have?" she said, bringing in the toast and cheese.

"A reminder from the electricity."

"When are they coming?"

"Tomorrow." He tried to appear casual. "I guess I'll have to go to London."

"Where Daddy going?" Kate said quickly.

"To London—I'll bring you back something."

"A dolly," the child said excitedly.

"What will you do?" Coral said.

"I'll try the bank first—I'll find a way."

"You know how I hate this place."

"I know."

And he prepared himself for her to follow with: you can always get away but I'm stuck here . . . My hands are tied . . . I'm the one that's always left behind. Instead she said, "When you're up could you look around?"

"I'll go and see some real estate people."

"Try somewhere near a park."

"I'll try darling."

"This isn't just you saying things to keep me happy? You will do something."

"Yes," he said quietly.

"We've got less than two months."

"You know how I work," he tried to sound convincing. "Leave things until the last week. Then I get something."

She didn't reply. He was nearly there, he thought.

"You won't forget."

And he was safe now.

"I'll do my best darling," he said and got up. "I'd better shave."

There was some hot water left in the kettle. He emptied it into a tin mould that she used to make cakes in, mixed a bit of cold water from the tap, and shaved in front of the mirror, above the dishes.

He tried to tidy his sideburns and realized that his face looked odd. It was the eyes. The left one set at an angle. He saw it as well in the baby. Around the small mirror was the kitchen window with old spiderwebs. Cuts in the snow skiers made climbing a hill sideways. And for a moment he was back to the pressure the cold made on his forehead. He was in a sleigh sitting behind the swaying rump of a horse held in its tight harness, with Holly. Past white fields with the telegraph poles just protruding. I could tell, she said, when you held my hand to take my coat off. And Jasmine. It snowed all that day in Montreal. After the lecture they went to the Berkeley and drank Brandy Alexanders until it was time to go. The expensive gloom of her parents' apartment. The thing like a curled bulrush that she took from out her hair. And Lily. How quick it was with her ... She had her own car. Her father owned an entire small town in Northern Ontario. He wondered what would have happened to his life had he made one of them pregnant.

"Don't forget to empty the bucket," Coral called from the other room.

He took a spade from the shed, walked along the path to the back garden. Halfway down he selected a part of bare earth and began to dig. He emptied the almost full black bucket into the hole he made. Then shovelled the earth back into the hole. It splashed gently. Then the liquid overflowed and stained the earth. He came back into the kitchen. "I've emptied the bucket," he said to Coral. He washed his hands. "Is there anything left?"

She went to the dresser with the few dishes and from a Peter Rabbit saucer took out a halfpenny and a 3d. stamp. He put the halfpenny in his pocket, then went upstairs, into his room, and put on his one clean white shirt. He took down his trousers hanging from a hook on a hanger in the corner. They were the trousers of his one remaining suit. He saw how frayed the bottoms were. He took the small scissors from his desk and cut some of the hanging threads. He put on the trousers, his tie and jacket, and came down carrying the black winter overcoat that he bought twelve years ago when he was at university. He put it on. Coral brushed him down. The children were crowding around him.

"You look nice, Daddy," Kate said.

"You will look around," Coral said.

"Yes," he said, then smiled to the children.

"I'll bring you back something nice."

"A dolly?" Kate said.

"Something to eat."

Coral picked up the baby.

He kissed them all goodbye.

They went with him to the front gate, and watched him walk along the road away from them. Kate climbed up the wooden gate and said goodbye several times. And they waved to each other.

From a distance of ten yards, Coral thought, he was still handsome and looked neat and successful. There was the confident manner, the upright walk. He turned and waved back to them. From some thirty yards, she thought, he looked even better. He might have been an executive going off to the office, to work.

He looked for darkness in the windshield. He could tell quickly by the amount of darkness, the outline (like those outlines they had trained him to look at in a tenth, a twentieth, a fiftieth of a second), whether the driver of the coming car was alone or not. He didn't bother to put up his hand if there were two.

II

From Piccadilly, Gordon walked down Lower Regent Street and into the bank, across the light marble floor, to the short teller with the Italian-sounding name. They shook hands and asked each other questions as if they knew one another well.

"I've just come up for the day," Gordon said.

"How is the family?"

"Fine. And yours?"

"They're fine. We went to Connemara for a holiday." He smiled and took out some photographs. "It was wonderful— the best holiday we had."

There were photographs of some children by a pony, by a cottage. And the bank teller in a pair of shorts.

"May I see the manager?"

"I'll see if he is free."

He left his cage and out of it looked even smaller but long in the arms.

He came back smiling. "The manager is busy. But our assistant manager, Mister Henderson, will see you."

"Come in, Mister Rideau."

The assistant manager, unlike most North Americans, looked much older than his forty-two years. But his "Sit down, Mister Rideau. Cigarette?" had a professional warmth. "Now, what's the trouble?"

"I have an electricity bill just over twelve pounds that I must meet tomorrow or else they'll cut us off. Could the bank let me overdraw fifteen pounds? It will only be for a short time. I've got money coming in."

"I'm sorry. It's impossible," the assistant manager said. "I can't let you have a pound." He lowered his voice. "*He* gave me strict instructions." And his eyes indicated the frosted glass partition of the other room.

"But I've been with the bank for seven years."

"*He* doesn't consider you a banking proposition."

They were both silent. The assistant manager looked uncomfortable. "Are you a veteran?"

"Yes," Gordon said, "I was in the Army," and remembered a time in Montreal, after taking a girl home to the Town of Mount Royal, he flagged a cab and found he didn't have enough money to get back. He told this to the driver. "Are you a veteran?" the driver asked.

"I was in the Air Force," the assistant manager said. He crushed his cigarette in the green-glass ashtray. Then stood up and walked away from his desk. Gordon also got up. The assistant manager put his hands in his trouser pockets.

"I'm sorry I can't let you have the money. Take this. Pay it back when you can. *Please.*"

"Thanks, I'll pay it back soon as I can."

"There's no rush."

He wondered if the assistant manager was now going to give him a lecture. But they shook hands and said goodbye.

Outside, walking up the Haymarket, Gordon took the bill out and saw it was a five-pound note. He was delighted. Imagine getting money from an assistant bank manager he had never met. But a moment later it also registered on him that the probable reason he got the money was because the assistant manager had never laid eyes on him before.

At a small kiosk he bought a pack of tipped Gauloises, a box of matches, an *Evening Standard*, then walked along Piccadilly to Lyons Corner House. He went into the Wimpy side, found an empty table by the wall, ordered two hamburgers and a black coffee. Around the centre counter, North Americans were staring at other North Americans. It might have been the drugstore back home, except they were on good behaviour.

III

The alarm clock woke Mr. and Mrs. Black at seven, even though Mr. Black wasn't going to work. He went to shave, and used the foam lather of the company whose assistant accountant he was. Then he sat down in the room with the Van Gogh print on the wall, the souvenir ashtray from Clovelly, the silver napkin rings, the photograph of himself in the Home Guard, while Mrs. Black did his porridge and the two pieces of toast in the kitchen.

"You won't get excited," Mrs. Black said as they were having their second cup of tea.

"No dear."

"She could have her old room. The children could sleep in the spare room. And there's the camp bed."

Mr. Black put on the jacket of his dark suit, the homburg hat, the black coat. He was a handsome if stern-looking man with dark, straight hair and a lean face, but there was a strain about it, the result of a lifetime of bronchial trouble.

"Do you want to take anything for the train?" Mrs. Black said, standing by the glass-enclosed cabinet with her Mary Webb novels and his *Lord Jim,* James Agate, *The Quest for Corvo,* the books on accountancy.

"I have the paper."

"I hope it goes all right," Mrs. Black said at the door.

"I'll be back for tea. Goodbye dear."

The train went by Eltham, Kidbrooke, Lewisham. Mr. Black turned to the *Telegraph's* crossword "_ _ _ _ _ _ _ _ _ is mortal's chieftest enemy" *(Shakespeare).* He tried "dying." But that wasn't long enough. Neither was "boredom." "Temptation" was too long…

At Charing Cross he changed to a tube that took him to Victoria, and here he had to wait another ten minutes for a train to Horsham. At Horsham he took a taxi to the cottage. It was 10:20 when he opened the front gate, but he didn't go to the front door. He went around the side of the cottage, where he surprised Coral hanging up the children's washing.

"Hullo," he said quietly.

They smiled, then they kissed. And one could see a family resemblance.

She opened the kitchen door and led him into the warm room where he took off his coat.

"How is Mummy?"

"She sends her love."

He gave the children some toffee candy.

"Gordon is in London," she said. "He had to go up on business."

"Daddy is going to bring me a dolly," Kate said.

"We haven't had our milk," Coral said. "I could make tea without it."

Mr. Black sat in the worn red chair. His breathing was audible. "You can't go on like this," he said quietly.

Coral quickly took the children into the next room and closed the door behind them.

"Why don't you leave him," Mr. Black said. "I'll see that you and the children are looked after. I'll get you a house—"

She didn't reply.

"He's no good," he said. "He'll only drag you down."

"I can't leave him," she said.

"If he wants to go on like this there's no reason why you and the children—"

"He's got no one except me and the children."

"I'll get you a house—" he began, but he knew it had not gone right. This wasn't the way he had rehearsed it.

"I think you must hate me," Coral said.

"I don't hate you," Mr. Black said. But he was at a loss as to what to say next.

Kate came into the room, followed by the crawling baby. Kate had a drawing. "This is for you Grandpa." He took the drawing and gave the child a half-crown. He also gave Coral three one-pound notes. She immediately went next door to the grocery and came back with milk, sugar, and some biscuits. They sat in the warm room and had tea while Mr. Black told her about a cousin who had gone to Rhodesia to run an Outward Bound school. That an uncle had become manager of a bank in Plymouth. And another cousin had gone to Canada as a physical training instructor. It was time, he said, he was leaving. They walked slowly up the road to the Shell garage, where Mr. Black took a taxi. Kate kissed him. So did Coral. "Goodbye Daddy," she said.

IV

For half an hour Gordon sat in the cubicle by the wall of the Wimpy watching other people. Then he went downstairs to the washroom. He turned the hot tap of the sink and began to wash his hands.

"You can always tell a McGill man. He washes his hands *before—*"

Gordon turned to see a grinning boyish face. I don't know him, he thought. Aloud he said. "Of course. It's—"

"Not fair surprising you like this. I'm Hugh Finlay," the man said still grinning.

"Hugh Finlay," Gordon said. They shook hands. "What are you doing over here?"

"Passing through. I'm on the way south, to France."

They were both in their middle thirties, McGill graduates, in London, but there the resemblance stopped abruptly. Hugh Finlay was blond, ruddy, and radiated bodily comfort.

"I heard you were over here," Finlay said. "I was going to go to the bank to get your address. You know we're having a reunion?"

"No," Gordon said. "No, I didn't."

"It's our tenth anniversary."

They returned to the cubicle and ordered two coffees.

"You've worn well, Hugh," Gordon said.

"The reward for leading a healthy life," Finlay said. "You married?"

"Yes. We've got two kids."

"Do I know her?"

"No. She's an English girl. We live in the country. How about you?"

"I was engaged to Sally Boston. The Boston Biscuits. They give a quarter of a million each year *anonymously*. But she was too good. She's like an angel. If she saw somebody poor, she'd cry." He took out some coloured snapshots from his jacket pocket. "This is my yacht at Cannes. Here's a picture of Garbo on it. Here's some of the girls I had on board last summer. She's only sixteen. Hard to believe. Do you know any addresses of girls?"

The pretty West Indian waitress came with the two cups of coffee. Gordon insisted on paying.

"How about coming to the reunion?" Hugh said suddenly. "Lot of the gang you know will be there."

"Do you think it will be all right?"

"I know it will. I'll phone Charlie Bishop."

While he was gone, Gordon tried to remember Hugh Finlay at McGill . . . but he couldn't.

"I talked to Charlie. He said sure, swell. We've a couple of hours. How about if we got some fresh air. I've a rented car outside."

They were driving through Hyde Park when Hugh Finlay said, "I saw a friend of yours last week. Mary Savage. Except she's not Mary Savage any more, she's Mary Troy. Remember Jack? You'll see him at the reunion."

"How is Mary?"

"Exactly the same. She does some kind of social work."

"What's Jack doing?"

"Selling beans . . . millions of them. They've got a place by the river. Fifteen rooms but no kids. I think they're planning to adopt one."

V

Because her father left her the money, Coral decided to go into London with the children. She washed them and herself, got them dressed, caught a green bus to the station, then a train to Victoria.

From Victoria she took a bus to Kensington Gardens, and walked through the Gardens. A man was flying a kite, ducks flew over. The children chased the wood pigeons. She liked London. It was the only place she wanted to live. But what chance had they? She decided to try the Town Hall. The receptionist led her into a separate office where a single yellow rose in a thin glass vase stood on the wooden desk. "Mrs. Troy will be here in a minute."

A tall, angular woman with dark hair and glasses came in. The woman was about the same age as Coral, perhaps a year or two older. "What's the problem?" she said.

"We have to get out of the place we're living in . . . in Sussex . . . and I wonder if you can help us find somewhere in London?"

"You have no alternative accommodation?"

"No."

"Have you funds?"

"No. We haven't."

"Does your husband live with you?"

"Yes."

"I'm sorry. I'm afraid I can't help you. We can only help if your husband leaves you."

Coral came out with the children and walked along Kensington High Street. Everyone, it seemed, would help her if he left her, or if she left him. Otherwise, what was the future? Moving from one rented place to another, from country village to country village or, with luck, to a provincial town. And she hated living in other people's houses.

She caught a bus to Trafalgar Square and walked among the pigeons. The children clung to her. Then along the Mall. She bought some choc ices and they had a little picnic of choc ices on a bench in St. James's Park. She wondered where Gordon was, who he was seeing, what he was doing. He always came back with money and food from these trips to London. But she suspected that he never told her the whole truth as to how he got it.

She was walking through the park—the baby in the push-chair, Kate holding her hand—when a truck, with a camera on the roof, stopped. A man and woman were inside. The man said, "Do you mind being in a film? Just like you are . . . with your children. Can you do that again? Thank you. Thank you very much." A few minutes later, further into the park, she sat on the grass, underneath a beech, by the water. The sun was out. Kate was feeding the ducks, the baby was on the grass watching. She suddenly felt extraordinarily happy. She hoped the truck would come back and take a picture of them now.

VI

Well-dressed men in their middle to late thirties were standing under the hanging flags or by the windows looking out to Trafalgar Square. They greeted one another enthusiastically. They came up to Gordon Rideau.

"Hi, Gordy, old man."

"Where have you been hiding?"

"Hello Gordon," Charlie Bishop said, and shook hands. "Nice of you to come. It has been a long time."

"Ten years."

"You don't look any different, Gordon."

Mike Gagnon, an energetic head of a publishing firm who was tipped while an undergraduate to be the next prime minister, came up. "Let us in on the secret Gordy. How do you keep so slim? You wearing a corset?" Mike's fine features were slowly being undermined by fat. "I go to the Y three times a week but I've still got this rubber ring." And he playfully slapped his middle.

Charlie Bishop hit his glass with a spoon and called, Quiet. Quiet. A short stocky man with glasses, almost bald, but hardly a line in his face. He was a director in the London branch of his grandfather's tar company.

"As you know," he said confidently, "this is something of an occasion. Our tenth anniversary. And while the main one is being celebrated in Montreal, it is fitting that we in London should get together and remember when we all were . . ."

"Single," someone shouted.

"*And* broke," another replied.

He waited. "The bond we established at McGill was something special. It's a different kind of loyalty to anything else. It's different from the wife or the kids. And I know that every time we come and get together like this that bond is strengthened."

"Hear, hear," came from several tables.

"This year I have a surprise. And by now you all must know who the surprise is. He's sitting here beside me . . . Somebody has pointed out that our year was a vintage year. And it's true. We've got more people in the Canadian edition of *Time* than any year since. But the only literary man we produced was Gordy. He has lived in England, in the country, since he left us. And he is difficult to get hold of. But when I heard he would be in London today I didn't have to do much persuading to get him to come to this reunion. Fellow classmates, I'm very proud to give you Gordon Rideau."

There was generous applause. Gordon got up.

"I first would like to say how pleased I am to be back with you."

"Hey, where did you pick up that Limey accent?" Jack Troy called out. Charlie Bishop detected something else in Gordon's voice and wondered why he was so nervous.

"Although this is the first reunion that I have attended, I've often thought of my college days," he said hesitantly. "I really had a good time. And I was just old enough to know it . . . I think what made us different from the other years was because we were all returning veterans. And it was difficult to pretend we were college kids straight from high school . . ."

He's not a good speaker, thought Charlie Bishop. His voice is too monotonous. But he seems to have the right idea. It looks like a short speech.

". . . and that nice secure feeling of walking under the avenue of black trees in winter, or in the fall sitting on the grass under the willow . . ."

Hugh Finlay seemed, at that moment, to be sitting on the grass under the willow tree watching the grey squirrels, the fallen leaves on the lawns, and waiting for a two o'clock lecture.

"One is always disappointed by change," Gordon said coming to the end. "And these reunions remain a tribute. To one's youth. To gaiety. To optimism. When things seemed continually fresh. And life was a pleasure. And it was all so very easy."

He sat down quickly to loud applause. Charlie Bishop leaned over and shook Gordon's hand. So did Mike Gagnon from the other side.

Then Charlie Bishop got up, thanked Gordon for his speech. "Before we leave the formal side," Charlie said, "I'd like us all to stand and remember those classmates who are not here with us."

They got up, some bowed their heads slightly. Charlie waited then nodded to Jack Troy. And Jack began to sing. Holding hands the rest joined in. There were tears in Hugh Finlay's eyes as, with the others, he sang.

For auld lang syne, my dear.
For auld lang syne.
We'll drink a cup of kindness yet
For the days of auld lang syne.

They broke up into small groups around separate tables. And as the afternoon went on, the food, the drink, being guest of honour did something to Gordon Rideau. He went around gaily from one group to another. And he found himself boasting about things that hadn't happened.

"The Russians have brought out my last two novels," he said, cutting into one group's conversation. "But I can't spend those roubles unless I go there."

To another. "They're making a film in Ireland. It's called *The Millionaire*. I did the script. It's an original."

A few moments later he tried again. "I won some prize in Australia. But I don't believe it. How can you believe a telegram that's signed Johnny Soprano?"

But after a while of this he felt their lack of interest. And that he was being left out of their conversation. The others were talking away and they wouldn't let him come in. He had the feeling that he was no longer wanted ...

If anyone was watching this convivial gathering he would have seen, through the smoke of cigarettes and cigars, Mike Gagnon get up from the table shortly after five and make his way across the room to the toilet. Gordon Rideau got up and followed him. They were in there for a few minutes. Then they came out together, not talking. Some ten minutes later, Charlie Bishop made his way to the toilet. And Gordon left his chair soon after Charlie disappeared. They came out together, Charlie somewhat red in the face.

In the next half-hour Gordon followed three more into the toilet, and reappeared with each one.

The talk around the table where Gordon Rideau sat was noticeably subdued. A short while later he got up and said he had to go. "It's a great reunion," he said to Charlie Bishop. He wanted to shake Charlie's hand, but Charlie withdrew his. "See you ..."

After he had gone, Charlie Bishop, Mike Gagnon, Jack Troy, and Hugh Finlay sat around without saying anything. They looked tired.

"Our great author," Mike Gagnon said finally.

"Maybe he's had a run of hard luck," Jack Troy said.

"How much did he hit you?"

"Three pounds."

"He got that from me."

"That four-flusher—" Hugh said, his voice shaking.

"You guys got off easy," Charlie Bishop said. "He hit me for five."

"*That little four-flusher.*" Suddenly Hugh lashed out at a glass on the table. Then he saw it was on the floor in pieces.

"Don't take it so hard," Charlie Bishop said. "There's another one next year. I won't make the same mistake."

"But why ... ?" Hugh said. "Why did he spoil everything?"

WE ALL BEGIN IN
A LITTLE MAGAZINE

W E LIVE in a small coastal town and in the summer, when
the place is looking its best, it becomes overcrowded
with people who have come away from the cities for
their annual holiday by the sea. It is then that we leave and go
up to London for our holiday.

My wife usually finds a house by looking through the
Times. In this way we had the house of a man who built hotels
in the poor parts of Africa so that wealthy American Negroes
could go back to see where their grandparents came from.
Another summer it was an architect's house where just about
everything was done by push-button control. A third time, it
was in a house whose owner was in the middle of getting a
divorce—for non-consummation—and wanted to be out of
the country.

This June she saw an ad saying: DOCTOR'S HOUSE
AVAILABLE IN LONDON FOR THREE WEEKS. REASON-
ABLE RENT. She phoned the number. And we agreed to take it.

The advertised house was central, near South Kensington tube station, not far from the Gardens. The taxi took us
from Paddington—how pale people looked in London on a
hot summer's day—and brought us to a wide street, stopping

in front of a detached all-white house with acacia trees in the front garden. A bottle of warm milk was on the doorstep. I opened the door with the key and brought our cases inside.

The phone was ringing.

"Hello," I said.

"Is this *ABC*?" a youthful voice asked.

"I'm sorry," I said. "You have the wrong number."

"What is your number?"

"Knightsbridge 4231," I said.

"That is the number," the voice said.

"There must be some mistake," I said. "This is a doctor's house."

"Is the doctor there?"

"No," I said. "He's on holiday."

"Can I leave a message for him?"

"Are you ill?"

"No," he said. "Tell him that David White rang. David White of Somerset. He has had my manuscript for over six months now. He said he would let me know over a month ago. I have written him four times."

"I'll tell him," I said.

"If he needs more time," the young man said hesitantly, "I don't mind—"

"OK," I said and hung up.

"I don't know what's going on here," I said to my wife.

But she and the children were busy exploring the rest of the house.

It was a large house and it looked as if it had been lived in. The front room was a children's room with all sorts of games and blackboards and toys and children's books and posters on the walls. There was the sitting room, the bottom half of the walls were filled with books in shelves. There were more books in the hallway, on the sides of the stairs, and in shelves on every landing. There were three separate baths. A breakfast room where a friendly black cat slept most of the time on top of the oil-fired furnace. And a back garden with a lawn, flowerbeds on the sides, a pond with goldfish, water lilies, and a copper beech tree at the end.

The phone rang and a shaky voice said, "May I speak to Doctor Jones?"

"I'm sorry, he's on holiday."

"When will he come back?"

"In three weeks," I said.

"I can't wait that long," the voice said. "I'm going to New York tomorrow."

"Would you," I said, "like to leave a message?"

"I can't hear what you're saying," the voice said. "Can you speak up? I'm a bit deaf and have to wear a hearing aid. The doctors have a cure for this now. If I'd been born two years later I would have been all right."

"I said, would you like to leave the doctor a message?"

"I don't think that will do any good," he said. "Could you look in his office and see if he has a poem of mine? It's called "Goodbye." If it is in proof, don't bother. I'll wait. But just find out. I am going over to teach creative writing in night school so I can make some money to come back here. The poem will probably be on the floor."

"Hold on," I said.

I went into the office at the top of the house. The floor was cluttered with papers and magazines and manuscripts with letters and envelopes attached. On a wooden table, a large snap file had correspondence. A box had cheques for small amounts. There were also several pound notes, loose change, a sheet of stamps, and two packages of cigarettes. (How trusting, I thought. The doctor doesn't know us—supposing we were crooks?) There was typing paper, large envelopes, a typewriter, a phone, telephone directories, and some galleys hanging on a nail on a wall. A smaller table had an in-and-out tray to do with his medical work, more letters, and copies of the *Lancet*. The neatest part of the room was the area where stacks of unsold copies of *ABC* were on the floor against the far wall.

"I'm sorry," I said on the phone. "I can't see it."

"Oh," he said. He sounded disappointed.

"Well, tell him that Arnold Mest called. M-E-S-T."

"I've got that," I said.

"Goodbye," he said.

"You won't guess," I told my wife. "The doctor edits a little magazine."

"We can't get away from it," she said.

Early next morning the doorbell woke us. It was the postman. He gave me several bundles. There were letters from different parts of England and Europe, and air mail ones from Canada, the States, Australia, and South America. There were two review copies of books from publishers. There were other little magazines, and what looked like medical journals, and a few bills.

As I put the envelopes and parcels on the chair in the office and saw the copies of *Horizon* and *New Writing*, the runs of *Encounter*, *London Magazine*, and a fine collection of contemporary books on the shelves right around the room, it brought back a time twenty years ago when I first came over.

There was still the bomb-damage to be seen, the queues, the ration books, the cigarettes under the counter. And a general seediness in people's clothes. Yet I remember it as one of my happiest times. Perhaps because we were young and full of hope and because we were so innocent of what writing involved. A lot of boys and girls had come to London from different parts. And we would meet in certain pubs, in certain restaurants—Joe Lyons, the French pub, Caves de France, the Mandrake—then go on somewhere else. I remember going over to see another Canadian, from Montreal, who was writing a novel. He had a studio, by the Chelsea football grounds (we could always tell when a goal was scored). I remember best the cold damp winter days with the fog thick—you could just see the traffic lights—and then going inside and having some hot wine by the open fire and talking about writing, what we were writing, and where we had things out. We used to send our stories, optimistically, to the *name* magazines. But that was like taking a ticket in a lottery. It was the little magazines who published us, who gave encouragement and kept us going.

I remember Miss Waters. She was in her late forties, a pale woman with thinning blond hair and a docile tabby cat. She edited a little magazine founded by her great-grandfather. She had photographs of Tennyson on the wall, of Yeats and Dylan Thomas. And wooden pigeon-holes, like the sorting room at the post office, with some of the recent back issues. She didn't know when I was coming. But she always greeted me with: "How nice to see you. Do come in."

She walked ahead, into the dark living room. Suggested that I take my winter coat off. Then she would bring out a decanter of sherry and fill a glass, then take out a package of *Passing Clouds*, offer me a cigarette.

I was treated as a writer by this woman when I had very little published. And that did more than anything to keep up morale. And after another sherry, another *Passing Cloud*, and she had asked me what I was working on and seemed very interested in what I said, she told me that her great-grandfather paid Tennyson a thousand pounds for one of his short poems, and two thousand pounds to George Eliot for a short story. (Was she trying to tell me that there was money to be made out of writing?) Then she stood up, and we went into the other room. It was very neat and tidy. Magazines on a table laid out as at a news agent's, books as in a library.

"Is there anything you would like to review?" she asked.

I would pick a novel or two, or a book of short stories.

Then she would say, "And help yourself to four books from that pile."

That pile consisted of books that she didn't want reviewed. She had told me, the first time, to take these books to a bookseller in the Strand who would give me half price for them, and later sell them to the public libraries. But before I could get the money from him I had to sign my name in what looked like a visiting book. And I saw there, above me, the signatures of the leading Sunday and weekly reviewers—they were also selling their review copies for half price.

And I remember how I would come to her place—with the brown envelopes lying behind the door—broke and depressed. And when I left her, I left feeling buoyed up, cheerful. There would be the few pounds from the review copies. Money enough for a hamburger and a coffee and a small cigar. And there was something to do—the books to review. She always paid in advance.

And before Miss Waters there were others. The press officer at the Norwegian embassy—he ran a Norwegian little magazine, in English, from London. And another one, from India, also in English. My early stories appeared in both. And when I got a copy of the Indian magazine I saw that my Canadian characters had been turned into Indians. And there was another editor who would ask to borrow your box of matches. Then, when you got back to your flat, you found he had stuffed a pound note inside the box.

They are all gone—like their magazines.

And something has gone with them.

Those carefree days when you wrote when you felt like it. And slept in when you wanted to. And would be sure of seeing others like yourself at noon in certain places.

Now in the morning, after breakfast, I wait for the mail to come. Then I go upstairs and close the door behind me. And I make myself get on with the novel, the new story, or the article which has been commissioned by a well-paying magazine. I take a break for lunch, then come back up here until four.

Once in a while I might take a day off and go on a bus to see what the country is like. I forget that there is so much colour about. Or, for a change, take a train for the day to Plymouth. But otherwise, it is up the stairs to this room. All my energy now goes into work. I light up a small Dutch cigar, and sometimes I talk to myself. I feel reasonably certain now that what I have written will be published. Writing has become my living.

Of course there are still the occasional days when things are going right and the excitement comes back from the work. Not like in those early days when writing and the life we were leading seemed so much to belong together. I had complete faith then in those little magazines. What I didn't know was that what they bred was infectious. They infected a lot of young people with the notion that to be involved with literature was somehow to be involved with the good life. And by the time you learned differently, it was usually too late.

On Friday I had to be up early. In the morning I was to be interviewed, in a rowing-boat on the Serpentine, for a Canadian television program on the "brain drain." And later I was to meet my publisher for lunch.

It was very pleasant on the water early in the morning. The sun made patterns. People going to work stopped to watch, while I rowed the interviewer, the cameraman, the sound-recordist, and their equipment—and was asked why wasn't I living in Canada, and why did I write?

I met my publisher in his club. He is an American, from Boston, bald and short. We had a martini. Then another. Then we went into the dining room. Smoked salmon followed by duck with wine, then dessert. And ending with brandy and a large Havana cigar.

He asked me what type would I like for the book, could I send him the blurb for the dust jacket? He told me the number of copies they would print, that one of the Sunday papers wanted to run a couple of extracts before publication. He told me some gossip about other writers, publishers, and agents. And what was I writing now? And which publishing season would he have it for?

I left him after four and caught a taxi back to the house.

"How did it go?" my wife asked.

"OK," I said. "How was the zoo?"

She began to tell me, when we heard a noise. It sounded as if it was coming from the front door. We went to look and surprised a man with a key trying to open the door. He was in his late fifties, short and stocky and wearing a shabby raincoat.

"Is the doc in?" he said timidly.

"No," I said. "He's on holiday."

"Oh," he said. "I've come up from Sussex. I always have a bed here when I come up."

He spoke with an educated accent.

"I'm sorry," I said. "But we have the place for three weeks."

"I always have a bed here when I come up."

"There isn't room," I said.

"My name is George Smith," he said. "*ABC* publish me. I'm a poet."

"How do you do," I said. "We'll be gone in ten days. Come in and have a drink."

While I poured him a brandy, I asked what was the name of his last book.

He said he had enough work for a book and had sent the manuscript to—and here he named a well-known publisher.

"But I haven't heard," he said.

"That's a good sign," I said.

"Perhaps they have lost it," he said. "Or they are, like Doc, on holiday."

He brought out a small tin and took some loose tobacco and began to roll his own cigarette and one for me.

"How long," I asked, "have they had it?"

"Nearly five months," he said.

He finished his brandy. I poured him some more.

"I would ring them up and find out," I said. "Or drop them a line."

"Do you think I should?"

"Yes," I said.

I went to the door to see him out, and instead walked him to the bus stop.

The street was full of mountain ash, and red berries were lying on the lawns, the sidewalk, and on the road.

"I had a letter from T. S. Eliot," he said. "I kept it all these years. But I sold it last month to Texas for fifty dollars," he said proudly. "My daughter was getting married. And I had to get her a present."

I asked him where he would stay the night.

"I have one or two other places," he said. "I come up about once every six weeks. London is my commercial centre."

I went and bought him a package of cigarettes.

"Thank you," he said.

The red bus came and I watched him get on.

When I got back my wife said, "Well, do you feel better?"

"No," I said.

It went on like this—right through the time we were there. An assortment of people turned up at the door. There was a young blond girl—she wanted to lick stamps for literature. There were visiting lecturers and professors from American and Canadian and English universities. There were house-wives; one said, over the phone, "I'll do anything to get into print." There were long-distance telephone calls. One rang after midnight and woke us up. "Nothing important," the voice said. "I just wanted to have a talk. We usually do now and then. I've had stories in *ABC*."

There was, it seemed, a whole world that depended on the little magazine.

I tried to be out of the house as much as possible. I went to see my agent. He had a cheque for four hundred dollars, less his commission, waiting for me, for the sale of a story. He took me out for a meal, and we talked about the size of advances, the sort of money paperback publishers were paying these days, the way non-fiction was selling better than fiction. I met other writers in expensive clubs and restaurants. We gossiped about what middle-aged writer was leaving his middle-aged wife to live with a young girl. And what publisher was leaving his firm to form his own house. I was told what magazines were starting—who paid the best.

Then I would come back to the phone ringing, the piles of mail, and people turning up at the door eager to talk about the aesthetics of writing. I didn't mind the young, but it was the men and women who were around my age or older who made me uncomfortable. I didn't like the feeling of superiority I had when I was with them. Or was it guilt? I didn't know.

Meanwhile my wife and kids enjoyed themselves. They went to the Victoria and Albert Museum, the National Gallery, the Tate, and came back with postcard reproductions that they sent to friends. They went to a couple of Proms, to a play, had a day in Richmond Park, Hampton Court, and a boat ride on the Thames.

When the time came to go back, they didn't want to.

But I did.

I had passed through my *ABC* days, and I wanted to get away. Was it because it was a reminder of one's youth? Or of a time which promised more than it turned out to be? I told myself that there was an unreality about it all—that our lives then had no economic base—that it was a time of limbo. But despite knowing these things, I carry it with me. It represents a sort of innocence that has gone.

On the Saturday morning waiting for the taxi to come to take us to Paddington Station, the phone rang, and a young girl's voice wanted to know about her short story.

I said the doctor was away. He would be back later. She ought to ring this evening.

"What time?"

"After nine," I said.

"Have you read the story?" she asked. "What do you think of it?"

"We just rented the house," I said. "We were here for a holiday."

"Oh," she said. "You're not one of us?"

"No," I said.

Then the taxi came. And the driver began to load the cases into the back of the car.

I DON'T WANT
TO KNOW ANYONE
TOO WELL

FIRST HEARD of Al Grocer as a legible signature at the end
of this typewritten letter.

Dear Mr. Bonnar,
I should like to ask you quite well in advance if you would
be agreeable to act as my guide while I'm in Cornwall
for a week at the beginning of September. I operate an
original service for independent radio stations throughout Australia. We offer them tape recordings of various
aspects of European life. For the 1967 season our project
is a series of journeys. And after reading your excellent
article on Cornwall we have decided to include *A Journey
into Cornwall* on our list.

I hope you can come with me, and together we can
shape a thirty-minute travel-interpretation of this (your)
region. I would be prepared to pay for your services, and I
think it would be fun to do. And I hope you can find time
to do it with me. By the way, to lug the equipment (and
ourselves) around, I'll rent a car because I think of this
in terms of my own pleasure and comfort, plus the great

benefit of being mobile in our work. At any rate, may I
have your initial reaction at this time.

Cordially,

Al Grocer

I wrote back saying I'd be delighted. It seemed a fine way
of seeing the country and having a holiday as well. For though
I've lived in Cornwall for five years, I haven't been around
much. I don't drive.

On Friday I got Sam England to take his taxi and we
drove over to St. Erth to meet the train. It was a fine, bluster-
ing kind of morning with whitecaps in the bay. And I could
see the shadows of the low clouds moving over the far shore
fields, leaving patches of light green, dark green, and brown.
Al Grocer had sent me a brochure of his company. It included
a photograph. From the photograph he looked to be an
undistinguished crewcut, in his thirties. But the man I finally
approached— the only one left standing on the platform—
was clearly in his fifties. Medium height, stocky, bald. He was
neatly dressed in a navy blue blazer, grey flannels, a white shirt
open at the neck. And on a pale face he had very large black
sunglasses.

"Mister Grocer?" I said. "Good to see you."

"Ditto," he said, dragging the word out. And his accent had
a trace of central Europe in it.

He smiled. And his mouth showed, contrary to what I
expected, one of the finest sets of teeth I have ever seen. We
shook hands firmly. Then he put his arm around my shoulder
and left it there, something I do not entirely take with strangers. It was, I discovered, one of his mannerisms. A few days
later I introduced him to my bank manager to cash a personal
cheque of his, as he was running short. In less than five minutes after meeting the manager he was putting his arm around
the bank manager's shoulder.

"Call me Al," he said, and changed his glasses for another pair that he brought out of his blazer pocket. I caught a glimpse of bulging eyes. "I better make sure the porters don't throw the equipment around, it's sensitive."

There were no porters. The portable recording machinery was dumped on the platform, and the train moved off to Penzance. I helped him carry the equipment up the steps and across the covered, brown, wooden bridge above the tracks. He was breathing hard and I could smell scent, a kind of bay rum.

"How was the trip?"

"Not bad," he puffed. "I really go for these toy English trains."

"Your first time in England?"

"No. Twenty-five or thirty years ago I lived in Southampton—for three months. Someone got a disease on the boat taking us to Australia. They took us all off the boat and put us in quarantine. Until we all got the disease. Guess who got it last...?"

On the way back we had to share the taxi with an elderly couple who were staying at the Tregenna Castle. We drove up the long drive of trees to the plateau, and the taxi stopped. Mister Grocer opened the taxi door and got out, surveying the grounds, the country house of a hotel, the fine view of St. Ives with the harbour, bay, and the Atlantic below.

"I'm going to like this place," he said, taking off his glasses and inhaling the air.

"This isn't where you're staying," I said. "This is the most expensive hotel here. You asked for bed and breakfast. I've got you a place for fifteen shillings a day—it's clean."

He put his dark glasses back on and returned into the taxi visibly disappointed. I had a feeling this kind of thing had happened to him before. And for some inexplicable reason I wished there and then that Mister Grocer could have stayed at the Tregenna Castle.

My wife took an instant dislike to him. She had gone to some trouble and expense to get a duck and spent most of the day getting it ready.

"What's this?" he said. "Rabbit?"

"No," my wife said, "it's crow."

He looked so startled that I found myself saying. "It's duck. It's been done in wine." And for my wife's benefit, "It's delicious." But the damage had been done.

Next morning he came around after breakfast. He had changed and was wearing a fawn gabardine jacket over a dark blue sport shirt, light blue sport trousers, and the black sunglasses. Apart from his bulging eyes, his other features were fine, though age and fat had started to undermine them. "How do you like the bed and breakfast place?"

"Just fine."

I fixed him up with a place run by a couple of artists. They had a terraced house and took in people, since they couldn't make a living from painting. But I was a bit worried if Mister Grocer would take to their bohemian ways.

"Would you like a walk?" I said.

"You're now about to get one of Bonnar's conducted tours," my wife said sarcastically from the kitchen. I had never known her to take such an instant dislike to anyone.

We were walking towards Carbis Bay—it's a pleasant walk: on the side of a slope, overlooking the bay, alongside flowering gorse, blackberry bushes, and wild garlic—when he said, "William, you having trouble in your marriage?"

"No."

"It's no good, William, I can tell. I'm sensitive to people's voices. I can walk into a room and spot immediately by the way a person talks whether he likes me or not. And I could tell from the way your wife spoke that you've just had a row..."

"But we haven't."

We walked on, through a stile, in silence.

"You married?"

He shook his head. "I had a girl once, in Poland. When the war came an uncle in Adelaide said he would bring her out for me. I would come later. He did bring her over. Three years later he helped to bring me. When I came, I found my girl married to his son." He stopped, plucked a wild garlic—"I made films in Poland,"—and put the green stem in his mouth. "Before the war, historical pictures—I used to be quite well known."

After about a mile the path leads to the door of the Carbis Bay Hotel. It was a very hot day, the tennis courts were deserted, there wasn't anyone on the close-cropped lawns. We went inside the hotel. No one there either. I suggested that he wait while I try to find out if we could have some tea or coffee or a beer out on the lawn or the balcony. I finally found a student in the kitchen who said he was working here for the summer. He said they didn't provide refreshments for non-residents during the season. I told this to Mister Grocer. But it was obvious that he had his mind on something else.

"Is there anyone about?"

"No."

He walked behind the reception desk and calmly helped himself to a considerable number of hotel envelopes and hotel writing paper. Then he sat down by a table in the empty lounge, made himself comfortable, and began to write a letter.

"I like good hotel stationery," he said.

When we returned to St. Ives, he fumbled in his fawn jacket pocket.

"I've lost my Biro."

So I took him to Woolworth's. He tried out several plastic pens at a shilling each, but didn't like them. "They are much too cheap."

We came out and walked along the front.

"I think we can get a Biro," I said, "in Literature and Art."

"*But I've got one.*" And he brought out from his fawn jacket pocket one of the plastic pens that were on sale in Woolworth's.

"What's the matter," he said good-humouredly. "Haven't you ever taken something without paying for it?"

We rented a car from the North Star Garage. We planned to start next morning. For the first day we would go outward to Land's End along the north coast, and come back by the south. We decided it would be best to start early and return to St. Ives, from wherever we were, to sleep.

We met in the car park by the cemetery. He was there, looking closely through a copy of the *Times*. And he encircled with his pen possible stories that he might record. *The oldest water wheel in England was in the West Country*—that would make an item, he said. *The man who breeds worms for a living.* Then he transferred these into a notebook that was marked "*Ideas.*" On its front page in his large clear writing was:

What is precious is never to forget
The essential delight of the blood.

"I've got the front of this book full of quotations and jokes," he said, turning the pages. "Listen to this. What did the young rabbi say to the old rabbi in the French pastry shop as he passed the cakes? *Have another Ghetto.*" And he laughed infectiously.

It was raining when he drove out of St. Ives and in a matter of minutes we were on the moors. The sea was beside us on the right. The moor on the left. And the rain kept coming across like folds of a pale white curtain.

"It's wet in England," he said thoughtfully.

Our first stop was at a filling station. The man who ran it was an old-timer, one of the survivors of a mining disaster. Mister Grocer came in carrying his portable tape recorder in a green sling over his shoulder. And he began to flatter the man. But the old-timer stopped him. "I've been interviewed many times on radio and television. You just tell me what you want..."

Mister Grocer asked him questions. They rehearsed, twice. Mister Grocer checked his equipment. He locked the door. He stuffed paper into the doorbell. He put up a "closed" sign in the window. And just as everything was set to record, Mister Grocer had an attack of nerves. So he had another rehearsal. The old-timer was right-on with his replies, while Mister Grocer fluffed his.

"I must take a tranquillizer," he said and swallowed a pill. He had worked himself up into such a state that I was ready to suggest that I interview the old-timer.

Then the interview started. And once he began, the voice that spoke into the microphone was authoritative, distinct, and without a trace of anxiety. It was the anonymous "interview voice" that radio and television have made familiar. As soon as he finished he relaxed. And you could see he was no longer interested in the old-timer, in mining, in this part of Cornwall. All he wanted to do was to get away from here.

"That's the start," he said, walking back to the car. He was full of nervous excitement and kept patting me on the shoulder. "The hard part is always the start." I said it was the same in writing. As a parting shot he told the old-timer the only obvious lie I could detect—that he would let him know when it would be broadcast. But driving on to Land's End he said that he came from a wealthy family just outside Warsaw. That his people were in wood. "My father had forests." And when he made a bit more cash in Australia he would go back for a visit. "I would like to see what the place looks like. We had a magnificent white house—I was born there. We had an Alsatian on a long leash attached to an overhead wire—he patrolled the grounds..."

And I didn't believe a word of it.

I could see St. Just come out of the mist. And in the town complete silence except for the squawks from the jackdaws and gulls. This is a part of Cornwall not touched by tourists. Instead of *Bed and Breakfast*, the signs here said *House for*

Sale. Empty square, large Wesleyan chapel, squat church. And right beside them small fields with cows and horses, barns and dung. A gull flew low down a wide empty street and the mist lay on the surrounding hilltops with stooks of corn on the slopes. Around the perimeter: abandoned tin-mine chimneys and the Atlantic.

We went to the Western Hotel—I had once met the owner. Mister Grocer had me rehearse with him, before we came to St. Just, all the facts about St. Just that I thought he ought to know, until he had memorized them word-perfect—he might have been an actor learning a part. And, for a few minutes, he did talk intelligently about St. Just with the hotel owner. He rehearsed the interview. Then, again, went into a flap. I was posted outside to keep guard. Doors were locked. And just as soon as the interview was over he wanted to get away from here. It was as if he had done something he knew he shouldn't and was afraid of being found out.

By the end of the second day I was beginning to have doubts whether this little holiday trip would last the week. I was convinced that Mister Grocer was on the verge of a nervous breakdown. He turned up around ten that night at the door of the cottage with his bags and portable equipment, sweat on his face. "William, I'd like to move."

"What's wrong?"

"Nothing's wrong. But the place—it's not for me."

My wife gave me a knowing glance. She was brought up in a London suburb and doesn't approve of the mild bohemian life that flickers here in the summer.

"Why don't you take him to Mrs. Richards'?" she said.

I walked him over to Mrs. Richards', helped carry his stuff. On the way down he suddenly stopped, put his bags on the road. I thought he was tired. "William, I forgot to pay at the last place. Could you, for me?" And he took out a couple of pounds.

"Sure," I said.

"Tell them I had to go to London, unexpectedly. And didn't have time to pay or say goodbye."

I left him at Mrs. Richards' and went to the other place and saw Leo—one of the owners.

"Leo. Al Grocer had to go to London. Here's what he owes."

"*Grocer*. That friend of yours is some character."

"What's up?"

"He came into my room last night, said he had angst. Said he wanted to tuck me in and kiss me goodnight."

Next morning when I got to the car park he was putting away the *Times* and his notebook in the dashboard compartment.

"Is Mrs. Richards' place OK?"

"Fine, William," he said cheerfully. "It's healthy the food here—I've broken out in pimples."

We drove out. The rain had stopped, and there was a fresh morning smell to the air. He suddenly became concerned about my welfare. "You must get out of Cornwall—the place is too slow. You have been spoiled living here. You won't be able to survive in a city. I'm not joking. And the longer you live here, the harder it will be. Come to Australia. With your education you could make money over there—like mud."

He watched me smoke a cigarette, with disapproval. Finally, he said. "You smoke your cigarettes too much. You must throw more of a cigarette away. You sell yourself cheap ..."

We headed for the south coast in sunshine. Over the car radio a crooner was singing.

Tear a star from out the sky
And the sky feels blue ...

In Falmouth he interviewed three housewives and got their recipe for making a pasty. In Helston he got the mayor to talk about the Flora Dance. Then came cursing out of a public lavatory.

"England's finished—there's no reason for a civilized country to have *such* toilet paper."

In Bodmin he saw, at a magazine stall, that Daphne du Maurier lived in Cornwall. He bought one of her books. Read about a dozen pages while we were having tea. "She's a very good writer. I wish I had time to go to a library and get some background reading on Daphne du Maurier. She interests me very much." And he went to the hotel's phone and rang her up. But she wouldn't see him. As we drove across Bodmin Moor, he tossed her book out of the window.

A couple of miles later the car broke down. The clutch burnt out. We left the car, on the side of the road, on the moor. Hitchhiked to the nearest phone, and rang up the garage. Then got a lift to St. Erth and walked over to the station. Al Grocer wanted to go in a first-class compartment. I told him on these one-track lines they were exactly the same. Anyway, we had bought a second-class ticket. But he wanted first. He had a stubborn streak in him.

And just when it seemed I had enough of him (he pocketed my change when I paid for lunch; he would never buy a round when we stopped off at a pub; and I began to think of the whole thing as a fiasco), I began to like him. I can't explain why. But I found I was looking forward to seeing him again the next day, and being in his company. Perhaps it was no more than knowing he was going away. Or maybe because neither of us belonged here, and we had come a long way to be thrown together. Or maybe the explanation was even simpler: certain things had now happened to both of us—we had a past in common. I told this to my wife. She thought I was crazy. She said she didn't want Al Grocer around any more and wouldn't care if she never saw him again.

He came to the door on his last night. A face made sad by the large bulging eyes. Neatly dressed in a grey suit, and very apologetic." . . . you mind, William, if we have a few drinks?" He held up a bottle of whisky. And for my wife he brought a miniature cherry brandy. She relented.

As he entered he said excitedly. "I've taken a room for my last night here—bet you won't guess—?"

"The Tregenna Castle?"

"No, not quite. The Porthminster."

It wasn't a bad evening. He was very good at telling a story, especially against himself. Near the end he began to get introspective. "I wonder why I feel insulted after a day interviewing people—I meet people all the time—but I've never got to know anyone—you know what I'm getting at?"

"It's a job," I said.

"There's something about the business—it makes you lose something of yourself as a human being—something of your dignity."

But he had drunk too much and went upstairs and was sick. It was past midnight when I suggested that we'd better call it a day. He said he enjoyed his stay in Cornwall and enjoyed meeting both of us very much.

"Now, could you get me a taxi?"

I told him it was only a three-minute walk to the Porthminster, and I would walk him back. He insisted on a taxi. I didn't think anyone would bother to come at this time for such a short distance—and I was right. But he wouldn't have it. "I'll get a taxi," he said defiantly, and walked unsteadily out of the room to the phone. I could hear him putting on his interview voice.

"You know who I am. I'm *Al Grocer—Al Grocer—*"

"He says Al Grocer," my wife said, "the way other people say 'happy Christmas.'"

"—*Al Grocer* will put Cornwall on the map—All *Al Grocer* wants is a taxi—to take him to your Porthminster Hotel— where he's staying—" He must have tried a half-dozen places, going through the same routine. Finally a taxi agreed to come.

And he came back to the front room. "I had to throw a bit of that personality stuff around," he said deprecatingly, "it comes in useful," and sank back into one of the chairs. I could see headlights sweeping the dark street. So I went and hailed the taxi. The taxi man had got out of bed and all he had on was a coat over his pyjamas and slippers. He apologized—with one hand by his mouth—for not having time to put in his false teeth.

But Al decided he didn't want to go. I helped him up and steered him to the door. He kept on about "dignity." Then, with great effort, he pulled himself together and said very precisely, "Come up tomorrow morning, William, and have breakfast with me at the Porthminster."

I did go up next morning. He was back to the navy blue blazer, grey flannels, and those large black sunglasses.

"You know, William, I've put something of yours in my quotation book." He turned some pages. "I got it from your novel. '*I don't want to get to know anyone too well,*'" he read slowly, "'*When I do I don't like them.*'"

I was going to explain that it was just a character talking—but he didn't give me a chance.

"It's very true," he said quietly. "Sad, isn't it."

Then he asked me if I would carry his bags down to the station while he carried the portable recording equipment. I didn't mind, but as we walked down the slope I couldn't help feeling that the reason I was asked up for breakfast was to carry his bags down for him. And immediately I was annoyed with myself for thinking this. To make up for it, at the station, I went over to the paper kiosk and bought him a copy of the morning's *Times*.

"Business can wait," he said with a laugh. And with a grand gesture flung the paper to the corner of the compartment. And shook my hand a long time. Large black sunglasses on a pale face, leaning out of the train, was the last I saw of him.

Ten weeks later I received a glossy picture postcard from

Sydney. On the front was a coloured photograph of its most expensive hotel. On the back he had written:

I am resting up here after a very rough ocean voyage. I have a few ideas for 1968. How would you like to come over and do a journey through the outback? Will write again and send address.

    Cordially, Al

A WRITER'S STORY

T THE BEGINNING of 1952 we were married. And in the spring we left London (two uncomfortable rooms in a cold house in a northern suburb) for the south of Cornwall, and rented a granite house on the lower slope of a hill. It had a high-walled garden with palms, bamboos, copper beech, and hydrangeas. Wild roses were on a frame bent over to form an arch. Blackberries grew on top of the wall. And between two trees was a hammock.

The house was once a schoolhouse. And in the front room, where we would eat and sit in the evenings, there was a long table with fixed benches on either side, and cut in the dark varnished wood were generations of children's names.

I worked in a large building attached to the house. The only furniture was a small stove where I burned wood in winter, a chaise longue where I read the landlord's little magazines (*Blast, Tyro, Horizon*) and the novels of Henry Green that were in a bookcase against the white wall, and a table where I wrote. The building must have been the gym or the assembly hall, for there was a raised platform at one end. And it had a high ceiling and large windows.

From a window overlooking the road I could hear the stream that went by outside and see, in the field opposite, a light pink house surrounded by trees with white blossoms, and, further away, the small green fields, separated by irregular hedges, sloping gently upwards. And in the distance a farmhouse.

From a window on the other wall I could see—over the garden and over the slate roofs and chimneys of the village—the water in the bay, the long sweep of the far shore. At dusk the land was often coloured purple. And we could hear the curlews as they flew back to the rocks at the sea's edge, and hear them again the first thing in the morning when we were still in bed. That gentle melancholy sound of a curlew flying over the house on the way to the fields above.

Sam, our landlord, looked like a Tolstoyan farmer. He always wore baggy trousers, worn shirts, a wide leather belt, and large working-men's shoes. He was tall and broad but he had a small head and a close-cropped ginger beard. For such a big man he had a gentle voice, and he spoke well and smiled easily.

He lived with his wife in a cottage on the moors. They believed in the simple life, in living off the land, in natural foods. They had these handsome blond children running around in bare feet. And because I had an MA and because he wanted something better for his kids than the local school, I signed a form that said I would look after their education. But it was my wife who taught them how to read and write.

By the time we knew him, he must have been in his middle forties. I had a feeling that he had lived quite a different kind of life before coming here. It was his voice which told it all. Years later someone told me that Sam was an Old Etonian. That's part of Sam's story that I don't know.

I only know that he was kind to us. He would arrive, on a bicycle, in the morning, his lunch in a brown paper bag. He always brought something for my wife: endive, new potatoes, a cabbage, a cauliflower, duck eggs, or honey that he collected.

We would all have coffee in the front room. Then he would go into the back of the gym, which was partitioned off and quite separate from where I worked. And here he would do his paintings. "My pot boilers," he said with a smile. But he was still hopeful that he would make a breakthrough and become known. When he did show me twenty or thirty canvases, it looked like a class at an art school—every picture was painted in a different style.

If Sam, dressed like a peasant farmer, was getting away from his past, so was I. The navy blue blazer with nickel-plated buttons, the grey flannels, the pipe—they belonged to the last four years at university and to three previous years, in uniform, in the war. But behind them were the streets of Lower Town, the houses with stables in the back. A working class community of French Canadians and immigrant Europeans that I was running away from. I just had a first novel accepted and thought of myself as a writer. I expected being a writer would be a continuation of the life I knew at university, where I edited the literary magazine, had poems and stories on the Montreal radio, and wrote the novel in my final year. Things appeared to follow one another, and fall naturally into place, without my having to try very hard. The war ... university ... novel accepted ... getting married. And now coming here to write the next book.

But for the first few weeks we took it easy. The early spring days were warm and sunny. Few people were about. The place had an air of nothing happening, of people gently living out their lives. Rooks and gulls flew slowly by. It was so quiet. And full of colour. The sea. The sky. The yellow sand beaches. Things growing in the fields and in the hedgerows.

Around ten in the morning Charlie would come up the granite steps to bring me the *Times*. He thought I was a painter. And if the back pages of the *Times* had a photograph of some disaster (like the Lynmouth flood, an air crash, or a fire) he would open the door, grin, and say, "This make good picture."

"Yes, Charlie."

Later I found out that Charlie, though in his thirties, couldn't read.

Or else Sam would come in to tell me some story he heard in the village. "You can write about that," he said.

I tried to write.

I spent hours at the wooden table in the large high room. And I didn't know what to write about. That's the trouble with going to university, I thought. I didn't have to try hard enough. The results for a little effort were too immediate and too great. You think you're a writer because those at university say so and make a fuss. But now that I was on my own—?

"You must write," I told myself. "It will come if you write."

But what to write about. I didn't know.

I thought at first that, at twenty-seven, I had run out of material. But as the weeks went by I realized it wasn't that at all. I didn't know what my material was.

I sat at the table, smoked (the pipe kept going out), read the little magazines, went to the windows.

What a pleasant place to be idle in.

I decided to take a notebook and go out. I walked to the sea's edge, and made notes. "The way the sun appears on the water on a hot summer's day. The blue water sparkles. Then it seems as if it is raining sundrops. They are hitting the water—slanting down—golden moving streaks—just like rain."

"I walk by the tideline," I wrote, "and I can see my footsteps behind me. But a little while later the footsteps disappear in the moist sand leaving no trace."

Then I sat on the granite pier and tried to describe the colours of the sea, the changing colours of the land as the clouds passed over.

My wife asked me at lunch, "How's the writing going?"

"Fine," I said.

On Sundays we went for walks in the country. She knew all the wild flowers. She would tell me their names. And I would repeat. But when we went out the following Sunday, I had forgotten. So she would name them again.

"What did you do as a child?" she asked.

What did I do, I wondered.

"We had other flowers," I said.

We passed a field with chickens. Horses in another. It was so still. So quiet.

"See the mole-hills," my wife said.

I didn't know they were mole-hills.

"That's buddleia," my wife said. "Butterflies like it."

She was right. There were butterflies resting on this bush. The sun caught them. Some with their wings spread, others drawn up. I counted twenty. And there were more.

"Those are Red Admirals," she said. "That's Tortoiseshell. That's a Peacock—"

But on Monday morning I was back in the large, high room by the wooden table. It was much better when I was out looking at things.

That is how I met Mrs. Burroughs.

I was out with my notebook. And she was standing by her front gate with a letter in her hand.

"Are you going to the post office?" she said. "Will you take this for me?"

After three more times taking letters for her she invited me into her house.

We walked along the gravel path with the garden on one side. Mrs. Burroughs' ankles were swollen and she had difficulty in walking. She used a cane. She was a large woman, slightly bent, with grey hair combed tight to her head and in a bun at the back. She had a large face, almost like a man's, thin lips, a strong jaw with loose skin under it. But her china-blue eyes were delicate. They slanted upwards.

"I don't go out much," she said quietly.

It was dark when we came into the house. I thought, at first, it was because we came in from the sunlight. But the walls of the rooms were painted brown. And they had dark Victorian oil paintings on them. Cows by a stream. Trees in a field. In front of the fireplace was a highly polished copper screen. And hammered out in the copper was a sailing ship. On a dark wooden side table, in a glass case, were three exotic stuffed birds with long tails. Their feathers were blue and green, but the colours had faded. The brightest things in the room were various glass bottles, glass vases, on the window sills. They were all the same ruby colour but with different designs.

"Sit down," Mrs. Burroughs said. "I heard you are at the old schoolhouse. And you're a writer. What are you writing?"

"I have a novel coming out," I said.

The phone rang. She didn't appear to hear it.

"The phone is ringing," I said.

"Oh," she said. And quickly went out of the room. I could hear her shouting from the next room. When she came back she sat down in her chair and said:

"What are you writing *now*?"

"Nothing."

"Why not?"

"I don't know."

She looked puzzled.

"You mean you don't know any stories?"

I didn't know what to say.

"I know lots," she said. "I'll tell you." And she did.

Every time I came up to see her she would show me into the front room, ask me to sit down, and tell me something else from her past.

It began eighty-one years ago. Her father was a farmer. She was a teacher and taught in a country school. Then she married Mr. Burroughs, who had a timber business. They moved into Penzance and had two daughters and a son. She packed up the teaching and ran the accounts. As they made money, they put the money into land and houses. They had properties all over Cornwall. When her husband died her son ran the business. Then the youngest daughter, Shirley, died when she was in her thirties. And Mrs. Burroughs didn't go out of the house after that. She didn't get on with her older daughter, Brenda.

"I don't go to see her often," Brenda told me, when I met her a few months later. "When I do, Mam begins to cry and says: why aren't you Shirley?"

I would sit in the darkened room with the Victorian paintings and watch how the light from the windows caught the ruby glass, while Mrs. Burroughs talked.

"Last year," she said, "I went to Jean's—my granddaughter's—wedding. One of Jean's girlfriends had a quarrel with her boyfriend. They split up. And she didn't have anyone to take her to the wedding. So she hired a boy from an agency— someone she had never seen before—to take her. At the wedding I saw this woman. I remembered her when she was a child. Her father and mother—they had their own farm— were devoted to each other. But they didn't have children. Then when she was in her forties she got pregnant. The baby was born. But the mother died in childbirth. The father was out in the fields. When he heard, he went and shot himself. And there was this child, now a woman and married, at the wedding. Isn't that a good story for you to write?"

"Yes," I said.

"I have a cousin," Mrs. Burroughs said. "She was going out with this boy. He worked as an accountant. Very neat. But the family didn't think he was good enough. So there was opposition to the wedding. But they did get married. Then the war came along. The Second World War. The man was called up. And he cut his throat because he was frightened of being killed in the war."

I'd go and see Mrs. Burroughs on Saturday mornings because her grandson came in from Penzance to play the piano for her. They were old tunes, mostly waltzes.

"It reminds her of the time when she was a girl," he told me.

I'd be in the front room, looking out over her garden; the sounds from the piano came from the other room, while Mrs. Burroughs talked.

"My daughter's husband is called Jack," she said. "His grandmother—when she was a girl—fell in love with Mr. Doo. Mr. Doo was an artist. But he was poor. So she married Mr. Wilsher. He was very rich and old. They lived together for seven years. And then Mr. Wilsher died. And she then went and married Mr. Doo. And they lived happily. Then Mr. Doo died. And Mrs. Doo lived in that pink house opposite you. She had butlers and gardeners and servants and cooks. All these people to wait on her. And all she could talk about was her darling Mr. Doo.

"Her daughter was brought up as a lady. And when she was getting on she fell in love with a young man—he was thirteen years younger. He worked on a farm. They married. And after they married, the daughter began to look more and more like a gypsy. And the young man dressed and behaved like a gentleman."

"That's a good story," I said.

"I have lots more," Mrs. Burroughs said.

It was at Mrs. Burroughs' that I met Mr. Oppenheimer. A neat man, about five foot two, bald, and with glasses. He was dressed in a hand-stitched tweed suit, a handmade shirt, and a woollen tie. Mrs. Burroughs told him I was a writer.

"I've met a lot of writers here," Mr. Oppenheimer said. "I used to visit D. H. Lawrence and Frieda on Sundays when they lived at Zennor."

"How was Lawrence?"

"*D. H.*" Mr. Oppenheimer raised his voice. "He was a gentleman. One time I rode over on a horse. It was a hot day, and the horse gave me a rough ride. When I got there I must have said some swear words. D. H. got angry. "'No need to say words like that here, Oppenheimer. There is no need.'"

"Arthur, my gardener," Mrs. Burroughs said, "also thought Lawrence a gentleman. Because when he went out there with a pony and trap to deliver a loaf of bread, Lawrence always gave him a shilling tip."

"After D. H.," Oppenheimer said, "there was Harris. And after him, another writer, Johnson. He was always talking about money. He stayed only a year. How long are you staying?"

"I don't know," I said.

I walked back with Mr. Oppenheimer to his cottage.

"I've known Mrs. Burroughs for over forty years," he said. "Very tight with her money. Never gives anything away."

How could I tell him that she was giving me all these things from her past.

"She can't hear very well," Oppenheimer said. "But if you start talking about money. She'll say wait—I'll just get my hearing aid. She had a grand-niece getting married in Canada. She told me she sent her a pound as a wedding present. *A pound*. Come inside and have a drink. I start the day with a small glass of brandy. The doctor told me to take it. It warms the system up."

His cottage was small and untidy. There was a dog, a terrier, also old, sitting by the electric fire. There were papers, magazines, and books piled everywhere. Often when I would come down to visit Mr. Oppenheimer I would look in at the window to see if he was in. The place was in a mess, plates and cups still on the table. And Mr. Oppenheimer, sitting in a chair with his feet up, reading a book.

He told me why he came here. His family owned freighters in Wales. He began to work in the Cardiff office. Then he got a spot on one lung. "The doctor told me to go to a warmer climate. Or else I wouldn't make old bones. I'm seventy-six," he said proudly. "I started a restaurant here just after the First World War. But I don't have anything to do with that now. I still have my office there. Come and see me."

I did go.

His office, above the restaurant, was as untidy as the cottage.

"Augustus John sat where you are sitting and drank a half bottle of whisky. And little Stanley Spencer—he came up to here." Mr. Oppenheimer stood up and put his hand under his chin. "I don't think he changed his collar once in the three months he was here. Have you heard of Guy Gibson? During the war?"

"Yes," I said.

"I gave Guy Gibson piggybacks on the sand," Mr. Oppenheimer said. "He used to come here as a child. Have some more brandy."

His hand shook as he poured. But it was because of arthritis in his fingers. It was painful for him to shake hands.

"Tell me about D. H. Lawrence," I said.

"D. H. He had a red beard. He worked at night. In the day D. H. went for walks on the moors. He was very good with his hands. He fixed things in the cottage. Why don't you come and see my house in the country. I've got a lot of land around it."

I said I would. But as he had bought the house for his daughter Mary and her husband, George—and only went there, reluctantly, on weekends—I never did go to see the place.

But on Monday afternoons I would go to see him at his cottage. I'd say.

"How are things, Mr. Oppenheimer?"

And he would say, "Have some more brandy."

This time he began to laugh. "I shouldn't laugh," he said. "But George had something else go wrong. George decided to cut some of the old trees—I shouldn't laugh—there are fourteen acres. He got the wood." And Mr. Oppenheimer began to laugh again. "I shouldn't laugh," he said, tears in his eyes. "He got the wood and started to cut it. And *phlewt*—half of his finger flew off. I shouldn't laugh at this. But he couldn't find the piece that flew off."

"What happened?" I said. I wondered why I was laughing.

"Mary got the ambulance. They rushed him to Penzance hospital. But it was too late. They couldn't sew the two pieces together."

Next morning, sitting at the wooden table in the high room, I thought how rich Mr. Oppenheimer's talk was and Mrs. Burroughs' talk. Compared to Sam's and mine. Sam never once talked about his Old Etonian past. Just as I didn't talk or even refer to my past. I was like Sam. We were both trying to cut out our pasts, to cover them up. And it made us boring.

The next time I saw Mr. Oppenheimer he said, "I don't have the dog any more. I took him out for his walk. We went along the harbour. The dog always peed against the railing. This time he went on the wrong side of the railing. There was no rail. He flipped over. Fell into the harbour. The tide was out. He broke his back."

Besides visiting Mrs. Burroughs and Mr. Oppenheimer, I also found two places that I would make for on my walks. One was in the country, just off the road. It had a broken-down gate, then a slope up, a field of green grass, and at the top of the slope, this house. An ugly house. With two dormer windows downstairs and two upstairs, and a white door that was always half-open. All the paint was peeling. The curtains were grey, half-drawn, and falling to bits. But there was something marvellous about a broken-down place with a sign at the front gate that said *Venton Vision*. No one lived in the house now except the animals: a goose, some cows, chickens.

Then, in December, with a mist closing in, in grey light, I found this field of anemones. The flowers were not very high above the ground. But the colours stood out. There were blues, purples, deep reds, light reds, and whites and pinks. Low colours, rising from the green, moving from side to side in the wind. Some were wide open with their dark centres. Others in bud, others opening. Very delicate colours, in the grey light, the mist closing in. And here and there a tall dead stalk from last summer's thistles. A lovely field. And no one picked them.

And I couldn't get over seeing the anemones, and the surrounding green fields, because it was December. I think of December as snow, ice, double-doors, double-windows, and skating on frozen rivers. I would come here just to look at this field. And wish I was back to the snow, the crisp air, the harsh glare on sunny days.

I went to see Mrs. Burroughs to tell her about the field of anemones. I found her crying.

"What's the matter, Mrs. Burroughs?"

"I'm remembering the happy times," she said.

She was holding a photograph of herself, before she was married, as a teacher with her class.

Meanwhile the problem was getting clear. How was I to earn a living if I couldn't write my next book? I started to make lists. Of the people I grew up with in Ottawa. Of the popular songs I knew when I was at school. Of the streets, the streetcar lines, the market, the library, the parks. But the money was running out. The novel was due in two months. It was time to leave.

I went to see Mr. Oppenheimer. The door of his cottage was locked. I looked through the window. Things were just as I last saw them. The newspapers, the magazines, the books.

On Saturday morning the taxi came to take us to Penzance station. We said goodbye to Sam. He still dressed like a Tolstoyan farmer, smiled easily, and talked of his pot-boilers.

We wished each other luck.

I told the taxi driver to go to Mrs. Burroughs'. As I went along the walk I could hear her grandson playing the piano. And as soon as I came in she said. "You haven't been up for a couple of weeks. Sit down. I have another story for you."

"I can't stay, Mrs. Burroughs."

But she interrupted or else she didn't hear what I said.

"You know the farm that you can see from where you are? That farm was run by Mr. and Mrs. Brill. She died when she was fifty-five. And six months later Mr. Brill had a heart attack. And he died. The relatives were saying how sad it was. How he tried and couldn't live without her.

"When the relatives came to divide the valuables they found a camera with a half-used film in it. They had the film developed. And it was full of pictures of Mr. Brill and his girlfriend—she was someone else's wife. There were pictures of this woman in his wife's kitchen. In her favourite chair. And Mr. Brill had made plans for them to go away to London. *Now* the relatives were saying the heart attack was the best thing that could have happened."

"What has happened to Mr. Oppenheimer?" I said. "He's not at his cottage."

"He fell in the street," Mrs. Burroughs said. "He is gone to live with his daughter in the country. We won't see him again. That's what happens. The family takes over and the friends don't see you any more. When that happens to me, I'll have to go and live with my daughter Brenda. Then no one will see me."

"Oh, you've got lots of time yet, Mrs. Burroughs."

"I don't know," she said quietly.

"I came to say goodbye," I said.

"Where are you going?"

"To London."

"When?"

"Now."

I could hear her grandson playing *Morgenblätter*. Since living here I had learnt the names of a lot of things.

"Do you like my red glass?" Mrs. Burroughs asked.

"Yes."

"Take the one you like."

"I couldn't do that."

"Why not. They will only fight over it when I'm gone. Do you like this one?"

And she gave me a red glass vase with a pair of cockerels etched in it.

I returned to the taxi with the red glass.

"Look what Mrs. Burroughs gave me," I said to my wife.

"It's beautiful," she said.

But she was looking out of the window as the taxi drove along the coastal road. On one side—the earth with the small green fields, the yellow gorse, a stone church with old gravestones. And on the other—an immense sky against the thin flatness of the sea.

My wife took my hand. "I'm glad we are leaving," she said. "Now things will begin."

CLASS OF 1949

THE END of January is quiet and empty in this seaside town. Martha is away at university in Manchester. A nine-hour train ride from here, on the fastest train. She has just phoned, as she always does on Friday evening. Ella has come back tired from school. She is doing A levels but buys magazines in order to read: "I was pregnant at 15"..."Are my kisses a match for his"..."My husband beats me." She has gone up the stairs to her room and put on a Joni Mitchell record. For I can hear:

> *The wind is in from Africa*
> *Last night I couldn't sleep*
> *Oh, you know it sure is hard to leave you, Carey*
> *But it's really not my home*

I was sitting in a comfortable chair, by the side of the open fire, waiting for the news to come on the television. Emily was on the settee, in front of the fireplace, knitting a red sweater for Ella. The black kitten was chasing a shallot as if it was a ball, knocking it from one paw to another.

The phone rang. "I'll go," said Emily.

"Who was it?" I said as she came back into the room.

"Someone wanting the old people's home. That's the second time today. If it's not someone wanting matron then it's Linda's, the hairdresser." She took up her knitting. I listened to the clock on the mantel above the fireplace.

Maybe I'll go to Amsterdam
Maybe I'll go to Rome

The phone rang again. Emily went quickly out of the room. I could hear her voice becoming louder. She came back excited.

"It's Victor," she said.

"Victor. Here?"

"Yes. He's at the Sheaf. I told him you'll go down and bring him back."

"I guess there is no way I can get out of this," I said as I put on my coat. But as I walked down the slope in the light rain—past the terraced houses, a few had lights on in the front rooms; by the closed post office, the closed summer restaurants—I remembered it was Victor who was responsible for my coming here in the first place.

I met Victor in 1946 in Montreal while going to McGill. We were two from the thousands of returning servicemen and women who went to university just after the Second World War. I remember that winter looking out from the top window of an apartment opposite the campus. It was snowing. And bundled-up young men and women in blue and mustard and black overcoats were walking to and from a lecture. Furthest away, through the dark trees—the arts building, the engineering, the library—bits of light, bits of orange. There was no sound. Just the snow falling. And the moving greatcoats.

Victor would have got to McGill war or no war. But a lot of the others depended on the Veterans Act—fees paid by the government and sixty dollars a month to live on. When Victor came in his car to pick me up for dinner with his parents and saw the basement room I had by the boiler on Dorchester next to the railway tracks, he put it down to some eccentricity on my part. Then he drove through wide streets with trees and lawns and elegant houses, to the paintings on the wall of Emily Carr, the first editions in the bookcase, the butler bringing in the drinks. It was through Victor that I met the rich and powerful English families of Westmount and Outremont. In those days I was attracted by the rich—their houses, their possessions, the way they lived. Perhaps this is what I found interesting in Victor.

But there was something else. We both wanted to be writers. And we were convinced that the first step was to get out of Canada and go over to England. To get over I needed money. That meant putting in for a fellowship. I said I would do a thesis on "The Decay of Absolute Values in Modern Society." And got five thousand dollars spread over two years. Victor got his father to give him a chunk of capital in the form of Bell Telephone shares, Canada Packers, Canadian Pacific, and Dominion Tar.

I am trying to be as brief and accurate as I can of those early postwar years. The girls wore their skirts and dresses long, and our jackets had padded shoulders. We had youth and high spirits—but they were held in check. When we graduated the principal made a speech saying what a fine generation we were, how we fought the enemy of civilization and made the world safe for democracy, and now we would take our place as useful citizens. The person they thought most suitable to give the convocation address was the chief of the Boy Scouts—I cannot remember a thing he said.

Next day, Victor flew to England. Two weeks later I took a freighter to Newcastle. We met up in London. Victor had rented a cottage in Cornwall for us both. London, he said, would be too hot in July and August. It was a marvellous summer. The wartime restraint suddenly went. And in its place I felt an exhilarating sense of personal freedom.

In September we went up to London. To a flat in Swiss Cottage. We were both writing first novels in different rooms on typewriters. The house was broken up into flats. In the others were middle-aged European refugees. And workmen were still repairing the bomb damage. We went to Soho, to the pubs, the drinking clubs, the small restaurants. We met painters, writers, editors. It was very pleasant.

Now and then Victor would say we were invited for the weekend to some large country house. (They were relations or acquaintances of his family.) And I would rent tails from Moss Bros., and we would go by train into the country, to the lengthy meals with many courses and wines and the mothers complaining that England was dull, that their daughters were not having the time they had. Then the Hunt Ball, champagne, dancing all night to the Harry Lime theme. And back to the seedy flat, to ration books and queues at Sainsbury's for the small egg, the Irish sausage, the cube of butter, the bit of cheese and meat. While the pile of typewritten pages for our novels increased. We both knew we had two years to live like this and finish our books. Then get them published and go on as writers—or else return to Canada.

The Sheaf was ahead. There was one room with a light. From the window I could see an open coal-fire. Two people by a table. The rest of the room was empty.

As I walked in, Victor called my name, got up, and smiled. We shook hands. He continued smiling. I saw that his once white teeth were discoloured. That his blond hair was grey. And I wondered what changes he could see in my face.

"This is Abdullah," Victor said, and introduced a small young Arab, very fine features with a dark moustache, neatly dressed in a brown suit.

"When did you get here?"

"Late this afternoon," Victor said.

"Will you have the same? Is it draught?"

"Yes."

I went to the bar and ordered three draught Guinness. Abdullah came up. "I'll bring them back for you," he said. I returned to the table and sat down opposite Victor.

"I didn't think you would still be here," he said. "I thought you would have gone back to Canada."

"We've been waiting for the kids to finish school. Martha is at university in Manchester. Ella is in her last year here. So we'll be able to move soon. What made you come down?"

"I thought Abdullah ought to see a bit of Europe. We've been in London the last two weeks. Going to art galleries, plays, movies, walking around—"

"It was very tiring, all that walking," Abdullah said.

"I decided to take us away from London for the weekend. We took a train to Truro, hired a car, and drove here."

"Where are you staying?"

"At the first hotel that had a car park opposite."

"That would be the Porthminster," I said. "Did you remember it?"

"No," Victor said.

He took out a package of cigars and gave me one. Then brought out a gold lighter and we both lit up. He seemed reluctant to talk. So I said, "My hair is a bit longer than it was."

"At least," he said, "it's the same colour."

"Emily and the kids wanted me to have it like this. So I let it grow. I didn't like it at first. In summer some of the places here have signs in their windows, *"no undesirables."* It means boys and girls with long hair who do not have much money to spend. I began to feel I might be undesirable. Abdullah, have you been to England before?"

"No. This is the first time for me out of Morocco."

"How long will you stay here?"

"Just the weekend," Victor said. "We leave Monday for London, then fly to Amsterdam for a few days. Then a couple of weeks in Paris. He learned English himself," Victor said proudly. "In three months."

"You speak very well," I said. "What do you do in Morocco?"

"I register births and deaths," Abdullah said. "I begin when I get back. It will be my first job. As assistant."

We finished the draught Guinness.

"Let's go back to the house," I said. "Emily is waiting to see you."

We went out of the pub. The tide was out. The widely separated lights along the front and the pier were reflected in the shallows. Up ahead, in the dark, were clusters of lights from the houses above the harbour. It felt damp and cold.

"I walked around with Abdullah earlier," Victor said. "A shame the boats are gone."

"It's become a tourist town," I said. "You're seeing it at the best time of the year. In summer you can hardly walk."

We went along a dark street. I stopped beside a cottage.

"Pop Short lived here," I said. "Remember him?"

Victor was silent.

"He let you read a first edition of *Lady Chatterley*. He used to ask after you. He told me there was a White Russian colony here after the First World War. Like we were after the Second. And I guess there will be others like us later on. Pop showed me a Fabergé egg that he got from the White Russians. He died last year. He was ninety."

We walked along a bit further on the wet cobblestones. I stopped beside a street light. There was an opening with stone steps going up.

"Do you remember this?"

"No," Victor said.

"It's where we had our first cottage, halfway up the steps. We were charged two pounds a week for it. At that time we didn't know we were overcharged a pound because we were Canadians. The rooms were damp. The gaslight came from small wire baskets. The toilet was outside in the courtyard."

"I remember that," Victor said hesitantly.

We walked a little further along. "This used to be Maskell's. He would put aside cigarettes for us. The cigarette paper had a thin pinstripe, like on a shirt. He died some years ago. And the Gay Viking? Here. We would go for coffee in the morning. Meet other people and have long talks. The Saint and Elsa ran it. They're both dead."

"I don't remember," Victor said.

"Victor's here," I shouted as soon as I got into the hall. Emily came out of the dining room, smiling. Victor was also smiling. He opened his arms.

"Emily."

"Victor."

They embraced and kissed.

"What a surprise," Emily said. "Here we are thinking no one comes to see us. And here you are."

"You haven't changed," Victor said.

"You've got taller," she said.

"It's these new shoes. They have thick heels. It's the latest fashion. This is Abdullah."

We introduced Ella.

"You remember Victor?"

She stood there smiling.

"How could she," Emily said. "She wasn't born."

I took their winter coats and hung them up. And we went into the kitchen where Emily had laid out the table.

"Someone gave us this pâté for Christmas," I said. "We were waiting for an occasion to open it. Do you know what it is?"

"It's pork," Abdullah said, chewing it slowly. "In my country I'm not supposed to eat it."

"It's very good," Victor said.

I helped myself to a hard-boiled egg.

"Do you remember Tom Slater? We met him in one of the Soho pubs. He wrote short stories—"

"I don't remember him," Victor said.

"He died nine years ago. He was thirty-six. He used to come down with his wife to see us. He knew I liked sardines. So he would bring a different tin of sardines every time he came down. He said he told a friend of his about my liking sardines. "That used to be the way you could tell a gourmet," the friend said. "Now, it's hard-boiled eggs.""

Abdullah laughed.

"Aren't these plums good. Have some more," I said to Abdullah.

"As you see, Victor, we are still here," Emily said. "We seem to sit here waiting for something to happen."

"We'll get out soon," I said quietly.

"I've heard that before," Emily said.

"We have a chance. Now that the kids have grown up. Ella finishes school this year. Then we'll be able to go."

"But where will we go *to*—?" Emily asked.

"You two sound like characters in a Beckett play," Victor said.

No one spoke. Then Emily said sharply, "How *could* you come back here, Victor?"

He didn't answer. He went on eating, looking not at all at ease.

"Do you remember Keith Haydon," I said. "He came over a few years after us and became an authority on nuclear strategy. He used to write articles, appear on television. He died last year in Venice."

"That's a shame," Victor said.

"And remember Len Mason? One time the three of us were walking along Sherbrooke Street after a late lecture. It was winter. Lots of snow on the ground. We told him we were going to be writers. And he said he was going to be an actor. So we said we would write plays for him. Len did become an actor. He acted in Canada and over here and in the States. He was killed two years ago while driving a car on a highway."

"I'm sorry to hear that," Victor said.

"How do you live in Morocco?" Emily said changing the subject.

"I have a house in the Arab quarter. I designed the inside of the house. Also had my own furniture made up. It's got lots of rooms. Now and then I have some European friends staying with me. But most of the time I only see Moroccans."

"What do you do in the morning?" I said.

"I go shopping. Buy food."

"Do you still cook?"

"Yes. But I have a cook and a houseboy."

"Is it hot there?"

"It can be during the day," Abdullah said. "But at night it freezes."

"What do you wear?" Emily asked.

"He wears a silken—" Abdullah smiled mischievously at Victor.

129

"It's something I got in Japan," Victor said nervously. "A karate suit."

"It's like the old men wear," Abdullah said, still smiling.

We went into the other room. I put more coal on the fire. Emily came in with the coffee. I brought in some whisky and brandy and began to pour the drinks. Victor took out the package of small cigars and offered me one. "I used to smoke one cigarette after another," he said. "Now I smoke one cigar after another."

"What do you work at, Victor?" I said.

"I'm a dilettante," he said lightly. "I do several things. But as an amateur."

"Then you're a professional dilettante, Victor," Emily said.

"No," Victor said. "I'm not professional at anything."

"But you could cook—very well," I said.

"He is doing a cookbook," Abdullah said proudly.

"I'm supposed to be doing one," Victor said. "But I don't think I will. Just putting down one recipe after another would be boring. I paint most of the time."

"What kind of paintings do you do?" said Emily.

"Landscapes."

"Like what painter that we would know?"

"Like Corot."

"That's a name to conjure with," Emily said.

"I like being an amateur," Victor said. "The good paint-ers and writers I know—they lead such miserable lives. I was going through immigration at London Airport. And the offi-cial looked at my passport and asked me, What do you do? I said writer— I still say that sometimes. What have you writ-ten? he asked. *Nothing*, I said."

We all laughed.

"He let me through."

And for a moment he was like the Victor I knew. The one who used to make me laugh. But just as quickly he went back into his shell of not talking freely and looking uneasy. A few minutes later he stood up. "I think it's time we went to the hotel."

"I'll walk you there," I said.

Back with Emily in bed. She said, "I was looking out of the window. And I saw three people coming up. And I thought, supposing Victor's married. And he's bringing his wife . . . Do you think Abdullah is his boyfriend?"

"I didn't ask. But I guess so."

"I thought he liked girls?"

"He did," I said. "I knew of three at McGill and one over here. Just before I met you he began to see a lot of this girl. I don't remember her name. She was a Canadian in London from the same background as Victor. About your height, only very dark hair, high cheekbones, a nice smile. She looked a bit like Claudette Colbert. *Very* sympathetic. One night he came to the flat I had in Notting Hill Gate (Victor was then living in Chelsea) to tell me that he had just left this girl. And she told him she was pregnant. He didn't know what to do. He said he would marry her. Victor has a great sense of doing the right thing. "'The trouble is,'" he said, "'I have enough income from my capital for one person to live. But with two—I'll have to get a job.'" So he went and signed up as a salesman to sell encyclopedias. He did that for a month. Didn't like it. Then the girl told him it was a false alarm. And that was the end of that."

We lay in bed for a while, not speaking.

"He's not giving much away," I said.

"Maybe he knows what writers do," Emily said.

"I don't think so," I said. "I remember when he finished the novel and showed me the typescript. The characters were lifeless. I asked him why didn't he write about people he knew. About his family, about Montreal, his private school, McGill. He said he didn't want anything to do with Canada or anything connected with it. I don't know anyone who hates Canada so much. And how can you be a writer if you reject your past? Seeing Victor, I can see the person I was."

"Yes," Emily said. "He can tell little lies. He said we haven't changed. I know we have. It's the kind of small talk you used to make. Why say things you don't mean?"

"It's a form of politeness," I said. "I wonder what would have happened to Victor if that dark-haired girl was pregnant?"

"But he's happy with his life," Emily said. "'The nice thing about these trips,'" he told me, "'is that at the end I can go back home to Morocco. To my house and my Arab friends.'" I think he's very lucky to live in a place he likes."

I didn't reply. I expected her to go on and say: we're about the only ones who live in a place they don't like. Instead she said, "I think Victor disapproves of me. Every time he looked at me, I felt it."

"I also think he disapproves of me now," I said. "For not living better—for not getting on."

"Well you have written a few books since you last saw him."

"But he's not curious about our life at all," I said. "He hasn't asked me one question as to what I've been doing these past twenty years. It's as if he looks at the way we live—and doesn't want to know. And he has forgotten a lot. I walked down the street with him, showing where we had the cottage that first summer—where Pop Short lived—Maskell's—The Gay Viking. All he said was: I don't remember. I don't remember."

"Perhaps that's why he was able to come down here," Emily said. "He doesn't have much to lose."

Next day, Saturday, they didn't arrive until noon.

"I've been walking up and down the street," Victor said. "I couldn't find the house. All the houses look so much the same."

"I've found Morocco in Ella's atlas book," Emily said, and showed Abdullah the map. "Are you anywhere near the coast?"

"We are about three hundred miles from the coast. Beside the mountains."

From the window I could see the sky was still overcast. "I hope you'll get a bit of sun while you're here," I said to Abdullah. "Then you'll be able to see the colours."

"I like the way it is," Abdullah said. "I have never seen anything like this."

"Why don't we go for a drive across the moors," Victor said. "Stop at a few pubs. Then I'll take you and Emily out to a meal."

I got in front with Victor. Emily was in the back with Abdullah. And in a matter of minutes we were on the moors. The small green fields with the grey broken-stone hedges. The hedges with gorse and hawthorn on both sides of the road. Last year's bracken a light rust colour. Some deserted tin-mine chimneys.

"In Morocco," Victor said, "you have these wild flowers. One day they are all yellow. Next day they are pink."

"I suppose you find this drab."

"No," he said. "I wouldn't mind getting out here and doing some painting."

I could hear Abdullah telling Emily, "My father has two dozen head of cows, some chickens and sheep."

"If a Moroccan sheep saw this green grass," Victor said, "it would go ga-ga."

We drove along the turning road. There was a drop to the green fields below us on the right while the moors went up on the left.

I can hear Emily with Abdullah in the back. "Have you any brothers and sisters?"

"I have thirteen brothers and sisters. My father has fifteen wives. But only four at a time. When my father comes in and tells the women to start cleaning and cooking—I know he is getting a new wife."

"He has written an autobiography," Victor told me. "That's all in it."

I hear Emily say, "Why have you written your autobiography?" and Abdullah saying, "Because I have had a very interesting life. I find life much more interesting than fiction."

"How old are you?" I asked Abdullah, turning my head.

"Twenty-three."

"How long have you and Victor known each other?"

"Five years."

We come to Zennor and Victor stops the car by the Tinners Arms and we get out and see the old squat church. No clock but a sundial. Inside the Tinners we stand and drink Guinness and take in the atmosphere. On the wall there is a painting of a stallion.

"It's an Arab," Abdullah said.

"How can you be so sure?" Emily said.

"See the smooth lines. Your English horses are more heavy in the stomach."

A group of young people sit at the far end where a fire is going. I recognize one as the son of a painter Emily and Victor and I knew twenty years ago.

"Are you one of the Sparks?" I asked him.

"Yes," he said, standing up and saying my name. We shake hands. He is the same age as Abdullah and twice as tall.

"Your mother and father," I said, "brought you over to see us when we lived in Mousehole."

"When I was in diapers," Sparks said laughing.

I introduce him to Abdullah. "He's from Morocco."

"I was there last summer," Sparks said. "I was thrown in jail. My friend, the chief of police, got me out and then I was in even worse trouble."

There is an immediate rapport between the small Arab and the tall country-faced young man.

While Abdullah is talking to Emily, Sparks tells me:" Abdullah—it's like Fred over there. You see all these mothers come running out of their houses calling: "'Come here, Abdullah, you naughty boy.'"

"He's just like his father," I said when we were getting back in the car, "outgoing—giving of himself."

"He tried to say goodbye to me in Arabic," Abdullah said.

We drove over to Mousehole. (We were covering old ground that Victor knew.) We came there just after Emily and I married. Lived for a year in a large granite house on the side of a hill. It had a nice garden with bamboos, copper beech, and palm trees. In the morning, when we were still in bed, we could hear the melancholy sound of curlews flying over to the fields above. And again at dusk when they flew back to the rocks at the sea's edge. Victor was living in St. Ives and he would come on Friday night for meals that Emily made. Our novels were finished and were making the rounds of the publishers ...

Now, we were looking through the bare hedge at the granite house in silence. Emily wanted to get away. "Some things are best left undisturbed," she told me. Victor showed no interest at all.

"Let's go," he said, "and have a meal."

The little village was very clean, the colours as fresh as paint, the streets deserted. But we were too late for lunch.

We drove into Penzance. The restaurants were shut. Finally we find one open in Market Jew Street. It was packed. Every seat taken. People were standing up. I saw stairs. I suggested we go up the stairs. Here it was all empty. The tables nicely set with white tablecloths and facing a wall window overlooking Market Jew Street.

"I see the advantage of a university education," Emily said.

"Now," Victor said, "we'll have a feast."

The menu was brought to us by a stocky middle-aged waitress. She had white shoes on, and gave the impression that there was still lots of life in her yet. We all agreed to have soup and scampi.

The waitress came carrying the bowls of soup close to her breasts. And she was singing, "*Isn't it romantic—*"

The soup was terrible. The scampi wasn't very good either. But we were hungry.

The waitress came back with a bottle of standard fish sauce, her hips swaying.

"Let's try some of this exotic sauce," Victor said, putting his knife into the bottle.

"I'll have some too," I said.

"*Isn't it romantic—*" she sang.

Abdullah didn't like the scampi. The waitress went back and sat down by another table. I guess she had her eye on Abdullah. But Abdullah was looking out into Market Jew Street.

"In Morocco," he said to Emily, "the people would be on the road and the cars on the pavement."

An old man came up and sat down at a table.

"Hullo, my handsome," the waitress said loudly. And went over carrying a cup of tea.

That night in bed Emily said, "Yesterday, early Friday, it was raining. And you know how it is here sometimes. You think it's all coming down on you. I just wanted to talk to someone. And there was Mr. Care outside his nice pink house with a broom. And I said, You're not going to change the colour? No, he said,

I've been away for a few days. I'm just tidying up. Where did you go? To Brighton. My son is a vicar there. He is the vicar for the crematorium. And I remembered our neighbour with her obsession about the dead. It was all getting me down. Then Victor phones to say he's here. And the next day I am out driving in a car across the moors and there were the green fields and this very English landscape. And sitting beside me is a dark little Arab. Suddenly life seems to have all sorts of possibilities. If this can happen—there's hope. I was so excited I was almost jumping up in the back seat. Thank God for Abdullah. Victor is too glum for me. And his talk is so superficial. I don't suppose you would have anything to do with him now if you met him."

"I don't suppose either of us would," I said. "He didn't expect to find us here when he came. I don't think we'll even exchange postcards when he gets back."

"That happens all the time," Emily said. "People who know each other when they are young drift apart. Are they coming tomorrow for lunch?"

"Yes," I said.

"I'll do a roast chicken and make a nice dessert."

"Fine," I said. "And I'll get some wine."

Soon after they arrived at noon, I brought them upstairs to this room. It seemed necessary, for me, that Victor should see what I had done with all those years. I showed him the books. For twenty years they seemed so few. But I tried to make it look better by showing him the various editions. Knowing his predilection for the exotic I showed him an article on some of the books in the *Bangkok Post* of 2 August 1970.

"This is nice," Victor said as he read it.

"Do many people come to see you?" Abdullah asked.

"A few."

"What do they want?"

"I think they want something to happen to them. Then they go home."

"Do you write about them?"

"Sometimes," I said. "People are very generous. They let you into their lives. So you don't want to hurt them by what you write. In any case I write about people I like or have liked. And only about people I know. Their visit is only the tip of an iceberg."

The meal went all right. Victor kept touching his chin when he talked. Abdullah was much more at ease. He told us that he was circumcised when he was six, that the Jews and Arabs were cousins, and what was all this stupid fighting for.

After lunch I took them both for a walk. "That's Emily's garden," I said. "There used to be a greenhouse but the storm blew it down. Underneath the pear tree there is a little cemetery of children's animals—part of Martha's and Ella's childhood—two cats, one kitten, two hamsters, a goldfish."

I walked them through the twisting back streets and around the harbour. "You have seen the small stone cottages," I said to Abdullah, "and the kind of terrace houses we live in. Now I'll show you how other people live here."

We got in the car and I told Victor to drive out of the place. Then down a road with trees. And through a wide gate. And there were the fine lawns with the large house at the end. The sides with trees. And a sheer slope down to the sand and the water of the bay. Abdullah could not contain his excitement. "Shall I take some pictures?" he asked Victor.

"I don't think the light is good enough," Victor said woodenly.

And I wondered why Victor hadn't taken any pictures of where we lived or of Emily, Ella, or myself.

"You might remember Henry Nicolle," I said to Victor as we walked towards the house. "He was a painter. We went to his first show in London in 1949. His widow still lives here."

But Victor didn't remember.

The front door was shut. I looked inside the front room with the paintings on the wall, the antique furniture. "I guess no one's in," I said.

But Victor had already gone back to the car. He looked impatient to get away. Did it remind him of the house in Westmount, of summers in Murray Bay, St. Andrew's Ball, Sherbrooke Street, McGill? I didn't know. When we got in the car he said, "I'll drive back to say goodbye to Emily."

For a while Victor and Emily looked at each other in the hallway. Neither knew what to say. Then they embraced and kissed. "If you are ever in Morocco," Victor said. And Emily laughed. "Yes, Victor—"

I went out to walk them back to the car park. It was dusk. Most of the houses were in darkness.

"You'll be able to get back to work," Victor said.

"The importance of work is highly exaggerated," I said. "Sometimes I think it is just another con trick." I didn't know if I believed this or not. Or was I trying to tell him that I understood his life. "It's probably just another way of passing the time."

He didn't reply.

When we got to the car, Victor turned and said, "It's been fun."

He said this with something of the gaiety that I remembered. I shook hands with both of them, and walked quickly away.

For the next three days I came up here and tried to get on with some work but couldn't. Victor's visit had made me dissatisfied with the sort of life I was living. Why am I chained to this desk? I asked myself. What's so important about writing? Victor was living a much freer life. He had travelled and continues to travel all over the world. But when I make a trip it is back to Canada—to keep in touch with the past. Another chain. I deliberately remain uninvolved with things here because I don't want to lose the past—to put too many layers between. While Victor—? I suddenly envied his life. I don't mean living in Morocco or his house or Abdullah—I envied him his freedom. Chains and freedom, I thought. Chains and freedom.

But on the fourth day the visit began to fade. Things here were getting back to the way they were before. Emily came up at ten thirty in the morning with a cup of coffee and a biscuit. And I began to go on with the writing where I left off.

A week later I had a letter from Montreal, from the Graduates Society of McGill, letting me know that this year was our silver anniversary. "Dear Classmate," it began. "Yes indeed it is hard to believe that a group as young as we are graduated from the old alma mater twenty-five years ago! But that's the way it is!"

BY A FROZEN RIVER

I N THE WINTER of 1965 I decided to go for a few months to a small town in Northern Ontario. It didn't have a railway station—just one of those brown railway sidings, on the outskirts, with a small wooden building to send telegrams, buy tickets, and to get on and get off. A taxi was there meeting the train. I asked the driver to take me to a hotel. There was only one he would recommend, the Adanac. I must have looked puzzled, for he said, "It's Canada spelled backwards."

He drove slowly through snow-covered streets. The snowbanks by the sidewalk were so high that you couldn't see anyone walking. Just the trees. He drove alongside a frozen river with a green bridge across it. Then we were out for a while in the country. The snow here had drifted so that the tops of the telegraph poles were protruding like fence posts. Then we came to the town—a wide main street with other streets going off it.

The Adanac was a three-storey wooden hotel on the corner of King and Queen. It had seen better times. Its grey-painted wooden veranda, with icicles on the edges, looked old and fragile. But the woodwork had hand-carved designs, and the white windows had rounded tops. Beside it was a new beer parlour.

Fifty years ago it was the height of fashion to stay at the hotel. It was then called the George. The resident manager told me this, in his office, after I paid a month's rent in advance. His name was Savage. A short, overweight man in his sixties, with a slow speaking voice, as if he was thinking what he was going to say. He sat, neatly dressed, behind a desk, his grey hair crewcut, and looked out of the large window at the snow-covered street. The sun was shining.

"Well," he said slowly. "It's an elegant day."

His wife was a thin, tall woman with delicate features. She also hardly spoke, but would come into the office and sit, very upright, in a rocking chair near Mr. Savage and look out of the window. The office connected with their three-room flat. It was filled with their possessions. A small, bronze crucifix was on the wall. Over the piano a large picture of the Pope. There were a few coloured photographs: a boy in uniform, children, and a sunset over a lake.

141

I rented the flat above. I had a room to sleep in, a room to write and read, and a kitchen with an electric stove and fridge. To get to them I would go up worn steps, along a wide, badly lit corridor—large tin pipes carried heat along the ceiling. But inside the rooms it was warm. They had radiators and double windows.

I unpacked. Then went to the supermarket, by the frozen river, and came back with various tins, fruit, and cheap cigars that said they were dipped in wine. I made myself some coffee, lit one of the thin cigars, and relaxed.

I saw a wooden radio on the side table in the sitting room. A battered thing. I had to put twenty-five cents in the back. That, according to a metal sign, gave me two hours' playing time. But that was only a formality. For the back was all exposed, and the twenty-five cents kept falling out for me to put through again.

Listening to the radio—I could only get the local station— the town sounded a noisy, busy place, full of people buying and selling and with things going on. But when I walked out, the first thing I noticed was the silence. The frozen, shabby side streets. Hardly anything moving. It wasn't like what the radio made out at all. There was a feeling of apathy. The place seemed stunned by the snow piled everywhere.

I quickly established a routine. After breakfast I went out and walked. And came back, made some coffee, and wrote down whatever things I happened to notice.

This morning it was the way trees creak in the cold. I had walked by a large elm when I heard it. I thought it was the crunching sound my shoes made on the hard-packed snow. So I stopped. There was no wind, the branches were not moving, yet the tree was creaking.

In the late afternoon, I made another expedition outside. Just before it got dark, I found a small square. It began to snow. The few trees on the perimeter were black. The few bundled-up people walking slowly through the snow were black. And from behind curtained windows a bit of light, a bit of orange. There was no sound. Just the snow falling. I expected horses and sleighs to appear, and felt the isolation.

That evening I had company. A mouse. I saw it just before it saw me. I tried to hit it with a newspaper, but I missed. And as it ran it slipped and slithered on the linoleum. I was laughing. It ran behind the radiator. I looked and saw it between the radiator grooves, where the dust had gathered. It had made a nest out of bits of fluff. I left food out for it. And in the evenings it would come out and run around the perimeter of the sitting room, then go back behind the radiator.

Birds woke me in the morning. It seemed odd to see so much snow and ice and hear birds singing. I opened the wooden slot in the outside window and threw out some bread. Though I could hear the birds, I couldn't see them. Then they came—sparrows. They seemed to fly into their shadows as they landed on the snow. Then three pigeons. I went and got some more bread.

On the fourth day I met my neighbour across the hall. He rented the two rooms opposite. He wore a red lumberjack shirt and black lumberjack boots with the laces going high up. He was medium height, in his forties, with pleasant features. And he had short, red hair.

"Hi," he said. And asked me what I was doing.

"Writing a book," I said.

"Are you really writing a book?"

"Yes."

"That must be very nice," he said, and invited me into his flat. It was the same as mine, except he didn't have a sitting room. The same second-hand furniture, the used electric stove, the large fridge, the wooden radio.

I asked him what he did.

"I work in a small factory. Just my brother and me. We make canoes. Do you like cheese?"

"Yes," I said.

He opened his fridge. It was filled with large hunks of an orange cheese.

"I get it sent from Toronto. Here, have some."

I met the new occupants of the three rooms behind me next morning. I was going to the toilet. (There was one toilet, with bath, for all of us on the first floor. It was in the hall at the top of the stairs.) I opened the door and saw a woman sitting on the toilet, smoking a cigarette. She wasn't young. Her legs were close together. She said, "Oh." I said sorry and closed the door quickly. "I'm sorry," I said again, this time louder, as I walked away.

A couple of days later she knocked on my door and said she was Mrs. Labelle and she was Jewish. She heard from Savage that I had a Jewish name. Was I Jewish? I said I was. She invited me back to meet her husband.

The people who rented these rooms usually didn't stay very long, so there was no pride in trying to do anything to change them. But Mrs. Labelle had her room spotless. She had put up bright yellow curtains to hide the shabby window blinds. She had plastic flowers in a bowl on the table. And everything looked neat, and washed, even though the furniture was the same as I had.

Her husband, Hubert, was much younger. He looked very dapper. Tall, dark hair brushed back, neatly dressed in a dark suit and tie and a clean white shirt. He had a tripod in his hand and said he was going out to work.

"Savage told us you were a writer. I have started to write my life story—What the photographer saw— I tell all. You wouldn't believe the things that have happened to me."

His wife said that the mayor was trying to get them out of town. "He told the police that we need a licence. It's because he owns the only photograph store here. He's afraid of the competition. We're not doing anything illegal. I knock on people's doors and ask them if they want their picture taken at home. He's very good," she said," especially with children."

After that Mrs. Labelle came to the door every day. She knew all the other occupants. And would tell me little things about them. "He's a very hard worker," she said about the man who made canoes. "He doesn't drink at all." Then she told me about the cleaning woman, Mabel. "She only gets fifteen dollars a week. Her husband's an alcoholic. She's got a sixteen-year-old daughter—she's pregnant. I'm going to see her this afternoon and see if I can help. Be careful of Savage. He looks quiet, but I saw him using a blackjack on a drunk from the beer parlour who tried to get into the hotel at night. He threw him out in the snow. Dragged him by the feet. And Mrs. Savage helped." She complained of the noise at night. "There's three young waitresses. Just above me. They have boys at all hours. I don't blame them. But I can't sleep. I can't wash my face. It's nerves," she said.

Then I began to hear Mr. Labelle shouting at her. "God damn you. Leave me alone. Just leave me alone." It went on past midnight.

Next day, at noon, she knocked on the door. She was smiling.

"I found a place where you can get Jewish food."

"Where?"

"Morris Bischofswerder. He's a furrier. Up on the main street."

I went to the furrier. He had some skins hanging on the walls. And others were piled in a heap on the floor.

"Do you sell food?" I said.

"What kind of food?"

"Jewish food."

He looked me over.

He was below middle height, stocky, with a protruding belly. A dark moustache, almost bald, but dark hair on the sides. He was neatly dressed in a brown suit with a gold watch chain in his vest pocket. He was quite a handsome man, full lips and dark eyes. And from those eyes I had a feeling that he had a sense of fun.

"Where are you from?" he asked. "The west?"

"No, from England."

"All right, come."

He led me through a doorway into the back and from there into his kitchen. And immediately there was a familiar food smell, something that belonged to my childhood. A lot of dried mushrooms, on a string, like a necklace, hung on several nails. He showed me two whole salamis and some loose hot dogs.

"I can let you have a couple pounds of salami and some hot dogs until the next delivery. I have it flown in once a month from Montreal." He smiled. "I also like this food. Where are you staying?"

"At the Adanac."

His wife came in. She was the same size as Mr. Bischofswerder but thinner, with grey hair, a longish thin nose, deep-set, very dark eyes—the hollows were in permanent shadow—and prominent top teeth.

"He's from England," he told her.

"I come from Canada," I said quickly. "But I live in England. The place I live in England doesn't have snow in winter. So I've come back for a while."

"You came all the way from England for the snow?"

"Yes."

They both looked puzzled.

"I like winters with snow," I said.

"What have you got in England?"

"Where I live—rain."

"Have you got a family?" Mr. Bischofswerder said, changing the subject. "Is your mother and father alive?"

"My mother and father lived in Ottawa, but they moved to California eight years ago."

"I bet they don't miss Canadian winters," Mrs. Bischofswerder said.

"We have a married daughter in Montreal and five grandchildren," he said proudly, "four boys and one girl."

"Sit down," Mrs. Bischofswerder said. "I was just going to make some tea."

And she brought in a chocolate cake, some pastry that had poppy seeds on top, and some light egg cookies.

"It's very good, isn't it?" she said.

"I haven't had food like this since I was a boy," I said.

"Why are you so thin?" she said. "*Eat. Eat.*" And pushed more cookies in my direction.

"I wonder if you would come to *shul* next Friday," Mr. Bischofswerder said.

My immediate reaction was to say no. For I hadn't been in a synagogue for over twenty years. But sitting in this warm kitchen with the snow outside, eating the food, Mrs. Bischofswerder making a fuss, it brought back memories of my childhood. And people I once knew.

"I'll come," I said.

"Fine," he said. "If you come here around four o'clock, we'll go together. It gets dark quickly."

That night the Labelles quarrelled until after two. Next day, at noon, Mrs. Labelle knocked on the door. "He didn't turn up. This woman was holding her children all dressed up. I told her to send them to school."

"Is this the first time?"

"No. It's only got bad now. He's an alcoholic."

She began to weep. I asked her inside. She was neatly dressed in dark slacks and a small fur jacket. "My sisters won't have me. They say I've sown my wild oats."

"Would you like some coffee?"

"Thanks. We had a house in Toronto. I have in storage lots of furniture—a fur coat—real shoes—not shoes like this. And where would you see a woman of my age going around knocking on doors? I'm sure I'm going to be killed. He calls me a witch. I found a piece of paper with a phone number. And a name—Hattie. I called up and said to leave my husband alone. I found another piece of paper. It said Shirley. They're all over him. He's a good-looking guy. And when he's working—these women are alone with him. You know—"

That afternoon, while I was writing, the phone went. It was Mrs. Labelle.

"I'm in someone's house waiting for him to come and take the picture. Can you see if he's in? He hasn't turned up."

I knocked on their door. Mr. Labelle was sitting on the settee with a middle-aged man in a tartan shirt, and they were both drinking beer out of small bottles.

I said she was on the phone.

"Say you haven't seen me," he said.

"Yes," the other man said. "Say you haven't seen him."

But Labelle came after me and stood by the open door. "Why don't you just say hello?" I said.

He went in and I could hear him saying, "I'm not drunk. I'm coming over." He hung up and closed the door.

"I'll tell you," he said. "Man to man. I'll be forty-one next month. And she's fifty-eight. We've been married fifteen years. I didn't know how old she was when we married. Then she was seven months in a mental home. I used to see her every day. At two. I had to get my job all changed around. But I'll tell you what. I knocked up a woman two years ago. And she heard about it. The child died. She can't have children. She won't give me some rein. I've had her for fifteen years. Don't worry," he said. "I won't leave her. You may hear us at night. I shout. I'm French Canadian. But I'll look after her."

He went back and got his camera and tripod. And he and the other man went down the stairs.

Ten minutes later she rang up again.

"Is he gone?"

"Yes," I said.

That evening around nine, there was a gentle knock at the door. It was Mrs. Labelle, in a red dressing gown. "He's asleep," she said. "Thank you very much. He hasn't eaten anything. I make special things. But he won't eat."

It was quiet until eleven that night. I could hear them talking. Then he began to raise his voice. "Shut up. God damn it. Leave me alone. You should have married a Jewish businessman. You would have been happy."

On Friday afternoon I put on a clean white shirt and tie and a suit and went to call on Mr. Bischofswerder. He was dressed, neatly, in a dark winter coat and a fur hat. We walked about four blocks. Then he led me into what I thought was a private house but turned out to be the synagogue. It was very small. Around twenty-four feet square and twenty feet high. But though it was small, it was exact in the way the synagogues were that I remembered. There was a wooden ark between a pair of tall windows in the east wall. A few steps, with wooden rails, led to the ark. The Ten Commandments, in Hebrew, were above it. A low gallery extended around the two sides. In the centre of the ceiling hung a candelabra with lights over the reading desk. There were wooden bench seats. Mr. Bischofswerder raised one, took out a prayer book, and gave the prayer book to me.

"Shall we start?" he said.

"Aren't we going to wait for the others?"

"There are no others," he said.

And he began to say the prayers to himself. Now and then he would run the words out aloud so I could hear, in a kind of singsong that I remembered my father doing. I followed with my eyes the words. And now and then I would say something so he would hear.

I had long forgotten the service, the order of the service. So I followed him. I got up when he did. I took the three steps backwards when he did. But most of the time we were both silent. Just reading the prayers.

Then it was over. And he said, "Good Shabbos."

"Good Shabbos," I said.

On the way back, through the snow-covered streets, it was freezing. Mr. Bischofswerder was full of enthusiasm.

"Do you realize," he said, "this is the first time I've had someone in the *shul* with me at Friday night for over three years?"

For the next seven Friday nights and Saturday mornings I went with Mr. Bischofswerder to the synagogue. We said our prayers in silence.

Then I went back with him to his warm house. And to the enormous Sabbath meal that Mrs. Bischofswerder had cooked of gefilte fish with chrane, chicken soup with mandlen, chicken with tzimmes, compote, tea with cookies. And we talked. They wanted to know about England. I told them about the English climate, about English money, English society, about London,

Fleet Street, the parks, the pubs. How I lived by the sea and a beautiful bay but hardly any trees.

And he told me how the trappers brought him skins that he sent on to Montreal. That he was getting a bit old for it now. "Thank God I can still make a living." He told me of the small Jewish community that was once here. "In 1920, when we came, there were ten families. By the end of the last war it was down to three. No new recruits came to take the place of those who died or moved away. When we go," said Mr. Bischofswerder, "all that will be left will be a small cemetery."

"Have some more cookies," his wife said, pushing a plateful towards me. "You have hardly touched them. You won't get fat. They're light. They're called nothings."

Mrs. Labelle knocked on my door. She looked excited. "I'm selling tickets," she said. "The town's running a sweepstake—when will the frozen river start to move? Everyone's talking about it. I've already sold three books. Will you have one? You can win five hundred dollars."

"How much are they?"

"Fifty cents."

"I'll have one," I said.

"Next time you go to the supermarket," she said, "you'll see a clock in the window. There's a wire from the clock to the ice in the river. As soon as the ice starts to move—the clock stops. And the nearest ticket wins."

She gave me my ticket.

"Good luck," she said. And kissed me lightly on a cheek.

She looked, I thought, the happiest I had seen her. My ticket said: March 26th, 08:16:03.

That night I noticed the mouse had gone. No sign of it anywhere. It was raining. The streets were slushy and slippery. But later that night the water froze. And next morning when the sun came out it was slush again. The snow had started to shrink on the roofs; underneath the edges I could see water moving. I walked down to the river. It was still frozen, but I saw patches of blue where before it was all white. Crows were flapping over the ice with bits of straw in their beaks. The top crust of the river had buckled in places. And large pieces creaked as they rubbed against each other. Things were beginning to break up. It did feel like something was coming to an end here.

Next day, just before noon, Mrs. Labelle came to the door. She looked worried. "Savage told us we have to leave. I went to see him with our week's rent in advance. But he said he didn't want it. He said we were making too much noise at night. The waitresses make noise, but he doesn't mind them. I don't know where we'll go. We've been in Sudbury, in Timmins, in North Bay—"

"It's OK," Mr. Labelle said, coming to the door. "We'll be all right," he said to her gently. And started to walk her back towards their door. Then he called out to me, "If we don't see you, fellah, good luck."

"Same to you," I said.

"But where will we go, Hubert?" Mrs. Labelle said, looking up to his face.

"There's lot of places," he answered. "Now we got some packing to do."

After the Labelles had gone, it was very quiet. I had got the reminders I wanted of a Canadian winter. I had filled up three notebooks. It was time that I left. I went down to the office and told this to Mr. Savage. He suggested that I stay until the ice started to move.

But I left before it did.

I took a light plane, from the snow-covered field with a short runway. From the air, for a while, I could see the small town. But soon it was lost in a wilderness of snow, trees, and frozen lakes.

THE GIRL NEXT DOOR

I N OCTOBER 1976 I came back to Ottawa and rented three rooms in an old house on Cobourg Street just below Rideau. It wasn't anything—plain bare rooms with brightly coloured wallpaper—but the windows looked out over a small park. And that made all the difference.

For the first two days—apart from going out to buy some small cigars and groceries—I stayed in and looked at the park.

It's a lovely little park . . . made for the human scale. People look right when they are in it. The two Lombardy poplars. One, at the edge of the park, by the sidewalk, in front of the window. The other, towards the middle of the park but off-centre, raised, where the earth formed a mound. And on top of the mound, on a small plateau, a gazebo. And beside the gazebo—with its open arches, its sloping brick-coloured roof—this other, very tall, Lombardy poplar.

I could not only tell a wind's direction by the arrow on top of the gazebo but, from the near poplar's leaves showing their light green underside, I could also tell its strength. Elsewhere there were maple trees—young and old—their leaves in autumn colours, some lying thick, underneath, on the grass.

I was quite happy to stay by a window. There was always something moving. A leaf from a maple, people walking, grey and black squirrels, boys throwing passes or kicking a rugby ball, others rolling from the gazebo down the slope. Pigeons, sparrows, and the occasional gull flying slowly over.

I watched until the park lights came on. Then it was too dark to see. That's when I switched on a small radio and listened to the news (the local, national, international), the sports, the time, the temperature, the weather forecast, and the commercials in between.

On the third day I woke up, drew back the curtain, and there was snow. It was the first snow I had seen in years. I made some coffee, lit up an Old Port cigarillo, and watched a man dressed in black with a black umbrella above his head walk through the all-white park. The wind picked up some loose leaves and moved them swiftly on top of the snow. Fascinating to see fallen leaves lifted then carried by the wind across the snow. They look like small birds. They are small birds.

I decided to go out. I had no destination. I walked along Rideau to the Château Laurier. In the lobby I took off my coat and sat down in a leather chair, as if I was waiting for someone. There were others also sitting down and watching.

I left the lobby as the bell in the Peace Tower was ringing ten and walked across Confederation Square, down Elgin, to the National Gallery, and found this Monet.

There was a Renoir to the left, of a mother and child. And a Braque to the right, of the Port of Antwerp. And elsewhere in the room: a red landscape of Vlaminck, a red nude of Duchamp, a Derain, a Léger, an Epstein, some Cezannes, Pisarros, Sisleys, and Gauguins, several Degas, and a Van Gogh of some irises.

But it was this Monet, *Waterloo Bridge: The Sun in a Fog* (1903), that I kept coming back to see.

When I was close to it, it was just paint. But when I went back, about ten feet, the sun was round at the top coming

153

faintly through the fog. The sun was orange on the water in the front and further away, on the water through an arch of the bridge, while the darker shapes, of the bridge, the barges, came visibly through.

At the end of the second week, Lynn moved into the apartment next door. I had pulled back the curtain and saw that the little park was almost hidden by fog. Only the gazebo— the arches filled with fog—and the near poplar and the near maples were visible. The rest was fog and the sun trying to come through. When a taxi drove up, a slim girl with long hair that almost hid her face came out. She was about five foot six or seven, dressed in jeans, a black sweater, and a black duffle coat. The taxi driver helped bring in her few things.

Next evening I knocked on her door.

"I saw you move in yesterday. I live in the next apartment."

"Come in," she said quietly.

The room was like mine. But she had put up art posters of Chagall and Picasso. And a Snoopy poster that said:

No problem is
So big that you
Can't run away
From it.

There were picture postcards and a row of paperbacks by the wall. There was a small wooden table and two wooden chairs.

"I haven't had time to do this right. Would you like coffee? It won't take long."

She filled an electric kettle and plugged it in. I noticed that she was left-handed.

"How long have you been here?"

"Two weeks."

"Will you stay?"

"I don't know. How about you?"

"I've got to sort myself out," she said.

I saw Jung's *Modern Man in Search of a Soul,* Sylvia Plath's *The Bell Jar,* books on psychology, poetry, philosophy, and art books on Klee, Magritte, Kandinsky, Munch.

"I go to the National Gallery," I said. "They have a lovely Monet."

"I like Monet," she said.

"Where are you from?"

"From New Brunswick," she said, "near Fredericton, in the country."

"I've been to Fredericton," I said, "about ten or eleven years ago. I deliberately go to places—some I know, some I don't—and isolate myself because I want to work. Why don't we go to my apartment? I have a bottle of wine and some records."

I put on Bix Beiderbecke and Sidney Bechet. And she took off her shoes and began to dance in heavy white woollen socks. She danced, for a while, by herself. Then she came over and stretched out her hands.

"Dance."

I got up and we danced. She was very firm, no fat at all.

After that we would see each other every day.

She had dark straight hair that she parted in the middle that almost hid her face. Now and then I caught a glimpse of her blue eyes, the longish straight nose, a small mouth, and, occasionally, a shy smile. When she smiled she also seemed to look amused. I liked her from the start.

After I told her I was a writer she would turn up at the door with a piece of paper and say, "Do you know this?"

When Spring comes round
If I should be dead,
Flowers will bloom just the same,
And trees will be no less green than they were last Spring,
Reality doesn't need me.

She wouldn't read it aloud, but give me the paper that she had written it on. It was through Lynn that I got to know the poetry of Pessoa and Osip Mandelstam. She also gave me several paperbacks of Herman Hesse. I think he was her favourite. But I didn't get very far with Hesse. I didn't try. I don't read much when I'm writing. And I was working on a long story, a novella, and I was often thinking of that even when I wasn't writing.

She would come to see me in the morning, in bare feet, a Hudson's Bay blanket draped around her shoulders.

"Walking in bare feet," I said, "that's the quickest way to get a cold."

"It's the way I grew up," she said.

She would light a cigarette and we would have coffee together and talk about writers, books, painters, movies, music, the weather…

After the coffee she would go out shopping. She always asked me if I wanted anything. About twice a week I would ask her to get some apples, grapes, tins of soup, salmon, coffee, rye bread (if she was passing Rideau Bakery), or nuts, if she was going near the mall. She always came back with a small white paper bag full of warm nuts from the Nut House. That's another thing we had in common. We both liked nuts.

She also went out every day for walks. And she would come back and tell me what she saw. She didn't tell me right away. There was this reserve—the silences—the shy smile—then she would say:

"I saw some gulls. Against the snow they looked dirty."

Or else I would have to guess what took place when she said, "I went to the cafeteria at the National Gallery to have a cup of coffee and listened to the conversations around me. People talk a lot of nonsense—don't they?"

"Do you know anyone in Ottawa?"

"Only you," she said.

"Why did you come here, Lynn?"

"I had a quarrel with my boyfriend. He's white. But he works for a black revolutionary organization in Africa. We were together nearly a year. I let my heart rule my head. Because I was in love with him I became interested in politics. Then we had a quarrel. And he left."

"What did you do before?"

"I went to college for a while. Then to art school. I was trying the wrong things. I left art school after two years. They were all on an ego trip."

"Can't you go home?"

"There's only my father. We don't get on. He wanted boys. But he got three girls. I'm the eldest."

"How old are you?"

"Twenty-three."

"You're young," I said. "You still have your life ahead of you."

"I don't know," she said. "There are times when I don't see any point—"

I thought, if I was twenty years younger it would be different.

"I'm the wrong person for you," I said.

She didn't say anything. But she appeared at the door more often. And now I found that she began to stay too long. Her visits became more like interruptions. I would say, "Yes, come in, Lynn. But you can't stay long. I have to do some work."

Finally I said, "I'm sorry, Lynn—I'm busy."

She went away. But the next time I became annoyed.

"Lynn—I can't see you. I'm working."

"Work. Work. That's all you do. What's so important about work?"

"Without my work," I said, "I'm nothing."

She walked away, slamming the door.

I didn't see her next morning. But in the afternoon the phone rang.

"Hello."

Silence.

"Hello," I said. "Hello—"

I thought I heard a voice but far away.

"—Is that you, Lynn?"

Silence.

Then quietly she said, "I'm going to kill myself."

"Where are you?"

"In a phone box—by the Château Laurier."

"Stay there. I'll be right over."

I got a taxi on Rideau and saw Lynn inside the phone booth, leaning in a corner with her head down. Her hair hiding her face. I put my arm around her and brought her to the taxi.

"I'm sorry," she said when we were inside her apartment. "I'm all right now. I feel tired. I'll lie down. You can go now."

Next morning she came around for coffee—in her bare feet, the Hudson's Bay blanket around her—and we talked as if nothing happened. She asked me if she could do any shopping. Was there anything I wanted mailed.

"No thanks," I said.

When she came back that afternoon from her walk she came back with a small present, a jar of honey, that she wrapped up very neatly in Snoopy wrapping paper.

She left me alone, but not for long. The following day she came around and wanted to talk. We did for a while. Then I had to say, "You'll have to go now. I must get back to work."

She went out. A few minutes later a piece of paper was pushed underneath the door. On it she had written, "I'm going—and I won't come back."

That afternoon I found myself going to the window, looking out to see if I could see her.

She did come back as the light in the park was fading.

"Where did you go?"

"To the Château Laurier," she said. "I sat in the lobby and watched people. I did that for an hour. Then I went to the

National Gallery and looked at the Monet. Then I walked. I walked until I got cold. So I went into department stores to keep warm. What's wrong with me?"

"Nothing," I said. "Just wait. Time has to go by. Things have to happen."

"You're lucky," she said. "You are doing what you want to do. I don't know what I want to do. I like going out for walks. I like looking at things—paintings, reading books." Tears appeared in her eyes. "Isn't there a place for someone like me?"

I went over and kissed her.

"Yes," she said quietly. "There's always that."

For the next three days it went more or less all right. She still went out for her walks. But instead of telling me about them when she came back, she showed me sketches that she did. Of the market, and people in the market, of people crossing near the cenotaph, of the mall, the frozen Rideau river with the snow, the trees, and the white Minto bridges.

On Friday she came in, around noon, with her sketchbook and a pencil. She wrote something on the paper, tore the piece off, and gave it to me. It said,

"I can't talk."

"Of course you can," I replied.

"No," she wrote. "I woke this morning and I wanted to speak but I couldn't."

"It will come back," I said.

Silence.

"Has this ever happened before?"

"No," she wrote.

Silence.

"I had a letter from my boyfriend," she wrote. "He wants me to come to Toronto."

"Why don't you go?"

"Do you think I should?" she wrote.

"Yes," I said.

She must have packed before she came to see me, for when I saw her again, a half-hour later, she was ready to leave.

"Thanks for talking to me," she said. "You don't know how much all those talks we had meant to me."

And I felt bad. All I could think of was how abrupt I was with her. How little I did give of myself.

I watched her go with her few belongings into a taxi.

A month later I walked to the National Gallery to see the Monet again. And as it was a particularly cold day I decided to go to the Lord Elgin, into Murray's, to have a cup of coffee. The large room was crowded with civil servants having their morning break. I found a seat by a table in a corner. It was pleasantly warm. The coffee was hot. I sat and smoked a small cigar and looked at the lights near the ceiling. They were set in round wooden circles, like wooden crowns. I noticed a lively group of boys and girls come in. They were talking and joking together. They all looked excited, handsome. Lynn was one of them. Her hair was short. She wore a bright yellow sweater. A tall young man was beside her. And like the others, she smiled and laughed a lot.

TO BLISLAND

SUNDAY MORNING on a hot warm August day. And we were in a train that was going to London. Two hours later, at Bodmin Road, we got off in the country. A long outside platform with upward-sloping green fields, trees, and hedges. The sun shining on them.

We crossed the tracks, to the other side, by the covered wooden bridge, and to a waiting small green bus.

Marie carried a carrier bag. I another. Hers had a carton of six eggs that she had boiled with onion skins to make the shells dark brown, a jar of gooseberries that she had cooked the night before, some panties, socks, soap, and writing paper with envelopes and stamps. I had several comics, grapes, apples, bars of chocolate, a paperback, and a kite.

It was warm in the bus. We were the only passengers. After twenty minutes it drove along a country road, then a small bridge, over a narrow river, and onto the main road.

Fifteen minutes later we came to the town. It was deserted. The bus went, slowly, up the rising main street. (The houses, the buildings, looked as if they had resisted change.) At the top, at crossroads, we got out and began to walk along a straight wide road.

On the side we were walking were small houses with small front gardens and, at the back, farmers' fields.

On the other side was a continuous brick wall. Behind the brick wall, cut grass lawns and, further away, Victorian brick buildings. The brick buildings had many windows and fire escapes—an institution, looking stark against all the greenery around it.

About a quarter of a mile down the road, the brick wall had a gap. A drive went from this gap, down a short slope, to a small new bungalow-like building.

Carol was sitting outside on a wooden bench.

She saw us.

We both began to walk quickly towards one another.

"Hullo love. Happy birthday."

Tears appeared in her eyes.

"You both look so handsome," she said quietly.

Marie wore a light blue summer dress with short sleeves. I had a light grey summer suit with a dark blue sport shirt open at the neck. Carol was all in black—black trousers and a long black sweater. Her black hair almost hid her face.

"We got some things for you—"

I took the kite. It was made and painted to look like a red butterfly.

"I don't think we can fly it today. There's not enough wind," I said.

"We brought a picnic," Marie said. "Shall we leave the other things in your room and tell Mister Patrick? Is he on today?"

"Yes," said Carol.

We went into the bungalow-like building, into the corridor. It was dark. A door was open, the office, and an outgoing young man in a white coat was sitting behind a desk. He was medium sized, stocky, with dark hair.

Marie went with Carol further along the corridor to her room.

I went into the office.

"We thought of taking Carol out for a picnic."

"It's a good day for it."

"Can you suggest anywhere?"

"Have you been to Lanhydrock?"

"We were there a few weeks ago."

"Altarnun—?"

"We have been there as well."

"There's a nice spot—just down the road—you can walk it from here. Down a hill. Go to the railway tracks. Then walk along the tracks. No trains run there on Sunday. And you will get to a river. It will be cool by the river."

"How is she?"

"Some weeks there is a step forward. Others not. At least she hasn't gone back."

Marie appeared with Carol.

"What time do you want her back?"

"Not later than five," Mr. Patrick said.

"Could you order us a taxi for five?"

"I'll do that," he said. "Have a nice time."

Carol didn't say a word.

We walked along the short drive, to the opening, then along the main road. On the horizon, the white grey hills of China clay.

"Have you been down this way?"

"No," Carol said.

"They've made a poster for Carol," Marie said. "They put it on the inside of her door. It says 'Happy Birthday.' Everyone signed it. I remember my eighteenth birthday. My mother made a large party, invited all my relatives, and I didn't like it at all."

"Have you still the room to yourself?"

"No," Carol said. "They put someone in with me on Tuesday."

"How old is she?"

"Seventeen."

We walked along the side of the road, down the slope, in silence.

"Someone else came in on Tuesday—" Carol said. "His name is George. He sits beside me at the table when we eat. He did the poster."

"Mrs. Smith asked after you," Marie said. "So did Flossie. And the woman in the paper place always asks how you are getting on."

Where the road levelled out we came to the railway tracks. We left the main road and walked between the tracks. There were trees on either side and overgrown grass. After a while the trees became thicker and the earth sloped more steeply down. There was a path near the top of the slope. We walked on the path, between the trees. It began to get dark. And we could see water.

It was a strange light. The sun (not able to come through the trees except for a shaft here and another some way along) left the top parts of the trees a bright yellow-green. Halfway between the tops of the trees and the river the light changed from bright to dark. The river was dark—dark green, dark blue, with large rocks in it. Sounds carried. We could hear boys and girls talking and splashing somewhere ahead. A dog barking. It was very still. We were walking in the dark light while above was this bright light yellow and light green. And all the colours seemed softened.

We sat on the trunk of a fallen tree, on the slope, where we could see the river. And had a picnic from the hard-boiled eggs, apples, grapes, and bars of chocolate.

"You look better," I said.

"I don't take the pills."

And she brought out, from her trouser pocket, some small red pills.

"They give them to me. I put them in my mouth, but I don't swallow. If they find out I will be in trouble."

"I'll take them," I said. "And get rid of them. If they get to know about this they may not let you go out."

"What's the girl like that is in the room with you?" Marie asked.

"She lies on her bed most of the time," Carol said. "They brought her in because she took an overdose."

"What's wrong with George?" I asked.

"He broke all the clocks in his house. Then the mirrors. Then the windows . . . How's Min?"

"She had kittens," Marie said. "In the cupboard under the stairs. Five this time. Four ginger and one black and white."

"I miss Min," Carol said quietly.

"We painted your room," I said, changing the subject.

"I don't know," she said. "Sometimes I think home is my room here."

We got up and walked by the river stepping over rocks and fallen branches and smelling the mud. The river turned. And as we came around the turn the sun had come through a gap in the trees ahead and we could see, in the shaft of light, a boy, two girls, and a dog. The boy was splashing in the water with the dog. While the others sat on the rock. They were in bright sunlight. The water, near them, a light bright blue. While all around it was dark.

We clambered up the slope to the railway tracks and into the sunlight, and walked farther along the tracks until we came to a road. The fields, on either side, were lush with grass and wheat. We came to an avenue of trees. They led to wide lawns and banks of flowers. And behind them, slightly raised, a large stone house with farm buildings. We walked on the lawns, picked some flowers. There was a small bridge over a stream. When we crossed the bridge we dropped the white and light pink flowers in the water.

Then we walked towards the farm buildings. They looked very old and used. A large pile of cut wood was neatly stacked by a barn. Others had machinery. In a stable a white horse with blue eyes had his head out of the stable door. He stood there not moving.

There was no one about.

We walked to the house. From the front it had a magnificent view over the lawns, over the trees, and onto a valley with the higher fields and trees on either side. The house was dark. It looked tatty, as if it had been lived in a long time.

"It looks so feudal," Marie said.

We crossed the lawn to go out on the far side. And crossing the stream we saw the flowers that we had dropped at the start, passing by, carried on the slow moving water.

Some way down the road were two neat cottages.

"My grandma worked on an estate like this," Marie said. "She was a teacher on the Royal Estate at Windsor. But that was nearly a hundred years ago."

"I would like a small cottage in the country, near here," Carol said. "I'd have a goat and a cat or a dog. I would grow my own vegetables. And I'd get better, if I can be left alone for a while. If no one bothers me. If there is no noise . . . I looked in an estate office window in Bodmin. There are cottages at two thousand pounds. When I'm twenty-one, I'll be getting five hundred pounds from the policy—maybe they will take that as a deposit—"

"Yes," I said. "That's a good idea."

We came to crossroads. One sign said to Bodmin, the other said to Blisland.

"Let's go to Blisland," Carol said.

"It's too late," I said looking at my watch. "We have to get you back by five."

"I don't want to go back."

"We'll go to Blisland another time," Marie said.

By the time we came back to the town we were all tired.

I tried to find a restaurant or a cafe. But all of them were closed. I saw a filling station open. Part of it had a small room with several tables with plastic tops.

We went in. We all had coffee in silence.

Then two motorbikes drove up. And four young people in white crash helmets and black leather jackets and jeans came in. When they took their helmets off I could see they were two young boys and two young girls. They talked loudly and laughed a lot. They had soft drinks standing at the counter. One of the girls went to the juke box and put some money in. The music came out loud and clear.

Nothing's gonna change my world
Nothing's gonna change my world

We remained sitting, not saying a word. Marie and I finishing our coffee. Carol hunched over looking down at the table.

"What's wrong, love," I asked Carol.

"It's the noise," she said. "I can't stand it."

Nothing's gonna change my world
Nothing's gonna change my world

I got up and awkwardly we left.

Outside it was warm. I started to walk briskly. I was first, then Marie, then Carol. And Carol became further and further away. I stopped to wait for her.

"I don't want to go back there," she said.

"You can't come home yet."

"I'll never come home," she said.

We were approaching the hospital when I saw Carol leave the side of the road and start to walk towards the middle.

A car, coming from the opposite direction, blew its horn.

"Carol," Marie shouted.

I ran over to Carol to try to make her come to the side of the road. But she shrugged me off.

More cars were coming at speed. They blew their horns. They took evasive action. One angry driver leaned out and shouted.

"Do you want to get killed?"

We were near the opening in the wall that led to the short drive and the bungalow-like building. The taxi was there. We waited for Carol. She came, slowly, away from the centre of the road and walked through the opening.

"I'm sorry," she said quietly. "Thanks for all the nice things. I had a lovely time. Will you come next week?"

"Yes," we both said.

"You better go in, love," I said.

We kissed outside the door.

She stood there with a plastic bag that had the remains of the hard-boiled eggs and the apples.

We went into the taxi that would take us to the railway station. As it drove away we waved.

And she went inside.

WHY DO YOU
LIVE SO FAR?

"WHY DON'T you go out?" Emily said. "Do you know it's over a week that you haven't been out of the house?"

"I went out on Tuesday to the post office."

"I meet people in the street. They all ask, 'And how is Joseph?' What can I say? He's working. He's up in his room. He's busy. Why don't you go out and see people?"

"It costs money to see people," I said. "If I meet anyone they say let's go in for a drink. I'm too old to go bumming."

"So what do we do? Play cards, read newspapers, and watch television. I'm tired watching television."

"You're tired when we go to bed."

"You expect me to be excited just because we're going to bed? Why don't you go out for a walk now? You'll feel better. Walk around the harbour, or through the town, go to the library."

"I hate this place," I said. "All I can think of is how to get us out. I've got a sign up on the wall of my room, *You've got to get out of here*, facing me all the time. I don't want to end my life in this cut-off seaside joint."

The phone rang.

"You answer it."

"Now you don't even want to answer the phone," she said and went out of the room to the kitchen.

I went up to this room, looked at the collection of picture postcards stuck on the large mirror. (When I look in the mirror, to see myself, the postcards give a 3-D effect.) They were from people scattered over North America, Africa, and Europe. I've stuck them on with Sellotape with spaces of glass in between. I even have a postcard of Carnbray in with the others. A summer's day ... palm trees ... the sea a shade darker blue than the sky ... a large green-and-white yacht in the harbour ... people on a sand beach ...

As a postcard, I thought, I could like this place.

I went to my desk and looked at the pieces of paper listing what payments I expected to come in. They added up to £325. But I had learned not to count too much on other people paying when they said they would.

Next morning Emily had a letter from her mother in London, and with it came a money order for ten pounds for Christmas.

I got a small tree and put it up in the front room. I went and got some ivy and Emily put it around the room, on the walls near the ceiling. Cards began to come in. And I went out and had a drink in a pub with people I hadn't seen for several months.

On the evening of December 23rd we were waiting in the front room, which looked very nice and warm. We had the fire going in the fireplace. There were some coloured balls hanging from the lights. There was this nice-fitting red carpet. It's a splendid room with a large bay window and we only use it when people come, or perhaps in summer, for it's too cold. Emily had made some sandwiches and I got a bottle of sherry and wrapped it in coloured paper, and bought some extra glasses. We were waiting for the people Emily had been evacuated to during the war. They lived near Truro. Since our marriage they've sent a chicken for Christmas and I've given them a bottle of sherry. We sat in the large second-hand chairs with the scratched sides where the cat sharpened its claws, waiting for them to come. It was past seven. I thought they were late.

"They have to put the cows away," Emily said, "and do a lot of things before they can leave."

A few minutes later we heard sounds outside the front door.

"That's them."

"No," I said, without knowing why. And it wasn't.

It was a wizened, hunched-up little woman, determined, thrusting her face forward. It was not a pretty face, although it had new blondish curls.

"Does Joseph Grand live here?"

It wasn't so much a question as an assertion. And it was said by my sister Mona from Meridian. I hadn't seen her for ten years.

Afterwards, she said I just stood there not saying anything but shaking my head.

I went outside and saw Oscar. He looked like a gentle wrestler. A squat little man with sleepy eyes, a hat on, a camera around his neck, a brand-new black coat and black gloves.

I shook Oscar's hand.

"Why didn't you write or phone or send a telegram?"

"I wanted to," Oscar said, "but your sister didn't let me."

I looked into the taxi, half-expected to see my father and mother inside.

"I bet you're surprised," Mona said excitedly when we were inside with the bags and hung up their coats. Oscar kept his hat on.

"Why didn't you let me know when you got to London?"

"We didn't want you to go to any trouble," Mona said.

Oscar said: "I've got a movie camera—I wanted to record the expression on your face when you saw your sister."

I steered them into the front room. Mona lit a cigarette.

"You don't look like your pictures, Emily," Mona said. "You've lost weight," she said to me. "It suits you. The last time I saw you, you were fat. I thought you had heart trouble."

Then the kids were introduced.

"This is Martha—this is Ella—this is Rebecca—"

"They're like dolls," Mona said.

"—this is your Uncle Oscar and your Auntie Mona. They've come all the way from Meridian in Canada. How was the trip?"

"Terrible," Oscar said. "We had to change twice on the train. You know it took longer to come down here from London than to fly from Montreal over to England. Why do you live so far?"

"If you sent a telegram or phoned," I said, "I would have told you what train to get. You wouldn't have had to change—"

"I told her," Oscar said.

"I didn't want to put you to any trouble—shall we give them the presents?"

They brought their new bags into the front room and brought out gay bunny pyjamas for the kids. They gave Emily a Norwegian ski sweater.

"He always wears black," Mona said. "Why, I don't know. So I thought I'd get him a white sweater."

It was a splendid sweater with a turtle-neck.

"You smoke?" Oscar said. And gave me several red-and-white flat tins of duty-free cigarettes.

"Thanks. Why didn't you write from Canada?"

"We didn't know if we were coming or not. You know your sister. She was terrified of flying."

"Everyone told us to go to Miami," Mona said. "At this time of the year, England, they said, would be full of smog, fog, accidents."

"It was a toss-up," Oscar said, "whether to go to Disneyland or to come here."

"Didn't you know *some*thing was in the air when I didn't write?" Mona said.

I didn't say anything to that. I couldn't remember when she last wrote.

"Here," Oscar said to the children, taking out his wallet from his back buttoned-down pocket. "From your Grannie and Grandpa in Canada—your Chanukah gelt." And he gave them two pounds each. Our kids never had so much money.

My sister looked at the Christmas tree, the decorations, the cards.

"Do they know about Chanukah?"

The kids were silent.

"Your Daddy will tell you." Then back to me in the same low disapproving voice: "You celebrate Christmas?"

"We sort of have a tree—and I give out the presents on Christmas Day."

"I always say, how you want to live your life, that is your business," Mona said.

The kids went upstairs to their rooms to try on their pyjamas.

"What would you like to drink?" I said confidently. It was the first time that year I had so much drink in the house. "Scotch, gin, sherry, beer—"

"You have no rye?" Mona asked.

"No."

"I won't bother."

"Oscar. What'll you have?"

"I don't care for the stuff."

"Won't anyone join me in a drink?"

"I'll have some sherry," Emily said.

"Let me taste," my sister said. "It's not bad. I'll have a drop."

"How's Maw and Paw?" I said.

"The same," she said. "Maw still works at the hospital." Then suddenly brightening up, "If they could only see the kids—Paw's got to go in for a checkup when we get back. You should see how nervous he was when we told him we were flying."

I remembered the last time I saw him. We were waiting for the taxi to take me to the station. He was in his shirt. A towel around his head. He was in the middle of shaving. "I hope I'll still be here next time you come," he said and began to weep. "Sure, Pop," I said. How pathetic and kind he looked. Then we saw each other in the hall mirror. He pointed to his weeping face in the glass. "I look like a Chinaman."

I suggested to Emily that Mona and Oscar might like to have some coffee.

Mona hunted in one of their bags and came out with a jar of instant coffee and gave it to Emily.

"We drink a lot of coffee, and I heard you can't get good coffee over here."

"We've got instant coffee," Emily said.

"Oh, you have," Mona said, puzzled. "Well, we like it strong."

As soon as Emily was out of the room, my sister said:

"I thought you said she was *half* Jewish."

"I said that long ago, because of Maw. She asked me where did I get married? Who was the rabbi? Now she knows. I know she knows. She said if this happened in her time the family would be sitting shiva."

"I always say, the way you live your life, that's your business," Mona said.

Emily came back with the coffee, and she also had some hamburgers in buns that she made earlier and heated up.

"Gee, these taste good," Oscar said.

"They're like we make them," Mona said, somewhat surprised.

I was surprised how she had aged. I knew she was two years younger. But she looked in her forties. Except for her body, which was very slim. She sat hunched, her back curved, jaw thrust forward, smoking one cigarette after another.

I heard a car go up. We live on the side of a hill. Mona stopped eating.

"What was that?"

I told her.

She heard a rail outside the house rattle. People hold onto it for support as they walk up the hill. But it was loose.

"And what was *that?*"

We were all quiet.

"I heard something—it's upstairs," she said.

I went upstairs.

"Nothing," I said.

"Are you sure?"

"I've got to do this every night," Oscar said. "You should see the locks on our doors. And the bolts. And the chains. When I go away after breakfast she locks the double doors with double locks—they're special locks. Then the chains. And then the bolts. She even has a gun and a dog."

"But what for?" I said.

"I don't know," Mona said quietly.

"You weren't like that," I said.

"Let me tell you," Oscar said, with a sleepy grin. "You've got some sister."

Just before nine the farmer and his wife came. And it became a small party. They drank several gins too quickly. They gave us a chicken and pressed tongue. I gave them the bottle of sherry. They left presents for the kids under the tree. They thought it was marvellous to come and find people who had only twenty hours before been in Canada. The farmer's wife—bright faced, plump—and Mona found something to talk about.

"—I also had my gallstones out."

"Mine burst," Mona said, "as the surgeon was putting it on the tray."

But they couldn't stay, as they had to get back to the farm.

Though the room had become much warmer, Oscar had not taken his hat off all evening. He had removed his suit-jacket, sweater and tie. With his hat on his head he went to sleep in the chair by the fireplace.

As soon as Mona saw that Oscar was asleep she said:

"What do you do about teaching the children religion?"

"We don't," I said.

"Our kids celebrate Chanukah. They all wear Mogen Davids around their necks—*This* is the Star of David, Emily," Mona said, showing her the thin gold chain around her neck. "In my home I have two sets of dishes. I light the candles on Shabbos. We eat bacon—but outside, in someone else's house. You might think that was hypocritical. Do you light the candles on Friday night?"

"If I did that, Mona, I'd feel hypocritical."

"Who did you name Rebecca after?" Mona quickly changed the subject.

"After Aunt Rocheh," I said. "You may not remember her. She's the one that never married. I think she died when we were kids. How did you get Francine?"

"After Fruma—Oscar's grandmother."

"Fruma is Frieda or Fanny," I said.

"No," she said. "You can take anything from the Fs..."

"But why just the Fs...?" I said.

"Well, it's got to be *like* Fruma—you can have Faith, Felicity, Fawn."

"They don't sound like Fruma to me."

"They don't have to sound, long as the first letter's the same. For instance, your Rebecca is after Auntie Rocheh. Then you could have had Roxana, Roxy..."

"That's the name of a cinema," I said. "Who's Lance after?"

"He is after Oscar's grandfather Laybel—he could have been Lawrence, Lorne..."

"What about Lou or Lionel?"

"They're old-fashioned."

Mona stubbed out her cigarette and immediately lit up another. I had noticed earlier the area of nicotine on her finger, but it was while I gave her a light that I noticed her hand was shaking.

"We don't let Francine go out with any English boys in Meridian. We send her away to Montreal during the holidays. She also learns Hebrew."

"Girls in Canada," I said, "learn Hebrew?"

"Why not?" Mona said aggressively. "I believe in God. Don't you?"

"No."

"Don't *say* that," Mona said. "You must *never* say that."

"Don't believe him," Emily said, trying to calm her down.

"I believe in fate," Mona said, "that between Rosh Hoshannah and Yom Kippur your fate for the year is decided."

"I don't go along with that," I said.

No one spoke.

Then Mona chuckled. "It's a good thing Oscar's asleep, otherwise he'd never forgive me for talking like this."

We gave them our bedroom. We slept on a mattress in my office with coats over us. This arrangement was all right for tonight. But tomorrow we'd have to try and get some sheets and blankets from the woman next door.

Emily and I were trying to get to sleep. Our eyes seemed level with the gap at the bottom of the door that showed the light from the hall.

"She must have been saving that up for a long time," Emily said. "I wanted to like her."

"I know," I said. "I've never felt terribly close to my sister."

Fifteen years ago, in Montreal, I was asked to leave the middle of an English 10 class.

"Someone to see you," the Dean's secretary said.

And there in the dark cool hall, under the arts building clock, was my mother. A bit frightened but dressed nicely in a small blue hat, a new black coat, and dark gloves. She had come up, on her own, from Ottawa to try and make me change my mind about coming to Mona's wedding. I don't know what excuses I gave for not going. And I don't know why I chose my sister's wedding to make a stand.

My mother took me out for a meal, in a small restaurant on St. Lawrence Main, which I enjoyed. It wasn't as good as her cooking, but it seemed ages since I had Jewish food. And the signed photographs on the wall of Max Baer, Al Jolson—her, all dressed up, across the table—the food—brought back my childhood on Murray Street; the stillness of the house on the Sabbath, with my mother, a handsome woman, sitting out the afternoons by the window. She wept—she may even have given me a few dollars—and I said I would come.

At the wedding I remember my father coming down the aisle with Mona. He was about the same size as Mona, but looked smaller, in a double-breasted blue serge suit which was cut down to fit him from one of my uncle's discarded suits. His lips pressed tight, near to tears, a little frightened. Away from the house he always looked lost.

Then the reception downstairs in the vestry rooms. There was something like three hundred guests. Most of them I didn't know. Perhaps I had, even then, gone further away from home than I thought. (The way the waiters were openly helping themselves to the booze—the way the people were stuffing themselves.) It seemed to me—at university because of the Veteran's Act, sixty dollars a month, which meant eating peanuts in the last week—that my mother, who had cleaned out her bank account for this wedding, was feeding a lot of strangers.

I remember the young rabbi sitting in front of me, eyes moving continuously. He was new, "from outta town." And ate very quickly. Then he got up to make his speech. He talked of Mona, whom he had never seen before.

"Mona, today you are a princess. Oscar, you are a prince."
Earlier that week Princess Elizabeth and the Duke of
Edinburgh had got married.

Then he sat down, mumbled quickly and indistinctly his
after-eating prayers, gave a few little shakes of his body, and
vanished.

Next morning Emily and I and the kids were up early. The kids
were very excited. Oscar and Mona came down after ten. Said
they slept well. Didn't eat very much but drank endless cups of
coffee that Emily kept making, and smoked cigarettes.

It was the coldest winter England had for over a century.
And though there have been Christmases in this resort where
I have been able to walk about without a coat, this time we had
fires going in every room. Fortunately our lavatories didn't
freeze, though the neighbours' did.

Oscar became a great favourite with the kids. He had a
way with children. He sat two of them on one of his knees. He
told them stories about Canada and their summer cottage by
a lake.

". . . We've also got a speedboat and we go through the
lakes. You could come up and stay at the cottage with us and
have some of Mona's blueberry pie and see the animals. You've
never seen a skunk. They come right up to the cottage . . ."

He spoke in a sleepy, genial way. The kids loved him.

"Why don't you go back?" he said.

"We'll see—maybe next year."

"You owe it to the kids," he said.

Mona began to speak in Yiddish. "Was it a question of
money?" Emily and the kids just looked on, puzzled.

"It's a bit more complicated," I said in English.

"How about if we take the kids back with us?" Oscar said.
"We'll take Martha and Ella. We'll look after them and they
can go and stay with us in the summer at the cottage."

Martha and Ella were hugging Oscar.

I didn't think for a minute he was serious.

"Look," Oscar said. "We can take them back for nothing on our tickets. We'll feed them, look after them. It's not a question of adopting them. They're yours."

"We'll see," I said to the two excited kids. It hurt, the way they were so willing to go away from us.

Whenever Mona didn't want the kids to understand something she began to talk in Yiddish. Until I finally decided to send the kids into the other room. Only to have Rebecca come back upset.

"They're whispering," she said. "They've got secrets."

It was nearly noon and we hadn't left the kitchen table. I suggested I might take them out, show them the place, and get some fresh air, so as to give Emily a chance to clear up and do some shopping.

It was freezing outside. There was no one out. The puddles in the narrow streets were frozen. The long fine sand beaches were empty. The water in the bay was grey. No boats in the harbour, only a few gulls were huddled together at the harbour's entrance, facing the wind.

"You should see it in the summer," I said.

"I can imagine," Mona said, huddled up in her Persian lamb coat. "It sure is a nice-looking place."

Oscar took coloured moving pictures of Mona and myself and the kids. And of the empty streets, the empty restaurants, the empty beaches, and boarded-up shops. Then we came back with rosy cheeks and sat around the fire in the dining room.

"It's healthy, the fire here," Mona said, lighting up a cigarette. "Not like our place—so stuffy."

I went outside in the courtyard with the coal-bucket and came back with it full to the top.

"You know what you remind me," Mona said, "you coming in like that—with the pail of coal?"

"I know," I said. "Paw."

There were times when I went out to get the coal from the shed in the courtyard that I remembered my father coming up from the cellar in the house on Murray Street, with a bucketful of coal for the Quebec stove in the hall. Just as there were times, upstairs in my room, when I was making out a list of payments to come and remembered him and his black book with his list of people owing him money.

"Do you remember you telling me: don't let boys touch you between *here*," she drew a line across her neck, "and *there*." Another line at the knees. "And you remember when you were at university and I saw you in Montreal. You had written that song. When you met me you gave me twenty dollars. I said no. What, you said, it's not enough. And gave me another twenty."

I didn't remember either of these.

Instead, I remembered when she was about eight or nine. When she was hit with a stone from a slingshot. It cut her head. They had to shave her head. And she wore a beret. She wore it in school. And the kids made fun of her.

"And you remember my wedding?" Mona said. "You remember Betty's fiancé, Sam? He was supposed to take a movie of the reception. But all he took was pictures of Betty…"

I didn't remember that either. I remembered Mona being sick. The doctor came to examine her. He gave her a large bar of chocolate for being a good girl. She gave me some. And we went upstairs and ate it in her room. Later, I watched the long, thin, white-yellow worms come out of her mouth and lie slowly twisting on the floor.

Mona and Oscar had never seen Christmas before, except in the movies. So I briefed them.

"This is the way it's going to be tomorrow. We wake up in the morning. We say happy Christmas to each other. Then the kids come down. We have breakfast. Then go into the front room. And I read out the names and give out the presents."

When they heard this they went out and came back loaded with presents that they wrapped up in their room and put under the tree.

"I arranged for a taxi to come on Boxing Day," I said. "We'll drive around and see some of the country around here."

"I thought you told Maw you had a jalopy."

"I might have said that," I said, "for Maw's sake."

In the evening we sat around and watched television.

"They've got the same programs here," Mona said, "as we've got in Meridian."

"They're American shows," I said.

We watched a quiz show for children. "Your TV is so much better than ours," Mona said. "It's so educational."

But they were mainly interested in the commercials.

After the news I switched off and we sat around the fire, drank coffee, and smoked cigarettes.

"Why don't you go back to Canada?" Oscar said.

"It takes money to get out of here," I said. "And maybe, now, I've lived too long away."

"With your education you could have been a doctor," Mona said. "It's true," she said to Emily.

"But I'm a writer," I said. "How many doctors has Canada got—thousands. How many writers? A handful. It's easier to be a doctor than a writer."

"Yeh, I know," Mona said sadly. "But it's hard."

I went and got some whisky—no one joined me.

"In a year's time I figure I'll make enough money to retire," Oscar said.

"Talk, talk," Mona said. "That's easy."

"You'll see if I don't," Oscar said. "I'd be halfway there if it wasn't for her operations. You know, she's had half a dozen already."

"It's true," Mona said.

Oscar, I knew, was in the scrap-metal business. But he bought anything that he could sell at a profit. He would fill up his warehouse and then load up a truck and drive the stuff to Montreal or Toronto and sell it.

"I've got to ring her up *every* night," Oscar said, "when I'm away from Meridian."

"We've got a system where we don't have to pay," Mona said. "If we don't want to talk but just let the other one know that he arrived in Montreal or Toronto—Oscar asks person-to-person and makes up some name like Johnson. "'May I speak to Mr. Johnson,'" he says. And I say, "'I'm sorry Mr. Johnson is not in.'" And I know he got there all right."

"You think *that's* something," Oscar said. "We know a woman who rings up Montreal long distance to get her kosher meat. She'd call up the butcher and say, "'Is Chuck in?'" And of course the man would say that Chuck wasn't in. But he knew that meant she wanted chuck that week."

"We've got three properties in Meridian," Mona said. "So you could come and stay there. I know it's a small out-of-the-way place. But until you find your feet."

"Thanks," I said.

But I didn't see much point in exchanging one small town for another. I desperately wanted to get out of this seaside town and live in London again. It's a cosmopolitan city that I miss. I try to go to London as often as I can, but it's expensive. Even so, a few days in London and I come back as if I had a shot in the arm. I feel sharper in London. I go through the streets and feel like singing. I do sing. I go to bed in London feeling slim and not the way I feel here, as if I'm carrying a large body with lots of weight and deadness.

"I've got to get us out," I told them. "There are times I've just got to take myself away from here. So I take a train to Plymouth. And just to walk down straight streets again. Until about noon it's fine. After that, I know I've got to come back to this place."

"Do you miss London, Emily?" Mona said.

"It's my home town. There are days here when I feel life is going by—day after day the same—and you're waiting for something to happen."

"Like us coming," Oscar said.

And we all laughed.

On Christmas morning the kids were up early. Emily had filled up their stockings by their beds when they were asleep. And by the time we all came down for breakfast the kids were excited and some of that excitement went over to us. We all said happy Christmas. And after some coffee we went in the front room. It looked cold outside, no snow but the puddles were frozen. Emily had the large open fire blazing away in each room.

I began to call out the presents. The children's first.

"This is for Rebecca from Uncle Oscar and Auntie Mona—I wonder what it is?" And the excited child undid the parcel and showered Mona and Oscar with kisses. "Who's this for—?"

Martha, just over nine, got a toilet set from them. There were things for cleaning her nails, plucking her eyebrows, putting on nail polish, and some perfume. The others got the most expensive dolls in the place. I know, I saw them in the store window. It embarrassed Emily more than it did me. There were boxes of candies from Emily's relations, reading books, and colouring books for the children, toys, bits of jewellery, and soap, and lots of handkerchiefs.

Around two we sat around the table in the dining room, all seven of us, for dinner. Emily brought in the turkey. "It's nearly twelve pounds," I said. And all the kids said "Ah" and looked excited.

"You think that's big," Oscar said to the kids. "If you come to Canada you'll have turkeys twice that size. You remember," he said to Mona, "the turkeys we had that time?"

"Canadian turkeys are a little bigger," Mona said politely.

On the last night we were sitting around the fire, watching some play on television. I decided to switch off. I went out to get some more coal in the bucket. When I came back Oscar was saying:

". . . one thing we got for sure. A place in the ground. It's six feet long, three feet wide." He moved his hand as if he was measuring. "And six feet deep."

I noticed Emily getting flushed. She turned her head away from Oscar. "Stop it. Stop it," she said quietly.

"It's all the same," Oscar went on, taking no notice. "We'll all have it in the end."

Emily turned her head away from us all. "I'm sorry," she said. And, weeping, got up and went out of the room.

Mona and Oscar looked astonished.

"Is she upset?" Mona said.

"No," I said, sarcastically.

"She's got to accept this, you know," Oscar said. "It's no use running away."

"She doesn't accept it," I said.

"But we all got to die," my sister said.

"I think," I said, "you brought back her father."

"So?" Oscar said. "I buried my mother."

"Maybe you better go and speak to her," Mona said.

I went. Emily had stopped crying, although her face looked as if she hadn't. I put my arms around her and kissed her.

"I'm sorry," she said. And I kissed her again. "It was a lot of things. It was suddenly as if I realized that she, they, being a Jew—as if I was an outsider and we weren't close, man and woman, like we are when she goes on talking Jewish. This is my house she's in and I suddenly felt we'll die and they are able to believe in something—that you are part of, and I'm not. And there isn't anything I could do about it."

I kissed her again. "Let's go back in."

We did.

"I'm sorry," Emily said.

"He's going to put us all in a story," Mona said, "just watch."

"I don't care," Oscar said. Then turning to me, "If you can make a buck out of it—that's okay with me."

I phoned up London and fixed them up with a room in the Strand Palace. "It's so much with a bath and so much without," I said.

"We'll have without," Mona said.

They were going to London because Oscar wanted to do a round-up of some of the places he knew when he was a soldier over here in the war.

"I'll cry when I say goodbye," Mona said. "I don't know why. I'm not like him. I'm like Paw. I cry."

We had to wait for the train at the station. Mona looked at Oscar. And Oscar put out his hand to shake mine.

I felt a piece of paper in my palm. I looked and saw it was a five-pound note.

"Thanks," I said, and gave it back to him. Since two of the kids were with us there was no scene.

"My pocket is deeper than yours," Oscar said, still holding the note out for me.

I put my hand in my coat pocket. Then put my hand in his pocket.

"It *is* deeper," I said.

Then the train came. I went in with their luggage and got them an empty compartment and kissed my sister. She wept, without a sound, her face screwed up. And I thought how like my father she looked. I shook hands and embraced Oscar.

They rang up that night to say they got in OK and the room was fine, the hotel was fine and a blizzard was on. I told them to go to Bloom's in Whitechapel for a meal.

Next night Mona spoke to Emily. They decided to go back tomorrow morning. London, they found, was expensive.

("There are no bargains.") The weather was miserable. And they missed their kids.

On the morning they were to take off, we returned the bedding to our neighbour, cleared the rooms. Nothing had really changed. And again that feeling of being cut off, and the need to get out of here. Luckily one of the payments came through. So I took myself off to Plymouth. Went to see the new books and the new magazines at W. H. Smith's. Had some coffee and doughnuts at Joe Lyons. Saw a bad movie. Had a meal. And came back. On the following Monday we got a letter from Mona. On page two she said:

... Dad was operated on this morning and it's a good job they did as both doctors said he wouldn't have lasted four months. I never saw such a big stone that he had in his bladder. The doctor said he got through better than average. We saw and spoke to him but he was in pain and got his hypo so thought we had better leave so he could rest. Poor Mom she looks terrible and it's taking a lot out of her. As soon as I hear any more will let you know.

On January 22nd came another letter.

It has been some time since we heard from you and hope all is well. Saw Dad yesterday afternoon and he got his stitches out and is looking better. I saw the doctor and asked him how he is getting along and he said as well as can be expected. Dad seems confused at times though. We brought the children yesterday and he was happy to see them. He's well looked after.

February 2nd, Meridian.

Hope all is well with you. Haven't been down to see Dad the last while and every time I spoke to Mom she seemed upset so yesterday afternoon I got the cleaning woman to watch the children and went down to see him. I also saw the doctor. He says Dad is coming along but is confused and that he doesn't know if he'll get better. He wants to put him in a rest home if he can get him in. The other day he went out in his pyjamas and it was below zero. I don't think he realizes he's in hospital. He recognizes us all but talks as if we were still living on Murray Street and gets confused.

February 25th, Meridian.

Dad was moved to the nursing home on Friday and went down yesterday to see him. He seems much happier and I don't know if he realizes where he is or not. At night they put a restrainer on him so he won't get out. Thursday morning at the hospital they found him outside at the parking lot. It was his fourth time out.

March 10th, Meridian.

Hope all is well and what's the matter I haven't heard from you? Saw Dad on Thursday and he was so happy to see me. Apparently he got out again so when I was there the director of the nursing home spoke to me and asked me to tell him not to go out and he got angry with me and said how can I get out as you see I'm lying here.

April 6th, Meridian.

Last week he got out with just his clothes and slippers and the nursing home is past the exhibition grounds and he walked to Bank Street and went in a restaurant (he had no money). They gave him a cup of coffee and phoned the nursing home and an orderly came with a taxi and got him.

"For some reason he wants to get out," I said to Emily. "But once out he doesn't know what to do. It's at the opposite end of town from where we live. He doesn't know how to get home from there. I don't know why, but I'm proud of him running away like this . . ." Tears were coming to my eyes. And with Mona's letter I went upstairs to my room. There was the sign. *You've got to get out of here,* facing me on the wall. The mirror with the postcards.

I went to the window. It overlooked a small valley of cottages. There was a funeral taking place in the street immediately below. The hearse with the glass sides had driven up outside a small stone cottage. Men in black brought out the light wood coffin. And heaped it with bright yellow flowers in the hearse. The mourners walked behind it. They seemed to walk like mechanical toys.

I stood at the window, over to the side, so they couldn't see me and watched them go by.

From this window I have now watched several funerals. They were all of people I didn't know.

A VISIT

THE PHONE woke us.

We let it ring. And looked anxiously at one another.

"Answer it," Emily said urgently.

I got out of bed and ran up the stairs to the office in the attic. At this time of night it could mean only one thing, someone was calling from Canada.

"I have a call for you," the operator said. "Go ahead."

"Gordon," an excited woman's voice said. "It's Mona."

"Hullo Mona."

"Did I get you out of bed?"

"Yes. It's after three in the morning."

"I'm sorry," she said. "Nothing's wrong. But I thought I'd ring to let you know that I'm coming over with Ma on Wednesday. We're flying from Montreal."

"I thought Ma was to come on her own?"

"It's the first time for her in an airplane. She asked me if I could go with her. Is that OK?"

"We can put Ma up," I said. "But there's no more room."

"I don't mind where you find me a place," she said. "I thought I'd bring Chuck as well. It will probably be the only chance he'll have."

"July is the height of the season," I said. "It will be difficult to find a place."

Suddenly I felt cold in the almost dark attic room. The only bit of light, moonlight, came from the uncurtained windows. And I could see the slate of the roofs glistening, the stars.

"I don't mind where you put us up," she said. "Any hotel will do, Gordon. As long as it's near you. Is that OK?"

"Yeh," I said. "That's great."

"Are you sure?"

"Yes," I said. "That's fine. What time have you got?"

"After ten—I'm sorry I got you out of bed. You're sure it's OK?"

"It's fine," I said.

Back in bed I said to Emily. "You heard the conversation. My mother is coming over with my sister on Wednesday. I told her to spend the first day in London and come down the next so they won't be too tired. Mona is bringing her boy."

"I could hear you say fine, fine," Emily said. "And I knew you didn't think it was fine at all."

We lay on our backs unable to sleep. I didn't know what Emily was thinking. But I guessed she was as anxious about this visit as I was. For neither she nor the kids had met my mother. All these years, I thought, I managed to keep the two sides of the family apart.

"Where do you think we'll get them in?" Emily asked.

"We can try Miss Benson down the road. It's only for a couple of weeks."

"Remember when your sister came with her husband? They walked in from Canada unannounced."

"I remember."

"You don't think they will do something like that again?"

"No," I said. "I told Mona to stay Wednesday in London. They won't be here until late Thursday afternoon."

But I was wrong.

I DON'T WANT TO KNOW ANYONE TOO WELL

They arrived on Wednesday. No one to meet them. They opened the door and stood in the hall, looking tired and nervous. Mona grey in the face, Chuck vacant, Mother neat and self-contained in her navy blue suit. As I came further down the stairs, I called out to Emily, who was in the kitchen. There was some kissing, and tears from Mother, Emily, Mona, and the children. I paid the taxi driver. We moved into the front room. And they sat down exhausted.

"Why didn't you stay the day in London?" I asked Mona.

"We couldn't get into a hotel."

"How many did you try?"

"One," she said. "Then they told us at the air terminal that if we rushed we might get the train for down here. You should have seen how fast that taxi went. We got to the station. No time to get tickets. We ran to get on the train. It's been like that since we left Montreal."

Mona lit another cigarette.

"I was told back home not to go Air Canada. That BOAC was better. *She* got the tickets. She said we're going first class. I told her no. Our tickets were economy. She insisted they were first. At Dorval the British plane had engine trouble. Another scramble. I was going around getting nervous, while she goes on as if she has all the time in the world. When they said we *had* to go Air Canada—I just stood there and laughed."

"It was a very good flight," Mother said. "I enjoyed it. She looks like a Raport," she said about our eldest girl, Martha. "Except the Raports are dark and she is blond. Kate must look like your side of the family, Emily. Judith looks like one of us."

They brought out their presents. Emily made tea and, on the quiet, sent out Martha to get some fish for supper. Mother said she wouldn't eat meat, it wasn't kosher, only fish. I got Chuck and Mona into Miss Benson's. And they went there after supper. Mother had our bedroom. Emily and I would sleep on the mattress in the attic-office. I thought I'd better see if Mother had settled in.

I saw her, sitting up in bed, giving candies to the kids. She looked refreshed and excited. She was patting the bed around her and saying:

"Come, sit down. And I'll tell you—"

Next morning when I went to open the front door to get the milk, there was Mona and Chuck.

"Hi," Mona said. "We've been up early. I couldn't sleep. Neither could he. He came and sat outside my door until I got up."

Mother came down. She said she slept well. And while Emily was making breakfast she and Mona opened their purses, gave the kids five pounds each and ten pounds to Emily and me.

"Where is the nearest bank?" Mona said. "I need to cash some traveller's cheques."

"Me too," Mother said.

When they came back they had bags filled with grapes, peaches, apples, oranges, cherries, bananas, pears. I don't remember having so much fruit in the house—not since I lived in Canada.

"People live differently over here," Mother said. "It's more slow. I like it."

She was curious about British money. And in no time she was doing sums in her head faster than any of us. They had bought postcards—showing the harbour, the beaches, the bay—to send to people in Canada. Mother insisted that Mona write hers for her since she wrote English phonetically. (I remember her criticism of my last book: "Why do you always write about bed people?" Or the time after Father died she wrote: "He was not used to going out with the hearse"—meaning horse.) And they soon got into an argument. Mona wanted to write the same message on each card. Mother wanted each one to be different. You would think they disliked each other the way they were talking.

"That's a lot of cards," I said in an attempt to break up the squabble.

"I've sent twenty-five," Mother said. "And I'm not finished. Everybody likes me. All my friends are millionaires."

"That must be comforting," I said.

"It's true," Mother said.

"I stayed at the Queen Elizabeth," Mona said. "$31.75 a night. Hamburgers and chips cost $3.75."

"The way you do your washing," Mother said to Emily, who had come in from the courtyard, "and hang it on the line and pull it up. It's just like the old country." And when she saw the enamel casserole with the purple-blue cover, "I haven't seen one like that since I left Poland." We looked at the bottom. It said *Made in Poland.*

But I remember in Canada when I asked her why did she leave Poland. She wouldn't say except something about taxes being high. When I said I'd like to go to Poland and see where she and Pa lived, she said, "It would be better if you didn't go. If you could do without."

And here she was excited because of seeing washing on a line, an enamel casserole, and narrow cobblestone streets.

The kids took them to the beach. They stayed there until late afternoon. Mona swam and lay on the sand. Mother walked by the tideline and picked small, delicate, pink shells that she brought back to her room. In a few days they looked much better, especially Mona, more relaxed. And they had caught the sun.

"We met this couple on the beach," Mona said. "They're on holiday from Scotland. They pay forty pounds a week rent for a house here. He earns fifty pounds a week—he must save up. They have a car—it cost them twelve hundred pounds—is that a lot?"

"Guess how much this tan is costing me?" mother interrupted.

"I don't know," I said.

"Take a guess."

"Five hundred dollars?"

"Seven hundred and fifty," she said with pride.

Chuck was left with us. He didn't like to go outside. He was frightened of steps, of a hill, and the beach. The first time he saw the sand he couldn't understand why we didn't fall through it. And when he was left on his own he would talk in these two voices. One was high, the other low. He would talk rapidly, in a singsong. High. Low. I couldn't make out what he was saying. The first time I heard him I asked.

"What are you doing?"

"Talking to myself," he said quietly.

He liked to watch television. The Americans were sending two men to land on the moon. And Chuck knew all the astronauts' names and what they had to do. He knew every stage of the journey into space. He rushed in.

"Halfway—moon gravity—"

He would stand in front of the television, only a few feet away. When he became excited he would bring his hands up by the side of his face, fingers wide apart, and they would quiver.

On days that it rained we sat around the breakfast table listening to the noise on the roof while Mona told the kids' fortunes in their tea leaves. She had complete faith in doctors and tea leaves. And mother asked Emily for the recipes of some of the things she had baked—cakes and desserts—so that she could make them for her golden age club when she got back. She showed us photographs. They were of elderly ladies sitting, all dressed up, by long tables with white tablecloths.

On the fourth morning it was drizzling. I was coming down the stairs. There was a nice smell of cooking from the kitchen. I saw Chuck at the bottom.

"You're *fame-us*," he said to me as I came down. "Me see you on TV *fame-us*." Then he looked at his face in the hall-mirror and said to himself "Fame-us. Fame-us."

Inside the front room Mona continued to chain-smoke. Mother was in a chair by the window, looking out. She looked at the valley of granite cottages, the houses on the other side of the hill.

"I like this," she said.

It was a summer light rain. It gave the slate roofs of the cottages a blue colour.

"Could you live here?" I asked her.

"It's nice. But not for me. I'm used to a different life."

She looked around the room, at the shabby furniture, the damp walls, the shelves of books, the worn red carpet.

"Did you ever think of changing your job?"

"And do what?"

"You could work yourself up and become a journalist."

"Journalists come down to interview me."

"But what have you got?" she said. "No home of your own. No new furniture. Children need nice clothes. Appearance *is* important."

I didn't think it mattered much. But perhaps it mattered more than I ever admitted. Else why did I always meet people who came from Canada, to see me, in a pub. Then take them for a conducted tour of this seaside town, ending with a call on a rich acquaintance who had a large granite house with a drive, wide lawns and gardens, above the bay. So they could go back with that. Was that so different from what she was saying?

"You remember Lionel?" Mother said.

I said nothing.

"I betcha he makes thirty thousand dollars a year. Maybe more. And his brother, Jackie, the one you played ball with. He makes forty thousand dollars, at least."

And Mona said, "Cousin Lily's daughter got married. You should see what they got. They have black leather Mediterranean chairs and settee. They have a new sports car. They pay two hundred dollars a month and they have a swimming pool. And it's so nice. Music comes in all the rooms—all the day.

"It's wonderful," Mother said. "I'm telling you—it's wonderful."

Emily had come in to join us. I wanted to change the subject. Mona had put out a cigarette and lit up yet another.

"Why don't you ease up on the smoking," I said to her.

"I tried. But I can't. It's my nerves. I need a cigarette. I tried candies but they don't work. What can I do?"

"Many men smoke," I said. "But Fu Manchu."

Only Emily laughed.

"You should go and see Israel," Mother said. "It's wonderful. For three hundred and fifty dollars you stay at the David Hotel. You have a table full of fish. You take what fish you want. You pay no more. No tips. Nothing. It's wonderful."

"But you haven't been there," I said.

"People who have tell me," she said quietly.

I went out of the room and when I came back Mother was saying: "I have had two proposals so I went and asked the doctor. He said what do you need another man to get sick on you and you have to look after him. I'm sixty-seven but I look sixty-one or sixty-two."

I didn't expect to be but I was taken back by this.

A few moments later tears appeared in her eyes. "Next year will be the fiftieth anniversary of my getting married." She rubbed the back of her hand against her eyes.

"How old is Chuck?" I quickly asked Mona.

"Twenty," she said.

"What are you going to do when he gets older?" Mother said.

"What do you mean?" Mona came back.

"You should get out of Meridian," Mother said. "Go to Toronto—you might meet someone there. You ought to marry again."

Chuck came in very excited.

"Landed on moon. Landed."

Then he went back, to the other room, to watch television.

"What do you and Gordon do, Emily, on Saturday nights?" Mona asked. "Do you go out?"

"We stay in and watch television."

"That's just like Chuck and me. That's what we do, every Saturday night."

Next morning it was bright and sunny. We were sitting around the kitchen table having breakfast. Mother was talking. She was telling the children: "—your grandfather was an architect. He came over to Montreal in 1904. He stayed a couple of years. But he didn't like the life. So he went back to Poland."

When the phone went.

Emily answered. She spoke quietly, didn't say much, and hung up.

"That was my mother to say Florrie died," she said and went into the back kitchen.

"I knew someone was going to die," Mona said. "Because of the birds. They were so loud this morning. They woke me up."

"Those are gulls," I said. "They are with us all the time."

"I thought it would be one of us," she said.

I went to see Emily. She was standing in the sunny court-yard against the whitewashed wall crying.

Mother, Mona, and Chuck went with the kids to the beach.

I remember Florrie. We spent our honeymoon at their farm, about forty miles from here. Emily was evacuated from London during the war. She came to Cornwall with her name on a luggage label around her neck. Florrie picked her out, at the station, from all the other kids because she said she was dressed in a nice fawn coat. She lived the war years with Florrie and her husband, Morley. Helped to bring the cows in, helped with the milking. Bicycled and walked around the country roads, the fields with the derelict mine shafts. "I used to write letters to my parents," Emily said, "saying I hate it here, take me away, they make me work. Now I look upon it as one of the happiest times of my life. I was lucky—it's like having a bonus. Now Florrie is dead and something has ended."

And I remembered Florrie coming every Christmas with our Christmas goose or turkey. "A dear little family," she called us. And the last time, when we told her we were all going up to London for a holiday and would be on the Cornish Riviera Express, Florrie said she would come out and wave a white tablecloth. We all stood in the corridor of the train looking out as we came near the place where Emily grew up. And there, in the distance, the white tablecloth moved slowly in the breeze—as we waved our handkerchiefs back.

The funeral on Sunday was in a Methodist Chapel. Very plain except for the organ. The chapel was packed. The singing was loud and excellent. And I sang as loud as I could because Florrie was the only one who said I could sing. Everyone else says I can't keep a tune.

Then we went to the cemetery. There was this tall church on top of a hill with the cemetery on the steep grass slope. There were fields with hedges and trees on both sides. As we stood by the open grave, a cow was going across the field opposite us. Emily saw faces of people she knew twenty-five years ago. And she showed me the gravestones of Florrie's father, of Morley's mother and cousin. Trees, grass, fields. It somehow felt right, here, in the cemetery. And I envied people who knew where they were going to be buried.

When we came back and opened the front door we could hear singing. Mother and Mona were in the courtyard clapping their hands and singing with the kids.

Oh, how we danced
On the night we were wed …

We didn't want to see them. So we went upstairs to the attic room. Emily went to the window and looked out at the deep blue water in the bay, the stone cottages, the far shore fields.

"I hate the sea," she said and began to cry. "I wish I belonged to something. I don't belong to anything. There's your mother, your sister, and yourself—you all belong to something. Even if you have run away from it. And there's Florrie and Morley—they belong to something."

I thought, where do I belong? Where does Emily? Mother? Mona?

Although it was after six in the evening the light was still bright. The sky had high summer clouds. And they were lit up by greens, light pinks, and orange. A gull was making its honking noise close by. And further away it was answered by another.

I could hear the children, inside, around the piano. They were playing a duet and singing loudly, "Things ain't what they used to be."

There was still another week to go but I was marking off the days. I found myself coming up to the attic to get away from the constant talk they kept up. Even the kids no longer listened to what they were told and had stopped being on their best behaviour. Judith had one of her little bursts of temperament and answered Emily back. When Mona heard this she said, "Judith, you remind me of me. What's the matter honey? You don't look pleased."

Emily was also becoming edgy. When she asked me to do something. And I said I would do it later.

"You're like your mother," she came back sharply. "You both live as if life goes on forever. But I don't think that way. I know there isn't much time. When a week goes by and I haven't done something, I feel I've squandered a bit of my life. But both of you think you have all the time in the world."

They could have stayed another week with us. But I told them they ought to see London while they were over here. They didn't want to very much. I said I would phone and get them a room in a hotel. It had to be central as Chuck couldn't get on a bus.

"How about twenty-five dollars a night?" I called from the phone.

Mona agreed.

Mother was against it. "Twenty-five dollars just to sleep in a bed?"

In the end I got them something cheaper.

"Type me out a list of what to see," Mona said. "Put, first, *Fiddler on the Roof*. And I want to travel on the train first class."

The last morning came.

"How time flies," Mother said at breakfast. "It went so quickly."

Mona came in without Chuck. She seemed to shrink physically in size and become anxious. Except for the tan, she looked like she did when she arrived. "I can't get Chuck out of bed," she said. "He's hiding under the bedclothes. He doesn't want to get up today. He thinks if he doesn't get up we won't have to go."

"I'll go and get him," Mother said.

And she did. She came walking back with him, holding his arm in a tight grip so that she took most of his weight.

"Look at us," she called out. "We are going steady."

When the taxi came, Mona and Mother wept as they kissed the kids.

We went with them to the mainline station.

"It's like Europe," Mother said as the taxi drove through the country. "It looks so nice here, the fields, the trees."

Mona and Chuck looked lost. I had a feeling, even then, that they were waiting for me to say: why don't you stay the last week here?

But I didn't say it.

At the mainline station we had to wait for the train. I walked up and down the platform. Mother came over.

"You wear your heels down the same way as your father."

And when I went to kiss her goodbye she offered me her face sideways—just like Kate, I thought.

Coming back in the taxi, Emily and I were silent for several miles. Then Emily said:

"She came too late."

"Yes," I said.

The hedges, the small green fields, were by us on both sides. Then the first glimpse of the sea and the hovering gulls.

When I opened the front door one of the kids was playing "Happy Birthday" on the piano. I had forgotten it was Emily's birthday. The kids had set the kitchen table. In the middle there was a chocolate cake with small candies. And birthday cards were on the dresser.

We sat in our places around the table. Emily lit the candles on the cake. Judith pulled the curtain across the window. It was nice by candlelight.

We joined hands and sang "Happy Birthday."

Then Emily stood up and took a deep breath.

"Make a wish," Kate said excitedly.

Emily hesitated. Then blew out the candles.

We all applauded.

Judith moved the curtain and let the daylight back into the room.

Then we began to eat.

THIN ICE

IN THE SPRING of 1965 a book of mine was published. And it got more notice and sold more copies than all my previous books combined. It was translated into several languages. The CBC and the BBC made half-hour films because of it. It went into paperback. Money began to come in from various places. Someone in Madrid wanted to use extracts in an English for foreigners textbook. Someone in Halifax wanted to make a recording of it for the blind. I was interviewed for British newspapers and magazines. Articles were written. I received a number of invitations: to open a new primary school in Cornwall, to give talks, to give readings. And one invitation came from the head of the English department of a university in the Maritimes offering three months as resident writer beginning in January. As I didn't know the Atlantic provinces and as I wanted to be back in Canada, I decided to go.

I arrived by plane on January 6th. I was met at the airport, which consisted almost entirely of fields of snow piled high and long drifts. "I can't remember when we've had so much snow and such cold weather," the head of the English department said. "We're blaming the Russians."

His face reminded me of an Indian chief but he smiled easily and was smartly dressed in a black winter coat, a white scarf, and a black Astrakhan hat that he wore tilted to the side. He drove, in a large low car with chains on the tires, to the best hotel in the city and led me to the top floor, to two comfortable rooms.

"Will this be all right?"

"Yes," I said.

Suddenly the life of a near-recluse that I had lived before changed. I was interviewed for the student newspaper, the town's daily paper, the local radio and TV. I was invited to contribute a regular article to the local monthly magazine. The commercial radio station would phone up and ask what did I think of a particular current topic? And what I said on the phone was taped and then broadcast. There was a display of my books and manuscripts (in glass cases) in the university library. The main bookshop in the place filled a window with my books. I gave talks and readings to a variety of women's and men's clubs. The leading Jewish businessman, Pettigorsky (he owned the largest department store), gave a dinner in my honour at the Jewish community centre. After a filling meal (that included soup and mandlen, chicken, blintzes, and lokshen kugel), and I had made my speech and everyone was standing up and drinking and smoking, Mr. Pettigorsky came over.

"It will take you a while to get used to living here," he said apologetically. "The first year you'll hate it. The second won't be so bad. After you have lived here three years you won't want to leave."

But I liked it from the start.

I enjoyed going to the various teas, luncheons, and dinners. I liked being asked to meet visiting VIPs who were passing through. Besides professors and undergraduates, I was also meeting judges, politicians, engineers, surgeons, scientists, army officers, restaurateurs, businessmen.

And I had this warm office in the arts building that over-looked the snow-covered campus and the city. I would go to the office, twice a week, and there would be people outside the door waiting to see me. I was like a doctor. Undergraduates would come—possibly with their ailments, but they would express it differently. Girls would say: "My boyfriend's too shy to come, but I've come," and say that he was trying to write a novel.

I was the first resident writer the university of this town had. And, after the early hectic weeks, it was mainly people not to do with the university who came to see me.

The first were two Army officers' wives from the large Army camp some miles outside the city. They told me that they were from Toronto and Vancouver and were only temporarily at the camp. They were going to put on a musical and wanted my approval. They intended to use the tunes of familiar songs—"Somewhere Over the Rainbow," "You Made Me Love You," "It's All Right with Me"—but they would put their own words to the tunes. And these words were to be witty comments on local events, especially Army camp gossip.

"We thought of beginning," said the lady from Toronto, "by having a voice come over the loudspeaker. It would be a pilot on Air Canada speaking to his passengers: 'You are now approaching the Maritimes—please put your clocks back fifty years.'"

Most of the others wanted to tell me things.

When I was having a haircut the barber thought I should know the best ways to hunt duck and moose. A scientist, in charge of a unit to help the surrounding farmers improve their productivity, came over after a reading and said,

"This is a true story. I thought I would tell it to you. Perhaps you can use it. There was this priest. He lived in the country near here. He was middle-aged. And he liked women, especially girls. Whenever he went to visit people who were sick in hospital or at home—if they were girls—he put his hand underneath the covers. Things got so bad that the local mothers got together and wrote to the bishop. Finally the priest was moved. And he was replaced by a much younger man. This young man didn't have the other's habits. But he began to ask for things. He said he needed a new car. The old one was too old. He wanted the house redecorated. Some special food he liked had to be flown in from Montreal. He wanted the best cigars. After a while the people again wrote to the Bishop this time complaining at the money this young priest was costing them.

"Being chaste is expensive, the bishop wrote back."

And Peter, the young owner of a Chinese restaurant where I sometimes went to eat, told me that before coming here he attended university in Red China. He thought I should know the best way to steal chickens off a chicken farm.

"You get this candle," Peter said. "It only comes from China. When you light it it gives off smoke. And you let the wind blow this smoke over to where the chickens are. You do it at night. One whiff and the dogs go to sleep for twenty minutes. So do all the chickens. They just lie down and go to sleep. You get a handkerchief and put it around your mouth and pick up these sleeping chickens and put them in your truck. Twenty minutes later, when they wake up, you are miles away—"

I listened to the strangest confessions, humiliations, suffering. And, as if to balance them, an amazing endurance.

By the beginning of February I was so well known in the town that strangers in the street would smile and say hello. A tall blond woman with glasses came up to me: "I saw your picture in the paper—it looks like you." Kids stopped throwing snowballs to call out: "I know you Mister—you write books." When I went into a restaurant heads would turn.

Meanwhile the invitations kept coming in.

One of the early ones was from the professor of English at St. Vincent's—a teachers' college which was affiliated to the university. But as it was a hundred and sixty miles away, I kept putting it off. Until the head of the English department told me that St. Vincent's was after him to get me to come.

"It will be the usual thing," he said. "A small dinner before. Then you give your reading at the college hall. And there will be a party afterwards."

I agreed to go next Friday.

Four days later, in the faculty club, he came over. "I've just got back from St. Vincent's. They're very excited about you coming. They've got posters stuck all over the place. There is a piece about you in their local paper. And they have put you up at the best hotel."

He ordered coffee and doughnuts for both of us.

"The board of governors asked me to tell you that you can be resident writer with us for as long as you like."

"That's very nice," I said.

I was to fly to St. Vincent's at noon. But fog came on Friday morning. The planes were grounded. The train no longer ran, although the tracks were still there.

I took a small green bus from the bus station. Four other passengers were on the bus at the start, but they got off at the small towns on the way. For the first hour the roads were clear. Then it began to snow. The wind increased. It turned into a blizzard. Fewer cars and trucks were coming from the opposite direction and more were abandoned by the sides of the road. The driver kept stopping to wipe the windshield. The snow was coming down so fast and thick that the wipers were not clearing it. Then he stopped at a filling station to get a tow truck.

"We'll never get to St. Vincent's today," he told me.

"But I'm supposed to give a reading—"

"It's impossible. I can't get through."

I rang St. Vincent's, told the professor of English the position. He said he understood, that the weather was bad there as well, and it would be best to postpone it.

I went back to the bus and sat inside.

"How about going back?"

"Nothing is getting through *either* way," the driver said.

The tow truck towed us for about an hour and a half—where, I don't know—as I couldn't see for the falling snow. Finally we arrived in a small town. The street lights were on but there was hardly anyone in the street—snow covered everything.

I asked the driver when he would go back.

"Soon as the roads are open. There will be an inspection tomorrow morning at nine."

I said I would be there.

I went to look for a hotel but as soon as I stepped off the main road I sunk to my knees in snow. I walked that way until I came to cross streets—the road was covered with freshly fallen snow but it was hard-packed underneath. I finally found a sign on a drab-looking wooden building that said it was a hotel.

"Can I have a room for the night?" I asked the man.

"It's eight dollars a night," he said.

"OK," I replied. And waited for him to give me the room key.

"Is that all your luggage?"

"Yes," I said holding on to my attaché case.

"If that is all your luggage you will have to pay in advance."

"I'm the resident writer at the university and I was on my way to St. Vincent's to give a reading when the blizzard came—"

"Is your car outside?"

"No. I came by bus."

"And that is all your luggage?"

"Yes."

"You will have to pay in advance—eight dollars."

I paid him the eight dollars. It seemed a long time since I was treated this way. I took the key and went up the creaky stairs to room two on the first floor.

It was a small gloomy room—the kind I used to have in my early days when I was poor. A bare light hung from the ceiling. And I needed it on all the time. There was an iron bed, a rickety wooden dresser. No chair. A cracked enamel sink with only one tap working. And every time I turned on the tap it made a wailing noise. The wallpaper was stained. I felt cold. I went over to the thin green-painted radiator. No heat. There were two grey blankets at the foot of the bed and a disinfectant smell when I pulled back the covers.

I felt hungry and tired. I looked in my attaché case and took out the toothbrush, the toothpaste, the shaving lather and razor, and the copy of my book that I brought for the reading. But in my rush, or absent-mindedness, I had forgotten to take my cheque book. Not that I would have had any luck cashing a cheque here.

I took out all the money I had and counted. It came to nineteen dollars and some change. If I'm stuck here another night that's another eight dollars. The ticket back is ten dollars. That left me a dollar and the change. I counted the change— thirty-seven cents. No need to worry, I said, I might be able to get away tomorrow. What I need now is food (I had been five hours on that bus) and a good night's sleep.

I went out to find a restaurant. It was still snowing. I went to the main street. The stores were on one side. The other side consisted of open fields covered in snow and some trees that were almost hidden. I went into a small supermarket and bought a loaf of bread, a tin of sardines, and two apples. That left me forty cents to spare.

I came back to the room. I ate the bread and the sardines sitting on the bed with my coat on. Then I dipped pieces of bread in the sardine oil. And washed it down with an apple.

I lay on the bed with the coat and the grey blankets over me. I thought that now that I was earning my living from writing and giving readings I was past things like this.

I went to sleep. And when I woke I was hungry. I ate the rest of the bread with the last apple. I remembered from my hard-up days that it was important to have something to keep up morale. I went out, found a small restaurant, had a cup of hot coffee and asked the woman if she sold any cigars singly.

"These," she said, "are twenty-five cents each."

I looked at it wondering if I had enough.

"This one is fifteen cents."

I took the fifteen-cents cigar, smoked it slowly. The tobacco was kind of green. I took a long time over the coffee. Then went back to the room in the hotel to lie down. Instead, I went to sleep.

Next morning when I woke up I was cold. I brushed my teeth and shaved in cold water and went out. The snow was still falling but it wasn't so thick. I walked to the bus station. The bus was in the garage. I found the driver—a different driver—in a stand-up eating place next to the bus depot. He was finishing his breakfast.

"No—no buses today," he said. "Next inspection tomorrow."

"What time?"

"Around nine in the morning."

"I know the ticket back cost ten dollars," I said. "Could you give me a ticket. And I'll pay when we get back?"

"We don't run the company on those lines," he said.

I felt hungry and light-headed.

"I'll buy you a cup of coffee."

"Thanks."

He paid for his breakfast and handed me the saucer with the cup of coffee.

"I'll see you tomorrow," I said.

When he had gone—in my nervousness—I spilled half of the coffee before I had my first sip.

I went back to the hotel.

"I'll stay another night," I told the man.

"That will be eight dollars."

I paid him.

All I had left was the ten dollar bill. I put it in my back buttoned-down pocket.

"How cold is it?" I asked the man.

"Thirteen below. But near here it's been thirty-five below."

Saturday morning, I thought, I'll go to *shul*. It will be warm. There might be a bar mitzvah or some kind of kiddush afterwards.

"Is there a synagogue here?"

"No," he said, looking suspiciously at me.

"Where's the nearest church?"

He gave me directions.

It was a wooden church painted grey in a snow-covered field. There was a narrow path freshly cleared to the door. A few cars and a few trucks were sunk in the snow by it.

As I opened the door a man in an ill-fitting blue suit said: "Bride or groom?"

I must have looked puzzled. For he said:

"What side are you? Bride or groom?"

"Bride," I said.

"To your left."

I went to the left side and sat down on the wooden bench at the back beside the Quebec stove that had large tin pipes going up and across near the ceiling. I don't know what kind of church it was but it was very plain, very austere. There weren't any religious figures or stained-glass windows. About thirty people were separated by a wide aisle. Those on one side looked at those on the other. We all had our coats on. Up ahead, slightly raised, were the bride and groom. And the preacher in a plain grey suit. There was a small wooden organ to the right where a woman was playing.

The wedding ceremony didn't last long.

Afterwards the guests walked in ones and twos along the snow-covered street—icicles hung from the boarded-up houses—down a turning to the main street and to a better hotel. And at the top of the stairs, in the centre of a large room, the bride and groom were sitting, side by side, on chairs against a wall. The guests came up to them, in ones and twos, with their presents.

I stayed near the door. There was food. A buffet. I guess that friends and relations of the bride thought I belonged to the other side. Just as the other side thought I belonged to the groom.

"Where are you from?" a man asked me.

"Out of town," I said.

I didn't stay long. Long enough to have three ham sandwiches and two cups of coffee.

Then I went back into the street.

For some reason I couldn't find the hotel where I was staying. The town wasn't that large. If you walked five minutes in one direction on the main street that was it. There were several side streets to the one main—but I kept getting into places that ended in dead ends.

I managed to get back to the main street. The place was now packed with people walking, people shopping. Outside a music store, over a loudspeaker, someone was singing, "Everyone's Gone to the Moon."

I felt like a vagrant.

I saw a bit of ice on the road and with a run I went down it. I was hungry and cold. But when I came back to the room my cheeks were rosy.

I lay down on the bed. Because of these last few years I had forgotten how it was to be poor. Now that I was back in it, I was hungry. All that had happened to me since the last book was published seemed some kind of fraud. I was a writer. In my world nothing is certain. I needed this reminder, I told myself.

Now, I must get myself out of it. I tried to remember what I used to do. I went though the pockets—of my suit, my overcoat. Not a cent. In my hard-up days I always left a coin or two in the pockets. What could I sell? There was the copy of my book from which I was going to read at St. Vincent's.

I went out again. I couldn't find a bookstore. But I did find a secondhand place that had a lot of junk (mostly furniture) lying inside in heaps all over the place. There were some battered paperbacks on the floor.

A woman finally came.

"Yes."

"I'd like to sell you this book," I said.

She picked it up, turned a few pages. I hoped she wouldn't come across the parts I had marked with a pen that I usually read.

She closed the book. "Fifty cents."

"It sells for $5.95. And it is almost new."

"Take it or leave it."

I took it.

If I had to stay another night I could try and sell her my watch. But she would never give me eight dollars for it—of that I was certain.

With the fifty cents I went out and got myself a hot dog and a cup of coffee. And wondered what I would do tomorrow if I couldn't go back.

Outside it had stopped snowing. I went to the hotel room. I felt hungry and cold and went to sleep.

Sunday morning I slept in. I looked at my watch—ten to nine. I didn't have time to wash or shave. I walked as quickly as I could to the small bus depot. The bus was outside, its engine running. The door was closed. The driver was not inside.

Two men, also unshaven and unwashed, were standing by the door.

"Is it going?"

"Yes," they said.

I went into the office and gave the driver the ten-dollar bill. He gave me a ticket.

When I came out the two men asked me if I could buy them a cup of coffee as they hadn't had any breakfast and they were broke.

"Sorry," I said.

I got back to the university town at noon. That evening I was a guest at a dinner party given in the Army camp, in the officer's mess of the Black Watch. There were fourteen of us, some with wives in evening dress. The young officers wore their dress uniforms. We sat in tall straight-backed chairs around the table. The lighting was by candles. We were waited on by two waiters. There was fish and white wine. Roast beef and yorkshire pudding with red wine. Then champagne with some exotic dessert.

I looked at the others. They were young, attractive, well-fed, well-dressed. How secure they all appeared. And how certain their world.

But outside I could see the snow, the cold, the acres of emptiness that lay frozen all around.

GRACE & FAIGEL

I N OCTOBER I was on my way to Ottawa to give a reading
at Ottawa U. But when the taxi brought me to Montreal's
Central Station, I realized something had gone wrong with
my watch during the Atlantic flight, for I arrived forty minutes early. There was nothing to do but wait. I didn't mind
that. There were these small purple-blue lights, and soft music
being played, and plenty of room. In the soft light the men
and women walking by were well-dressed. They wore bright
clothes. They looked carefree. It was very pleasant just to sit, to
look and listen. Or to walk along the marble floor. The signs,
by the newsstand and cafeteria, were in French and English.
The public telephones were of the kind that you touched the
numbers, no dialling. And when you touched a number, it
gave off a delicate plaintive note. It was so different from the
run-down English stations I had left behind.

Then on the train, sitting in a soft seat, by the window,
looking at the trees. With the sun on them they looked like
coloured smoke. How smooth the train moved. How comfortable, I thought. How clean. What luxury.

I am forty-nine. And since I was twenty-five I have been
living away from Canada in England. It was in England that

I met my wife, had our children, watched them grow up. But every so often I leave wife and children and make these visits to Canada.

In England we live an isolated life. The apathy of a seaside town in Cornwall, out of season, is hard to believe unless you have ever lived in it. So these trips to Canada. They shake up the system. I always come back to England wanting to do things. And for the first two weeks I do phone London, send cables, write letters. But then the life that we live in Cornwall takes over. I begin to feel cut off. And soon it is as if I have never been away.

I looked at the young woman on the seat across the aisle. She was reading a paperback with a large *L* on the cover. She had a small boy of about eight opposite her. He was half-sitting on the seat and standing up. He began to recite, in a rush: "A Cub Scout always does his best thinks of others before himself and does a good turn every day I promise that I will do my best—"

He stopped. His eyes looked upward. Then he repeated the words just as fast. And stopped in the same place. The woman said something to him. The boy said quickly, "to do my duty to God to the Queen help other people and keep the Cub Scout law."

He laughed. And pushed himself back onto the seat, his feet dangling.

She stood up and, from a small travelling bag in the rack above her, took out a book, a pencil, and some pieces of paper. And gave them to the boy.

She was tall, on the thin side. She had blond, short hair close to her face and two wisps curled upwards beneath her ears. She wore a tight green sweater and a Scotch plaid skirt with a large safety pin on its side. She sat down and went back to her book. As she read her mouth twisted into a frown.

I saw that the paperback was Doris Lessing's *The Story of a Non-Marrying Man*.

She caught me staring. She smiled. And her face changed. She looked beautiful.

"Do you like the book?"

"Yes," she said.

"I met Doris Lessing," I said. "She wanted us to have her house one Christmas and New Year because she was going to be away in Scotland. Who else do you like?"

"Graham Greene," she said.

"Have you read Henry Green?"

"No. What has he written?"

"*Living. Loving. Caught. Back. Concluding.* I hadn't heard of him either until I went to England."

"Do you live there?"

"Yes," I said. "I was in London yesterday."

"How was London?" And she smiled again. Her face looked radiant.

"It was raining when I left," I said. "What's his name?"

"Justin," she said.

The next thing I knew I left my seat and came over and sat beside her. Justin's large brown eyes stared at me.

"Do you want to see a trick?"

I took his pencil and held it in the middle by my thumb and first finger, and slowly began to move my hand up and down. The pencil appeared to be bending.

"It's in here," Justin said. And opened his book, turned a few pages, and there it was illustrated.

"He's advanced for his age," she said.

"You know any other tricks?" Justin asked.

I stared into space. Then I put my two hands together, fingers apart. I slid the middle finger between the opposite fingers, turned one hand right over, and wiggled the two middle fingers, that stuck out, on opposite sides.

She was laughing.

Justin said, "What do you call *that?*"

"Milking the cow," I said. "Why don't you go over to my seat and see if you can see any animals from the window. I'll give you a cent for every cow that you see, two cents for every horse, twenty-five cents for every goat. And a dollar if you see an elephant or a lion."

"Boy," he said. And took his pencil and papers and went eagerly to the window on the other side.

I looked at the large safety pin on her tartan skirt.

"I think," she said, "it's the weight of the pin that keeps it down. I don't usually talk to people on a train. Not for long. But you have an interesting face. What do you do?"

I said I was a writer.

"Can you tell me your name?"

I told her.

"I'm sorry," she said. "I have not heard of you."

"No reason why you should," I said. "What's your name?"

"Grace."

"What do you do?"

"That's my trouble," she said. "I don't do anything well."

This time I smiled. "The only other woman who said that to me turned out to have a very strong character."

"Oh, I'm a bitch," she said. "I know it. I'm selfish. I'm difficult to live with. I lived for a year in England. I used to knock around with the jet set in Knightsbridge. They were a bunch of layabouts just preening themselves. I worked in Selfridge's."

"How old are you?"

"Twenty-nine," she said. "I'll soon be thirty. Are you married?"

I said I was.

"Is your wife in England?"

"Yes."

"I'm getting a divorce," she said.

We were coming towards Ottawa. I called to Justin: "How many animals did you see?"

He came over, adding up pencil marks. "Ten cows," he said slowly. "*And* six horses."

I gave him a dollar.

"Wow," he said to his mother. "I've now got a dollar and a quarter."

He carefully folded the dollar and put it into the back pocket of his jeans. Then went back to the window on the opposite side.

"Besides England," she said, "I've been to South and Central America."

"I've only been to England and Canada," I said. "Wasn't it a lucky accident for us to meet?"

"I don't think these things are *accidents*," she said. "I think we were intended to meet. We have good vibrations," she said quietly.

"I'm coming here to give a reading—on Tuesday night," I said. "I'll be staying with my mother while in Ottawa. Let's meet tomorrow."

"All right."

"How about in the morning? In the lobby of the Château Laurier. Ten o'clock. Is that too early?"

"I'll be there," she said. "I'm here for the weekend to see my parents. It's a kind of duty. They live just out of Ottawa. The last time I saw them was in August."

She took a piece of Justin's paper and, in pencil, wrote her parents' phone number, then her address and phone number in Toronto.

We were coming towards the new Union Station. I took her case. We got out of the train and walked into the clean, all-glass station. It was quite empty.

"Anyone meeting you?"

"No," she said. "I'll have to phone my father at the office. He'll come and get me."

"I'll take a taxi outside. Will you be all right?"

"Yes," she said and smiled. "I'll see you tomorrow."

The taxi went down Rideau to Cobourg and stopped by the small park with the gazebo, the poplars, the maples, and the yellow dead leaves on the grass.

When my mother opened the apartment door I kissed her on the cheek.

"I expected you yesterday," she said. "You look tired. Why didn't you phone when you got to Montreal?"

"The plane was late," I said. "There were no trains. I had to spend the night in a hotel."

"Which one?"

"You wouldn't have heard of it," I said. "The big ones were full. The room I was in had no heating. I was so cold I couldn't sleep. I put on a heavy sweater, socks, and my coat on the bed, and I was still cold."

"I have something that will warm you up," she said.

And brought out a third-full bottle of brandy from her fridge. She keeps everything she can in the fridge. And what she can't she pushes in the cupboards. There were so many tins, jars, bottles, and plastic bags filled with food—it was like a siege.

She poured herself a bit of brandy.

"To life," she said.

The brandy was cold.

"It will soon warm you up," she said. "*Watch.*"

"I'm not cold now."

"How is everyone?" she asked.

"I'll tell you later. How are you?"

"I've got high blood pressure, I've got to take pills every day. But why do we have to talk about unpleasant things?"

Above her head, on the wall, was a photograph of how I looked when I was twenty.

I brought out presents from my bags—English honey, English marmalade, packs of tea—and gave them to her.

"You shouldn't have bothered," she said. "Come and sit down and have something to eat."

"How is Esther?"

"Fine. She rings me every morning at eight to see if I'm still alive. There was an old lady here. She was dead four days before they found her. Since then Esther rings in the morning, after lunch, and at night. Anyway, I've got good neighbours. Mr. and Mrs. Budnoff—they are on one side—and someone from the Gatineau on the other. I don't know him. In front there's Mrs. Nadolny. We all wear the same suits."

It was only then I realized that she was talking about the cemetery on Metcalfe Road.

She returned from the kitchen with a large banana. "I've bought some bananas for you," she said. "If you have two or three a week, it's good for the heart and protects you from high blood pressure."

That night I couldn't sleep—and my mother's apartment was warm. Perhaps it was jet lag. But I kept looking in the dark, at the electric digits telling the time in the bedside radio . . . watching the minutes, the hours, change . . . and thinking of Grace.

Next morning I was in the lobby of the Château Laurier ten minutes early. She didn't come through the doors until twenty past ten.

"What an early hour." She was out of breath. "My mother drove in."

"I nearly gave you up."

"I left word at home in case you telephoned."

She had on the same clothes as yesterday but wore, on top, a hand-knitted woollen jacket. She looked cold.

"Let's go," I said, "and have some good hot coffee."

We crossed the War Memorial (I saw them putting this up, I told her) and walked down to the Lord Elgin and into Murray's. We sat at a table by a window and had coffee. Outside it looked cold, blustery, deserted.

"When I was seventeen," I said, "I saw the Lord Elgin being built. I worked in a government building across the road. The Department of National Defence. It's not there any more."

"I didn't come to Ottawa until I was five," she said. "I don't like the place. It depresses me. I went around with the cocktail crowd at Rockcliffe. They liked me because I was pretty. I became a revolutionary at university. I met my husband there. He was a Che Guevara character. He wore a black beret and a black leather jacket. I was gun-running in South America. Some of my friends who were caught were tortured."

"What do you do now?"

"I work in a lawyer's office and go to school at night to learn Greek." She smiled. "I'm learning Greek because of my Greek workman. But it's so difficult. I'm seriously thinking of marrying him."

She must have seen an expression in my face for she quickly said, "He's not a workman. He's an architect."

As if that made any difference.

I lit an Old Port cigarillo, drank some coffee, and remained silent.

"Will you come back to live in Canada?"

"I hope to—in the Spring," I said. "I have to go back to England and sort things out."

"You don't talk about your wife."

What could I say. "She's pretty," I said.

"Is she English?"

"Yes."

"You're the first Canadian I have liked," she said. "All the others have been Europeans. You must meet my friends in Toronto. George and Isabel. They've been very good to me. George was my lover for a while."

"While he was still with Isabel?"

"Yes."

"Lucky George," I said.

"Yes," she said. "Lucky George."

"Do you like sex?"

"I like the power it gives me over a man," she said.

We came out of Murray's, arm in arm, and went across to the National Gallery. It was enclosed in scaffolding. All the rooms were closed except for a small Matisse exhibition of drawings by the stairs. The best paintings were the picture postcards on sale downstairs. I got her a Francis Bacon *Pope*. She didn't like it. She preferred Lawren Harris's *A Side Street*, of old houses in winter.

From there we walked up to the mail.

She was shivering.

"I didn't bring enough warm clothes. I don't like the cold. I have bad circulation."

She saw Fisher's. She wanted a Scout cap for Justin and she was told she could get it there.

I remembered Fisher's. When I started university I bought a black winter coat from them. But they were on the other side of the street. I'm sure they were.

After she paid I asked the young man who served her. "Wasn't Fisher's on the other side?"

"That's the old store," he said, "before my time."

We came out.

"Hungry?"

"Yes."

"Where shall we go?"

"You choose."

"Let's go to Albert Street," I said. "There used to be a couple of Chinese restaurants."

We went into the first one. We were the only customers. We had soup to warm us up. Then sweet and sour.

"You're under-nourished," I told her.

"I don't like eating by myself," she said. "I've been living an isolated life these last few years in Toronto."

Halfway through the tea and cookies I leaned over the table and kissed her.

"That's the second time I've been kissed this visit," she said. "My father had some people in last night for a drink. And this friend of my father's said, 'Are you Grace? How you've grown.'" "And kissed me."

"Can you come to Montreal next weekend?"

"I'll see if I can. I have a friend in Montreal. I could come and stay with her. But I've got to think of the money."

By the time we came out of the Chinese restaurant it was twenty past four. The light was fading and it was colder. We walked along the empty street towards a bus stop. The wind lifted loose papers about.

"Do you like Stephane Grappelli," she said, "and Django Reinhardt?"

"Yes. I have their record," I said. I didn't say it was a present from our eldest daughter for our twentieth wedding anniversary. "Le Jazz Hot."

"They've made a lot of records," she said. "Do you like Alan Stivell?"

"The Celtic Harp. Yes, I have the record." Again I didn't say it belonged to our youngest daughter.

We walked about twenty yards along Queen Street.

"I can take a bus from here," she said.

I put my hand in my raincoat pocket and saw that my mother had put in a bus ticket.

"Here," I said.

"You are prepared for anything."

"When will I see you again?"

"Tomorrow, I have to be with the family. And I'm going away early on Monday morning—"

"I'll ring you sometime tomorrow," I said.

She was shivering. I put both arms inside her woollen jacket and drew her closer. We kissed.

"What would people in Ottawa say if they saw you behaving this way in the street?"

"I couldn't care less. Are you still cold?"

"Not now," she said. "I'll see if I can arrange things for Montreal."

Then the bus came. We kissed, awkwardly, goodbye. But I was singing as I walked back to my mother's place.

Next morning, just after breakfast, I phoned her.

"I was going to ring you tonight," she said quietly.

"Can you come to Montreal?"

"I can't talk freely," she said, "the telephone is where my parents can hear every word."

"I'm the same way," I said. "I have taken the phone into the bedroom—but I have to sit on the floor to talk."

"I won't be coming to Montreal," she said.

"In that case I can fly to England from Toronto," I said. "I'll come to Toronto—"

"But I'm working during the day and going to school at night. I don't think you're thinking clearly. You are living a very isolated life while you are over here. I told you that I'm considering getting married again—"

I didn't say anything.

"Ring me before you fly," she said. "And I'll write to you in England. And when you come back I'll see you."

Later, I thought, how silly. But for two days I felt excited and happy. As though I was experiencing something I thought I had lost.

My mother finished another long telephone conversation. "That was Mr. Laroque," she said. "He does memorial stones. He phones me every few months and asks: Anyone sick—anyone dying? Everybody here is trying to make a living. Have something to warm you up. The lecture isn't until tonight and you're already nervous."

She brought a bottle of Bristol Cream from the fridge and gave me a glass full.

The reading went all right. Though at the start I was blinded by the lights and my mouth and lips became dry.

When it was over around twenty people—mostly students—came down from their seats and asked me to sign copies of my books.

As I was getting near the end I noticed a plump middle-aged woman, in a brown cloth coat, with glasses and grey hair, standing about ten feet away, and staring. A grey-haired man was beside her. The woman's lips were pressed tight. She didn't move, just stared. Then she said:

"Don't you remember me?"

I thought—I have never seen this woman before.

She said a name. It didn't bring back anything.

I felt awkward. "I'm sorry," I said.

Behind her was a small thin woman. The first thing I noticed was her eyes—large, dark eyes set in a white face. Then how smartly she dressed. She had on a new camel-haired coat with black leather boots. And there was a nervous vitality about her. Although her shape belonged to that of a young girl, she was clearly in her late twenties or early thirties. She had high cheekbones, a wide mouth, very good teeth. And dark red hair cut close to her head.

As soon as the grey-haired woman and her husband walked away, the small woman with the large eyes came up and said, "I'm Faigel Shore. I enjoyed this evening very much."

She spoke with an accent which I couldn't place.

"It's nice of you to say that," I said.

"I've heard other writers come here and talk," she said. "They say how wonderful their work is. But you sounded different. Honest."

"Aren't you?"

"No," she said. "I tell lies."

"But why?"

"It makes life much more interesting."

The engineer was turning off the lights. Everyone else had gone.

"Why don't we go and have some coffee," Faigel said.

"All right. But I can't stay long. I'm expected at a party a professor is giving for me."

As we were walking through the leafy streets of Sandy Hill, I told Faigel that I knew these streets, that they were part of my childhood.

"But your parents come from Poland?"

"Yes," I said.

"Then we have a lot in common," she said. "I was three when I left Poland after the war. My mother and father fought with the Polish resistance. We all went to Australia then to England before coming to Canada. I went to school in England. We lived there six years—in London—just off the Fulham Road."

"I know where it is," I said.

"You know what I miss—from England?"

"No," I said.

"Kippers. I liked eating them raw—with juice squeezed from a lemon and pepper on top. And with brown bread. It tastes like smoked salmon."

"I thought I was the only one who did that," I said.

She put her arm through mine.

"We have a lot in common," she said.

I expected that we would have coffee in a restaurant on Rideau Street. But she crossed Rideau and began to walk into Lower Town. She stopped in front of a run-down wooden house which was divided into two apartments.

"This is where I live."

It looked shabby on the outside. The grey wooden steps and grey veranda, with wet fallen leaves, needed repairing and painting. Inside was worse. The wallpaper was peeling, the curtains were old and torn. There were books, magazines, paperbacks, all over the place. Things were in cardboard boxes.

"It's a mess, isn't it?" she said. "But I can't throw anything away."

She pushed aside unwashed dishes in the kitchen and put some coffee on a small electric stove. The light was a bare bulb hanging from a wire from the ceiling.

"Come, sit down here," she said.

It was her bed—a mattress, on the floor, with a patch-work cover full of colour, made-up of small snowflake shapes. Beside it were boxes of matches, burnt-out matches, saucers for ashtrays, candles, and loose change scattered on the bare floor. How it brought back those early years in England after the war. And people I once knew with little money.

Faigel took off her camel-haired coat—she had on a smart black suit—then her leather black boots. And went around in her stocking feet.

When she goes out, I thought, she takes such care to look nice and neat but she lives in such disorder.

"Clothes are very important," she said, as if guessing my thoughts. "They tell a lot about a person. When I'm depressed— I go and buy something new to wear."

"Where's your husband?"

"He works all week at a mining camp north of here. I work in a library. We live quite separate lives during the week. He has his women friends. I have my men friends. But he comes home for weekends. We spend our weekends together. I like my husband very much. I can't find any milk or sugar—"

"I have coffee black."

"Good. So do I."

She brought the coffee in two cups without handles and lit a cigarette and one for me. She sat, opposite, on the bed, her legs crossed underneath her.

"You write so beautifully," she said. "But if I may make one criticism—you never tell enough. Especially with sex. You say people go to bed. Then it's done. I want to know details."

That would be telling about my wife, I thought. "I don't know why I don't describe details," I said.

"You belong to the nineteenth century," she said. "What films do you like?"

"Antonioni," I said, "and Ray."

"Have you not seen *Jules et Jim*?"

"No."

"You must. What about books. What do you re-read?"

"Turgenev," I said. "And you?"

"Proust," she said. "I also shoplift, about once a month. I've taken cocaine. I've slept with my husband and with another woman in the same bed. I'm just going to change into something more comfortable."

What is she telling me this for, I wondered. Is this the way the younger generation get to know one another? Instant intimacy.

She came back wearing a silk blue blouse with black buttons in front—the top three she left undone. And I could see a lace see-through bra.

"I'm not on the pill," she said. "I tried it. But I put on weight."

"Then what do you do?"

"I'm very cautious," she said.

Cautious, I thought. Shoplifting, cocaine, three in a bed. We kissed.

"Do you like large breasts?"

"Yes," I said. "But most of the women I have known had small. What are you, 36?"

"No, 34."

I moistened a finger and ran it lightly over her lips—it was part of my wife's pre-lovemaking.

But Faigel said, "Are my lips dry? I don't wear lipstick."

"They are not dry," I said ...

"Stop it," she said. "You are working me up. We have gone too far already."

She sat up on the bed and lit another cigarette. "You haven't told me about your wife."

I now knew what she meant when she said she had "men friends." I had a feeling that when this point was reached, the others told Faigel about their wives. But what was I going to tell her?

"She's attractive," I said. "Intelligent."

"I expected her to be that," Faigel said. "What else?"

"She's not well," I said. "She had a lump in a breast removed— about nine months ago. But why should this interest you?"

"I'm *very* interested," she said. "My mother died from cancer. I go for checkups every six months. Does it affect sex?"

I hesitated. "Yes."

And to change the subject I said, "Do you like Stephane Grappelli and Django Reinhardt?"

"I don't like jazz," Faigel said. She looked at her wristwatch. "I think you had better go. I have to get up early."

She left the bed and walked across the room to a cluttered table. It wasn't only the neatness in her dress, the care she took with her appearance, that stood out. But also the style with which she moved in these shabby rooms.

She came back carrying a small diary-like book. "I can't see you tomorrow," she said looking in the book, "I have an appointment tomorrow. It was made a long time ago ... And my husband flies in on Friday night ... How about next week on Tuesday? I can see you on Tuesday. Let's have an appointment for Tuesday."

"I don't like appointments," I said quietly.

She took no notice. She wrote in the book and said, "We'll come together on Tuesday. I look forward to that."

And I left her.

When I came out, to my surprise, I saw that the clock in the Peace Tower said it was almost half past one in the morning. In any case I had forgotten the address of the professor's house.

For the next three days I enjoyed myself. After living cut off from people, I felt as if I was suddenly thrown into life again. I didn't think anything of going a hundred and twenty-five miles to Montreal for dinner with a film director who was interested in one of my stories and coming back later to Ottawa that night. And I like the fall—the colours, the trees, the fallen leaves, and the thin veneer of comfort that modern machinery and money give.

My publisher arranged for me to give another reading the next week. But on Saturday morning I received a cable from England—sent by our neighbour—to say that my wife was not well, could I come back. The earliest flight I could get on was Sunday.

I didn't phone Grace. But I did try to phone Faigel. I tried several times, even from the airport. But I guess she didn't answer the phone when her husband was home. Or perhaps they had gone away for the weekend.

My wife was in bed when I returned. After three days she was able to get up. But Canada had a mail strike. The mail strike went on for six weeks. And by the time it was over there didn't seem to be any point in writing to either Grace or Faigel. What was there to say.

I remember the merchant navy man who joined the train at Truro. He was going to Glasgow. He had just left his ship at Falmouth. His wife didn't know he was coming back today. He hadn't seen her for three months.

"I have her picture on my cabin wall," he said. "For the first few days of the voyage she's nice and big. But as the weeks go by—she gets smaller and smaller ..."

Perhaps, I thought, even when we are with people it's a kind of pretence. Nothing really matters.

CHAMPAGNE BARN

DIDN'T NOTICE the birds until I saw them flying. Red-winged blackbirds. A flutter of black. Then a flash of red on the black. Lovely to see. I'd follow a bird as it came level with the window, then watch it go quickly back and disappear from sight. Then I'd look ahead to pick up the next flutter of black, then the flash of red on the black, and follow that for as long as I could.

I was on a train from Montreal to Ottawa. It was early June.

On the second day in Ottawa the local CBC people came to interview me in the small park opposite to where my mother lives. I was sitting on a park bench talking to the camera.

"That new building. Across the road. It's for senior citizens. But when I was a kid it was the terminus of an Ottawa streetcar line called Champagne Barn—"

When a thin old woman came up. She walked right into the film and said to me. "Aren't you Mrs. Snipper's boy?"

"Yes," I said.

"You look like your mother. I'm a near neighbour of hers in the senior citizen building."

Then she noticed the camera on the tripod, the camera-man behind it, the sound recordist.

"Who are these people?"

"From television."

"Have they come to take a picture of our building?"

"No."

"What are they doing?"

"Interviewing me."

"*You.* What for?"

"I'm a writer."

She didn't say anything after that. Just had a good look and walked away.

When the interview was over I went across the road, through the glass doors of the senior citizen building, to the elevator. Mr. Tessier was also waiting. As we were going up he said, "I've seen a lot of people die here since I first come five years ago."

"How many?"

"Sixty-eight," he said.

I got off at the second floor, where my mother had her apartment, and Mr. Tessier went up to his on the third.

"How did it go?" my mother said soon as I came in.

"All right. Except a thin, tall lady came up in the middle of the interview and began talking to me. She said she was a neighbour of yours."

"That's Mrs. Sobcuff. She has to know what's going on. Come, sit down and eat."

I went to wash my hands in the bathroom.

"I can't eat all that fish."

"It's delicious," my mother said.

"But I can't eat two pieces."

"Try."

I began to eat a piece of fish with a sliced tomato and sliced cucumber.

"Eat with bread," she said.

"I'm trying to watch my weight."

"You're not fat."

I finished one piece. And began the other.

"Why don't you eat?"

"I had something earlier," she said. "I eat a little bit but every two hours."

And to prove her point she came back with a piece of hot chicken on a plate.

She ate quickly.

"Slow down," I said.

The phone rang.

She had it beside her on the table.

"We're in the middle of eating," I said. "Let it ring."

"No," she said. "Hullo. Yes. Hullo, how are you?"

She walked with the phone into the next room, her bedroom. And I could hear her say: "Did you go to Rideau Bakery? Did you get bread? What did you get? Rye. Was it sliced?"

She talked like that for twenty minutes while everything got cold.

When she came back she said, "Without the telephone I don't know how I would go through the day. It takes up three or four hours. That was Esther. She would like to take you out for a meal. She'll pick you up at six."

"How is Esther?"

"Her health isn't very good. But she phones me every day."

It had been hot and sticky. A few minutes before six I went down to the entrance of the senior citizen building to wait for Esther. And a sudden summer storm. The wind increased. The poplars began to sway and rustle. The sky got darker. And the rain came slanting across the park.

When Esther drove up I ran to get in beside her.

"We need this rain," she said. "I know a good place in Eastview. The food is excellent. It's French."

Esther's my spinster cousin. In her late forties. Around five foot eight and a hundred and fifty pounds. Large, dark eyes, black hair, heavy bones. Her nicest feature is her eyes. She was made a fuss of as a child, as she was the youngest. Then, when she was twelve, her brother Hank was born. And the fuss was all about Hank. Esther worked in the office of my uncle's wholesale fruit and vegetable business in the market. She did the accounts, saw that the drivers had the right load to deliver, checked the money when they cashed in at night.

I liked going to the market and to Uncle's store. It was always a bit dark when I walked in. But there was the immediate smell of rotten fruit and crates lying all over the wooden floor. Hank would throw me apples and oranges until my pockets were full. Esther would give me a hand of large bananas to take back. And, when no one was looking, Uncle would slip me a dollar and say: "Go and see a movie."

Uncle died while I was away in England in the war. And two years ago Hank died from cancer. Then Esther sold the business.

"How are things?" I asked her.

"I wish I could have a rain check," she said. "I sure would live it differently. I had to go to a doctor for an examination. He said it was the first time he had seen an intact hymen in someone of my age."

This was the first time Esther had talked to me like this. I guess I was too young before.

"Things have changed," she said, "since the business was sold. I don't get up early any more. I go to the library. I take out books. But I can't remember what I read. In the evenings I stay up. I've got some Bristol Cream. I drink that and watch television. I get so involved with what's on. I talk back to it. Throw things at it—"

The rain stopped as we drove into Eastview. The sky got lighter. The grass, the trees, the painted wooden houses looked full of colour. She parked the car by a small wooden hotel.

The restaurant was on the ground floor. There were round tables with white tablecloths. The two waiters wore some kind of theatrical soldier's uniform. We both ordered steak and mashed potatoes and vegetables.

It arrived covered in gravy.

She tasted hers.

"It's cold," she said. "*Waiter*."

I tried mine. It wasn't cold.

A waiter finally came to the table. "The meat is cold," Esther said. "The potatoes are cold. I would like it changed."

He took our plates away without saying a word.

"Why shouldn't I tell them to take it back?" she said angrily. "We used to sit like dummies before. Not any more. If you keep quiet and don't make a fuss—you go under."

After what seemed a while the waiter returned with both plates.

She tasted her steak.

"It's better now," she said quietly.

I tasted mine. It was just the same.

"Yes," I said. "Much better."

Esther drove me back to the senior citizen building. When I came in Mother was reading the *Journal*.

"How did it go?"

"Fine," I said.

"Did you have a good time?"

"Yes."

"What did you have?"

"Steak, potatoes, and vegetables."

"Esther will be home now," she said. "Why don't you give her a ring and tell her you had a good time."

"But I just saw her."

"It won't hurt to ring her up and talk to her."

"But I only left her fifteen minutes ago. And I was with her a couple of hours before that."

My mother picked up the receiver and dialled.

"Hullo, Esther. Yes, he said he enjoyed himself very much. Thank you. It's very good of you. All right. We'll talk again tomorrow."

She hung up.

"The important thing," she said, "is for people to think well of you. So they will have good memories of you."

"They don't remember for very long," I said.

And to change the subject I asked her, "Where are my things? Where's the officer's uniform?"

"I gave them away when I moved into here," she said. "What's the use of carrying all those things along."

"I wish you hadn't given away the uniform."

"But you weren't here," she said.

The phone went.

"Hullo, Sonia. Yes, he looks fine—"

This time she was on the phone for over half an hour. When she came back she said, "That was Sonia. I'll be going with her to Toronto for a wedding. Then we'll come back through Montreal. I'll be away about five days. Why don't you move in here instead of staying at the hotel? Why spend all that money just to sleep? You have everything you want. And it's quiet. Here are the keys."

That's how I came to be living in a senior citizen place in Ottawa. I was thirty-eight. Everyone else was over sixty-five. Most were in their seventies and eighties.

Next morning I rang up Harvey Reinhardt.

"Have you had breakfast?"

"No," I said.

"Let's have breakfast. I'll pick you up in half an hour. OK?"

"That'll be eleven thirty."

"Yeh. I'll pick you up and we'll go to Nate's and have breakfast. OK?"

"OK," I said.

Harvey Reinhardt is the only one left in Ottawa from the old Lower Town gang. Just before eleven thirty I went down to wait outside the front glass doors. Mr. Tessier was also standing there, his shirt sleeves rolled up.

"It's going to be a hot day," Mr. Tessier said. "It's almost eighty now."

We looked at the small park opposite, at the still trees, the grass. It was very quiet.

"I played in this park when I was a kid," I said.

"When I was a kid," Mr. Tessier said, "it was a cemetery. When they widened the road they dug up skeletons."

Harvey Reinhardt drove up in a large olive-green car sending a wake of dust behind him.

"When did you get in?"

"A few days ago."

"You look the same," he said.

So did he. His straight black hair had thinned. But the stockiness, the grin, were the same.

"How long is it since you were here?"

"Five years," I said.

"Before we go to Nate's," he said, "I want to stop for a minute in Murray Street."

He drove by Anglesea Square—where Harvey and I used to play touch rugby—by the Bishop's Palace, Brebeuf School, and into Murray Street. One side of the street had all the houses knocked down. The other side still had the houses I knew when we both lived here. But the doors and windows were boarded up. Sparrows flew in and out from the roofs. Harvey's old house had become a store with a plate-glass window and *REINHARDT FOODS* painted on it.

"Are you still in the butcher business?"

"No," he said. "I let my brother Albie have it. I set it up for him. He pays me two hundred dollars a week. I realized early on that there was more money to be made out of the by-products than in meat. For a while I made smoked meat, salami, hot dogs—then I got bored with it. I'm in hides. I'll take you out there later."

And he grinned.

"I'm the biggest hide man in eastern Canada."

I followed Harvey into Reinhardt Foods. The room was arranged as a supermarket selling only meat and poultry. The brother was not around so Harvey took me into the back. There was a room with carcasses hanging on hooks. Another room had meat in large vats soaking in brine. Sawdust on the floor. But the only activity was coming from another room. Beside thick wooden tables five men were energetically hacking away at hunks of meat. Separating the meat from the bone. They didn't look at us all the time we were there. They just went on attacking the meat.

Back in the supermarket Harvey's brother appeared.

"When did you get back?"

"A few days ago."

"Staying at the Château?"

"No, in a senior citizen place."

He looked puzzled.

"It's where my mother lives. But she's gone for a few days to Toronto."

He gave Harvey a cheque. As we were going out he said, very proudly, to me, "We supply the prime minister with food. We've got two smoked turkeys in the back. You know the address on Sussex Drive? Go and take a look."

"I believe you," I said.

From there we went into Nate's on Rideau Street. It was much cooler inside than in the street. Harvey ordered large plates full of smoked meat, chips, pickles, and rye bread.

"Not bad, uh?" Harvey said, eating a forkful of smoked meat.

"Delicious," I said.

"They get it from us," he said. "I never thought you would be a writer. Christ, I thought Gunner would be a writer—not you."

"How is Gunner?"

"He's a professor at some university. He comes back every winter and we go skiing. We still go to Camp Fortune, Fairy Lake, Ironsides—"

And I remembered the last time I went with them. But that was more than twenty years ago.

"I want my son Henry to go to university," Harvey said. "I told him he could learn about literature, art, science, philosophy, economics. But he wants to be a butcher. He likes it all. The blood, the killing, the whole lot. It must be in the blood."

He brought out two thick cigars, gave me one. And we had second cups of coffee, smoking the cigars in the air-conditioned room. A large blown-up photograph of Trudeau was on the wall opposite.

"I'm still a socialist," Harvey said. "But you can't be a socialist in a capitalist economy."

He carefully took out a large wad of bills from his back pocket, paid for our breakfast, then put the money in the back pocket and buttoned it down.

I felt the sticky summer heat as soon as we went out.

"How long are you here for this time?" Harvey asked.

"Just a couple more days."

"Next time you're here," he said, "I'll take you out to see my plant. It's in the country. I built it all myself—the machinery—the conveyor belts—the whole process."

We got back into his car.

"The government health inspector is after me," he said mischievously. And grinned. "I'm a polluter."

I like Harvey. I like his style.

He drove slowly through the streets of Lower Town. "Before," he said, "the small park, the playground, the streets and houses—all fitted together. Now, they knocked down a lot of the wooden houses—left gaps—and put up these high-rises. Suddenly the park is too small. The playground is dwarfed. Nothing seems to fit."

From Lower Town he drove over the Minto bridges to Rockcliffe and stopped at the lookout. We got out. It was warm and silent. The trees. The grass slopes. A heat haze over the river. Everything here looked so right and in its place.

"I've got a problem," Harvey said. "My daughter Clare won't eat. She's a sweet affectionate girl. But if you ask her to eat something—she refuses. If you insist, she gets angry, loses her temper. I don't know how she keeps going. To get her to eat a cracker or a small piece of cheese we have to go through a whole performance—talking and coaxing. And when she finally does have a spoonful of something, I have to behave as if I've just won first prize in a sweepstake . . . We've been butchers for three generations. I love food. And what she's doing is like a personal insult. She told me that she thinks life is pointless. I can understand someone in their thirties or forties or 241 fifties saying that. But a sixteen-year-old girl."

"When my sister Mona was growing up," I said, "she didn't feel like eating either. She kept to her room. She would go and close the door and stay there. Then we tried to get her to come outside. We had this dog kennel in our backyard. And she used to go in that. My mother would leave out some food for her. In front of the kennel. But she didn't touch it. This went on for weeks. Until my mother put a toy blackbird in the grass by the food. Mona began to show some interest in this bird. And from that day she got better. It took a little while, but she began to eat . . . I miss red-winged blackbirds. I don't see them in England."

"Don't they have blackbirds there?" Harvey asked.

"They have lots," I said, "but I haven't seen any with red on their wings."

We drove for a while in silence. Then Harvey said, "We ought to spend a few days together. I'll tell you the story of my life. And you can write it. It will be a best seller. We can go fifty-fifty on it. I'll show this society up for what it really is. I can tell you things. Christ, did you know we were the poorest family in the street? We burned the furniture one winter to keep warm. When the electricity was cut my grandfather got some tallow and made candles, big candles, and we did our homework by this light. Did you know about that?"

"No," I said.

"And when I started going to high school they gave three things free at the cafeteria: Heinz ketchup, hot water, soda crackers. This combined together made a delicious soup. This was my daily lunch. I'll tell you things that go on in business that you won't believe. Everyone bullshits. *This is the best. That is the best.* It's all bullshit. If you want to get on you either have to screw somebody or charm somebody . . . When the kids were small I advertised for a nanny in England. She gave me the baloney about being an Oxford grad. She came over. She had beautiful manners. She had character. But no money. What's the good of having good manners, talking nicely, if you've got nothing to eat? Christ," Harvey said, "why live now in England? That country is on the skids. The last good time they had there was during the war."

"I'm thinking of coming back here," I said.

We were now back outside the senior citizen building. The heat haze had gone with the afternoon and it felt cooler. Small, pink clouds were in a clear blue sky.

"My mother believed," Harvey said, "that there had to be rich people so the poor could live off them. Let me know when you're next in town. Give me a ring. I'll come and get you, show you the plant, and tell you about my life."

"OK," I said.

I left Harvey and went into Champagne Barn. It was like going into a quiet residential hotel. I decided to walk up the two flights of stairs to my mother's flat. The carpets in the hall. The copies of the *Citizen*, the *Journal, Le Droit* outside the numbered doors. Between the buildings there was a connecting passage with the walls all glass where some men sat in their shirt-sleeves and played cards. Above their heads, on the wall, were large posters of Betty Grable in a tight sweater and red lips, and another poster, of Ann Sheridan.

A woman went by and said, "Is that all you've got to do, play games?"

Next morning I was sitting by the window, looking at the park and thinking ("This is what I miss in England—trees. Living, as we do, by the sea and all that stone. It's as if something is missing in the diet. The lack of trees. When I'm with trees I feel better.") when a police car with its flashing light drove up, followed by an ambulance. Men went into the building and came out carrying a woman on a stretcher, an oxygen mask over her face. She looked very grey. She still had her hair in curlers.

Then they drove away.

I went downstairs. I went over to Mr. Tessier.

"I was just talking to her," he said. "About an hour ago. We were watching them pull down that house. And I said—it sure don't take them long to pull down a house."

"Have they taken her to hospital?"

"She's dead," he said.

I went to my mother's flat and made myself a cup of coffee. There were the reminders of the past on the walls and on top of the dresser. I looked through a drawer, and found my logbook from the Air Force. And a pile of unused cards. There were Get Well cards, Deepest Sympathy cards, Happy Birthday cards, Happy Anniversary cards, Speedy Recovery. Several said Congratulations on your Success.

Next morning my mother appeared just after six.

"Look what I brought you," she said. And excitedly took out pieces of wedding cake and assorted pastry from the reception, as well as salami, smoked meat, smoked salmon, hot dogs, bagel.

"I know you like these things," she said. "And what you get in Montreal tastes better than here. *Now* what would you like me to make you for breakfast. Some salami with a couple of eggs?"

"Just coffee," I said.

"What's wrong. Don't you like this food any more?"

"I do," I said. "But I don't want it now."

After the coffee I thought I would go out. It was my last day here. And Mother had started to make cookies for me to take back to England. She's happiest when she's cooking. Sometimes I think the only way she can reach you is through food.

I put on my light summer trousers, a sport shirt, and my favourite light shoes so well worn that the leather was split on top in several places.

"You can't go out like that," my mother said. "You've been on television. You've had your picture in the paper. Suppose someone sees you?"

Outside it was like walking in a hothouse. It had just gone seven. I walked by Anglesea Square. The row of poplars was still. But now and then their leaves caught a passing breeze. York and Clarence had all the houses bulldozed to the ground. And all that remained standing were the trees. And a signpost saying *Clarence Street*. Another said *York*.

On St. Patrick, Percy the Barber was closed. The door boarded up. But from a window I could see the layers of the years on the walls. Haircuts ten cents ... minnows for sale .. . Ken Maynard at the Français ... pictures of King Clancy ... Albert "Battleship" Leduc ... Howie Morenz ...

By the river it was quiet. The water hardly moving. The sun was coming through a haze. Trees. White bridges. A silver church steeple on the opposite shore. It was like an Impressionist painting.

Then in Murray Street. The wooden houses, with the wooden verandas, only on one side. As I came near Reinhardt Foods I began to hear the hacking. Then I saw the men. Their window was open. They were the same five men I saw before. By the thick wooden tables ... with the knives ... the choppers

... attacking the meat from the bone. Hack, hack, hack. While the birds sang. The black squirrels moved quickly and stopped on the grass. And now and again a breeze set the small leaves of the poplars moving. Hack, hack, hack ... Hack, hack, hack ...

I would carry that sound with me long after I left.

BECAUSE OF THE WAR

LEFT CANADA in 1949 and went to England because of the eighteen months I lived there during the war. I met my wife because of the war. She was evacuated to Cornwall from London. She also had a weakness for displaced Europeans who had left their country. And I am European—one generation removed. For almost twenty-seven years we were happily married, raised a family, then she became ill and died.

Soon after that the writing stopped. I'd go out in the morning to get the *Times,* do shopping, cook something to eat. Then go for long walks. Or I would sit in the front room, look out of the window, and listen to the wind, the clock, the gulls. The evenings were the most difficult.

After seven months I realized I couldn't go on like this. So I came back to Canada, to Toronto. A city I had never lived in before. I came mid-February (two months before a new book was to be published . . . it was the last thing I read to her in manuscript). I like Canadian winters. But after two weeks in Toronto I didn't want to go out.

I would only leave this room to walk to the corner store and buy two packs of cigarillos. And mail my letters. Then I would go to Ziggy's supermarket. The neat piles of fruit and vegetables. Such lovely colours. And in sizes I wasn't used to. The cheeses from all over. The different bread, bagel, salami, hot dogs—what abundance. Equipped with this I stayed inside, cooked, listened to the radio, made cups of coffee, smoked the cigarillos, and wrote letters to England, Holland, and Switzerland. I like a foreign city. But there was something here that made me uneasy every time I went out.

My publisher had got me this apartment. A large bare room on the seventh floor in the centre of Toronto. It looked shabby from the outside. But one wall was all glass. I watched passenger jets, high-rise office buildings, clusters of bare trees, and some magnificent sunsets. It was even more impressive at night. The lights inside the glass buildings were left on. They made the city look wealthy, full of glitter, like tall passenger liners anchored close together in the dark.

On my first day I went to a bank on Bloor Street to open an account. A small grey-haired woman with glasses came to the counter. "What is your job?"

I told her.

She lowered her head and mumbled.

"Unemployed?"

"No."

As she wrote my name, address, and other particulars, I could see she didn't believe I was in work. I wondered why. I had on a new winter coat. I was wearing a tie, a clean shirt, a dark suit. I had good shoes.

I walked to the Eaton Centre. From the outside it reminded me of Kew Gardens—one greenhouse above another. And seeing people moving sideways on the escalators—like something from *"Things to Come."*

I had come to get a telephone. And when I came out with the telephone I was on a frozen side street. I didn't know where north was. So I asked a woman in a fur coat.

"Don't talk to me," she shouted angrily, waving her hand. "Go away, go away—just walk along—"

I did walk along. The panhandlers kept asking, "Can you spare a quarter?" "Any change, sir?" Then told me to have a good day or else to take care. The cold wind blew loose newspapers down Yonge Street. It looked shabby and raw.

But inside it was different.

I'd come in from the cold to this well-heated building. Though the room was warm the air was dry. The toothbrush I left wet at night was like chalk next morning. And when I left out a piece of sliced bread ... In the morning I woke to a high-pitched sound. It was the dry bread drying even more.

In those first weeks I went for walks. And discovered a large Chinese section, a Portuguese, Italian, Polish, Jewish, Greek . . . with their restaurants, bakeries, butchers, bookstores, and banks.

On a cold morning I walked into a district of large houses, wide lawns, a small park. Icicles were hanging from the roofs. And on the lawns the snow had a frozen crust. It was garbage day. The garbage cans, and the tied black-green plastic bags, were on the snow at the edge of the lawns. In the road steam was rising from the manholes.

Because of the ice I was walking slowly through the park when I saw a red bird fly to a young tree. This small red bird in this frozen landscape looked exotic. I was watching this bird when three large dogs appeared. They attacked the garbage cans, ripped the plastic bags, and foraged. They did this, from lawn to frozen lawn, without making a sound. Then went away leaving garbage scattered and exposed.

Some days I gave myself destinations.

One afternoon I decided to walk to the Art Gallery of Ontario. At a busy intersection I had to wait for the lights to change. I looked up and saw a black squirrel on a telephone wire slowly crossing above the crowded street. No one else seemed to take any notice.

Because I saw the squirrel get across and because the sun was shining, I said to the man waiting beside me, "Isn't this a lovely day?"

"You too," he replied.

Late on a Saturday, I went and bought a paperback of *Heart of Darkness*, then walked back through fresh snow to the apartment. As the elevator started it began to vibrate. At the top it stopped. The door remained shut. I pressed the number seven button again. It went to the bottom. And stopped. The elevator door still wouldn't open. I tried all the buttons, the switches. Nothing happened except the lights went out. It was then that I realized I was trapped.

I began to call out.

I don't know how long I was there. The air had become stale. I thought: how awkward it will be if I die here. Finally someone did hear me. "OK fellah," I could hear him on the other side. "Don't worry. I'll get the fire department. They will have you out in a matter of minutes." And they did. They forced the door open. I was at the bottom of the shaft. And climbed out into the light and the cold air.

That's how I met Nick, the superintendent of the apartment. He was standing with the firemen. He looked distressed. "Not my fault. I start work yesterday. I no work weekend. Not my fault."

"Of course it's not your fault," I said.

After that Nick and I talked whenever we saw each other. His wife had left him. He had custody of their son. When he left for school in the morning, I watched them wave and smile until the boy finally turned the corner. Nick told me he was Yugoslavian. That he grew up with the Germans in his country. "I see people die. I see people hang. These things I cannot forget."

"I work for the two sisters. They need to fix here plenty. But they no like to spend money."

The two sisters came from France after the war and spoke English with a French accent. They owned the apartment and ran it from an office on the second floor. Every morning—Monday to Friday at ten—I'd go down to see if I had any mail. And be greeted by smiles and good mornings from one of the sisters. "Please sit down. A cup of coffee?"

Edith, the older one, despite her straight grey hair, looked the younger. She was tall, slim, with dark eyes deeply set. She had a long, intelligent face. But there was something awkward about her presence. Both sisters were generous, sociable. And both were elegantly dressed.

"These shoes," Edith said, stepping out of one and going easily back into it. "I went to Paris to get them."

"I too go to Paris for my clothes," said Miriam. She was stocky: blue eyes, black hair, a round face. She smiled a lot and liked to talk. But often when she started to tell a story she would forget the ending and stop in mid-sentence with a startled look.

Edith was separated with two children. Miriam was divorced with two children. They thought I was too much on my own.

"You won't meet people staying in," Miriam said, "or going for walks by yourself. Go to dances. Go to political meetings. Join something-" She forgot what she was going to say. Then in a flat voice said. "In this business you can tell a lot about a person from their luggage."

At the end of March I met Mrs. Kronick. She lived on the floor below. A small Jewish woman, seventy-eight, a widow. She came with her husband from Poland after the First World War. He died ten years ago. She had a son, a doctor, in Vancouver. But he rarely came to see her. Mrs. Kronick was still a striking woman, very independent. And she looked after herself. Every time I saw her she wore a different hat. But she couldn't tolerate the cold. I was in the lobby, waiting for the elevator, when she walked in from the outside. Her face was pale, her eyes watering.

"It's a Garden of Eden," she said, trying to catch her breath. "A Garden of Eden."

"What have you been doing, Mrs. Kronick?"

She was silent. Then quietly said, "Sewing shrouds."

"It's an honour," she added quickly. "Not everyone gets asked."

Next morning Edith knocked on the door of my apartment.

"Did you see what they did in the elevator?"

"No."

"Come, I'll show you."

On the inside of the elevator I saw, scratched on the metal, a badly drawn swastika. And on the inside of the elevator door: *Kill Jews.*

"They don't like us," she said.

Edith's student-daughter told me, "My mother wears dresses from Dior. She has a woman to help her in the house. But she can't throw away a small piece of cheese. She will wrap it up and save it. She also saves brown paper bags that she gets from shopping—to use again. It's because of what happened to her in the war."

Both sisters were delighted with Nick.

"He is so much better than the last one," Miriam said. "He never stops working."

"The last one was too old," said Edith. "He came from the Ukraine. After forty years here—he was still in the Ukraine."

"You must come and meet our friend Henry," Miriam said. "He is very intelligent. Come for brunch next Sunday." And wrote an address and drew a simple map. "Do you think you will be able to find your way?"

"In the war," I said, "I found my way to Leipzig."

On Sunday I took the subway north and travelled as far as it could go. Then began to walk. I had not seen a Canadian spring in thirty years and I had forgotten how colourful the trees were. The flowering crab-apple's pink and crimson; the horse chestnut with its miniature white Christmas trees. And all kinds of maples.

I was walking through a suburb, several cars were beside each house, but no sidewalks.

I walked on the road.

A car drove up, on the opposite side, and stopped. A man got out. He stared at me. Perhaps because I was walking. As I came opposite I called out, "Why didn't they build sidewalks?"

"I'll only be a minute," he said nervously. And ran inside the nearest house.

"This is Hannah," Miriam said.

And I was introduced to a handsome woman in her late fifties: thinning red hair, brown eyes, high cheekbones, a pleasant face, but there was a certain arrogance.

The man opposite was Henry, a professor of Russian at the university. He was wearing jeans and a blue sports shirt. I felt overdressed in a grey suit. Miriam had on an expensive-looking sack dress in pastel colours. Edith had gone to New York for the weekend. In the other room the table was set.

We were sitting in the adjoining room. A blue Chagall of flowers was on the wall. And faded photographs of young women with attractive faces in old-fashioned clothes.

Henry was around my age. He spoke English with an accent. I told him that he looked very fit.

"I go jogging every morning. I play tennis. I swim. You realize you are the only Canadian here. Hannah comes from Poland. She came just after the war. I came a few years later. What Russian writers do you like?"

"Chekhov and Turgenev."

He smiled. "And what modern ones."

"Babel, Mandelstam, Akhmatova."

"Yes," he said and kept smiling.

I felt my credentials were being examined.

"I have not long come back from Moscow," he said. "The status of a writer in Russia today is determined if he is allowed to visit the West. It is the highest accolade. It is higher than getting your book published."

And I remembered a Russian writer who came to see me in England. He was hitchhiking. And it was pouring with rain.

"What are you doing?" I asked him.

"Right now, I'm doing an article on suicide in Dostoevsky. Then I will lecture on it."

We went to the other room and sat around the table. In front of each plate there were wine glasses and tall thin glasses with a yellow rose in them.

Miriam came in with a platter of bagel and croissants.

"Don't let them get cold," she called out, "they are delicious."

I sat next to Hannah. She told me she was leaving tomorrow for Israel. "I know a lot of people but I don't like staying with friends or relatives. I will stay in a hotel. My mother told me: guests and fish stink after three days."

Miriam poured wine into the glasses.

"Why," Hannah asked, "is it so difficult at our age to find another person?"

"Once you have been married," Henry said, "when you meet someone who has also been married, you are both carrying trailers with you. It is this that makes it difficult."

"But people do marry again," Miriam said.

Then Hannah told us how someone she knew got out from Eastern Europe. "He was running across the border when he heard a whistle. He didn't turn around. He kept running. Then he heard the whistle again. He kept running. He expected shots. When he got to the other side he heard the whistle again. And saw it was a bird."

Hannah took a croissant.

"I don't know why," she said, "but people from Europe that I meet in Canada seem to be smaller. I don't mean in size."

"Because in Europe," Henry said, "things are small and intimate, therefore the importance of a person is exaggerated. And over there people talk better."

Miriam brought in ice cream with a hot chocolate sauce. Then waited until she had everyone's attention. "Today," she said with a smile, "I would like us to talk about happiness."

"You cannot generalize about happiness," Henry said. "What is true for one person is not true for another."

"With the truth you can go around the world," Hannah said. "My mother told me that."

"What is happiness for you?" Miriam asked.

"Moments," I said. "You're lucky when they come."

"For me," said Miriam, "it is getting to know another person."

"But Miriam, don't you agree," I said, "that it is impossible, really, to know anyone else at all. At the most it is just speculation."

"It's living with another person," Hannah said. "That's what people can't do without. Once you've had that you want it again."

"On a visit to a mental hospital," I said, "I met a patient. She was in there a long time. She was in there because she was always happy. If someone she liked died, she laughed."

Miriam suddenly stood up. "Such a nice day," she smiled. "Why don't we go for a walk."

So we did, the four of us. We walked on the road in the sunshine. Then Hannah said she had to leave as she had to pack. And Henry became restless. He said to me: "Can I drive you to where you live?"

When he had gone to get the car Miriam said, "Henry must be lonely. He is always the last one to leave a party."

The book came out and the publisher arranged a promotion tour. Everywhere I was taken to be interviewed there was a young rabbi ahead of me. He was being interviewed because he claimed to be "an authority on Death." There was also a singer making the same tour. In Vancouver she said, "I love Vancouver. In Calgary, I love Calgary, I love Ottawa, I love Montreal . . . it's beautiful, beautiful." A man from the States said: "I fell in love with Canada. I changed my nationality. I'm going to die here." People were going around saying "I . . . I . . . I . . ." At the end of the week I felt I had given enough radio and TV interviews to satisfy a minor head of state. But when an article appeared in the *Globe* I had a phone call.

"Do you remember Archie Carter from McGill?"

"Of course," I said, recognizing his voice and seeing a tall man with dark straight hair, thin lips, a sharp nose, a sharp jaw. He used to be an athlete, then something happened, for he had a limp. In our last year at McGill, Archie Carter started a small recording business. He got me to interview visitors as if they were visiting celebrities. Then they would buy the record to take home. In return Archie let me make recordings of the poems of Thomas Hardy.

"Can you come and see me. Or are you busy?"

"Of course I'll come."

"Today?"

"Yes."

He gave me his address.

It brought me to an expensive high-rise opposite a grove of young birches. A doorman, his war medals on a pale blue uniform, saluted me.

I pressed the button outside Archie's door. He called out: "Prepare yourself for a shock."

"I'm not the same either," I shouted back. When he opened the door I didn't recognize him. He was bald. He had put on weight. All those sharp features were gone. Only his voice was the same. And I wondered what he was seeing in my face.

We shook hands. He led me into a room with a glass wall overlooking the birches. He limped more than I remembered.

"What would you like to drink? I only have Italian wine. But it's a good one."

He came back from the kitchen with two glasses of red wine. We drank in silence.

"I have three daughters," I said. "When they were small a friend from London, a painter, would come to see us once a year. When he arrived he would give the three of them five pounds in separate envelopes. The last time he came he only had two envelopes. He had forgotten the youngest. So he quickly asked me for an envelope and a piece of paper. As I went to get them the youngest ran into another room. I could hear her crying. I thought she was crying because he had forgotten her. So I went in to tell her that people often forget . . . But the tears were trickling down her face. And she was sobbing. *He's got old. He's got old.*"

"I'm not a failure," Archie said.

"In the end, Archie, we're all failures."

"Oh, I don't know about that. Do you like the wine?"

"Yes."

"I'm in love with Italy," he said. "The food, the climate. Everything. I go there every two years . . . I got this foot in Italy. I was leading my company. A mortar bomb hit me. They had to remove the ankle."

"What happened after McGill?"

"I taught English for a while. Then I began to paint. I'll show you the paintings later." He paused. "Of course I'm mad." And paused again to see what I would say. I said nothing. "When it's bad it's just boring. It was the pain from the wound that brought it on. The first time was in the hospital ship going back from Italy to England. The next time was fifteen years ago."

"What happened—?"

He hesitated. "It's because I have an economic theory that I believe will cure the world's economic problems." He hesitated again and smiled. He had a pleasant smile. "I believe we wouldn't have inflation or unemployment or high prices—things would be more abundant and we would be a lot happier—if people didn't *gyp* one another."

"Did they put you into a mental hospital for that?"

"I went to Lakefield," he said, "before McGill. Some of my friends are ambassadors—people like that—scattered all over. I called up Cairo, Amsterdam, London—and told them about this theory."

"That still doesn't seem bad enough to be put away."

"But I called them at two in the morning. Some of them became concerned and called the police. It was the police who brought me in . . . I thought at this point I was a genius. The hospital I was in was full of people who thought they were geniuses."

He filled the glasses with more wine.

"A nurse in the hospital tried to make me pee. She got a jug full of water and emptied it into an empty jug. So I could see and hear it. She kept repeating this. I still couldn't go. But the other patients, who had been watching, all wet their beds.

"I have invented a word game that I intend to put on the market. I still think I'm not a failure, you know. But I must not forget. I must call this number." And he took out an envelope. And dialled very determinedly. "There is a studio going. And I must get this woman before she lets it to someone else."

He let the phone ring a long time before he hung up.

"What was I saying?"

"What happened after you came out of the hospital?"

"I began to paint. My shrink quite likes them." He brought several small canvases from his bedroom. They were gentle landscapes of fields and trees by a river. "What do you think?"

"I like the colours."

"I better phone that woman or else that studio will go. And I need a studio."

He dialled. No response.

"Remind me to try again."

"Yes," I said.

"It's good you are in Toronto. We have lots to talk about."

"I'm going to England," I said.

He looked disappointed.

"But I'm coming back."

I got up. "I'll ring when I get back."

"Fine. I better call that woman again."

He took out the envelope. We shook hands. And I left him dialling the number.

On the way back I saw Mrs. Kronick.

"What have you been doing?" I asked.

"I was walking down Yonge Street," she said, "and I thought of the people I knew who are dead. What have I done with my life?"

I didn't know what to answer.

"You have a son," I said.

"Yes," she said gently. "That's what I have done with my life."

The two sisters continued to ask me to small parties that they arranged for people separated or divorced. But I met Helen in the supermarket. I could not find the roasted peanuts in their shells. She was standing nearby. I asked her. And she walked over to show me where they were.

She was tall. Light blue eyes, a small fine nose, a small mouth, colour in her cheeks, short blond hair with a fringe. She smiled easily and had a pleasant voice. Because I detected a trace of an English accent in it I said, "Where in England are you from?"

"Devon—from Exeter."

"How long have you been here?"

"Thirty-four years."

"I've not long come from England."

The next time I saw her was in a small cemetery. I was

coming from my publisher. She was arranging flowers by a stone. "I don't come here often," she said. "It's my husband's birthday."

"Shall we go and have some coffee?"

"My car is here," she said. "Why don't we go home?"

There were oil paintings on the wall, books, and black and white photographs of a handsome-looking man.

"He was a very private person," she said. "It's almost four years. He had come back from a business trip when he had a heart attack."

She made me a cheese and tomato sandwich.

"I met Jimmy during the war. He was with the RCAF. We got married when the war was over and he brought me to Toronto. Then Jimmy's father died. And he had to run the family business. We had a very good marriage for almost thirty years."

Then she told me about her early life in England. How she was brought up by two grandmothers. The one in the city ran a theatre. The other, in the country, was a farmer's wife.

"Why don't you write it down," I said. "It would make a good book."

"I wouldn't know how to go about it."

"Talk into a tape recorder."

"I can talk to you," she said. "Leave me a photograph. That will help."

"No, I'll come up."

That's how it started. Twice a week I would leave the apartment and go there in the late afternoon. She would give me a drink. And talk into the tape. And I would ask her questions and she would answer. Then she would give me dinner. And do another hour of talking into the tape.

One evening there was a thunderstorm.

"Why not stay the night," she said. "There's a bed in the spare room or you can sleep with me."

As I got into bed she said, "I bruise easily."

Later she said, "I wanted you to know that you had a choice."

Did I have a choice, I wondered.

It was very pleasant having breakfast together. Then walking, in the early morning, down Yonge Street.

After two weeks Helen said, "Why don't you move in here? One room could be your study and where you work."

"I'll have to go to England first and settle things. Then I'll come back."

"The sooner the better," she said.

The two sisters decided to buy a small coffee and cake store for their children. But the children were hardly there. Only Edith and Miriam. And they seemed to be enjoying themselves. As I came in Edith said, "You must have a croissant. They are the best in Toronto …" "Did you know Nick will be leaving us?"

"No," I said. "But why—"

"He takes too many days off. He doesn't do his work."

Miriam came in. "You're just the person I want to see. We are having a small party on Saturday night. There will be some interesting people.

Henry will be there—"

"I have come to say goodbye."

"I don't like goodbyes," said Edith.

"Ella Fitzgerald used to sing:" I said,

Every time we say goodbye
I die, a little.
Every time we say goodbye
I wonder why, a little.

"That's Lamartine," Edith said. *"Chaque fois qu'on se dit au revoir, je meurs un peu.* Imagine being in a store like this in Toronto and quoting Lamartine."

"I'm sure that in small stores in Toronto—Czechs are quoting from Czech writers, Italians, Hungarians are doing the same. The Portuguese here are quoting from Portuguese poets—" I noticed grey airplanes in the sky. I could see them from the store window. They were coming in all directions. I counted a Dakota, six Mustangs with their clipped wings, two Bostons, a Lightning, a Tiger Moth, another Dakota.

"They're airplanes from the Second World War," I said.

"It must be from a museum," Miriam said in her flat voice.

I watched the low-flying planes. They looked so slow. Then they began to circle as if they were going to land.

I went outside to watch the airplanes and saw Nick coming across the car park. He was carrying a loaded shopping bag from the supermarket. I wanted to tell him about the airplanes. But he had his face down. As he came closer I could see tears in his eyes. I thought it was because he had lost his job.

"Tito is dead," he said. And walked by.

The airplanes had disappeared. There was not a trace of their presence. Only a seagull flew low between two high-rises.

I was walking by the store that showed the time in the capitals of Europe when I saw Mrs. Kronick on her way back to the apartment. She had on a smart black and white suit and a large black hat.

"I'm leaving, Mrs. Kronick."

She looked at me for a while. Then said, "When I leave a person, I don't care if I never see them again."

"But what about those you love?"

"Of course," she said, "with those you love there's always regret."

SOMETHING
HAPPENED HERE

I FELT AT HOME soon as I got out of the Paris train and waited for a taxi outside the railway station. I could hear the gulls but I couldn't see them because of the mist. But I could smell the sea. The driver brought me to a hotel along the front. It was a residential hotel beside other residential hotels with the menu in a glass case by the sidewalk. It had four storeys. Its front tall windows, with wooden shutters and small iron balconies, faced the sea. On the ground level was the hotel's dining room. The front wall was all glass. And there was a man sitting alone by a table.

It looked a comfortable family hotel. The large wooden staircase belonged to an earlier time when it had been a family house. The woman who now owned and ran it liked porcelain. She had cups and saucers on large sideboards, on every landing, as well as grandfather clocks and old clocks without hands. They struck the hour at different times. There were fresh and not so fresh flowers in porcelain vases. There were large mirrors, in wooden frames, tilted against the wall, like paintings. There were china plates, china cups, and china teapots on top of anything that could hold them.

My room on the third floor didn't face the sea but a court-yard. I watched a short man in a chef's hat cutting vegetables into a pot. The room was spacious enough but it seemed over-furnished. It had a large double bed with a carving of two birds on the headboard, a tall wooden closet, a heavy wooden sideboard, a solid table, several chairs, a colour television, and a small fridge fully stocked with wine, brandy, champagne, mineral water, and fruit juices. On the fridge was a pad and pencil to mark what one drank.

After I partly unpacked and washed I went down to the dining room and was shown to a table by the glass wall next to the man sitting alone. He was smoking a cigarette and drink-ing coffee. He had on a fawn shirt with an open collar and a carefully tied black and white cravat at the neck. He also had fawn-coloured trousers. He looked like Erich von Stroheim.

The proprietress came to take my order. She wobbled, coquettishly, on high heels. Medium height, a little plump, in her late forties or early fifties perhaps. She had a sense of style. She wore a different tailored dress every day I was there. A striking person. She had a white complexion and black hair. And looked in fine health. Her teeth were very good. There was a liveliness in her dark eyes. Every time I walked by the desk and the lounge she never seemed far away: doing accounts, dealing with the staff, talking to guests.

I gave her my order in English. I ordered a salad, an omelette, and a glass of *vin rosé*.

When she had gone the man at the next table said in a loud voice, "Are you English or American?"

"Canadian."

He began to talk in French.

Although I understood some of what he said I replied, "I can't speak French well. I'm English Canadian."

"I speak English," he said. "I had lessons in Paris at the Ber-litz school. My English teacher, she was a pretty woman, said I was very good because I could use the word 'barbed wire' in a sentence. My name is Georges."

I told him mine. But for some reason he called me Roman.

"Roman, what do you do?"

"I am a writer."

"Come, join me," he said. "I like very much the work of Somerset Muffin and Heavelin Woof. Are you staying in this hotel?"

"Yes. I arrived a half-hour ago."

"I live in the country. Since my wife is dead I come here once a week to eat. What do you write?"

"Short stories," I said, "novels."

"I read many books—but not novels. I read books of ideas. The conclusion I have come is that you can divide the people of the world. There are the sedentary. There are the nomads. The sedentary—they are registered. We know about them. The nomads—they leave no record."

A young waiter, in a white double-breasted jacket, poured more coffee.

"Do you know Dieppe?"

"No, this is my first time here."

"I will show you."

And he did. When I finished eating he took me along the promenade. A brisk breeze was blowing but the sea remained hidden by mist. He brought me to narrow side streets, main streets, and squares. He walked with a sense of urgency. A short, stocky man, very compact and dapper, with lively brown eyes and a determined looking head. He had a bit of a belly and his trousers were hitched high up. He carried his valuables in a brown shoulder bag.

In a street for pedestrians only we were caught up in a crowd. It was market day. There were shops on both sides and stalls in the middle.

"Look, Roman, at the *wonderful* colours," Georges said loudly of the gladioli, the asters, lilies, roses, geraniums. Then he admired the peaches, apricots, butter, tomatoes, carrots, the heaped strands of garlic and onions. He led me to a stand that had assorted cheese and large brown eggs, melons, leeks, and plums. And to another that had different sausages and salamis. On one side he showed me live brown and white rabbits in hutches. And laughed when, directly opposite, brown and white rabbit skins were for sale. The street fascinated him. He stopped often and talked loudly to anyone whose face happened to interest him.

We had a Pernod at a table outside a cafe that had a mustard and orange façade. He lit a French cigarette. I, a Canadian cigarillo. The pleasure of the first puffs made us both silent. Nearly all the tables were occupied, shoppers were passing, and music came loudly from a record store.

I asked Georges, "What do you think of Madame who runs the hotel?"

"*Très intelligente,*" he said, and moved his hands slowly to indicate a large bosom. "*Et distinguée.*" He moved his hands to his backside to indicate large buttocks. And smiled.

He had a way of speaking English which was a lot better, and more amusing, than my French.

He brought me inside an old church. He was relaxed until he faced the altar. He stiffened to attention, slid his left leg forward as if he was a fencer, and solemnly made the sign of the cross. He remained in that position for several seconds, looking like the figurehead at the prow of a ship. When he moved away he relaxed again. And pointed to a small statue of the Virgin with her arms open.

"Roman, the Virgin has opened her legs in welcome."

I was feeling tired when we came out of the church. The train journey, the sightseeing, the conversation ... but Georges walked on. He was heading for the docks. I said I would go back to the hotel, as I had some letters to write.

"Of course," he said, "forgive me. You must be exhausted. Tomorrow, would you like to see where I live in the country? I will come for you after breakfast."

And he was there, as I came out of the hotel, at eight thirty, sitting in a light blue Citroën, dressed in the same clothes.

"Did you sleep, Roman?"

"For eight hours."

I could not see the sun because of the mist. But the surf, breaking on the pebbles, glistened. As he drove inland it began to brighten up. He drove fast and well. And he talked continually. Perhaps because he needed someone he could talk English to.

He said he had been an officer in the French navy. That in the last war he had been a naval architect in charge of submarines at their trials.

"I was at Brest, Cherbourg, Toulon, Marseille. My daughter was born when I was stuck in submarine in the mud. My wife told me the nurse came to say, "'The baby she is lovely. But the father—it is dead.'" "And he laughed.

On a low hill, ahead, a large institution-like building with many windows and fire escapes.

"Lunatic asylum," Georges said. "Full of patriots."

The government, he said, had a publicity campaign for the French to drink more of their wine and appealed to their patriotism. After this whenever he mentioned anyone who liked to drink, Georges called him "a patriot." And if anyone looked more than that, "*Very* patriotic."

The asylum was beside us. A cross on top. And all the top windows barred.

"When I was a boy . . . this place made big impression. Before a storm . . . the wind is blowing . . . and the people in lunatic asylum scream. I will never forget."

He drove through empty villages, small towns. He stopped, walked me around, and did some shopping. I noticed that the elaborate war memorials, by the churches, were for the 1914–18 war. The only acknowledgement of the Second World War was the occasional stone, suddenly appearing in the countryside, at the side of the road, that said three or four members of the Resistance had been shot at this spot.

"I have been to America," Georges said. "I like the Americans. But sometimes they are infantile. Nixon—dustbin. Carter—dustbin."

He drove up a turning road by a small, broken, stone bridge that had rocks and uprooted trees on either side. "There is a plateau," he said, "high up. It has many meadows. The water gathers there for many rivers. Once in a hundred years the water very quickly goes down from the plateau to the valley and turns over houses, bridges, trees. Last September a priest on the plateau telephone the Mayor and say the water looks dangerous. But the Mayor, a young man, say it is only an old man talking. Half-hour later the water come down and drown thirty people and took many houses. It was Sunday so many people were away from the houses otherwise more drown. All happen last September. In a half-hour. But it will not happen for another hundred years. And no one will be here who knows it. The young won't listen. They will, after some years, build houses in the same place. And it will happen all over again."

In one of the large towns he stopped and showed me the cemetery where his family is buried. It was a vault, all stone, no grass around. Nor did any of the others have grass anywhere. On the stone was a vertical tablet with two rows of de Rostaings. The first was born in 1799. "He was town architect." A few names down, "He had lace factory . . . He build roads . . . See how the names become larger as we come nearer today."

"Will you be buried here?"

"No. My wife is Parisian. She is buried in Paris. I will lie with her."

He continued on the main road, then turned off and drove on a dirt road. Then went slowly up a rough slope until he stopped, on the level, by the side of a converted farmhouse.

"We are here," he said.

We were on a height. Below were trees and small fields—different shades of green, yellow, and brown. Instead of fences or hedgerows, the fields had their borders in trees. And from this height the trees gave the landscape a 3-D look.

Georges introduced me to Marie-Jo, a fifteen-year-old schoolgirl from the next farm who did the cooking and cleaning during the summer. Short blond hair, blue eyes, an easy smile. She was shy and tall for her age and walked with a slightly rounded back. While Marie-Jo barbecued salmon steaks at the far end of the porch, under an overhanging chimney, Georges walked me around. In front of the house, under a large elm, was a white table and white chairs. It was quiet. A light wind on the small leaves of the two near poplars. "They say it will rain," he said. And beside them a border of roses, geraniums, and lobelia.

We ate outside on a white tablecloth. I could hear people talking from the farm below. Further away someone was burning wood. The white smoke rose and thinned as it drifted slowly up. On top of the house was a small stone cross. A larger metal cross was embedded in the concrete of the front fence.

"I am Catholic," Georges said. "There are Protestants here too. My sister married a Jew. A Pole. From Bialystok."

Marie-Jo brought a round wooden board with cow and goat cheeses on it. And Georges filled my glass with more red wine.

"When I was young boy of seven we had great distilleries in my country. We hear the Russians are coming. We wait in the street. It is beginning to snow. But I do not want to go home. Many people wait for the Russians.

"Then they come. They look giants with fur hats and big boots and long overcoats. *Very* impressive.

"After a while—what happens? First the women. They say to Russian soldiers—you want drink? They give them drink. A little later, in the street, you see the women wearing the Russian furs for—"

Georges indicated with his hands.

"Muffs," I said.

"Yes, muffs, muffs. The women all have muffs.

"Then the French men give drink. Later, the French men you see in the street—they are wearing the Russian boots.

"The peasants—they *drowned* the Russians."

Marie-Jo brought ripe peaches, large peaches, lovely colours, dark and light, red to crimson. They were juicy and delicious.

"How did your sister meet her husband?"

"At the Sorbonne. My sister always joking. He serious. I did not think they would stay together. When she go to Poland to meet his family we are worried. We Catholic. They Jew. They have two children. Then the war. The Nazis. He is taken away. My mother, a tough woman, get priest and doctor to make fake certificate—say the two boys baptized. But my mother did not think that was enough. She tell me to take the boys to a farmer she know in the Auvergne. I take them. When I meet the farmer I begin to tell story. But the farmer just shake my hand. Say nothing. The children stay with him for the war."

"What happened to the Polish Jew?"

"He died."

We went to have coffee in the barn. The main room of the house. High ceiling with large windows and the original beams. To get to it from the inside you would go up some stairs. But you could walk to it from the garden by going up a grass slope. "All farmers have this for the cattle to go up and down," Georges said.

It was also his studio. On the walls were oil paintings by his uncle who was dead. Impressionist paintings of the landscape around here. "They sell for 40,000 francs," Georges said. "I have about thirty good ones. Some in the flat in Paris, some in the flat in Cannes. A few here." He also had his own paintings—on the wall, and one on an easel—like his uncle's but not as good.

Marie-Jo appeared with a jug full of coffee.

"I am working on book," he said. "I have contract with Paris publisher. Eleven years—! am not finished. It will be traveller's dictionary of every place in world that someone has written."

We had coffee. He lit a cigarette and went over to his record player.

"Roman—have you heard the Japanese Noh?"

I answered no with a movement of my face.

"Very strange. Sounds like a cat ... and a chain with bucket ... and a man flogging his wife. I was twenty, a midshipman on cruiser. We visit Japan. Suddenly I was put there, for six hours, listening to this."

He put a record on. "This is the cat ..."—a single note vibrated—"looking for another cat ..." Georges was standing, talking with gestures. "Now, the long chain with a bucket going down well ... it needs oil. This is a man flogging his wife..."

He stopped the record.

"The Japanese, they are different from the French. They believe the dead are with us all the time."

He showed me a photograph of his wife, Colette.

She looked a determined woman, in her late forties. A strong jaw, thin lips, blond hair pulled back on her head, light eyes.

"She had beautiful voice," Georges said. "One of the things I like in people is the voice. If they have bad voice it is difficult for me to stay long with them."

"How long is it since she died?"

"Three years."

He must have thought of something else for he said abruptly, "If you do not come into the world—then you cannot go."

He took me for a walk through the countryside. There were all kinds of wild flowers I didn't know, and butterflies, and some, like the small black and white, I had not seen before either. But it was the trees that dominated. And I like trees. Probably because I have lived so long in Cornwall facing stone streets and stone terraces.

I wondered why Georges was not curious about my past. He appeared not interested in my personal life. Though I did give him bits of information.

"How long will you be in Dieppe?"

"Two, maybe three days more," I said. "I want to go to England, to a flat I have in Cornwall, and do some work."

It was after nine, but still light, when we got back to Dieppe. "I know a small place but good," Georges said. And brought me to a restaurant opposite the docks called L'Espérance.

We were both tired and for a while didn't talk. I ordered marinated mackerel, a salad, and some chicken. And Georges ordered a half-melon, veal, and cheese. Also coffee and a bottle of red wine.

Two tables away a man and a woman, both plump, in their late fifties or early sixties, were eating with relish. The woman had a large whole tongue on her plate to start with, the man a tureen of soup. He tucked his napkin into his open-neck shirt. Then they both had fish, then meat with potatoes, then cheese, then a large dessert with whipped cream on top ... And all the time they were eating they didn't speak.

Beside them, going away towards the centre of the restaurant, were two young men. They were deaf and dumb. They were talking with their hands. They also mimed. When they saw us looking they included us in their conversation. One of the men looked Moroccan, with a black moustache on the top lip and down the side of his face. He was lean. And he mimed very quickly and well. He pointed at Georges' cigarette and at my cigarillo. And shook his head. He touched his chest and pretended he was coughing. And shook his head. He then showed himself swimming, the breast stroke. He was smiling.

He showed us that he was also a long-distance walker, getting up and staying in one place, he moved heel and toe, heel and toe, and that curious rotation of the hips.

"Roman," Georges said loudly. "The woman you see is fat. Her husband is fat. Look how they eat. Beside them two men, slim, young. They have to talk with their hands. They look happy—all the time the food comes—they are talking. But the two beside them—they do not talk at all—they concentrate on next bite. If I had movie camera—that is all you need. No words. No explanation. If I was young man, Roman, I would make films."

As he drove me to the hotel, Georges could not forget the scene in the restaurant. On the hotel's front door there was a sign saying it was full.

"Tomorrow," Georges said, "I no see you."

As tomorrow was Sunday I asked him if he was going to church.

"No, I do not like the clergy. The elm tree need spray. They get disease. I know a young man. He will do it. But I have to get him. And I go to see an old friend. He was officer with me. He now alone in Rouen. We eat lunch on Sunday when I am here. Two old men. I see you the day after."

And we shook hands.

Next morning, I opened the large window of the room. The sun was out. It was warm. A blue sky. After breakfast I decided to go for a walk. I crossed the harbour by an iron bridge. And went up a steep narrow street of dose-packed terraced houses. It looked working class. The houses were small, drab, unpainted. And the sidewalks were narrow and in need of repair. They had red and pink geranium petals that had fallen from the window boxes on the small balconies.

I passed an upright concrete church with a rounded top. It stood by itself, stark, against the skyline. I went through tall undergrowth and, when clear of it, I saw I was on top of cliffs.

They were an impressive sight: white-grey, sheer, and at the bottom pebbles with the sea coming in.

I walked along for about an hour, on top of the cliffs, when I noticed the path becoming wider as it started to slope down. The cliffs here went back from the sea and left a small pebbled beach. People were on it.

I was looking at the dirt path as I walked down because it was uneven and steep, when I saw a shrew, about two inches long, over another shrew lying on its side. The one on its side was flattened as if a roller had gone over it. I watched the head of the live shrew over the belly of the dead one—there didn't seem to be any movement. Then, for no reason, I whistled. The live shrew darted into the grass. And I saw the open half-eaten belly of the one on its side, a brilliant crimson. The colour was brighter than any meat I had seen at the butcher's.

The small beach wasn't crowded. The surf gentle . . . the water sparkled . . . a family was playing boules. Someone was windsurfing across the length of the beach . . . going one way then turning the sail to go the other, and often falling in. A man in a T-shirt brought a dog, a terrier, on a leash. Then he let him go into the shallows. Under an umbrella a young woman was breastfeeding a baby. Nearer to the water a tall woman with white skin and red hair was lying on her back, topless. People were changing using large coloured towels, while there was the continual sound of the low surf as it came in breaking over the pebbles and sliding back.

I had brought a picnic: bread, a hard-boiled egg, cheese, tomatoes, a pear. And a can of cider to wash it down. After I had eaten I took off my shirt, shoes, socks, and lay down on the stones.

A loud noise woke me. It was two boys running over the stones between my head and the cliffs. I sat up. I didn't know how long I had been asleep. The surface of the water sparkled. The click of the boules was still going. From somewhere a dog was barking. The cliffs, a few yards behind me and on both sides, had light green streaks in the massive white-grey. And high up, on the very top, a thin layer of grass.

The tide was coming in. I put on shirt, socks, and shoes, and walked over the pebbles to a paved slope that led from the beach to the road. I could now see a narrow opening between the cliffs. And as I walked up the slope the opening fanned out to show a suburb of houses with gardens, green lawns, and trees. As I came to the top of the paved slope I saw, across the road, on a stone, in French and English.

On this beach
Officers and Men of the
Royal Regiment of Canada
Died at Dawn 19 August 1942
Striving to Reach the Heights Beyond

You who are alive on this beach
remember that these men died far from home
that others here and everywhere might freely
enjoy life in God's mercy.

When I got back to the hotel the "full" sign had been taken down. Madame greeted me with a smile.

"You have caught the sun. I have surprise for you."

She soon reappeared with a thin blond girl of about twelve or thirteen.

"This is Jean. She is from Canada," Madame said proudly. "From Alberta."

"Where from in Alberta?" I asked.

"Edmonton," the girl replied in a quiet voice.

"How long will you be in Dieppe?"

"I live here. I go to school."

"When were you in Edmonton?"

"Three weeks ago."

"Is your father there?"

"No, he is somewhere else. He travels. I'm with my mother."

"Can you speak French as well as you can English?"

"I can speak it better," she said.

And she was glad to go off with Madame's only daughter, who was older and not as pretty, to roller skate on the promenade.

"She is charming," Madame said as we watched both girls run to get out.

"I went for a walk today, Madame," I said, "and came to the beach where in the war the Canadians—"

"*Ah.*" She interrupted and shook her head, then raised an arm, in distress or disbelief. She tried to find words—but couldn't.

"I have read many books about it," she said quickly. "Do you want to see the cemetery?"

"No," I said.

That evening, while in the dining room, I decided to leave tomorrow. For over three weeks I had been travelling in France. All inland, until Dieppe. It had been a fine holiday. I had not been to France before. But now I wanted to get back to the familiar. I was also impatient to get back to work. I had brought with me a large notebook but I had written nothing in it.

I said to Madame at the desk, "I will be leaving tomorrow. Could you have my bill ready?"

"Of course," she said. "You will have it when you come down for breakfast."

"It is a very comfortable hotel. Are you open all year?"

"In December we close."

"Has it been a good season?"

"I think I go bankrupt," she said loudly. "Oil—up three times in two months. It is impossible to go on—" She held up a sheaf of bills.

"I will tell my friends," I said.

"Is kind of you," she said quietly. And gave me several bro-chures that said the hotel would be running a weekly cookery course in January and February of next year.

Late next morning, with my two cases in the lounge, I was hav-ing a coffee and smoking a cigarillo, when Georges appeared. He saw the cases.

"Yes," I said. "I'm going today."

"What time is your boat?"

"It goes in an hour."

"I'll take you."

He insisted on carrying the cases to his car. Madame came hurrying away from people at the desk to shake my hand vig-orously and hoped she would see me again.

While Georges was driving he gave me a card with his address in the country, in Cannes, and in Paris. And the dates he would be there. Then he gave me a large brown envelope. I took out what was in it, a small watercolour of Dieppe that he had painted. It showed the mustard and orange cafe with peo-ple sitting at the outside tables and others walking by. On the back he had written, "For Roman, my new friend. Georges."

"When I get to England," I said, "I will send you one of my books."

"Thank you. I should like to improve my English. Perhaps I find in it something for my traveller's dictionary."

At the ferry I persuaded Georges not to wait.

"Roman, I do not kiss the men."

We shook hands.

I sat in a seat on deck, at the stern, facing Dieppe. The ferry turned slowly and I saw Dieppe turn as well. The vertical church with the rounded top, the cathedral, the square, the houses with the tall windows and wooden shutters and small iron balconies.

Then the ferry straightened out and we were in the open sea. After a while it altered course. And there were the cliffs where I had walked yesterday and the narrow opening. I kept watching the cliffs and the opening. And thought how scared they must have been coming in from the sea and seeing this.

The sun was warm, the sea calm. And when I next looked at the cliffs the opening had disappeared. All that was there was the white-grey stone sticking up. I thought of gravestones close together on a slope . . . You could see nothing else. Just gravestones. And they were gravestones with nothing on them . . . they were all blank.

On the loudspeaker the captain's voice said that coming up on the left was one of the world's largest tankers. People hurried to the rails with their cameras.

I went down to a lower deck and stood in the queue for the duty free.

DJANGO, KARFUNKELSTEIN & ROSES

I N LATE OCTOBER, on the morning of my fiftieth birthday, we had breakfast early—my wife and three daughters. On the plain wooden table: a black comb, a half-bottle of brandy, a red box of matches from Belgium, a felt pen, a couple of Dutch cigars, a card of Pissarro's *Lower Norwood under Snow,* and a record. They wished me happy birthday. And we kissed.

After breakfast the children went to school. We continued to talk, without having to finish sentences, over another cup of coffee. Then my wife went to make the beds, water the plants, do the washing. And I went to the front room, lit the coal fire, smoked a Dutch cigar, drank some of the brandy, put the record on, listened to Django Reinhardt and Stephane Grappelli—*The Hot Club of France.* And looked out for the postman.

The mimosa tree was still in bloom in the small front garden, as were some roses. To the left, a road of terraced houses curved as it sloped down to the church steeple and the small shops. And at the end of the road—above houses, steeple, shops—was the white-blue of the bay.

Directly opposite, past the garden and across the road, was Wesley Street. A short narrow street of stone cottages. I watched the milkman leave bottles on the granite by the front doors. Mr. Veal—a tall man with glasses, a retired carpenter, a Plymouth brethren ("I have my place up there when I die," he told me, pointing to the sky)—came out of his cottage holding a white tablecloth. He shook the tablecloth in the street. From the slate roofs, the red chimney pots, came jackdaws, sparrows, and a few gulls. They were waiting for him. Mr. Veal swirled the tablecloth—as if it was a cape—and over his shoulder it folded neatly on his back. He stood in the centre of the street with the white tablecloth on his back, the birds near his feet. ("I need to get wax out of my ears," he said when we were walking. "I don't hear people—but I hear the birds.") Then he went inside.

The postman appeared and walked past the house. This morning it didn't matter. My wife hung the washing in the courtyard and pulled up the line. Then left the house to buy the food for the day. The sun came through the coloured glass of the inside front door and onto the floor in shafts of soft yellow, blue, and red. I went upstairs to the large attic room. And got on with the new story ...

Within a few years this life changed. And for my wife it ended. The children left home. I would get up early—the gulls woke me—wondering what to do. (I wasn't writing anything.) Living by oneself like this, I thought, how long the day is. How slow it goes by. I went from one empty room to another ... looked outside ... such a nice-looking place ... and wondered how to go on. And there were times when I wondered, why go on?

Then a letter came from Zurich. It came from the people who worked in a literary agency. They told me that my literary agent was going to be seventy. They were planning a surprise party. Could I come?

At the airport a young man with curly brown hair and glasses, just over medium height, was holding a sheet of paper with my name on it. He was shy. (No, he hadn't been waiting long.) He smiled easily. He said he did the accounts.

"You have not met Ruth?"

"No," I said.

"How long is she your agent?"

"Fourteen years."

Zurich was busy. In sunny end-of-May weather he drove to the heights above, to a cul-de-sac of large houses. They had signs, *Achtung Hund*, except in front of the large house where he stopped.

As he opened the door there were red roses in the hallway, lots of them. And more red roses at the bottom of the wide stairs. The wall opposite the front door was mostly books. But in a space, waist high, a small sink with the head of a brass lion. Water came out of its mouth. There were more roses, as well as books, in the large carpeted rooms that he led me through. Then outside, down a few steps, to a grass lawn. People were standing in clusters talking and eating. A tall attractive woman with straight blond hair was cooking over a barbecue. She talked loudly in Italian. A man in his thirties—regular clean-cut face, black curly hair—was moving around slowly with a hand-held camera, stopping, then moving again.

The person from the airport came towards me with a lively short woman. She looked very alert, intelligent, and with a sense of fun.

"What a surprise," she said. We embraced quickly and kissed. Then we moved apart and looked at one another.

"This is very moving," she said quietly.

I could hear the whirr of the film camera.

"You must be hungry."

She linked arms, led me to the barbecue, and introduced me to Giuli—the tall blond Italian who was her housekeeper. (She would die, unexpectedly, in two years.) There were frankfurters, hamburgers, salad, grapes. I had a couple of frankfurters and walked to the lawn's edge and to an immediate drop.

The churches, the buildings, the houses of Zurich spread out below and in front. Across some water I could see wooded hills. And further away, hardly visible against the skyline, mountains.

More people kept arriving. I could now hear French and German. It was pleasantly warm. Sparrows flitted around us. Giuli, and others, threw them bits of bread.

That night cars brought the guests into Zurich. The birthday party was in a Guildhall near the centre. A narrow river was outside. The water looked black. I could see several white swans on it. The guests came from different parts of Western Europe. They were mostly publishers. But I did meet Alfred Andersch. A gentle man with a pleasant face, a nice smile ("Why write novels if you can write short stories"). He would die within a year. And Elias Canetti. A short stocky man with a large face, high forehead, thick black hair brushed back. (He would be awarded the Nobel Prize.)

There were speeches, toasts, in English. Then the guests went in line to another room where—on a long table with white tablecloths—there were lit candles and all sorts of food. Platters of shrimps . . . asparagus . . . a large cooked salmon . . . roast beef . . . the salads were colourful. I looked ahead to the far end where the cakes were. And saw, on the table, what I thought was one of the white swans from the river. As I came closer I realized it was made of butter.

Later that night, in the house, seven of us who were staying as guests sat with Ruth in the kitchen. We talked and drank. I was the only male. The women's ages spread from the late thirties into the seventies. The youngest was the girl from upstairs who rented a room and worked in Zurich. She was waiting for her gentleman friend to phone to let her know when he would be in Zurich. After she spoke to him she came down and joined us. She started to sing, "It's All Right With Me." She had a fine voice. We joined in. There were more Cole

Porter songs. And Jerome Kern. Then the older ladies sang, very enthusiastically, European Socialist songs. And went on to folk songs, mostly German. (Ruth was born in Hamburg.) The one that made an impression was a slow sad tune about the Black Death.

Giuli, sitting beside me, said in broken English how her husband, a pilot in the Italian air force, was killed while flying. And how lucky she was to find Ruth. Then, with more wine, she began to talk Italian to everyone and stood up wanting us all to dance. We formed a chorus line, Ruth in the middle. We kicked our legs and sang as we moved around the kitchen. Then, tired, we sat down. This time Ruth was beside me, a little out of breath. While our glasses were being filled again I asked her—what was she thinking when she saw those large bunches of roses all over the house?

And she said that during the last war she worked as a courier for the Resistance. They sent her to Holland. The Nazis tracked her down. "Things became difficult. I was on a wanted list. I had to stay inside my small room. I couldn't go out.

"In the next room there was a man called Karfunkelstein. He told me he was going to commit suicide. I asked him why.

"One can't live with a name like Karfunkelstein in these times."

"I managed to talk him out of it.

"Wait," he said. And left me.

"When he came back he had his arms full of roses and other flowers.

"For you," he said.

"And gave them to me.

"My small room was full of flowers. And I couldn't go out to sell a rose for food."

Four and a half years later, early this December, I saw Ruth again. I had been invited to Strasbourg to give a lecture at the university. After the lecture I took a train to Zurich. Outside the station I went into a waiting taxi. I gave the driver the name of the street.

He replied with the number I wanted.

"How did you know?"

"Many people go there."

This time no guests or flowers. But the same warm welcome. The young man who met me at the airport was still doing the accounts, still looked shy, and smiled easily. His hair was grey. I met the new housekeeper, Juliette. She came from France. About the same age as Ruth.

It was cold and foggy. At dusk I could see the lights of Zurich below. Juliette brought in some coffee and for over an hour Ruth and I talked business. She phoned up the Canadian embassy in Bonn and spoke to the cultural attaché about an East German translation. She phoned a radio station in Cologne about a short story that had been broadcast. We went over a contract line by line. Then Ruth said, "I must go and lie down for twenty minutes."

She went upstairs. I went into the kitchen and talked to Juliette while she was preparing the food. Juliette told me she used to be a photographer in Paris before the war. Then worked in London. She had a studio in Knightsbridge, and talked nostalgically of the time she lived there. A small radio was on. Someone was playing a guitar. I said I liked Django Reinhardt.

"I knew him," Juliette said. "My husband, André, was his best friend for some years."

Ruth appeared looking less tired.

"You didn't stay twenty minutes," Juliette said in mock anger.

Ruth and I finished the rest of our business over a drink. Then it was time for supper. The three of us sat around a small table in the kitchen, in a corner, by the stove. We had red wine. We clinked glasses and drank to our next meeting.

Juliette passed the salad bowl.

I asked her about Django Reinhardt.

"He couldn't read or write. He was a gypsy," she said. "Very black hair but good white teeth. You know how he got those two fingers? His wife was in a caravan making artificial flowers when there was a fire. Django ran in and saved her. His hand was burned ... Oh, he was a bad driver. He had so many accidents ... the car looked a wreck. One time he came to see us with a new shirt, a tie, and a new suit. He asked my husband what was the proper way to wear it. André showed him. Django stood in front of the mirror, wearing the new clothes, looking at himself, very pleased at the way he looked." (Juliette acted this out with little movements of her face and hands as she spoke.) "We listened to him play ... he would play for hours ... If I could have recorded it ... He only began to make records so he could give them to his friends. But he could be difficult. To get him to the recording studio on time my husband would say: 'Django, you are late ... the machinery is all set up ... there are people waiting ... they have their jobs.'" And Django would not go. André tried again. And Django got angry.

"I need my freedom. If I can't have my freedom ... it's not my life."

"Later he bought a Château near Paris. That life didn't suit him. He was ruined ... by money ... by women ... fame. He couldn't handle it."

Juliette stood up and from the stove brought a small casserole and served the meat and the vegetables.

"What happened to Karfunkelstein?" I asked Ruth.

"He probably committed suicide," she said in a flat voice. "In those days people like him did ..."

"On May 10th, 1940," she went on, "the Germans came into Holland. Next day there was an epidemic of suicides. There weren't enough coffins. They put them in sacks.

"I knew this young family. They had two small boys. The man was a teacher. His wife was in love with him. She would go along with whatever he wanted. And he wanted to commit suicide. He kept saying: "'Life as it is going to be . . . will not be worth living.'"

"I knew someone in the American embassy. I arranged for them to see him next morning so they could get out of Holland. But I wanted to make sure they would be there.

"I went to their house. The man was still saying that life without freedom to live the way he had lived would be impossible . . . when the youngest boy swallowed a small bulb from a flashlight. (At least his mother said that he did.) She was very worried. She asked me: What should she do? How could she get a doctor? After a while the child got better. Because I saw how worried she had been I thought it was all right to leave them for the night. I said I would be back in the morning.

"When I arrived, the two boys were dead. The man and the wife had sealed all the doors and windows. Turned on the gas. And they had cut their wrists."

When we had finished, Juliette began to clear and wash up while Ruth went into the other room to dictate letters into a machine for the secretary next morning. I went up to the room where I would sleep the night—a large bare room in the attic with a low double bed, books all over, and a wide window with a view of Zurich. I looked at the lights and thought of the people who had come to Zurich, from other countries, for different reasons. And how few of them stayed.

Juliette came to the door and said, "There is a Canadian film on television. Have you heard of it? It is called *Mon Oncle Antoine.*"

"It's the best Canadian film I have seen," I said.

"Then we shall all see it," she said.

I went down with her.

Juliette drew the curtains. Ruth put in a hearing aid. "I only do this for television," she said.

I looked forward to seeing the film again. I had seen it, about twenty years ago, in St. Ives on television and remembered how moved I had been by it.

"There is a marvellous shot," I said while the news was on. "It is winter. On the extreme left of the picture there is a horse and a sleigh with a young boy and his uncle. The horse has stopped. And on the extreme right of the picture is a coffin that has fallen off the sleigh. In between there is this empty field of snow. It is night. The wind is blowing . . . no words are spoken. But that image I have remembered all these years."

Mon Oncle Antoine came on. The first surprise—it was in colour. I remembered it in black and white. Then I realized . . . it was because in St. Ives we had then a black and white TV set. There were other disappointments. It might have been because of the German subtitles, or my memory.

I told them the scene was about to come on.

When it did—it wasn't memorable at all.

Was it because it was in colour? Or had it been cut? I remembered it as lasting much longer. And it was the length of the shot, in black and white, that made it so poignant.

When the film was over I could see they were disappointed.

"I remember it differently," I said. And told them how I had seen it on a black and white TV set.

"It would have been better in black and white," Ruth said.

"There may have been cuts."

"It seemed very jumpy," Juliette said. "You could see it had the possibility of a good movie."

That night in the attic, in bed, I heard midnight by the different clocks in Zurich. I didn't count how many. But there were several. Each one starting a few seconds after another. And thought about *Mon Oncle Antoine*. How it differed from what I remembered. I saw how I had changed that shot. Just as I had switched the candles from around the man in the coffin at the start. And had them around the boy in the coffin at the end. I had, over the years, changed these things in order to remember them. Is this what time does? Perhaps it was a good film because it could suggest these things.

And was this what Juliette had done when she told about Django Reinhardt? And Ruth with Karfunkelstein?

But some things don't change.

I remembered my wife having to go into Penzance hospital to drain off some fluid. It was in the last two weeks of her life. She hadn't been outside for over a year but in that front room where I brought down a bed. And from there she looked out at the granite of Wesley Street and Mr. Veal feeding the birds. Two men carried her out on a canvas and put her in the back of the ambulance.

When she returned she said, "It's so beautiful. The sky ... the clouds ... the trees ... the fields ... the hedges. I was lying on my back and I could see through the windows ..."

Early next morning Ruth drove me to the railway station. The streets were quite empty. The sun was not high above the horizon. And here it was snowing. The sun caught the glass of the buildings, the houses, and lit them up. And the snow was falling ... thick flakes.

"My aunt in Israel is ninety," Ruth said. "And drives her car. Isn't that marvellous?"

We were going down a turning road, down a slope, then it straightened out. I asked her, "Will you go on living in Zurich?"

"I don't know. The only other country would be Holland. I like Holland."

After she left I went inside the station and gave all the Swiss change I had to a plump young girl who was selling things from a portable kiosk. In return I had a bar of chocolate, a large green apple, and a yellow pack of five small cigars.

GWEN JOHN

ARLY in January 1984 I flew from Toronto to London.
Then a train to Sheffield. My son-in-law, Kevin, met me
at the railway station. And from there he drove out of the
city onto moorland that led to a valley and to a stone house in
Hathersage. Ellen, my eldest daughter, was having their first
child. And as her mother was not alive I wanted to be there.
The baby was a boy, Hugh. I stayed with them a week. Did the
shopping. Helped to prepare the evening meal. (Kevin was in
Chesterfield during the day, teaching science.) Took the dog, a
whippet named Gemma, out for long walks in the surrounding countryside.

It was a pleasant village in a valley, hills all around. A few
churches. A school. A short busy road. Above it, on the sloping fields, sheep. There was a butcher shop, a bakery, several
fruit and vegetable stores, an Italian restaurant, some old pubs
with early photographs of local cricket teams, and a good inn.
It looked like a village in a children's book. The postman on his
bicycle ... the farm off the main street with working horses in
the stables ... ducks by a stream that went by a playing field ... a
small library (a room in a house) open some afternoons.

An Air Force jet appeared low overhead. Then climbed and banked quietly above the hills. I saw coaches and cars arrive with hikers and climbers. And walked in a section, up from the lowest part, where the large houses were, with magnificent views of the hills. And, closer, the neatly cut bowling green with the delicate bandstand. Ellen told me that Eyam, a nearby village, was isolated in the Middle Ages because of the Black Death. People would not go in but leave food. And on a postcard (in a small newsagent post office) I read that Charlotte Brontë stayed in Hathersage, then used parts of it in *Jane Eyre*.

When it was time to leave, Kevin drove me to Chesterfield railway station. Across the moor . . . before the sun was up . . . frost was on the stubble. He went on to his school. I got on the train that arrived from the north and was going to Penzance. I couldn't see an empty seat. Everyone looked asleep. When I heard a voice say, "You can sit beside me."

Bright, alert. She could be in her late twenties. Her black hair all over the place—probably I had woken her up. Her face was pale with dark eyes. And she wore an elegant, dark-purple, woollen suit.

"You can have the window seat," she said. "I'm going to get some breakfast."

She came back with two fried eggs, toast, and coffee. I saw a small black case by her luggage. Perhaps a flute. After she had eaten, tidied up, we started to talk.

She had been visiting her parents in the Lake District. I told her I had just flown from Canada and was going to Cornwall.

The train was moving along. Past small fields. And, in the depressions, water. I remember the American student in the airport bus from Heathrow. In England for the first time, and excited by what he saw. "This is watercolour country," he said.

"Have you been to East Germany?"

"Yes," she said.

"How long were you there?"

"A year."

"I was there two weeks. Where were you?"

"Halle."

"I was in Halle a few hours . . . between trains. What were you doing?"

"Teaching English."

"Did you go to Leipzig?"

"Yes."

"When I was in Leipzig I was taken to the Thomaskirche and shown where Bach played the organ. In the aisle, on the floor, there's an area of aluminum where he is buried. And in the middle of the aluminum, in large clear letters, it had BACH. Someone had placed a red rose in a corner. The organ was at the far end of the church. It's small. The pipes look like children's crayons standing on end."

"My boyfriend is an organist," she said. "A good one. He came to see me. We went to Leipzig. In the Thomaskirche he was given permission to play Bach's organ."

Outside. A grey sky . . . low clouds . . . small fields . . . hedges . . .

"Where are you going?"

"Oxford."

"What are you doing in Oxford?"

"A Ph.D."

"In what?"

"English."

"On what?"

"Decadence."

I thought, how marvellous. On a train in England just after eight in the morning. And we are talking about decadence.

Neither of us was certain what it was. But she was interested what form it took in art. She thought it might be when something—a way of painting, of writing, a style—goes on after the life of the original is over.

Oxford came too soon. She got off. I was on my own until St. Erth, where I got off, walked across the covered wooden bridge, took the branch line that went by Lelant Estuary, then the coast, to St. Ives.

I keep coming back. To this place. To this house. Although now it is only the top floor and the attic that I rent. I keep coming back to these shabby damp rooms, with the paintings on the walls given to me by people no longer here. The old black gas stove, the small (rust-on-the bottom) fridge, the plain wooden table. I can't leave go of this place. The life that was lived here is no longer here. The ceiling is cracked and peeling and when it rains patches are wet. The wood of some of the windows is worn and splintered. It all looks used and worn-out and not repainted or repaired. Yet I feel comfortable here even though the life wasn't comfortable. Nor is it now.

I live opposite stone—stone cottages—stone terraced houses—street after street of stone—no trees.

But there are the windows. In the rooms on the top floor. And when I go up the turning stairs to the attic. And see the colours of the far shore fields, the sun over the bay, the light-house, the gulls, the low clouds moving from the land to the sea.

And, from the windows, on the other side, the back and front gardens of the larger houses farther up on the slope with the neat rows of vegetables, the poppies growing wild in the tall grass, the shrubs, the flowers.

And I like being here because I'm on my own. I do what I want to do when I want to do it. I get up—the gulls wake me—before the sun is above the horizon. Make breakfast (a grilled Manx kipper), have cups of coffee, read the morning paper. Listen to the radio. For the first few days that is all I do. Except for walks by the coast, the estuary, in the country (the fox-gloves), on the moor (the changing colours of the bracken), or through the town. I get fresh mackerel from the fishmonger, hot bread and saffron from the bakery. There is a familiarity . . . as if I have never been away.

But after a week, sometimes less, I am ready to leave. I've had enough. This slow pace, these uneventful days and nights, these spartan and used rooms. When I now walk through the town I see it for what it is—a backwater. A few more days . . . I feel strangely exhausted doing nothing. I go to bed, while it is still light, draw the curtains. And it's as if I'm in a small cabin, on a large passenger ship, on an ocean. The ship has its engines stopped. And it's drifting.

Gradually the pace that is here takes over. The tiredness goes. I go upstairs to the attic, to this familiar desk, and start to write.

I remain here, living like this, until I finish something, or a first draft of it. Then I fly back to Toronto, where I live a different life with Mrs. Garrens, a widow of forty-six. She has a large secluded house in three acres of grounds (lawns, gardens, trees), a gardener, a housekeeper. In winter we travel.

So these two lives. The one with Mrs. Garrens began four years ago—eighteen months after her husband, an industrialist, died. The one in St. Ives, in 1949, when I was twenty-four and living in London for the first time.

There was still food rationing, bomb damage, cigarettes under the counter, *The Third Man*, cheap Algerian wine, large Irish sausage at Sainsbury's. And a lot of displaced people.

I had come over to do postgraduate work at the University of London and rented two rooms above the Institute of Child Psychology in Notting Hill Gate. Opposite was a garage. The door beside the garage had *Theosophy* painted above it.

In my third week, I returned late from a party and couldn't get the key to open the outside door. I saw a light in the garage.

And walked across the street. A bare bulb hung from the ceiling and a thin man in a white shirt, in his sixties, was reading a newspaper and smoking a cigarette.

I told him I lived above the institute and couldn't get in.

He remained silent. Then said, "Come with me."

I followed him in the dark to the back of the garage where cars were parked.

"You want a Rolls or a Bentley?"

"Bentley," I said.

He opened the boot of a car, brought out a blanket, unlocked a back door, put the light on, gave me the blanket, and said goodnight.

It was all white inside. A shiny white, like satin. I stretched out across the back seat. It was like being in an expensive coffin.

When I woke it was raining. And almost nine next morning.

That evening I went to Chelsea to see Nicholas Kempster, who was with me at university and lived in a bed-sit on Oakley Street. He left a note on the door saying he'd be back in a few hours.

I went to wait in the nearest pub. It was dark and gloomy (the walls were painted brown) and empty except for an old man sitting by the side of the fireplace. He seemed to be staring into space. A pint of beer was on a small table in front of him. He didn't touch it all the time I was there. He had on an officer's fawn greatcoat, unbuttoned. His hair was grey and uncombed. I recognized him as Augustus John.

The next time I saw Augustus John was two years later, in a black and white photograph on the wall of a pub, the Globe, in Penzance. The others in the photograph were Maurice Mayfield (a war artist) and his attractive wife, Nancy, dressed like a gypsy. Maurice Mayfield tried to look and live like Augustus John. I knew this because, in those two years, I met Elizabeth. We married, and decided to come down to Cornwall. We rented a large granite house with a walled garden from Maurice Mayfield. When he heard what I was doing he let me have it cheaply.

So we lived in this fine large house (it was the finest house we ever lived in) while the owner and his wife and four young children lived in a small primitive cottage on the moors. Maurice would come in every morning on an old bicycle to his studio—a small partitioned section of the building, near the house, where I worked. He always wanted me to see his new paintings. They were of peasant or gypsy women. Stylized figures, often in black, like the one above our bed called *The Angel of Sleep*. Though I didn't care for his work, I liked Maurice. Years later, I was told he came from a working-class family by the London docks. You wouldn't have known from the way he spoke. The soft voice, the careful diction, the good manners. A large man with a small head, short red hair, blue eyes, a face that looked as if he had just caught the sun. He went around dressed like a peasant farmer. And he smiled easily.

He told me he was trying a new technique (beeswax) and wanted me to see what he had done. I didn't like any of them. Then I saw on the wall a small unframed oil of a woman's head and shoulders. She wasn't smiling. The hair was close to her head, parted in the middle and pulled back, to form a bun. She didn't have much of a chin. It was mostly in browns. But there was an immediacy, a human quality, that none of the others had.

"I like that," I said, glad that here was something I could be enthusiastic about.

"It's not by me." Maurice smiled. "It's by Gwen John."

It was the first time I had heard her name.

At Mousehole we lived on the slope of a hill in this cut-granite house, with the high granite wall around it, and the copper beech, bamboos, roses, inside. At night, in bed, we could see the roofs of the cottages sloping to the harbour. The boats, in the bay, fishing between the chimneys. We had little money. I went out with the fishermen from Newlyn and bicycled back after midnight. The moon on the water . . . heard a fox . . . an owl from Paul. Then going up the outside granite steps, wondering if we still had electricity. Two days later an elderly man, from the electricity company, came to disconnect our supply. I held the ladder so he could climb and do it.

That night we ate our meal by candlelight.

The fishermen left pilchards and mackerel outside the front door. The farmer, from the fields above, left broccoli, new potatoes, and lettuce. Ellen was born. The butcher, Mr. Brewer, left five shillings on her pram when she was asleep. Then the money ran out and there was little I could do here to earn any. So we moved: to London, Devon, Brighton. When things improved we went back to Cornwall and to this house.

A few years later I read that Augustus John had died. And on the television news caught a glimpse of Maurice Mayfield at the funeral. Then Maurice Mayfield died. Our children left home. Elizabeth died. I went back to Canada, to Toronto, where I met Mrs. Garrens.

It started as a business arrangement. Mr. Garrens had left instructions that he didn't want a memorial stone. But Mrs. Garrens wanted to do something. She told me he liked books and thought of having a book prize, in his name, to be given every two years to a promising writer. And she wanted me to select the writer. We continued to meet in her house to discuss this. Soon we talked about other things. The prize was never mentioned. We were both still young enough to miss the physical side of marriage. And we didn't like living on our own.

But I have this illness. What other men do with other women I can only do with my wife. And when she died I thought, now I have to learn to be promiscuous.

When I moved in with her it was Mrs. Garrens's life that I began to live. Not only the house with the spacious grounds.

But the large rooms with floor-to-wall white carpets, the walls painted a delicate green. The paintings on the walls. The one I liked was a drawing, a nude, by Matisse. The meals cooked by the housekeeper. The dinner parties. I also began to travel.

She took me first to France. (Mrs. Garrens grew up in the South of France and talked about the fields of blue cornflowers in the long grass that were part of her childhood.) I had never been to France. It was the country Elizabeth always wanted to see.

In Paris we stayed in a hotel by the Luxembourg Gardens. We often went into the Gardens. Then to a restaurant, then back to the hotel. We went to Marseille and did the same. We both seemed to have a lot of energy, especially early in the morning, as if we had to catch up on lost time. She would make a sound from her throat as she reached her climax. Then give me these quick little kisses all over my face.

At breakfast, she said,

"Your eyes go up when you're happy."

Next morning at breakfast she said,

"Your eyes tilt when you come."

On our last day in Marseille she asked,

"Is there any place you would like to see?"

I said Dieppe.

So we went to Dieppe. Went for walks by the coast. Had picnics in the countryside. And to a different restaurant every night. And sometimes we ate in the hotel where we stayed along the front. The bed was wide and high. And there were long mirrors on the doors of the wardrobe.

"I'm your last fuck," Mrs. Garrens said.

That's the way our life has gone. And I like the life we have together. But after seven or eight months, I become restless. Another month or two and I need to leave. I am pulled back (why, I don't know) to this pretty backwater, these seedy rooms, to being alone. And to work here.

This January I told Mrs. Garrens. "I need to go to St. Ives."

Mrs. Garrens doesn't like this. When I tell her I need to go she becomes anxious. We have little quarrels. And when I'm packed, the bags downstairs, waiting for the limousine to come up the drive to take me to the airport, I feel sad about leaving her.

We sit in the front room, having a drink and talking quietly.

She never uses my name but calls me 'you.'

And I always call her Mrs. Garrens.

I arrived back here on January 10th. There had been continual rain in England for weeks. Drizzle. The sky was overcast. It was raining now. And in the passing small fields there was flooding.

When I arrived in St. Ives it was grey and wet. The open railway station above the beach was deserted. I began to walk with my bags. The streets were empty. Just the sound of the gulls. The rooms, the attic, were cold. They were damp. There was no heat except from the gas rings of the black kitchen stove. I put the three on that were working. There was also a strike. The water was cut off. When it came on I was told to fill the bath. I would take saucepans of water from the bath to the kitchen, to make coffee, to wash the dishes, to shave.

I had caught a cold and had a temperature. I decided to go to bed. But I wanted something to read. I went to the small library. Saw a biography by Susan Chitty of Gwen John. I returned to the cold, damp, and dusty rooms, put on two sweaters, thick woollen socks, and several extra blankets. I went to bed in the narrow front bedroom, with the bottle of duty-free brandy that I had bought.

And began to read.

How Gwen John led a middle-class upbringing in Wales. Went to Paris to be a painter. Became a model to earn some money. Met Rodin. They became lovers. She was, for a while, happy. Then he discarded her. She wrote him letters every day. And waited in Luxembourg Gardens hoping to get a glimpse of him.

After that she withdrew . . . she continued to paint . . . but didn't look after herself . . . hardly eating . . . little money . . . she ended up in a shed at the bottom of a garden . . . the rain coming in from the roof.

The Second World War. The Germans invaded France. Augustus John was in the South of France with some of his women friends and several children. He was to drive and pick up Gwen John in Paris, then head to one of the ports. But he avoided Paris. And got on the last ship for England.

With the Germans invading, Gwen John left Paris. Got as far as Dieppe. Collapsed in the street. People thought she was a vagrant. Took her to a hospice, where she died. No one knows where she is buried. Augustus John was supposed to do a memorial stone. But he never got around to it . . .

SOAP OPERA

I PHONED my mother in Ottawa just after 6:00 p.m. No reply. A few minutes later I tried again. Then I took Fred, mostly beagle, out for his walk through the small park (at twelve he still has this rapid acceleration and expects me to throw a tennis ball for him to chase), around the reservoir and the wall of green trees that hide the ravine. In front, by the path, were the four saplings planted a few years ago with the name-plates: *In Memory of My Beloved Papa, Joseph Podobitko.* I wondered who Joseph Podobitko was. I had asked the Portuguese gardener who looked after the grounds if Joseph Podobitko had worked here. He told me that Joseph Podobitko didn't work here. He didn't know who he was, and it cost three hundred dollars to put up one of those saplings.

I came back to the house with Fred and phoned again. I tried the Civic Hospital. I asked if she was a patient. Silence. Then her voice (slow and shaky) said, "Hello."

"When did you go in?"

"This morning at ten." It was an effort for her to talk. "I'm just played out."

"I'll see you tomorrow," I said. "I'll take the early train."

That evening I phoned my sister Sarah in Carleton Place. She had come to Ottawa and had been staying with Mother for a week.

"I couldn't take it any more," Sarah said. "She doesn't want to live. She has given up."

"A person who calls an ambulance and gets herself admitted as an emergency case hasn't given up."

"But you don't know what she talks about."

"I'll take the early train," I said. "It gets in around noon."

"I'll be with her in the morning and you will be with her in the afternoon."

"Yes," I said. "We'll get together later."

My mother was on the fifth floor of the surgical ward in a room by herself. When I walked in she was asleep, propped up by pillows. I was dismayed at how she had changed. I brought one of the grey leather chairs to the side, sat, and waited.

It was a large air-conditioned room with two windows. The blinds were halfway down, the curtains halfway across. On a small table by the bed, a telephone. On a chest of drawers some flowers wished her a speedy recovery. On the wall a painting, a reproduction, of two rowing boats by a blue pier with the moon out. The room had another room within it. A private bathroom. All the walls were orange and cream. And the doors light blue. The large front door was opened as far as it could go. And on it a name-plate: *Donated by Mr. Thomas Sachs*.

She opened her eyes.

"Hello, Mother."

"Have you been here long?"

"No. It's a nice large room."

"I paid into Blue Cross," she said weakly, "for semi-private. But they put me in here. Do you think they made a mistake?"

"I wouldn't think so."

She looked up at the two standing metal forms beside her. One had a bag that was giving her blood. It was almost empty.

The other, water. And that was full. She watched closely, as I did, as the drops appeared.

"What did the doctor say?"

"That I have jaundice. That I'm bleeding inside. But they say they can stop that. He's a very nice man."

"Was Sarah here in the morning?"

"Yes."

"How is Sarah?"

"Hysterical. She looks at me and laughs. Then she cries."

We were silent. "Help me up."

I put my hand behind her back and eased her forward. I was surprised at the thickness of the spine, how much it protruded, and how light she was. She sat, with her head down, as if waiting for strength to return.

"I can't eat," she said in despair.

There were small cardboard containers on the table by her bed. "Would you like this?" It was prune juice. "This one?" Orange juice. "This?" A white-purple thing labelled *Ensure*. She answered by an almost imperceptible movement of her head. I put in a stubby straw, bent it near the top, and held the *Ensure* while she sipped it all. Then she reached, slowly, for the box of Kleenex on her bed and, carefully, dried the corners of her mouth.

Again we were silent.

"You will stay in the apartment?"

"Yes."

With a finger she pointed to the dresser by the wall. I opened the top drawer and saw a large beige purse.

"Take the keys ... Have you got the keys?"

I showed them to her.

"In the fridge . . . help yourself. There is coffee. Eat whatever you like. You have my permission."

"I'll water the plants."

"It would be better if I didn't have them."

"How much water do you give?"

"Not too much. Every two or three days."

"Anything you want me to bring?"

"The small key is for the mailbox . . . See if any mail. In the dining room . . . in the drawer . . . are two cheques. Six hundred dollars and something. Take the bank-book . . . pay in my account."

I said I would.

She wanted to be eased back to the way she had been.

"Mrs. Tessier, across the hall, takes in the *Citizen*. Tell her you are in the apartment and you will have the paper. I have paid three months in advance . . . I don't think I'll go back there. I'll go to some other place for a rest."

The large blue eyes. The grey hair, usually neatly combed up, was loose on the sides. She did not have her teeth in and her mouth looked small. I thought of her independent nature, the quick intelligence, and how she coped with things.

"I'm all played out," she said. "But I'm not tired of living."

She watched the blood and the water drip.

"It's working," I assured her.

But she continued to watch.

"Another doctor came," she said. "A young doctor. He asked me questions about my operations. He said I had some kind of anaemia that only Jews from East Europe have. Did you know about that?"

"No."

"He said the mother passes it to her siblings. Does that mean daughters?"

"Sons and daughters."

We were silent.

"Do you want to see anyone?"

She said no with her head.

"If anyone phones. If anyone in the building asks. Say I have gone in the hospital for tests. Don't say anything more. Just tests."

"Yes."

Again we were silent.

"I'm going to close my eyes now," she said.

The closed eyes made the socket bones more visible. Faint sunlight was on her face and on the far wall. I knew nothing of her life in Poland except what she told me. "I liked a young man, a red-head. He was a scholar. My mother and father didn't think he could make a living . . . At my wedding they threw money in pails . . . We had a large house and a servant. When I was coming to Canada she begged me to take her." Then the difficult early years in Ottawa that she doesn't want to be reminded of. And for the last twenty-one years on her own, in a senior citizens' building, opposite a small park. I thought again of her generous nature, how independent she was, and how she came out with unexpected things.

Her eyes opened.

"I need a bed-pan," she said in a low voice.

A white flex, with a white button on it, was held to one of the pillows by a safety pin. I picked up the flex and pressed the button. A snapping sound and a slight electric shock.

"When the nurse comes I'll go," I said. "And I'll come tomorrow. Sarah said she would be here as well."

I went over and kissed her on the forehead. "With jaundice I don't think you should kiss."

I opened the door of her apartment. In the half-light I could see the three small rooms. Brought the suitcase in, quickly drew the curtains, and opened the windows. All the clocks had stopped.

The place looked as if it was left in a hurry. In the kitchen, dishes on the draining board were upside down. In the bed-room the large bed was not made. A dress was on the back of the rocking-chair. Two-tone beige and brown shoes were under the bed. The calendar, by the window, had not been changed in two months.

She had kept everything neat and clean. Now a thin layer of dust was on the furniture and on the wooden floor. And on the leaves of the plants in the front room. The earth was dry. I watered the plants. Looked in the fridge. A few potatoes were sprouting. The pears were bruised and had started to go rotten. I couldn't understand why Sarah hadn't tidied up. There was some half-used cottage cheese, a bottle of apple juice, a tin of *Ensure*. The cupboard by the sink was packed with tins as if for a siege. I made a cup of coffee, brought it into the front room, sat by the table, and started to relax.

I had not been here on my own before. How small and still. And full of light. The chesterfield set, from the house, was too large. She brightened the settee with crocheted covers—bands of red, yellow, green—that kept slipping down. And cushions with embroidered leaves of all kinds. The same was on the chair, by the side of the window, overlooking the street and the small park. (The Lombardy poplars are gone. But the gazebo is there. And kids throwing a ball around.) On the other side of the window, against the wall, a large black and white television was on the floor. No longer working. Its use, to support the plants on its top. Beside it: the glass-enclosed wooden cabinet with her best dishes, best cups, saucers, the Chinese plate that goes back to my childhood, the Bernard Leach mugs and bowl that I brought back on visits from St. Ives. On top of the cabinet a family tree. Small, round, black and white photographs in metal frames hung from metal branches. Father and Mother, in the park by the river, some fifty years ago. Sarah and I . . . when we were around ten and eight . . . the people we married . . . our children . . . with their husbands their children . . .

The room's centrepiece was the nickel-plated samovar on the long wooden dresser, against the far wall, with the mirror above it. Two silver candlesticks were on either side. A brass pestle and mortar. A silver tray. And more plants, lots of them, just leaves in various shapes and sizes.

Above the settee, two small paintings of people at the Wailing Wall. Beside it a framed diploma-looking paper with a red seal at the bottom.

First Distinguished Service Award
Presented to
The Dedicated Men and Women
Past and Present Of
The Ottawa Burial Society

"What do you do?"
"Sew shrouds."
I had said nothing.
"It's an honour," she'd said indignantly. "Not everyone gets asked."

On the wall, a watercolour of St. Ives (signed Holland). It was done from the Malakoff, overlooking the harbour, before TV aerials were on the cottages. I grew up, in Ottawa, with this watercolour. And in all those years we didn't know what it was. In 1949 I left for England. Five years later I made my first visit back. Paid the taxi, walked into the house, kissed them, and saw the watercolour.
"That is where I live in England."
No reaction from either of them.
The phone rang.
"Hello."
"Annie?"
"No, it's her son."
"Where's your mother?"
"In hospital."
"Not again. What is it this time?"
"They don't know. She has gone in for tests."
The telephone was loud. I had to hold it away.
"Who shall I say phoned?"

"Tell her that Phyllis Steinhoff called. We belong to the Golden Age Club. We go and play bingo together."

"I'll tell her."

Silence.

"Your mother is a lovely woman. She is intelligent. And she is nice."

I went to the door, directly opposite in the hall, and knocked. Mrs. Tessier, small, gentle, dumpy, with brown eyes and glasses, opened the door. She always looked cheerful.

"Hello, Mrs. Tessier. I came because my mother is in hospital."

"How is your mother?"

"Not well."

"What is wrong?"

"They don't know. She is in for tests."

"You want the paper?"

"Yes."

She disappeared.

"You want the others?"

"No, just today's."

"How long you here?"

"Two or three days."

"I hope your mother comes home soon."

I decided to change the bed linen. The linen cupboard was packed tight with neatly folded sheets, pillowcases, and towels. I was taking out a couple of pillowcases when I saw a used brown envelope. It was unsealed. Inside were dollar bills. Twenties, tens, fives, twos and ones. I counted. It came to a hundred and eighty dollars. When I took out the sheets I saw more used brown envelopes, unsealed, also with money. I counted all the money. It came to $2,883. I put my hand between other sheets, pillowcases, towels. No more envelopes but a small battered cardboard box held together by red elastic bands. Inside, large silver coins that I remembered as a child. A double eagle on one side, two heads on the other. She had brought them over with the samovar, the candlesticks, the pestle and mortar, the silver tray.

It was humid and hot. I had a bath. Then phoned Sarah. She was staying with her daughter Selina and her family on the outskirts. I asked Sarah if she knew about the money.

"Yes."

"Do you know how much there is?"

"No."

"Two thousand eight hundred and eighty-three dollars."

"It's for her funeral. She told me what to do when she dies. I have to call Pettigorsky from the burial society right away. She wants no autopsy. The coffin must be the Jewish way. No nails. Shiva she wants private. At her place. Only the family. And she wants me to get someone to say Kaddish for her. I'll pay him from that money."

"She hasn't mentioned any of this to me."

"When I'm with her that's all she talks about."

Next day I walked to the bank on Rideau near the market and paid the government cheques into her account. Then to the Rideau Centre, got on a bus to the hospital. Sarah was sitting in a leather chair by the bed. Mother was asleep. She was having another blood transfusion. The water was dripping as well. Sarah saw me. "Hi," she said and smiled. We both walked quietly over and kissed.

"How is she?"

"Most of the time she sleeps."

"Has the doctor been?"

"Yes."

"What did he say?"

"He said, '"We are not going to let your mother die."'"

We were silent.

"She doesn't have cancer," Sarah said.

Another silence.

"Why didn't she keep the money in the bank?"

Mother opened her eyes.

"I couldn't put the money in the bank," she said slowly. "If I did I would have to pay more rent."

I sat her up. Got some juice and a straw. She didn't have the strength to hold it. When she finished and wiped her lips she said, "It is not necessary to put this in a story."

"I only write about people I like."

She wasn't convinced.

"Phyllis Steinhoff phoned," I said.

"You didn't tell her anything."

"That you were having tests."

Silence.

"And Dinka called," I said.

"Is she in Ottawa?"

"Yes, for the weekend. Do you want to see her?"

"No," she said quietly.

We were silent again.

"How old is Dinka?"

"She is four years older than me and she runs around like a girl."

"Did she marry again?"

"She did. But she asked him to leave."

Another silence.

"In your letter-box," I said, "you had a notice saying that men are coming next week to clean your windows."

"No," she said. "I don't want anyone to go in there. It's dirty. Write on a piece of paper Mrs. Miller doesn't want her windows washed. Then stick the paper, with tape, on the outside of the door. You get the tape in the dresser of the living room."

Another silence.

She wanted to be eased back, propped up by the pillows. I suggested to Sarah that as I'm here she might like a break and have coffee in the cafeteria.

When Sarah left I told Mother what was in the news. "Waldheim was elected President of Austria." She looked surprised. "The Blue Jays are not doing so good. It's their pitching." I showed her photographs of St. Ives that I took on my last visit. "Do you remember that summer . . . the two weeks you were there?"

"It was the best holiday I had."

"You used to walk along the beach and pick the small pink shells at the tideline."

"I still have them."

We were silent.

"I'm going to close my eyes now," she said.

When Sarah came we went out in the corridor.

"What else did the doctor say?"

"That she still has jaundice. Why, they don't know. He said they were thinking of doing an operation to find out. She is all for it. "'I don't want to go on like this,'" she said. "'If they can do anything—let them do it.'" But they think she is a poor risk and wouldn't survive. She's not eating."

A nurse came and woke her to take a sample of blood. I told Sarah I would go to the waiting room at the end of the corridor.

On the way I saw a young doctor.

"They took a piece of her liver," I said.

"When was that?"

"On Friday. How long will it take?"

"The pathologists are in a class by themselves. They take their time."

"I guess we'll just have to wait."

"I don't think whatever they find will make much difference."

In a room with the door open I saw a nurse by the bed of a patient. A tube was being shoved down her throat.

"Let me die."

"Swallow it, dear, as if it is a piece of bread."

"Let me die."

"I'm not allowed to. Now swallow it for me, dear, as if it is a piece of bread."

I returned to my mother's room.

"Selina is coming in a half-hour," Sarah said, "to pick me up for supper. She's invited you as well."

"You'll go," Mother said.

She knew I didn't want to.

Whenever I arrived from Toronto to see her, and after we had eaten and had a talk, she would say, "Call up Sarah. Call up Selina."

I said nothing.

"Do it for me."

Selina had been in Toronto for two days at a real-estate conference. (She is high up in the company.) And was coming from the airport to the hospital. We were walking from the hospital to Selina's car when Selina stopped.

"She's going to die."

"Yes," I said.

Selina was Sarah's only child. A tall pale woman with blond hair, a small face, a nice smile, blue eyes. She looked pretty but anaemic. And there was a toughness about her. The few times I did go to their house she inevitably forced a confrontation.

She had tried teaching, advertising. But she hadn't found what she was good at until she went into real estate. She was married to George (he was fourteen years older), who smoked a pipe, worked in the civil service, and spoke in a slow, deep voice. They lived in a large new house, in a windswept field, on a housing estate near a lake. The nearest place, Rockliffe, was some ten miles away. Their son, Scott, had his mother's eyes and complexion. But looked oddly serious. "He's very clever," my mother told me. Then, lowering her voice as if she

was going to tell me something she shouldn't, "He's a genius."
Scott's favourite reading was stocks and shares. But at twelve
he wasn't allowed to play the market. I once asked him if he
played sports. "Football," he said.

"What position?"

"Centre forward—I'm very good."

I don't remember the meal. It was afterwards—when we
went into the large sitting room with the Eskimo carvings, the
Indian paintings—that Selina started.

"This is the first time for you. All the other years you weren't
here. We had to take her to the hospital. See her through the
operations. While you were away in England."

"You're lucky," I said. "You know her in a way that I don't."

An awkward silence.

"Why did you go away?" Selina said.

"I had to."

"You didn't have to. You could have stayed and got a job in
the government."

"I had to leave," I said. "The family doctor told me to get
away."

"Why would he say a thing like that?"

"Because of her," I said. "He told me to get as far away from
home as possible. She was too strong. She dominated the rest
of the family. Because she could do things well she wouldn't
let anyone else do anything. I saw what she did to Father. And
he was devoted to her. She was trying to do the same to me." I
stopped from saying, and look what she did to Sarah.

Then George said, "When you come on a visit she doesn't
want us to know you are in Ottawa."

Another silence.

"Selina thinks we should sit shiva here," Sarah said.

"What's wrong with her apartment?"

"It's too small," Selina said. "Three people in there and
there's no room to move."

"But here—it's miles from anywhere."

"All the people who would come," George said, "have cars."

I thought I knew what was not being said. My mother's apartment was not only small, it was in a senior citizens' place. And I could see it was no longer going to be private, a small family thing, but a social occasion.

"I'll be here for the funeral," I said. "But I won't sit shiva."

"Why not?" Sarah shouted. "It's therapy."

"I don't believe in it."

"But for Ma."

"To remember someone," George quietly said to Sarah, "you don't have to sit shiva."

He had, on marrying Selina, converted to being a Jew.

"You don't have any feeling for this family." Selina was angry. "You just don't have it."

In my mother's apartment I couldn't go to sleep. I finished reading the *Citizen*. There were no books. Only those I gave her that she kept hidden, in the bedroom, in drawers. They were in mint condition signed to my father and to her. Then only to her. She is the only one in the family who reads my things.

I was looking for a photograph of my father—a studio photograph of how he looked before he came to Canada— and couldn't find it. But I did find a glass jar with the small pink shells that she collected on the beach in St. Ives. And faded cuttings—from the *Journal* and the *Citizen*, of my early books—that I had forgotten. Some large boxes of chocolates unopened. Horoscopes that she cut from the paper. (Sarah was also an Aries.) A flyer that said, "Your psychic portrait rendered by the combined skills of an astrologist and of an artist. Strategically placed in your home, it allows for meditation on self, and to work out one's destiny." And it gave two telephone numbers.

In her clothes closet, at the bottom, large leather purses. Brown, beige, black. And none looked used. Inside they had loose change and a wrapped toffee or two. There were small yoghurt containers filled with pennies. One had American pennies. The others Canadian. Some were bright as if newly minted. I saw a small hand-mirror. The glass was cracked. I remember it because of the black and white drawing on the back—a woman's face and neck and dense black hair. I last saw it as a child on her dresser in the bedroom. Now, the drawing didn't look right. I turned the hand-mirror upside down. The drawing became another drawing. A woman had her hand in her pubic hair. I felt an intruder. I didn't want to look any more.

Next morning I walked to Rideau Street and to the Rideau Bakery. On visits I always drop in to buy some bread. I bought a rye, to take back to Toronto, when one of the owners came in from the back. (We both went to York Street School.) He was talking to a well-dressed woman when he saw me.

"Going to see your mother?"

"Yes."

"This is Mrs. Miller's son," he introduced me to Mrs. Slover, a furrier's wife.

"Your mother," said Mrs. Slover, "is a very nice person." Then looking directly at me, "Are you a nice person?"

"No," I said.

"Give her my regards when you see her. She is a lovely lady." And walked quickly away.

The owner of the Rideau Bakery looked confused.

"And remember me to your mother," he said quickly.

"She is in hospital," I said.

She was asleep when I entered her room. There was only the drip. I went out in the corridor, towards the reception desk, when I met the surgeon. A stocky man with glasses from Newfoundland. He was in between operations. They were, he said, still trying to find out why she wasn't eating. I told him I had someone coming from England. Would it be all right if I went back to Toronto? How long would I be away? About five days. He hesitated. "That should be all right."

I returned to the room. When she opened her eyes I gave her some *Ensure* and said I would be going to Toronto as Henry, a friend from St. Ives, was due tomorrow evening. I'd stay the weekend. And be back to see her the following week.

"The surgeon has my phone number."

"Did you have a nice time at Selina's?"

"Yes."

We remained silent.

"I'm going to close my eyes now."

After she woke, I said I would leave, as I wanted to pack and close the apartment.

On the open front door I saw the name-plate.

"Who is Mr. Thomas Sachs?"

"A bachelor," she said.

In the Union Station, waiting for Henry to arrive, I was early and having a coffee. And think how lucky I was to have grown up with painters. Painters are much more open than writers. They seem to enjoy their work more—more extrovert. And Henry was like that. When I first knew him he and his wife, Kath, were working in a café opposite Porthmeor Beach. And Henry painted when he could. He had one of the studios (large, spartan) facing the beach. And let me use it. The tall end-windows (that looked out on sand, surf, the hovering gulls) had a wide windowsill. I had my typewriter on the sill and wrote while Henry painted behind me. I could hear him talking to himself. "Look at that green . . . That red sings . . ." And when the work was going he would sing quietly: "Life is just a bowl of cherries." Just that line. And when a painting was finished he wanted me to see it. I said I liked it. "But it is so still. Quiet."

"All good paintings," he said, "have a feeling of calm about them."

Henry began to paint in Germany as a prisoner of war. "I got canvas from the pillowcases. Oil from the odd tin of sardines." He also went hungry. After the war he married. Left a struggling working-class home in the provinces to come to St. Ives. He had a thing about those who were (like us) in St. Ives but who had private incomes or parents with money. This didn't bother me. I guess you have to be English to have this love-hate with class. I remember when one of our lot (money behind him) won a prize for one of his paintings. We met in the pub by the parish church and the War Memorial Garden. He bought Henry and me a beer.

When we left the pub Henry was angry.

"A half-pint of bloody beer. Christ, if I'd won that money I'd have bought everyone double whiskies."

After that summer, and those early years, we moved apart. I heard he was teaching in an art school near London. I read about his exhibitions in the paper. Sometimes I saw him, briefly, in London. It was still a struggle.

More years passed.

Then in the spring of 1980 I came to Toronto. I was living in a modest high-rise in Yorkville when Henry phoned. He was in Toronto. He had flown from Alberta and was on his way back to England. Could I come to this restaurant and join him for dinner.

The taxi brought me to a seedy street near Kensington Market. I went up a narrow worn-out staircase. Turned into a barn-like room. Lots of tables. No customers. A man was behind a small bar by the wall near the door. A woman, in a simple all-black dress, came towards me. I asked for Henry. She led me through a door to a room in the back.

It was all red. The wallpaper was a deep red. Red lights were on the walls. The tablecloths were red. The small lights, on the tables, had red lampshades. There was only one person in the room. Henry, sitting by a large red table and smiling.

"It's a brothel," he said.

We had a platter of seafood. We drank and talked. About our friends, our children, and what we had been doing. He had been a guest lecturer at Banff for two months. Things, he said, were beginning to pick up. But he still had to hustle.

After the meal we went into the other room, stood at the bar, drank with the proprietor and his wife. Neither could speak much English. She was telling me that her husband played football for Portugal when a slight man, in a light-grey summer suit, joined us. He must have had his meal somewhere in the large room. But we didn't notice. He said he was an American. After a while he said he worked for the CIA. Still later, Henry and the CIA man began to dance. I danced with the proprietor's wife. Then we all put our arms over the shoulder of the person on either side. The proprietor joined us. And we moved around the empty restaurant as a chorus line. Henry singing, "Life is just a bowl of cherries."

Out in the street we asked the CIA man where he was staying. The Windsor Arms. So we walked to the nearest main road and waited for a taxi to drive by. The grey light of early morning. It was cold and shabby. A gusty wind. Loose newspapers. And no cars. The CIA man began to take out dollar bills from his jacket pockets and threw them up into the air. The wind blew them away. Henry and I went after the loose bills ... on the road ... the sidewalk ... across the street ... and stuffed them back into the man's pockets. Then he took them out again and threw them in the air. And again we went after them ... Until a taxi finally came along.

Since then Henry has called that night magical. A word I never use.

This time he had flown from England to New York. Spent four days looking at galleries and museums. Then took the train to Toronto.

"It's marvellous," he said in the taxi. "I don't have to lecture or teach or flog my paintings. I can do just what I want to do. Enjoy myself. And I have enough money not to pinch and scrape. From here, I'll go to Vancouver. See Expo. Then fly back."

He liked Fred. I showed him his room. We both got dressed up. Henry in a light blue silk jacket, a silk shirt, light blue trousers, a black beret.

"How's your mum?"

"Dying."

"She knows you know," he said.

Henry is tall and stocky with a grey moustache and glasses. A woman I know, who saw us walking down Yonge Street, phoned up after he had gone and asked, "Who was that policeman you were with?"

We were having a drink before going out. His eldest son was acting in the West End in a Stoppard play. His youngest was studying languages in Munich. "And playing cricket for the MCC."

"I didn't know he was that good."

"The Munich Cricket Club. After a game if he's done well he will phone. If he doesn't phone I know he didn't get many runs."

It is only after we have told each other about our families that we get onto work.

"I've never been so busy," Henry said. "I can barely cope. I think it's to do with age. It is so strange to be so busy that there is never a minute to spare. Not until I sit down in the evening and fade out in front of the TV. I can hardly believe it. My early work continues to sell. I am so confused. I don't know whether to stop letting the last few things go or just treble the prices."

The taxi arrived.

He was excited.

"Where are we going?"

The taxi stopped on a badly lit street by some garbage. There was an open door, a worn-out staircase.

Henry was smiling. "It's the same place."

There was the man and the woman. They said they remembered us. I don't know if they did. The front barn of a room had no customers. We asked if we could go to the back. She said, in poor English, it was closed.

We sat, by a table, against a wall. And all those white laid-out empty tables stretched in front of us.

The proprietor sat in front of a large TV screen. It was raised and could be seen all over the room. Benny Hill was chasing some girls who kept dropping their clothes.

The woman in the black dress came to take our order. In a firm but friendly voice Henry said, "We'll have champagne."

The woman went away.

Henry looked relaxed and happy.

She returned to say no champagne.

"No champagne," Henry said. "Bloody hell."

"Last night a wedding. No champagne."

He looked upset.

"Shall we have a Scotch?"

"Yes," I said.

She went away.

We were silent.

"You know," Henry said, "I wanted to come and see you. Go to a restaurant. And just say: We'll have champagne. I remember at The Tinners . . . I was strapped for money . . . I was nursing a half-pint of bitter . . . When in walked John Friel. And it was the way he said, in that arrogant plummy voice of his, a bottle of champagne. I thought, someday I'm going to do that."

We started with Portuguese sardines.

I told him that last summer I went to Paris and Marseille with a woman who opened up France for me. And it was in a small fishing place near Marseille, called Cassis, where I had the best sardines.

"I was in Marseille," he said, "before France fell. I was in the cavalry. We went to a brothel. There were three of us. All young. We kept coming back. They began to charge us hardly anything. They were glad to see us. I wondered why."

"Did you come back to the same girl?"

"Yes," he said. "I decided that they had two-way mirrors. They made their money from those who watched my ass going up in the air."

"Did you like the girl?"

"Oh yes," he said. "I liked her."

Next night I took him to an Italian restaurant, on St. Clair West, where I knew the food was good, and Henry said he liked Italian food. And the same thing happened. He asked for champagne. The proprietor, who was our waiter, looked sullen.

He came back with a bottle of Asti Spumante.

"I don't believe it," Henry said. "That's no champagne."

We drank bottles of Asti Spumante and were having a fairly good time.

The proprietor remained sullen. Finally he walked out.

"He probably has a mistress," Henry said. "Or else he has gone gambling."

His wife was the cook. A small pretty woman in a low-cut dress. Black hair, very white skin, large dark eyes, perspiration above her top lip. She had to finish serving the meal.

"I stayed in London with Adrian Oakes," Henry said. "The night before flying over. He had a girl staying with them that he had just before breakfast. His wife doesn't mind. It's the upper classes. His father gave him a mistress when he was twenty. He's been used to it since. Not like us."

When we got back we walked Fred around the park. Ahead, in the sky, I could see Orion.

Back in the house we drank and talked about Peter Lanyon, Patrick Heron, Terry Frost, Alan Lowndes. And the crazy things we did.

"I remember," I said, "how we all got dressed up in suits to go to Peter's funeral. And one of your sons saw us walking in the street. "'You look like a bunch of gangsters,'" he said."

"Who is normal?" Henry asked. "Do you know anyone who is normal? My mother's sister was called Ida Bolt. As Ida Bolt she was quiet and passive. And no one took any notice. But she also called herself Jennie Dempsey. And as Jennie Dempsey she would wiggle her hips, pretend she was dancing to the radio, jump with excitement. A complete extrovert. When she died the only people who came were those she played the piano for in a mental hospital."

Near the end he said, "There's hardly anybody left in St. Ives. No one to talk to. Oh, I talk to a lot of people—but we don't go back very far."

Next morning, before seven, Henry was up. And we took Fred out for his morning walk. I have to give Fred a tennis ball so that he doesn't bark and wake up people. He gets excited as I open the door. And will leave the ball for me to throw. He doesn't wait but starts to run fast ahead. Then stops, crouches. And looks at me. When he was young, when I pitched the ball, he would catch it in his mouth. Now he misses. So I throw it over him or to one side so he can chase it. He also chases the black and grey squirrels. They always get to a tree before he can get to them. I don't think he would do anything. He just likes chasing. Then he goes off into his own world and will sniff the grass and not move for several minutes. I whistle. I call, "C'mon, Fred." Finally he does. Or else he goes on his back and twists his body on the grass.

Walking with Henry, he was noticing shapes and I was noticing colours ... then he saw Fred was waiting for us.

"He's smiling."

"He always has that expression on his face," I said.

We went to the galleries in Yorkville. Saw some early Hans Hofmann. "I wouldn't mind having one of those," he said. At another gallery he liked the Borduas and the Riopelles. As we came out from a gallery on Scollard we came out above the street.

"There's a painting right here," he said.

I saw a red mailbox, a green metal container beside it, a cluster of three glass globes at the top of a lamppost, a cherry tree in blossom.

"What do you look for?"

"Surfaces," he said. "That green beside the mailbox. That has a flat top. The red mailbox has a curved top. Then the cherry tree. The shape of the streetlights."

We went to the Art Gallery of Ontario. I knew some of the paintings. Van Gogh's *Woodcutters in Winter*. A lovely little Renoir landscape. We go up a ramp and, on the wall, beside us, Patrick Heron's *Nude* of 1951; Peter Lanyon's *Botallack* of 1952; and Henry's *A Snow Day of Grey* of 1953.

Henry looked pleased. "I didn't know it was here."

For lunch, in The Copenhagen, we ordered duck with red cabbage.

"Gino came to see me in Cornwall," Henry said. "I can't remember his second name. It's my memory. He was in the Italian army. In the last war. He fought on the other side. He came to see me because he likes my work. When I told him I would be in Toronto, he said to go and see a sculpture of his. Here's the envelope with the address."

In neat small writing: *Bell Canada H. Q. Trinity Square Building. Business Hours.*

We went to find it.

I don't know about Henry but I didn't expect too much. But there it was. Impressive. A tall piece of metal, with a gold coating, as a central column. And from it rods came out at right angles, as if from a spine. And these rods were close together. They went up and down the centre column. Not in a straight line but a gentle curve. And then back. The effect— when you looked at it or walked slowly around—was as if those rods were gently moving.

"Breathing," Henry said.

It went up several floors.

"It really works." Henry was delighted.

We both went to see where it had Gino's name. And what he called it. But there was no plaque, no sign, nothing to say that Gino had done it.

I asked a travel agent, on the first floor, whose door was open. She didn't know who did it. "It's just there." I asked a commissionaire on the ground floor. He didn't know.

When we left the building to walk to Union Station, both of us were angry.

I remembered the man in St. Ives who lived down the road. A widower, in his late seventies. It was a hot summer's day. I was coming back from mailing some letters when he suggested I go for a drive in the country with him.

"You could use a break."

He had a Riley. He drove up the Stennack, turned left at the blacksmith's. And there was Rosewall Hill with the decaying engine-houses on the slope of moorland. He drove towards Towednack. Ahead were low outhouses painted white, a piggery. And near them, this tall brick chimney, neatly made, tapering as it went up. Then, at the very top, it became wider. As he drove near it, he turned his head and said, "I did that."

After Henry left I tried to get on with some work, but I couldn't. I phoned the hospital. My mother was the same. As it was Sunday I decided to go for a walk. I walked north until I came to Roselawn. And saw fields on a residential street. They were Jewish cemeteries. On one side were the larger fields. Stones here had MDs and Ph.D.s after the names. There were several families called Kurtz. On one it had: "His name will live for ever." But it was the two smaller cemeteries, on the other side of the street, that I was drawn to. On a wooden board, the paint fading, one had *Poland*. The other had *Minsk*.

I sat, on the side opposite, on a green park bench. Looked at these two small cemeteries. And thought, this is where she belongs.

I walked back from Roselawn. Down Forest Hill Road ... down Oriole Parkway ... to St. Clair. It had taken over an hour and as it was a warm day, I sat on a bench in a small park on the corner of Avenue Road.

A few trees ... green benches ... I sat and smoked ... when I noticed a sapling with a metal name-plate. I went over. *In Memory of My Beloved Papa Joseph Podobitko.* This was a good twenty-minute walk from the reservoir and the little park where I lived. What was Joseph Podobitko doing here?

I phoned Sarah.

"She has stopped talking," Sarah said. "She just points with a finger. And I'm supposed to know what she wants. When I get the wrong thing, she just moves her head."

I talked to Selina.

"She's frightened of dying," Selina said. "You can see it in her eyes."

Next day I packed a white shirt, a dark tie, a suit, in case I had to stay for the funeral.

In her apartment. A feeling it's all coming to an end. The money was gone. I asked Sarah if she had taken it. She said she had.

After three days I had to return to Toronto. I went to the hospital to say goodbye. She looked thinner and smaller. But there was a youthful astonishment in her face. A luminous quality. The eyes looked very blue. She didn't have her teeth in. And the dark opening of her small mouth was in a smile.

This, I thought, is the way I want to remember her at the end. And I wanted it to end.

Weeks went by.

Selina phoned. "Why hold onto the apartment? It's paying rent for nothing."

"She needs to know she still has a place to go back to."

"She'll never go back there."

Two weeks later, Sarah phoned.

"You'll have to come and help me break it up."

"There's not much there," I said.

"I can't do it myself."

More weeks passed.

My mother started to get better. She started to take some food. Every time I now came to Ottawa another plant had died, something else was missing: the samovar, the pestle and mortar, the silver candlesticks, the silver tray, the silver coins. But she was getting stronger.

She was moved to a lower floor. They were going to try and build her up.

I dialled her number at the hospital.

"Hello," I said.

No answer.

"Hello."

"Hullo," she said, out of breath.

"How are you, Mother?"

"I'm fine." Still out of breath. "Are you in Toronto?"

"No, I'm in Ottawa."

"In Ottawa ... I just fell out of bed ... to get to the phone. I'll have to call a nurse ... I'm on the floor ... We'll talk later."

When I went to the hospital, I asked the staff nurse where her room was. She said she would take me.

"All the nurses are fighting to look after your mother."

I wondered why.

"Because she gets all the other patients involved. She includes them in whatever she says. And she doesn't talk about herself. She doesn't turn the talk to herself."

"A doctor came to see me," my mother said, after I sat down at the end of her bed. "He was the only one who said I was not dying. That I had something. That I hadn't given up.

"You know what I get from people—respect. Some people, whatever they have on their chest, they get it out. Dinka, if she had anything she tells it. I don't. I don't tell about my husband, my children, or any of my business. They tell all...

"I wish I had done something in medicine. In research."

And I remember a visit. A knock on her door. A thin elderly woman stood with her arm in a makeshift sling. "I was told to come and see you. I fell. You would know what to do." My mother examined the woman's hand, tried to move the fingers. Then announced, "Call an ambulance."

"Look what she has to read." She pointed to the books of the woman in the bed beside her who was out of the room. "Trash. You can tell she is common.

"Sarah...doesn't have a head. You and me we have heads."

I tried to interrupt.

"I'm not finished," she said.

"There is a little Chinese lady. I take pity on her. She can't talk English. If I go, she goes. She talks Chinese. I talk Yiddish. She has a bowl of noodles. She gets her a fork. And me a fork. And she wants us to eat out of the same bowl...

"A doctor who went away, on holiday, came back to see me. When he saw me he was crying. He was so pleased I was still alive.

"Where are you going? You don't have to go out.

"The Chinese lady. She is a little thing. Hardly eats. But I show her this pudding with raisins is good...by eating it. So then she eats. She doesn't know a word of English...just Chinese. But she can't walk well...something is wrong with her feet.

"A Polish man came up to me and began to talk in Polish. So I answered him in Polish."

"How did he know?"

"A nurse told him I came from Poland.

"Afterwards she"—indicating the bed beside her—"said, 'I see you have a boyfriend.'

"She's *prost* . . . common.

"We walk with our walkers . . . First the little Chinese . . . then me . . . then the Polish man . . . The nurses look at us. I tell them, this is a masquerade . . . a cabaret . . . They don't know whether to laugh or not."

I looked at my watch.

"What is it like outside?"

"The leaves are falling. The sun is shining. I'm going back to Toronto."

"How is the apartment?"

"Fine. I've taken my books that you have in the bedroom in the drawers."

"Good. I don't want anyone to have them."

I got up to go.

"You'll phone me tomorrow?"

"Yes. When do you finish lunch?"

"About twelve, twelve thirty."

"I'll phone you at one."

But it was she who phoned at nine.

"I just finished breakfast."

"What did you have?"

"Juice, an egg, toast. But I couldn't eat it all. Did you have a nice time?"

"Yes, now that you're better I don't mind being here."

"What will you do with the food left in the fridge?"

"I'll give it to Mrs. Tessier."

"That's good."

"Your plants . . ."

"My plans are to go back to the apartment. Will you go to the Château Laurier and get a bus to the airport?"

"No, I'll call a taxi and take a taxi to the airport."

"That's better."

"I'll write from Toronto."

Fred was the first to go. It was the end of October. A fine sunny morning. I was getting ready to take him out for what would be his last walk. He barked as he always did before he went outside. From his bark you couldn't tell he had cancer that had spread. Fred looked up and wagged his tail whenever I pet him. He was twelve and a half. It was a fine sunny day. The leaves on the ground were some of the colours of Fred, the browns. He had also white on his neck and some black on the sides, but mostly a light brown. I was waiting for the taxi to take us to the vet. Fred was sniffing the air. His head is up. His tail up and curling...

The next to go was Mrs. Tessier.

She died in her sleep. I read her obituary in the *Citizen*. Sometimes I would see her sitting in the all-glass connecting lounge, between the buildings, with a few other ladies who lived there. They all spoke French. She always looked jolly. Her feet not touching the ground. Her husband died a few years ago. A tall nervous man with glasses. He was also quiet. They had no children. Whenever I saw her she asked, "How is your mother?"

I would tell her.

"Will she come back?"

"I don't know."

And when I was to leave the apartment early next morning for Toronto, I would knock on her door the night before and give Mrs. Tessier anything perishable in the fridge. I would knock on the door and a tallish thin woman with grey hair, in a fringe, opened it apprehensively. She looked sullen. She must have been, like Mrs. Tessier, in her late seventies or early eighties. Then I saw Mrs. Tessier appear to the right, sideways, wrapping a dressing gown around her. She was naked underneath. And she was wrapping the dressing gown around as if she didn't mind being seen like this. The other lady was fully dressed.

After that, whenever I knocked, the thin sullen woman was always there, always apprehensive. Once I saw her going to Mrs. Tessier's door carrying cut flowers. Sometimes when I arrived, or was leaving, I heard light laughter from behind Mrs. Tessier's door. I didn't know what was going on. But I hoped they were enjoying themselves.

There was going to be a meeting with the doctor and the social worker. Sarah, Selina, and my mother would be there to decide where she would go from the hospital. I had to be in Halifax on business.

When I got back to Toronto I phoned her.

"You sound better."

"Of course," she said, "I'm eating."

"How did the meeting go?"

"You should see how mad Selina was when the doctor said if I want to go home I can try it. Oh boy, was Selina mad. She wanted me to go to some nursing home, an old age home, to an institution. Anything but to live in my home again."

"How about Sarah?"

"She said nothing."

"How do you feel?"

"I'd like to try and see if I can look after myself."

"I'll come and take you back. When will that be?"

"Next Wednesday."

"I'll come on Tuesday."

That night I spoke to Sarah on the phone. I asked about the meeting. "To get back to her place she put on some performance."

On Tuesday when I went to see her she was standing by the window with her walker watching a blizzard.

"I'll need my boots. Put on the light in the hall. I have no light in the cupboard. But you will be able to feel, at the bottom, the boots. Take a scarf from inside a sleeve from one of my coats."

When I came back next day, after lunch, she was dressed ready to go in a wheelchair.

I gave her the green and brown silk scarf. Then the boots. She put one on with difficulty. Then tried the other. It wouldn't go. She tried again. Then I tried. It only went so far.

"You brought me two right feet," she said. "How can I go like this?"

"It's not far to walk," I said. "From the taxi, over a bit of snow, to the front door of your building. You have your walker. There will be the taxi driver and me to hold you."

"Two right feet."

She thought that was very droll.

Without the samovar, or the plants, the apartment looked empty.

"It's so nice," she said. "It lights my eyes up. I feel so good. It's home."

"The plants . . ."

"It doesn't matter. This one is the healthiest. And this cutting from the rubber plant I think I can save."

She sat by the window looking at the snow-covered park. "Oh boy, Selina was mad. She wanted me to go to a nursing home. If I go to a nursing home I don't get any money from the government. This way I'll be able to leave some money to all the children.

"The sun is strong." She turned her head away from the window.

I phoned Selina at her office.

"She should be in a nursing home. I want my grandmother to live a few more years. And she will in a nursing home where they can look after her."

"She wants to be in her apartment."

"But what happens if anything goes wrong? Mummy is in Carleton Place. You are in Toronto. I'm the one who will have to look after her."

"She also said she wants to be back because of the monthly cheques."

"That's a cop-out. She doesn't want to lose her independence. That's what it's all about."

I phoned Sarah and asked if she would come and stay with Mother for a while.

"I'm too tired. The place is too small. Why? Did she want me to be there?"

"No. I just wondered if you thought of it."

I asked Mother, "What about having Sarah come and stay with you?"

"I don't think so. I feel better by myself."

It had rained during the night. Then it froze. On the train back to Toronto the smaller trees were bent over. Some were broken by the weight of the ice. But it all looked pretty. Mile after mile. I thought of a friend, a professor of mathematics at the University of Toronto. He has devoted his life to mathematics and to logic. I asked him, what did he make of it all.

He said. "Nothing lasts. Everything changes."

Was this why we keep making connections? Why do I connect Gino's sculpture, to that tall brick chimney, to those saplings with Joseph Podobitko, to Mr. Thomas Sachs on the door of the hospital room, to those little Jewish cemeteries on Roselawn?

But then, whenever I go to a new place and walk around to get to know it, I inevitably end up in a cemetery.

My mother had been in her apartment a half-year when I phoned to tell her I was going to England to see my daughters. I would be away several months.

"The children have to know they have a father," she said.

I told her I would come tomorrow. "I'll see you around one-fifteen."

"Any time. You will be a good guest."

She had put on weight, and now could walk without a walker. But she still looked frail.

The place looked clean. The two surviving plants looked healthy. But without the samovar it seemed empty.

"Selina has it in the basement," she said. "What is a samovar doing in a basement?"

She wanted to make tea. And did, taking her time. I brought in the cups and saucers. She brought in the teapot.

"When I came home ... everything was dirty—the dishes.

"Not any more the people who used to be—the apartments are empty."

She talked about Mrs. Tessier.

"People in the building told me because I wasn't in my apartment, Mrs. Tessier couldn't go to sleep."

"How often do you go to the hospital?"

"Once every two weeks. When the doctor looks at me— the big smile. He is so happy.

"If I was in a nursing home I would be dead."

She left the table and disappeared into the bedroom. Came back with several twenty-dollar bills. Put them in my hands.

"For the children."

She sat down, slowly, by the table. "You know the money I was saving for a trip to England."

We were silent.

"Only another seven years and you will get the old age pension. That's wonderful," she said. And began to take out her hearing aid. Then put it back in. "It should make a noise if it is working." I tried a new battery. It still wasn't working. She finally gave up and said she would get the nurse tomorrow to find out about it.

After that it was difficult to have a conversation. There were silences.

"Did you watch *Shoah* on television?"

She didn't answer. I didn't know if she heard.

"It's about European Jews being taken to concentration camps in Poland."

"No," she said quietly. "I watch *Guiding Light* and *The Young and the Restless*."

I must have looked puzzled.

"It's soap," she said, raising her voice.

I said nothing.

"It's soap opera," she said loudly.

And she was angry.

FROM A
FAMILY ALBUM

RETURNED to England to see my daughters who live in different parts. Early this March I returned to Cornwall, to St.
Ives, to see the youngest who was starting work as a French
teacher. While there, my late wife's mother, Christine, eighty-
one and on her own, had a fall near where she lived in Redruth.

I took the morning train. And bought two hot pasties from
the bakery in Redruth near the railway station, where I could
smell fresh bread, and flowers (yellow roses) from a seedy flo-
rist on the road to her cottage. And I had a tin of Canadian
salmon.

I always bring her a tin when I come over.

"I'll keep it," she said, "for a special occasion."

We sat in the small main room (a mixture of neatness and
disorder) with little daylight. Ate, slowly, the pasties. They
were still warm. She only ate half of hers.

Old Staffordshire plates were propped up on the dark
wooden dresser. And in front of them, photographs in simple
frames. A black and white of her late husband, Sydney, when he
was young. He is dressed for the occasion. Dark straight hair
combed back, a dark suit, white shirt, dark tie. He is smiling.

I remember him as a handsome man reluctant to take risks. Because of asthma, he was in the Home Guard during the war. And worked as an accountant in a company that made containers: for toothpaste, shaving cream, and shoe polish. When he went off in the morning, in his homburg, carrying the *Daily Telegraph* and a brown leather case, he looked elegant. But he had to stop, struggling for breath, before the station slope, and use his atomizer. He also worried about losing his job. And taught himself to be a carpenter. When we married he gave us a wooden folding ironing-board that he made without using a nail. And on the day the doctor told him he had six months to live he went straight home and built his coffin.

His younger brother, Albert, had been a lieutenant colonel in the British Army in India. After the war, Albert started a dating service in Brighton where he lived. When that didn't work he started a business assembling crucifixes on wooden crosses. Then sold them to Catholic institutions, hospitals, bookstores. When he became bored with that he left his wife and children in Brighton, bought a trailer to his car, drove to a field above a deserted beach in Cornwall, and wrote two novels which did not find a publisher. Sydney and Albert's favourite uncle, Stanley, was in the British Army. Sent to Canada. A Canadian winter finished him off. He is buried in a military cemetery in Quebec City.

Next to Sydney was a black and white photo of Christine when she was the manager of a small Express Dairy by the station. Outdoor-looking, lots of energy, active in sports and Girl Guides. She did everything in a hurry and, when angry, slammed doors. They both liked musicals, especially Harry Welchman. In the house she sang:

Blue heaven and you and I
And sand kissing a moonlit sky
The desert breeze whispering a lullaby

Only stars above you
To see I love you

In January 1952, Elizabeth and I were married. Then went to live in Cornwall. When we were leaving for our first holiday in London, the taxi brought us to Penzance open-air station. As we walked by the standing train, I saw an elderly man in a camel-hair coat get on. Sometime after the train started, while Elizabeth stayed in our seats with our ten-month-old Ellen, I went into the dining car to have a coffee. The only other person there was the man in the camel-hair coat. We got to talking. He said he now lived in the country near Penzance. And asked what I did. Having just had a first novel published, I said I was a writer. He said he was Harry Welchman.

The name meant nothing to me. I remained silent. He said: "I'm the Red Shadow." I said that I was brought up in Canada and had not long lived in England. He said, before the war, he was well known in the West End of London. Suddenly he began to sing, the opening lines of *The Desert Song*. And this medium-height, elderly man, red in the face, largish nose, filled the empty moving dining car with a magnificent sound. Then just as quickly he stopped, slightly embarrassed.

On Saturdays, Sydney went to the public library in Eltham High Street and came back with books for the week. In the front rooms, in with his books on accountancy, there were editions of W. H. Hudson, Conrad, and Thomas Hardy.

Chris went as far as elementary school but kept in touch with her teacher (a widow, Lily Hay) long after Lily Hay retired. Chris pronounced Michigan 'Mitch-igan.' Menu, 'mean-u.' And when, as a widow, she came with us on a day trip to Dieppe, her daughter said, "When you want to say everything is all right, OK, say *d'accord.*" When Chris said it, in public, she said *Dachau.*

Whenever she phoned from the lobby of a hotel, she put on what her daughter called her posh accent.

Beside the photograph of Chris there was a photograph of Chris's mother, Grandma, a Jehovah's Witness. When she was in her eighties. A tall woman, now stooped, in a new hat and coat, about to board a ship at Southampton for a Jehovah's Witness get-together in Germany. She became a Witness after her husband was killed in a road accident.

"Left with five small children, I didn't know what to do. I went to the Bible, opened it, and read: "'Go out and do good.'"

Then a photograph of Chris's late daughter, Elizabeth (my wife), when a schoolgirl. Someone had hand-coloured the blue summer-dress, the short blond hair, the blue eyes. She looks like her father. And smiles like him.

But the room, the cottage, was dominated by Chris's paintings. Unframed they were everywhere. On all the walls. In the entrance hall, in the main room, in the small kitchen, on the side of the stairs, in the toilet, and in the two cramped bedrooms upstairs. They were copies of other paintings. And they were all unbelievably bad.

One, a small seascape, she had not copied. I told her it was the best thing she had done.

"I painted it in Scotland while on holiday. You can have it. Why don't you take it?"

"I don't want to take it now."

It was a good visit.

She talked about her mother when her mother worked (before she married) as a teacher on the Royal Estate in Windsor. And how, after her mother died, she went to Windsor and was shown the handwritten punishment cards where her mother recorded who was caned, who was sent out of her class. She insisted on going up the stairs (one at a time, with her stick) and came back with copies of these punishment cards. They gave them to her as a memento.

"You can have them," she said.

I remember Grandma coming with Chris to see us in St. Ives. She always had on some little thing we had given her:

a silver maple leaf, a brooch, a scarf. She never tried to convert us to being a Jehovah's Witness. But after a visit we would find a copy of *Awake* on the piano. In summer she would walk down to the front and the harbour. And sit out the afternoon on one of the green benches. Listening to the Salvation Army Band at the slipway. When she came back, she came back smiling.

"Everyone talked to me."

Then all of us (the children as well) sat around the kitchen table having tea. And Grandma, her eyes opening wide, talked about her grandfather.

"The miser. He would sit at the kitchen table with tea in a glass and cut the flies that landed on the table with a knife."

And about a brother, Willie.

"He went abroad and married an African person. He sent us photographs of his fine and handsome children."

On another visit (as they were leaving) our Cornish neighbour, Martha Leddra, a spinster in her late seventies, a ship's captain's daughter, a strict Methodist, on her hands and knees scrubbing the outside granite steps to her house, called out to Grandma.

"We'll go off to the South of France, my girl, and you shall spend all my money."

The last time I saw Grandma was in Truro Hospital. Very alert. She said to Chris, who talked about her going home, "Do you think I ever will?"

As we said goodbye, Judith blew a kiss. And Grandma put both her hands to her mouth and waved them towards us.

Then Chris talked about her teacher, Lily Hay, who had died since my last visit. She looked shocked as she told me that Lily Hay's son, a doctor, had left his wife to live with a man. And because of that, Lily Hay left all her money (her husband had been a builder) to a society that arranged séances. Then she told me about her annual treat: going with her art class to London to see this year's Royal Academy exhibition.

Afterwards, a good meal at Simpson's in the Strand. And in the evening, a musical (this year it was *Spread a Little Happiness*) before coming back.

When I left her, I left feeling cheered up as I walked through the rundown streets of Redruth to the railway station. No train to St. Ives for two hours. I got on a train that was there going in the opposite direction—to Truro.

I hadn't seen Truro for several years. It hadn't changed. Not the turning road, the narrow sidewalk, down from the station. The bookshop at the bottom with books on trains in the window. The store where I would buy Manx kippers and homemade Kea plum jam. By the Cathedral, feeling hungry, I went into a restaurant that had red chequered tablecloths. It was crowded and noisy. And those inside seemed to know one another. On the walls were black and white faded photographs of people in old-fashioned clothes. On the wall where I sat, there was a photograph taken in a field. A slim young woman with dark hair. In one hand she had a wicker basket. In the other the hand of a girl in a white dress. The girl has curly blond hair. Beside the woman, a man with a cap on, jacket, grey trousers. About the same age as the woman. They look handsome, optimistic.

I sat and ate. All around others were also eating and talking. I wasn't curious about them. But I kept looking at these faded photographs.

I asked the waitress. She didn't know.

I asked the owner.

"No one knows who they were. Or anything about them. They were there when I bought the restaurant over forty years ago. And no one knew anything about them."

On my next visit she couldn't put on her shoes. Her feet were swollen. I got the shoes on but I couldn't tie the straps. She didn't want lunch. But asked if we could walk to the nearest pub, The Miners Arms.

She walked with a stick, and rested often. Along a narrow passageway—by the backs of terraced houses—the ground was uneven.

"This is where I fell."

The pub (opposite a fish-and-chip shop called The Jolly Friar) was old and small. The saloon bar empty. We sat by a polished wooden table near the door. She ate slowly, one crisp at a time. Took a long time over the shandy. And looked around the room with an intensity, an awkward fixed smile, as if she was looking at these things for the last time.

"I always come here to collect for cancer," she said. "They always were very good."

I phoned the doctor. She phoned the following afternoon.

"The doctor came. She left me all kinds of pills and tonics to take."

I met Avril on the next visit. A widow, short, energetic. Her husband had been a miner. He had given her a parrot, Lucy, now fifteen years old. Since Chris had her fall she came twice a day. Tidied, washed dishes, clothes, did the shopping, put the garbage out, mailed letters, went to the bank, paid the bills.

The following Wednesday, at noon, Avril phoned. She sounded upset.

"The doctor was here this morning. Chris has gone into hospital. The ambulance just drove away. She said to me, "'Don't be sad. I've had a good life.'"

Next morning I took the early train to Redruth, then walked through the town and into the country, to a small hospital at Carn Brea. It was at the bottom of moorland. Five other patients were on one side of a ward, in front of their made beds, waiting for the doctor. She was last, by a window. (The moor began a few yards outside). Washed, dressed, her hair combed. She looked better than she did in her cottage. In her lap a letter from my daughter Judith who lived in Norwich. And photographs of the two great-grandchildren.

Before leaving Canada I had arranged to see Ellen and her family in Derbyshire. Ellen wanted Chris to come and live with them.

"Could you bring her with you?"

"I don't think she is strong enough for the train."

"Then Kevin will come and drive her back."

"I don't think she is strong enough for that."

Three days later, on my way to Derbyshire, I got off at Redruth. Chris was in bed, sitting up. In a new woollen sweater that had large outlines of squares. It suited her. We talked quietly about the family. And just looked at one another. She looked younger than her years. When it was time to leave it felt awkward and incomplete. I said I would see her when I came back in four days.

Late Thursday I was back in St. Ives.

Friday morning. The gulls woke me. It was still dark. I made coffee, went to the attic, looked across the bay. The orange lights of Hayle and Camborne were going off and on as if faultily connected. Gulls, dark shapes, were over the roofs of the houses and cottages and narrow streets. Then the sun, not yet on the horizon, began to lighten the sky. Across the bay a mist began to clear. I could see the white-blue water of the bay. The browns, yellows, greens, of the far shore fields. Godrevy Lighthouse. And Carn Brea.

At seven the phone. The staff nurse said she had died in her sleep.

My daughters came. And what was left of Chris's family. A younger sister . . . her two children . . . a nephew, a director of Rolls Royce in Derby . . . Members of her local art class in Truro. And Avril.

Afterwards we packed into the saloon bar of The Miners Arms. Had coffee and sandwiches that Ellen had organized. (The sandwiches that she made from the tin of Canadian salmon she offered first). I had told Ellen that Chris wanted to come to this pub for her last outing. I also told her that Chris got better as she got older.

"I'll miss her," Ellen said. "She was, above all, straight."

I saw Chris's friends from the local art class. They had, like her, started to paint when they came here to retire.

Most had lived abroad.

I had met them once before. When Chris took me to the annual exhibition of her art class. It was held in a large house in the country (fields in front leading to a river). The woman whose house it was (a handsome woman, a widow. Her husband, a doctor, had been mayor of Truro) didn't belong to the art class, but grew up with one of the women who did. So she provided the food, the drink, the household help. And these large rooms with spacious walls.

It was a French evening. With aperitifs we had pâté de foie gras on toast. Then sat down to melon. Followed by lampreys in a dark chocolate sauce. The lampreys had no taste but a texture, that of crumbling liver. A delicious tomato salad (light mustard on top). Cheese from different regions of France. Wine from the Médoc and Saint Emilion. Everyone seemed to be enjoying themselves. We danced to the music of Sidney Bechet and Barney Bigard. And the songs of Yves Montand. While on the walls were these terrible amateur paintings.

I talked to a lively blond woman in her sixties. Colour in her face. Large eyes. She sat most of the time. She said she needed to have a new knee.

"I'm near the top of the waiting list."

We began to talk about dogs. I asked about her dogs.

"All gone to heaven."

I told her about the dog I had in Toronto.

"Who is looking after it?"

"There is someone."

"You married again?"

"Yes," I said. "It's my wife's dog."

"I was forty when my husband died. Had a heart attack. I couldn't fault him on anything. It's living on your own that's not nice. I was a planter's wife in India. We had to have six gardeners because of the caste system. One gardener wouldn't do another gardener's job if he was of a higher caste."

"Did you know Mrs. Goodhand?"

"Oh yes," she said. "We were friends."

"I liked her. But she found it difficult to adapt."

"You do come down with a bang when you return to England."

From The Miners Arms we walked to the cottage. There were too many to go inside. So we stayed outside on the gravel. In twos, threes, and fours. Not quite knowing what to do. Then Ellen came out from the cottage with one of Chris's paintings. Holding it, in front of her, her arms fully extended, she walked, directly, to a person. And, without saying a word, gave the painting formally. Then she turned. And walked back into the cottage. And soon came out holding another painting in front of her. And walked towards someone else. We watched in silence as she solemnly gave one bad painting after another. To all the relatives. To all the members of the art class. To Avril. I had the small seascape.

Twenty-nine years earlier, not long after his fifty-second birthday, Sydney died. We had not long moved to St. Ives. The children were small. I stayed to look after them, and my wife went up to London for the funeral. After she came back she said she had a pain in her right foot. Then she began to limp. The doctor gave her cortisone injections. And told her it was probably a reaction to the death of her father.

In the spring, she heard that an art class was being given in the St. Ives library. She signed up for it. And looked happy when she came back from buying the material she needed.

And excited as she went off to her first class. But she only stayed two sessions.

"As soon as the others arrive, they all know what they want to do. And they get on with it. I don't know what to do. An elderly man beside me has been going there for years. As soon as he comes in he arranges everything neatly, the way he wants. And begins to paint.

"That's a nice sky," I said.

"I can only do this one sky," he replied.

A year before she died she told me:

"After I finished school I wanted to go to art school. It was the only thing I have ever wanted to do in my life. But my mother and father didn't approve. They made fun of the paintings I did in my bedroom. When I said I was going to show them to a principal in an art college—to see if I was good enough to get in—they thought I was foolish.

"I brought my portfolio to the principal of St. Martins. He looked at the paintings and drawings. And said he would write and let me know within two weeks.

"I couldn't wait at home. I went to Cornwall. Stayed on the farm where I was evacuated to during the war. Went for walks on roads that I knew. And all I could think of . . . that what I'd be doing with my life . . . was being decided in London.

"When I came back I asked my parents if there was a letter? "They said no.

"Days. Weeks. Months. Passed. I did nothing. Something had happened to me.

"My father arranged that I work in the bank. I didn't last a year. Then I went to Teachers Training College. Then we met.

"After my father's funeral I began to turn out things for my mother. In their bedroom, in a drawer, I came across an envelope addressed to me. It was opened. Inside, a letter from St. Martins. It said I had been accepted."

MY KARSH PICTURE

I T WAS MID-JANUARY 1944 and I had returned to Ottawa
from the West—having received a commission as a pilot
officer—to spend a few weeks' embarkation leave at home
before going over to England. That, as it turned out, wasn't
exactly right either. For I was still to stay another seven weeks
in Canada, in a finishing school in Quebec, in order to learn
how to behave like an officer. But my mother didn't know this,
and she wanted to have a photograph taken while I was on
embarkation leave so she could be left with a picture when I
went overseas. And the man to take your photograph, if you
lived in Ottawa, was Karsh.

Though Karsh at that time was not the internationally
known figure he is today, he had already established himself
among the wealthy and influential people in Ottawa. Whenever I went to my uncle's on the Driveway, there was his
Karsh picture on the mantel in the living room, as there were
of my aunts and cousins. And though Karsh did not, I imagine, charge then as much as he charges now, whatever he did
charge was still more than my parents could afford.

The Jewish community in Ottawa's Lower Town was small
and provincial, but it had a well-organized grapevine. My par-

ents soon got wind that the person who did all the touching-up at Karsh's, a refugee, sometimes took private sitters in the evenings, and could produce photographs exactly like those of Karsh for a fraction of the price.

My mother arranged an appointment. And I went out on a freezing night to meet the toucher-upper in the Honey Dew on Sparks Street. His name I have forgotten (I'll call him Lou). But I remember him as a tall thin man with a sallow complexion and a melancholy look on his face. And he had thin, straight, sandy hair. He had with him a very short, roly-poly, amiable man called Zhavel, also a refugee, who was to act as his assistant. During the day Zhavel worked for a tailor on Metcalfe Street. We walked over to the arcade and the tall man looked around furtively before taking some keys out of his pocket and opening the door of Karsh's studio.

I had never seen so much equipment before. Wires, reflectors, lights, tripods, venetian blinds, drapes—it looked like my idea of a Hollywood set. I took off my coat. I had some cold cream put on my forehead. I combed my hair. And the toucher-upper, Lou, posed me on a small raised platform, holding my gloves in one hand, arm bent, elbow on my knee, a spotlight behind me to give the Karsh halo outline. I faced the camera.

Zhavel was holding up a light, standing on a chair a short distance to my left, so that half my face was in shadow, the other blinded. I could see he was standing fully stretched—his trousers were at half-mast. Lou looked in the camera, black hood over his head, did some adjusting, and put in a plate. Then, holding a rubber bulb in his hand, he came close to me, to the shadow side, and said, like the maestro,

"You like flying?"

"Yes," I said.

"Fine. Now imagine this. Imagine you are flying over Germany. And a battle that will decide the future of mankind is being fought in the skies. It is simply terrible. Stukas are diving.

Parachutes are everywhere. You are turning, firing. You are coming out of a dive. It is terrible.

"Planes are breaking up like little toys, bits go by your face. But you are determined to live. You are determined. You *look* determined. Look determined, please."

I tried to look determined. I was nineteen. And all my flying so far had been done in Tiger Moths and Ansons over stretches of prairie and foothills in Alberta.

"Got him?" Zhavel said from the chair. "I can't hold this light much longer."

"Yah," Lou said. But he didn't sound very enthusiastic.

Zhavel put his light down on the chair. And they had a huddle by the camera. I could hear bits of conversation.

"—he's a stoneface. What can you do?"

"Let me try…"

So Zhavel took hold of the bulb. And Lou climbed up on the chair to take charge of the light.

"Now," Zhavel said from somewhere to my left, slowly and intimately. "There is a beautiful girl. And you are very tired. You have fought forty times today. The ack-ack has made mincemeat of all your friends. You are fed up with war and all that business. And you are alone in your tent. And she comes in. She is wearing negligible clothes. And…"

"Zhavel, he's too young."

"If he's old enough to get killed he's old enough for this—she comes close to you and kisses you gently on the lips and says…"

"Zhavel, I know his father."

"All right. You try something then. The guy's a stoneface. Not a crease."

Lou said nothing in reply. And Zhavel again took over. He changed his approach.

"Look. How would your mother like to remember you? You're dead, see! And all they've got is this picture hanging on the wall. Do you want to leave them a picture with *no* expression? Nothing to say thank you for all the things you've done for me all these years? Don't you want your mother and father to look at the picture and get sóme joy? Think of something happy!"

"And double it," said Lou from behind the light. "You're not going to a funeral. Ask him about when he was a child."

"What was the first thing," Zhavel said, "you wanted to be? Think. Don't think too hard, but what was the first ambition?"

"I wanted to be," I said, "the man who swept the leaves from the street in the fall with a big broom and put them into a barrel."

"And now you've become an officer."

"Zhavel, quit horsing around with philosophy," Lou said sharply.

"I'll tell him a joke then."

"Which one?"

"About Yosel."

"That one takes you half an hour."

"How about the salesman with the rubber goods on the farm?"

"That's an Old Country joke—he's a Canadian boy."

They had another huddle. And when they came away from it Zhavel looked very sly.

"You are feeling miserable," he said gently. "You've got no money. Your girlfriend has left you for your best friend. You have been in an accident and you have your legs and arms amputated without anesthetic. You have lost buckets of blood. And you've got a toothache. Life isn't worth living..."

"It's no good," Lou said from the chair.

Suddenly Zhavel exploded. "*You're no good.* Your face is a cover. A garbage can. For what? I'll tell you. You're a liar. A rotten apple. A thief—I give up. The guy has only one expression."

"Cheese," I said.

"What, you like food?"

"As a matter of fact I do. But you're supposed to say cheese before you have your picture taken, sometimes."

"You like latkes?"

"Yes."

"You like smoked meat?"

"Yes."

"Well, you are alone with a plate of hot juicy smoked meat, lots of fat, and this beautiful girl, and she is making latkes with nothing on ..."

He must have pressed the bulb then, for the toucher-upper came down from the chair, and they had another long huddle around the camera.

When it was over, and I was putting on my coat, I asked Lou:

"Will it look like a Karsh?"

He led me to a room where in tanks filled with water were floating pictures of several Canadian and American generals, the royal family, and the pope.

"In two days you'll be floating there with them," he said.

Two months after the war ended I came back to Ottawa. The Karsh photograph was on the wall. There I was, gloves in one hand, halo behind my head. I heard that the toucher-upper had died of TB. No one knew what had happened to Zhavel.

BY THE RICHELIEU

NTIL I was eighteen I spent my summer holidays at the family cottage on the banks of the Richelieu south of Montreal and six miles north of the American border. Two miles away is the French-Canadian village of Île aux Noix. There is an island in the river, opposite the village, with a decaying fort and a moat with shallow water. Water lilies and a thin green scum cover the surface. During the last war the fort was used as an internment camp for aliens.

I imagine that until the road was built, during Prohibition, the river was busy. But though the channel is still occasionally dredged and the red and black buoys that mark its passage are sometimes repainted, I have seen few riverboats go by. The only traffic now comes from the small hired boats with the sport fishermen. For alongside the channel the weeds are thick—so thick that sometimes I have been stopped, as the keel or the propeller became entangled.

The countryside is not exciting to look at. Even from the water. It is flat with a few isolated trees and farm fences. The farmers have small fields. They are all French Canadian. They grow wheat, corn, potatoes. Some have chickens and pigs. The two hotels along the bank shut in winter. They are there for the

American businessmen who come down in the summer and fall to play cards, drink, and fish. For this part of the Richelieu has some of the best fishing I know. I've anchored by the red buoy, opposite the Grand Hotel, for muskellunge; trolled along the banks for pike; caught carp at night using a light and spearing them as they rose to the surface a few yards from the shore. There are also fine black bass and perch.

When I first knew the place it still hadn't been discovered by the tourists, although the signs were there—a cluster of stilt-cottages along the bank, nearer Montreal. And every spring afterwards, when I came down, the cluster of stilts grew and spread downwards to the border.

Until the arrival of the stilts, the people by the river's bank lived in a few proud old cottages. The one my parents had was built by a priest—so village rumour said—who came from Rimouski to retire after he won a lottery. It was made out of wood: dark green with white trimmings, and a wide veranda went right around. The main highway was a quarter of a mile away. Between highway and cottage were empty, gentle sloping fields. And between cottage and river there was a raised walk of rough planks. In spring the water came up the cottage steps so that I could take out the dinghy, the canoe, or the rowboat from the shed and push it down a few yards to float it. In summer I had to push the boats through mud. By the time I reached the deep water the bottom and sides of my feet were covered with mud and bloodsuckers.

Two miles down from the cottage, towards the border, the river had taken a small bite out of the land and left a cove. The banks of this cove are lined with magnificent elms. Whenever I was fishing or sailing near here I could see the hulk of a great house almost completely hidden by the trees. It was the largest house not only along the river but, I imagine, between Montreal and Montpellier. Sometimes I caught a glimpse of rough greystone, large windows, the wood a shiny black. I knew, as did everyone else around here, that the house belonged to the Dobells.

Like individual people, I sometimes think that families also have a zenith to their lives. So many generations have to be sacrificed in the climb upwards for another to have that bright interval at the top. After which there are others to take the decline down. From what I have read, and what my parents told me, I would say the Dobells were at their peak in the early 1920s. Arthur Dobell, who now had the house, was of the fifth generation. He rarely occupied it. Usually he was photographed at his place in Bermuda, or in Palm Beach, or somewhere on the Riviera.

My first meeting with him was accidental. It was a hot August afternoon. I had taken out the sailboat with the drop keel—which was a present for my sixteenth birthday from my father—and combined sailing across the river while at the same time trolling for pike. I let the line out, tied it to my big toe, and felt the pleasurable vibration of the spoon travelling through the water. Not far from the island I felt the bite. Then I saw him drift alongside. He looked like some seaweed with the sun shining on it. I had a spinner with three hooks. One of the hooks had got inside the edge of his jaw, through the flesh, and come out again. I could see the blue end of the hook clearly. I landed him and clubbed him to death. I didn't know how much he weighed. But when I held him, he stretched from the bottom of the boat up to my hip. Then the storm came. I had to tack several times to make any progress back. When the rain began I decided to shelter in the cove in front of the Dobell house.

He must have watched me, for he came running out. Helped me tie up, dismantle the mast, and brought me inside where I rang my parents. Then we stood by the large windows and watched the lightning over the river and the rain. It didn't look like easing up so he suggested that I spend the night there.

I had changed my clothes. Wrapped myself up in one of his expensive dressing gowns that had a silken Miami-Florida label sewn inside with his name. And sat in front of the fireplace. He had lit the set-logs and quickly they were blazing away. It was the most impressive fireplace I had seen. A cement roof and sides came out from the wall like a canopy and leaned into the room.

"My great-grandfather built it from pebbles in the cove," he said quietly.

Thousands of small round bluish-green stones were set in the cement.

The butler came with hot cocoa. I sat there drying out, feeling warm, and looked around the room. At the heavy curtains; the large oil paintings on the wall of the dead Dobells; the heads of stuffed animals, all with the same brown sad eyes.

"How heavy was the fish?"

"I dunno. But it's the biggest pike I've ever caught. Do you want it?"

"No thanks." And he smiled, a shy, understanding smile.

I was disappointed when I first saw him. He looked much smaller than his photographs, about five foot seven, slightly built. And his appearance was entirely commonplace. Yet I felt a curious sense of detachment about him. Though I knew he was in his late thirties, he looked amazingly young. Money, I thought, had preserved him, like it did this house.

"Do you like music?"

"I can play the trumpet," I said, "not well."

He went to the gramophone by the wall, lifted the lid until it locked in its hinges, took out a collapsible steel handle, wound it several times, then put on a record.

"Are you going to college?"

In the morning
In the evening
Ain't we got fun?

"No. Not till next year."
"What will you study?"
"Medicine."

The rent's unpaid, dear,
We haven't a sou.
But life was made, dear,
For me and for you.

"Isn't that Sir Nicholas Dobell—?"

I indicated the second-last oil on the wall. It was a rhetori-
cal question—the Kipling face, the weak eyes looking through
glasses, the high white collar were familiar to me from photographs. Nicholas Dobell had, along with Charlie Conacher
and Sweeney Schriner, been one of my schoolboy heroes. I
knew he had lectured in surgery at McGill, then went on to a
chair in Cambridge, and was knighted just before he died.

The record stopped.

"When you graduate," he said, "I hope you'll go and see
something of this world. I don't think these boys did. Not until
it was too late. It's not the same after thirty. You begin to look at
things differently. And things begin to flatten out ..."

And again I felt that curious feeling of tenderness emanate
from him and with it the sense that it was impersonal. It was
the kind that one usually gets from a doctor.

For the rest of that summer I was often in this house.

I went sailing in his yacht up and down the river. Sometimes we swam out to the white raft anchored in the middle
of the cove and lay there and got brown. And sometimes I was
with him for meals when the butler brought the food to one

of the wicker tables under the large striped beach umbrellas that were stuck like mushrooms on the lawns. He introduced me to various dishes. He taught me how to make a passable omelette. He taught me what little I know about wines. There was always a phonograph handy, portable ones on the yacht and in the house, which he would take out onto the lawns and keep playing records—they were only records of the twenties. It was in his library that I first came across Hemingway, Fitzgerald, and Faulkner. He taught me to drive his Plymouth coupe with the white tires and we raced along the highway, flashing by the empty fields, the slow river, the signs showing how many more miles it was to Morgan's. On weekends he took me into Montreal or Ottawa—and bought me a small present, usually a book—and then to one of his favourite restaurants, or to a country place by the lakeshore. Meals with him were always an event.

I guess all of us have a favourite period in our lives. That summer was mine. It was one of those times that now, looking back, I realize how much it influenced my life. What I sometimes tend to forget is just how easy it was to live it, without much thought. Although I did sometimes wonder—especially at dusk when I saw him on the lawns against the large house, a solitary figure watching the sun set over the river behind the trees—why someone as likeable and with so much money had no visitors. I had the feeling that he only used Île aux Noix in the sense of a retreat. That away from it he was quite a different person. Certainly the impression of an irresponsible playboy, created by the papers and gossip, did not bear out in what I knew of him.

The next summer he was away. I received a postcard from Antibes in June. A month later another card came from Saint-Tropez. In the fall I went to McGill and began my pre-med. Then the war came. I joined the RCAF and went overseas. And I heard no more of Dobell. When the war ended I went back to McGill, got my degree, then took six months off and visited parts of Europe and Africa that Dobell had told me about.

I intended to practise in the east—but things didn't work out that way. And after a few stopping-off places in Northern Ontario, I found myself in Vancouver, which was very pleasant. For ten years now I have built up a fairly successful practice, married, have a son and daughter, friends, and a fair amount of cash to do the things I want to do. Then last summer something curious happened.

I became homesick for the east. At thirty-four, with youth definitely over and middle age relentlessly approaching, I found myself turning more and more to my roots and the friendships those bred. And though I have very close friends on the west coast I felt that I wanted to go back to the places and the people with whom I'd had the formative experiences of my youth. I seemed to have reached a point where I wanted to take a look backwards and sum up an epoch in my life, so as better to go forward. I felt a curious lack of completion. The momentum of youth was dying down without generating a new passion. And although I'm interested in medicine, I cannot say that it grips me totally.

So I flew back. Spent the first three days in Montreal. Montreal was a reassurance. It had not changed too much. Not along the parts of Sherbrooke Street I knew or walking along St. Catherine...

The water still dripped from the gargoyles of Christ Church Cathedral and at noon the carillon at St. James's played its tin-penny tunes. At the corner of University, the man who sold the *Star* and *Gazette* (under the turning clock of the Bank of Montreal) looked, with age, even more like Ernest Hemingway. In Phillips Square the pigeons pecked at soaked bits of bread and in the pools of water the sharp reflections of Birks and Morgan's, the statue of Edward VII, and the taxis on either side, while a Jehovah's Witness stood with a copy of *Awake* in his hand. At night, the gay neon of the restaurants, the films, the delicatessens, the grey buses. And above them the three sweeping searchlights probing aimlessly through the low clouds. While at the end of each intersection the black shape of Mount Royal with the lit, stubby cross on top .

. . . Except it was a different person now seeing this. And though I kept bumping into acquaintances and bits and pieces of my past, there was the inevitable disappointment. I suddenly wanted to go back to Île aux Noix.

My father had sold the cottage just after Mother died and had come out to Victoria. There was really only Dobell. I sent him a telegram on the off chance that he might be there. When I returned to the Mount Royal that evening there was one waiting: LET ME KNOW WHEN ARRIVING CHAUF-FEUR WILL MEET TRAIN—ARTHUR.

The chauffeur who met me at St. Johns was new and had nothing of the servant about him. Although he wore the tra-ditional dark double-breasted suit and chauffeur's cap—on him it looked a masquerade. He was stout, short, and slightly bowlegged. The face, although clean-shaven, was swarthy. He looked like a well-fed peasant. We talked on the drive in. I said he was new. "A little over a year—You have pleasant journey—You are tired at end of day—"

His English was full of copybook phrases and he volun-teered on his own that he was Hungarian. Outside. A few lights of farmhouses and lights by the river and patches of water in the fields lit up by the moon. I asked after Dobell. He appeared non-committal. "He has waited to see you."

He was waiting in that room with the oil paintings and the stuffed animal heads on the walls. I was prepared for the usual signs of old age, but not what appeared a different per-son. He was thinner, and this made him even smaller. His face was long and sallow, empty of any kind of expression. He rose to meet me, and his legs, bent at the knees, dragged across the floor. His hands hung near his chest like a pair of lifeless claws, and they shook. The left hand more than the other. When we grasped hands, there was no pressure in his. He said, "It is good to see you."

But there was no emotion in his face. All vitality seemed to be drained out of him. I must have talked to cover up my embarrassment. But he stopped me.

"I imagine this is a shock to you."

The left hand began to tremble more than the other, and the right hand went over to steady it.

He still spoke quietly but the voice was coarse and less distinct. And looking at him I wondered if the brain was still active in the man and was only imprisoned by this shell of a body. I had, professionally, diagnosed as soon as I entered that Dobell had Parkinson's disease.

At supper, the chauffeur was also the butler; but Dobell hardly touched the food.

"Tell me what happened to you. I saw in the paper that you did graduate."

I told him of the west, marriage, the family, wartime flying. He listened. But there were many silences. And there was an unhappy quality about the silences.

The cook was also the maid. She was also new. A German girl who spoke a shy English, in her twenties, pretty, with prominent cheekbones and high breasts.

I waited for him to tell me his story. But he didn't. Sometimes while I was talking the trembling hands, forgetting to hold on to each other, would creep up to the chest, and then he would remember and bring them down again.

The room hadn't changed. Except that his portrait was added to the others on the wall. It was painted the way I remembered him.

He appeared to be exhausted quickly, and we went to bed early. I had the same room as that first time. There were dried pussy willows in the small ornamental brass vase on the dresser, and a picture of himself, as he used to look, on his yacht, with me beside him. In one corner were several of the portable phonographs, and stacks of old records.

I don't know what time it was when I woke up. My light was still on and the wind was blowing the curtain from the window. I heard a cock crowing. I looked at the window—it was dark outside—and saw my face in the glass. I waited, and heard it crow again. Only instead of coming from the outside it seemed to come from somewhere in the house.

I put on my dressing gown and went out. There was a small night light on in the hall and I could see from the landing straight down to the large room with the paintings and stuffed animal heads. The room was in shadows except for a wedge of light from the door to the kitchen, which was open. Then I saw the chauffeur come out of the shadow of a corner, in his bare feet and long winter underwear. He was shuffling in front of the cook, who also had her clothes disarranged, her hair loose, and who kept making furtive little gestures of trying to escape, while the chauffeur kept following. He continued to stalk, shuffling his legs, and holding his hands lifelessly up in front of his chest in a cruel parody of Dobell. Then suddenly he leapt up, arms and legs flung out, and gave a crow of a cock.

Finally he cornered her—gave one more pathetic shuffle, then a vigorous crow—and hugging her to him like a bear, he lifted her off the ground. She immediately threw her arms around his neck, her legs fastened around his buttocks. Then he carried her inside the lighted door of the kitchen. I returned to my room, went back to bed, and listened as the clock in the house struck two.

In the morning I was awakened by a cock crowing not far from the window. It was the real thing this time, it sounded asthmatic. Then it was answered by another cock, some distance away. I dressed and went outside.

The morning had a fresh, clean smell. The air cool. In front of the house leading to the elms and cove, the lawn was beautifully kept—the slugs moved like pieces of slow rubber across the cut grass—but where I remembered similar lawns on the sides and behind the house, there were chickens.

I watched the birds come running—heads forward, flapping wings, sometimes leaving the ground—as the chauffeur brought pails of food to the small, rough, wooden houses, while the roosters stood on the roofs of the houses, stretched up their necks magnificently, and crowed.

From the kitchen a nice smell of coffee and the cook greeted me shyly and asked if I would like three or four eggs with the bacon. Then the chauffeur returned.

"You like my hens? I ask Mister Dobell if I can have them. He say to me OK. In the back. We start in the back but soon they need more room. Now we have the sides."

The cook said something in German to the chauffeur.

"You like a drive, sir? Mister Dobell never wake until midday."

I suggested we drive down the river to where the cottage was.

There were stilts on either side of it, all deserted. The old road had not been mended and the car climbed and heeled and swung sideways as it went in and out of the large holes. I went down the gravel path. My parents' cottage looked shabby compared to the stilts. Two planks were missing in the raised walk. The grass had overgrown. The flagpole was no longer on the lawn by the mountain ash. I looked around and for a while it brought back sadly the happy time I had here. I peered inside one of the windows. Whatever furniture was there was draped in white sheets.

The chauffeur watched me.

"I used to live here," I said.

"Once upon a time ago?"

"Yes."

"You now come back?"

"No. I don't think I could, even if I wanted to."

We drove back in silence. Passed the low fields. A few horses were grazing. A child stood on a hay wagon. The wind lifted her skirt above her head. She waved in our direction. I waved back.

Back to the house, and a chicken squawked as it ran in front of the car. Dobell was sitting in a large chair on the flat stone porch looking out to the elms and the river. He was bundled up in a black winter coat, hands in a muff. From the kitchen I could hear the chauffeur and the cook talking in German. They had a radio on, and a girl with a husky voice sang about "Real Love."

The chickens were supposedly kept behind the wire fences, but some had come through holes, or over the top, and were invading the front lawn and the approaches to the river. I watched a honey-brown rooster head off a couple of hens, then, as they settled down to peck at the earth, he nervously lifted his neck and crowed. And he was immediately answered from the other side of the house. And then another crowed even further away, before he replied.

Dobell sat there motionless.

A duck waded in the shallows. And across the river, swallows became thick like carbon dust from a sharpened pencil. While in the marshes splashes of red flew slowly by, then settled black on the reeds.

Occasionally we spoke, but it was only small talk. Our thoughts remained and we had nothing to say, because there was nothing for either of us to discover in each other. I knew I would leave soon. And I also knew that I would not come back, except as a tourist.

A VIEW
ON THE SEA

I

THERE WERE four gulls on the side of the roof across the street. And they kept up a continual noise. Sometimes they just opened their beaks and whined and took a few steps forward and whined again, while another would mutter a few sharp tongue things I used to do on the trumpet. Then, for some unknown reason, one of them would start to honk and let out a full-throated piercing sound, its whole body shaking. That went on for a few seconds, and back to the muttering. Two of them seemed to be muttering in a kind of conversation. Until, again, the piercing sound, the background mutter, and the pitiful faraway whine.

It was too hot to close the window. So I kept it open. The Back street was on the level with the front door, and the window faced a pink-painted cottage where a couple, with two small boys and a grandmother and grandfather, were down. Last week it was a honeymoon couple—this time three generations. They quarrelled outside. They scolded the children. The gulls. The cars going by a matter of inches from the window, blotting out the light. The passing visitors with their portables full on. I decided to go out and to try and work at night.

I went into Connie's Expresso and took a small blue table by the door. On the walls were blown-up black and white photographs of the harbour and the front. They were taken some time ago when the place was still full of fishing boats. A young girl in a green smock stood behind the counter. She was tall, heavy-set, and with an oval, expressionless face. A portable radio beside her played uninterrupted music. I had a hamburger and gave the girl one and six. Then a cup of black coffee, and that came to another sixpence. The sign behind the counter said *American Style*, but there wasn't much meat in the hamburger, and the onion was fried. Still, the coffee was strong. I had another cup, and smoked a Gauloise, and looked out.

The water in the bay was a thick, deep blue. The sun brilliant. It showed up the fields on top of the cliffs of the far shore; the lower Towans with the bald patches in the coarse grass; the long line at the bottom of dazzling sand; and the white lighthouse in the bay, a milk bottle with a camera stuck in its throat. Two French crabbers, anchored beside each other in the deep water, faced the wind. But there wasn't much of a breeze. Tourists walked by the open door. In shorts, slacks, sandals, bare feet. Holding hands. It was all very informal. No rush.

A couple of tourists came into the restaurant. An elderly man and a slightly stooped woman. He had a cane and a small grey moustache. He went to the counter and brought back some tea and wholemeal biscuits to their table.

"Is that your radio?" he said to the girl.

"Why," she said, "is it too loud?"

"No," the tourist man said.

"I bring it here for company. At home I never listen to the radio—"

"Where do you live?"

"In the Back Road."

"You don't know how lucky you are," the tourist man said. "You've got the most beautiful bay in England and the finest sand beaches—This place is wonderful—"

"I think it's a dump," she said. "It's so boring. There's nothing for us to do—"

"Have you been to Land's End?"

"No."

"And you live here?"

"Born here and lived here all my life."

"You'll have to be a good girl and take a look at Land's End."

"I'm the eldest of nine," the girl said. "I have to look after the others—"

"Like a mother," the tourist woman said quietly to her husband.

They dunked the wholemeal biscuits carefully in the tea. Then ate the biscuits. Then drank the tea.

"But I wouldn't like to live in St. Just," the man said. "You know St. Just—"

"No," she said, "I've never been to St. Just."

"—it's a very sinister place. We went over this morning and we met a girl there. She told us she leaves St. Just every Friday and comes into Penzance and stays in Penzance until Sunday night—"

"Penzance is a bit of a dump."

"Would you like to go to London?"

"It's funny," the girl said, brightening up, "I've never wanted to go to London. The place I'd like to go is South America. Ever since I was a kid I've always wanted to go to South America."

"That's some way from here," the tourist man said.

The girl smiled. "I guess I'll just have to marry someone with lots of money."

I finished my coffee and went out.

It was very pleasant along the front. Cool air, the smell of the sea, and so much for the eyes. I walked by the stone building of the Salvation Army, Woolworth's, the Shore Café. Music was leaking out of the Harbour Amusements, and at its entrance a boy, twirling a stick, gathered pink candy floss from a machine while a child rode a wooden rocking horse for sixpence. In front of Literature and Art, tourists were picking their way through the picture postcards. And others were picking their way through earthenware pots, mugs, soup bowls, small stone lighthouses, souvenirs at the Arts and Crafts. But there weren't many in the stores. They were lying on the dry sand of the harbour; they swam and splashed and stood in the clear shallows; they sat in striped deck chairs, green benches, along the wharf. The clock in the church, by the urinal, struck eleven. And the sun came down brutally. It caught the glass of thousands of windows facing the bay; the bright paint of the cottages and hotels; the stone of the terraces; the two piers; the blue water, and the close-cropped greens, browns, yellows of the far shore fields. Everything appeared so vivid and sharp, as if all these colours had just been freshly washed. I walked along the harbour, by the rails. The tide was going out. It left the fine shell sand ribbed, and in the depressions bits of glistening water. Young seagulls, their feathers speckled brown and white, were foraging behind the outgoing tide. One had found a dead spider crab, and poked at its underside.

On the long granite pier a row of parked cars was being cooked and at the pier's end a small boy sat fishing, watching the water. Seaweed clung to the granite sides—small hands severed at the wrist—below the waterline they waved lazily from side to side.

I left the harbour at the slipway, walked up a narrow passage, by another car park; past a Methodist chapel that was now an art gallery; past white- and cream-washed cottages with *Bed and Breakfast* signs. And I came to the beach. Quickly, I went down the hot stone steps, and onto dry sand. At an empty stretch I took off shoes, socks, shirt, trousers—

I had on swimming trunks underneath—rented a surfboard from the beach stores, ran across the hot, dry, then damp sand, through the warm pools, until I came to the shallows. The water was cold. I waded in, ran some of the breaking water over my arms and chest, and as the next breaker came in to spend itself out, I plunged in. The shock of cold water lasted briefly. And when I stood up I no longer thought the water was cold. I went further out with the board, half swimming, to get to the deeper water. At chest high I stopped, my back to the incoming waves. I let two go by. They broke before they reached me, and I leaned back into them. But I took the third. I watched it gather behind me, the dark line in its upper part advance, then, leaping onto the board and kicking my legs I was lifted and flung downward—felt the wood smack into the stomach, as I remembered from childhood jumping on a sleigh to go down a slope—and pointing downward I was carried in a glistening white cascade as the wave broke around me and water crashed into my face and eyes. When I felt the wave losing some of its momentum I twisted my body and the board from side to side so that I went through the water like a drunken driver sending patches of spray from one side then the other as I curved into the shallows, skimmed along in a few inches, until I was deposited onto the wet sand.

I went back and forward like this for about an hour. Sometimes without the board. Just arms and legs stretched fully out, and as the wave carried me forward I rotated my hands once over, and my body followed, turning round and round in the salt water until I sank. Then, pleasantly exhausted, I walked back across the sand and lay down to be dried by the sun.

It was a magnificent beach, the finest I had ever seen. An elongated C, lying on its side, facing the breakers, the Atlantic, and the horizon. Within it was a smaller C made by a line of dead seaweed and pebbles that the high tide had left. The sand within this smaller C was a light tan colour, and damp. A few boulders were embedded in the wet sand. The outgoing tide had made small pools around the boulders. Children were playing happily in the pools. In a long strip that curved the entire length of the beach, in between the two Cs, people lay on hot, dry sand; or in the shallow crater-like holes they had scooped out of it.

The sun was beginning to burn. I turned over on my back and caught a light breeze. It ruffled the flags of England, Wales, Scotland, Ireland—on top of sandcastles that a tanned boy, his hair the colour of linen, had made not far away—and the seagulls' feathers he had stuck in others. And brought with it the sweet smell of suntan lotion.

Just above me, on the slope of earth above the beach, was a cemetery. Around me, scattered in clusters on the strip of hot sand, families were stretched out. Surfboards were standing upright, stuck in the sand, by their heads. The sun caught the boards and reflected their white tops. They looked like the tombstones on the slopes.

I told myself, I must remember that, and use it someplace. But I should have given it more thought. For the kind of images that one finds in a particular place are not as accidental as they appear. Surfboards around people lying on the sand getting brown—tombstones in a cemetery. Still, at the time I wasn't interested in this place. I was living in a book I was working on, set in winter, in Montreal.

For the next two weeks of July I did this walk and swim every morning. I would wake up around 9:15, just after the postman went by, have a light breakfast, then make up a list, do my shopping, wander around, have a coffee at Connie's, go surfing, then sunbathe on the beach. And in the afternoon, on the beach again, then more wandering around. In the evening I worked until half past two.

By the beginning of August I felt I knew the place and it gave one a wonderful feeling of possession and confidence. From the height of the terraces or the bus stop it looked picture-postcard but with a 3-D view; a small bent finger flung out from the mainland into the Atlantic with the inside of the finger, the harbour, and the outside, the beach. Then into the place—everyone walked on the road—a kind of valley with a lot of tight little streets and condemned cottages (with outside water taps and soapy water stagnant in the gutter) that were bought by tourists who came here with their savings to live out their lives, and pushed the locals into the council houses on the outskirts. There were brass piskies, brass galleons, for knockers; and low ceilings, and narrow stairs that went straight up soon after you opened the door—the double doors like horse-stables—and outside pipes painted to look like varicose veins. Castrated cats sunned themselves in the middle of the streets. And budgerigars were kept in cages. And as you walked on various levels it appeared all angles with small turnings off, dead ends, and narrow connecting tunnels. It reminded me of a doll's house. Except for the outsize barn shapes of the Methodist and Wesleyan chapels.

Then at dusk. Watching the long sunsets on the beach. When the wet sand was flaked pink and the pastel colours of the French crabbers, going across towards the shelter of the bay, were caught by the last rays of the sun. And later. The front lit as a stage set; lit from the inside like so many pumpkins. And in the dark water of the harbour the long brilliant scratches of yellow, green, faint red, white, from the streetlights and the cafés' neons. And still later. After midnight. Standing at the end of the pier. The moon out. The water sparkling. And I could hear the French sailors talking on the crabbers out in the bay.

When it rained the Scala (you could hear the soundtrack outside) and the Royal had lineups. The tourists huddled in raincoats on the beach, stood by the rails or in the narrow doorways, looking miserable like a lot of wet birds. I tried the library. It was small, drab, but not gloomy. The books were so old that it became a kind of grab bag. For the titles were rubbed out with use and neglect so that picking a book you didn't know whether it would be *The Gun-Shy Kid,* or a first edition of Kirby's *Golden Dog,* printed in Montreal, with illustrations, falling to bits.

Then there was the morning exodus from the bed and breakfast places. Entire families came down the various slopes that led to the beaches carrying picnic lunches, plastic beach balls, portable radios, towels, flippers, paperbacks, surfboards. And returned, tired, the same way, at dusk. Then dressing up for the night, sunburnt and tanned, they promenaded around the front, Fore Street, the two piers, the Back Roads, the island, went into a crowded pub, a café, a restaurant ...

It was very pleasant for a while to just wander around and mix with people who were here for the avowed purpose of doing nothing.

I have gone into this place at some length as it is this place, as much as anything, that is responsible for what happens. It was, at first, so colourful and remote, and so un-English, that I didn't think I could ever become bored with it. But I did. And it didn't take so very long.

For all its magnificent scenery, and sunshine, I began to miss people. It wasn't enough, I found, just being surrounded by tourists. I would wake up on a beautiful hot morning, a blue sky, hardly a breeze, and walk to the harbour. And watch ... But for all the buoyancy, the jazzed-up activity, the gaiety of the outward appearance, there was so much inertia to the place. You didn't have to do very much. The landscape did it all so brilliantly and monotonously.

And I was tired of seeing the same kind of person around me. Every two weeks a new batch would arrive. And you could trace the way their paleness and enthusiasm disappeared. It began on Monday morning buying postcards, writing them on the green benches of the front. Then soaking on the sand. By the third day their determined gaiety would have taken in an uneventful trip "around the bay" or "to the lighthouse" or "to see the seals." More soaking in the sun. And at night wandering through the streets, all eyes and comments about the smallness, the quaint cottages, the cobblestone streets with the names Virgin, Teetotal, Salubrious. And in the second week buying presents from the bric-a-brac shops along the front. And then a sudden flatness when they realized that, apart from what they had already done, there was little else for them to do. So that in the last few days they were looking forward to leaving this place for "home." Boredom is such an essential part of a seaside town.

I began to spend a great deal of time in the Harbour Amusements playing the pinball machines, when I could get a free one. I enjoy the colours, the balls moving, things lighting up, the *sput-sput* noises. Once you get a ball going there is something inevitable about it.

Perhaps it was because my writing wasn't going. I just lost interest in the book on Montreal. I could no longer become concerned with the antics of my hero, an optimistic Irish immigrant trying to survive his first Canadian winter.

At night I sit by the desk until my eyes become watery, and I get sleepy. I listen. The surf on the beach. Just one steady noise. The cars have stopped. The lights have been turned off. No sounds, except the sea. I go out along the Back Road to the beach. The breaking waves, white scars in the dark. They gash the black in several places. The gashes grow wider. They join. One white line the length of the beach. Then I come back. Go up the stairs. And to bed.

I tried all sorts of devices to snap out of this lethargy. I tried waking up extra early one morning and walked along the deserted front. But all that happened was that the gulls seemed extra loud. I saw several labourers walking to work, gas-mask webbing slung over their shoulders. And the *slap-slap* of water against the tied boats in the harbour sounded like bacon frying. Then, tired, I watched the sunrise coming from behind the Towans, over the bay. A sleepy policeman stood by the rails and watched it as well.

I tried going out with a few of the remaining Cornish fishermen. But they were old men, suspicious of my intentions. In any case the novelty of the physical act soon wore out—it was a kind of slumming.

In a moment of desperation, on a rainy morning, I went and had my ears syringed. Small, hard, purplish lumps came out with the warm water. And then to hear the resonance of one's voice. I went out, talking to myself, and listening to the sound of my voice, the different sounds the rain made on water, asphalt, wood. The wonderful sound of a car's engine, the sound of tires on the wet surface. And in Connie's hearing conversation all around me. Then back to the cottage. Hearing the clock in the room. The sound my shirt made as it crumpled. The rifle shots of my typewriter.

I found I would wake up and have to give myself small destinations in order to get through the day. And there were mornings I used to wake up with nothing to look forward to except perhaps a letter.

In the end it was this overwhelming boredom of the place and the tourists that made me seek out the people who actually live here. I don't want to sound self-righteous about this, for I owe them a great deal, but at the time I didn't realize that I was the one being used. They needed me as much as I needed them. For they suffered from another kind of boredom. And the way the residents fought theirs was by having parties.

There was a party of a kind every night but the main ones were on Friday and Saturday. They began at the Sloop. One of the most uncomfortable pubs I know when it is crowded. You stand in the narrow passageway and people brush against you and drinks get spilled. Before closing time bottles are bought and everyone makes his way to wherever the party is given. If you were a stranger and bought a bottle, you were invited back.

There was a wonderful feeling of comradeship, a kind of fantasy of brotherhood. People came down and were what they wanted to be. If someone called himself a writer or a painter, then you were that, and accepted as such by everyone. There was no examination of credentials. The bait was the sea, the peeling off of clothes on the beach, the three hundred miles from London, the Mediterranean colours; and a lot of people, like myself, anxious for some excitement.

These were the people Bill Stringer met at the round of parties in the summer of 1959. Abe and Nancy Gin—Baby Bunting—Rosalie Grass—Jimmy Stark (whom everyone called Starkie)—Hugh and Lily Wood—Albert Rivers—Carl Darch—Helen Greenway—Nat Bubis—Oscar Preston. As the professional writer he took pride in being, he had them down for characters that he would someday use.

II

The first of these I got to know were Nancy and Abe Gin. I met Abe at the Sloop at lunchtime. We got to talking, found we were both Canadians, and when the pub closed he invited me back to the Celebrity for a meal. Abe was a sentimental, generous Jew from Winnipeg. Romantic and wanting to be liked by everyone. He had come over to England in 1949 as an academic. Spent a summer holiday in St. Ives. Was bitten by the "creative life," and the people here. Decided to stay and paint. Unfortunately he hadn't much talent, or discipline. But he looked like the public conception of a painter. Especially in summer when he wore his faded blue jeans and black high-neck fisherman's sweater. The summer's crop of art students, shorthand typists, and tourists, who came to St. Ives for "the artists," inevitably fell for Abe's leonine face, curly black hair splashed with white, and large melancholy eyes. And at forty-three he went out of his way to encourage them. In winter he received a daily allowance of a pound from Nancy and spent most of his time in the Sloop nursing half-pints of draught beer and playing table-skittles. He suffered from indigestion and belched often; when anyone heard him he excused himself by saying "Oxford."

Nancy was a plumpish, short woman of thirty-six, pale anemic colouring to her face. But there was a strong structure about it. It was almost a man's face. It was far stronger formed than Abe's. She comes from one of the London suburbs, south of the Thames. And came down in the summer of 1950, just out of art school, on a holiday, and fell for Abe's considerable charm. They married. Had a rough time for the first six years. Until she realized that Abe would never be able to support them with his painting. She then opened, with borrowed money, the Celebrity, and runs it very efficiently. Chopin, Tchaikovsky, Brahms come steadily from the record player by the cash desk. And paper flowers and paper grass hide the lamps hanging from the ceiling.

As Abe has become less Jewish, Nancy seems to deliberately cultivate it. Her specialty is hot latkes, three for a shilling. And I've seen her mocking Abe, when he returns from the Sloop early to get another pound. "Well, Ginsberg,"—(normally she only called him "you")—"what is it you want?" She also affects Yiddish attitudes. I was with her in the Sloop one night sitting on a bench by a long table watching customers coming to the bar for drinks. "He has a marvellous capacity," she said of a red-faced man in a navy blazer. This, I discovered, had nothing to do with his ability at the bar, the dining table, or in bed. But his ability to make money. She is drawn to people with money. Although she is very generous herself (to those who come to her, especially if they are young and struggling painters and writers). You can see the mother hen spreading her wings. She wants to be involved. And she can do this only through other people's lives. Abe and Nancy no longer sleep together—at least so gossip has it.

I have found it difficult to meet anyone here for the first time without having some preconceived idea of that person. For all the people here seem to live on is gossip. They gossip continually, about one another, and of people they haven't met. I first heard of Baby Bunting when I asked Nancy about an invitation card that was on the mantel above the fireplace in her living room. It said:

TOMMY IS TWENTY-ONE

Sir Louis Behnke, Bt.,
invites you to a cocktail party
at the Riviera Hotel
St. Ives, Cornwall,
between 6 p.m.–8:30p.m.
on
Friday, August 6th, 1959
to celebrate
T. L. Hudson's
coming of age
RSVP

"Baby owns the Riviera Hotel," Nancy said, "and likes boys and innocence—but he's ambidextrous. Except that all his girls he calls Camel. His wife goes in for the same sort of thing. Every winter he makes a tour of the slum places in the North and picks up what good-looking boys and girls he can. Then brings them here in the spring. Makes them waiters and waitresses in his hotel. And proceeds to corrupt them. It's easy. He just stuffs them with expensive food and money. Gives them presents. Lets them use his Rolls. And when he's had what he's wanted out of them, he discards them. They can't go back where they came from. So they drift, from one seaside resort to another."

"Baby really comes from the English aristocracy," Abe said. "But he doesn't belong there. He's an eccentric. He says he bought the Riviera because he figures St. Ives is the safest place to be in, in England, when a bomb is dropped. He'll quote you bits of the Bible to prove it—"

"St. Ives is mentioned in the Bible?" I said.

"No," Abe said, "that a bomb will be dropped."

"Until then," Nancy said, "he takes rejuvenating pills, tries a few sexual experiments, and has a party every Friday at the hotel . . ."

That Friday night I went with Abe and Nancy to the Riviera Hotel. It faced the bay. There were about twenty French crabbers anchored in the deep water. With their lights on they looked like lit candles moving gently in the dark. The party was in a ballroom adjoining the one used by the hotel's paying guests. Before you came to the ballroom you had to pass through a long bar. A few couples were already on the floor dancing to a three-piece band; but most of the guests were in the bar.

I met Baby Bunting.

"Been here long?" he said.

"A couple of weeks."

He had got up from a green swaying couch that stood near the far wall of the bar, against a painted mural of old St. Ives dark with fishing boats. In his early fifties, tall, thin blond hair, a bronzed face with a small mouth, hardly any visible lips, glasses. He might have had a good figure once but he had put on weight.

"How long are you staying?" Baby Bunting said.

"I don't know—maybe the winter."

"Then we'll be seeing each other," he said, and went to greet another of his guests, Albert Rivers, a composer, of thirty-four, with blond wavy hair that had a bit of red in it, and a worn baby-face. Albert Rivers lived in a cottage on the moors, and came in on Fridays and Saturdays for the parties and free drinks. His total income for the year was a hundred and four pounds—not quite what Baby Bunting received every week.

The three-piece band was playing "Stardust" and then a polka, and a young, tall German—a student who was here for the summer to improve his English—was stomping around the room with a handsome young English girl on holiday.

A short, stocky man—with a shaggy mane of grey hair, a smug expression on his weak face—was talking to a pretty Canadian girl called Thelma Eskin. She was twenty-four, but her small nose, blond straight hair cut square with a fringe, and light grey eyes made her look even younger—until she opened her mouth and the teeth betrayed the youthfulness of her appearance. The man with the grey hair was called Nat Bubis, a painter. His father invented a lubricant that everyone uses. It cost about a penny a jar to make and sells for two shillings and sixpence. It has allowed him to have a fine house in Carbis Bay, a placid French wife who has borne him two daughters and whom he leaves for three or four months a year, a cook, a gardener, and one of the studios facing the beach with a bar in it, a TV, a large maroon fitted carpet. The girl lives in the Back Road, in one of the condemned cottages, on National Assistance. She has a small child. The father of the child moved to Paris on a Canadian government grant, to paint. She earns a few extra pounds a week by posing for Nat in his studio. And he takes her and the child for rides in his Bentley along the moors.

"Hello, Albert. How's tricks?" Nat said.

"I'm mellowing furiously," Albert Rivers said for the third time in the last half-hour to three different people who had asked him the same question. "I had a run-in with the Labour Exchange this ah-ah-afternoon. They wanted to know why I ha-ha-ha-haven't been paying stamps f-f-f-for the last five years. I told them I didn't ur-ur-earn enough. 'How much do you ur-earn, Mister Rivers?' the man in the Exchange said. 'Tu-tu-two pounds a week,' I said. 'Then how do you l-l-live?' he said. 'How do the birds live?' I said. He was so bwee-bwee— he was so bewildered he let me go."

They laughed and Albert Rivers felt he could move on.

As soon as he left them Nat said to the girl, "I wish Albert didn't feel that whenever he speaks he has to be funny."

"I know," she said. "I asked him earlier, 'When did you get back?' 'Last week,' he said. 'How was Italy?' 'M-m-m-marvellous,' he said, 'bloody marvellous. See N-N-Nipples and die.' Did you hear about Dolly?"

"What about?"

"She's going to have a baby."

Nat drew on his cigarette and exhaled. The smoke went into his right eye. He closed his eye and grimaced with his mouth. Then rubbed his eye. And for a moment looked as if he had just heard some very bad news.

"I thought Sam's sperms were no good," Nat said. "They're supposed to have no heads, or is it no tails—"

"She's not carrying Sam's."

"Oh," Nat said and looked anxiously around the room. "Whose—?"

"I don't know. Hugh told me that Dolly was two months pregnant."

In one corner of the ballroom a short slender man with a sunburned face, blond straight hair, blue eyes, and an air of alert gentleness was the banker of a homemade roulette wheel. He had an old portable gramophone and, with white chalk, had divided the green baize cover of the turntable into segments. The largest segment was exactly half of the turntable; it gave two-to-one odds. The smallest, a segment of only five degrees, paid twenty to one. The man spun the turntable and when it stopped he collected all the money from the segments and paid off the winners. The man's name was Hugh Wood. He had been a flying officer in the RAF during the war and now was a photographer. He photographed the sea, the coastline, the beaches, the farms, the moors. They were photographs without people. His wife, Lily, came from the same background. They met, just after the war, on the Lelant golf course, by the sand dunes, and the twelfth-century granite church. And two months later got married.

Both their parents belonged to a small colony of Englishmen and their wives who had gone out as young men and women to India, Burma, Africa, the Far East. And—as the Empire was coming to an end—had come back to live out their lives in West Country seaside towns. It was strange, at first, to see someone who had been in charge of a territory almost as large as Wales going through the turning narrow streets with his wife's carrier bag to do the shopping. Or the still-attractive wife of a former bank manager in Pakistan, washing on her hands and knees her outside granite steps. As I walked by she looked up.

"If my servants could see me now."

Money, the mild climate, the slow pace, the sea air, all helped to preserve them. They took considerable care with their appearance. And looked ten to fifteen years younger than they were. But they also looked as if they had some of the stuffing knocked out of them. Especially the men. The women tended to spend a lot of time playing bridge, the men golf. Some of their children, soon as they were old enough, left England for New Zealand, Australia, Canada. But for Hugh and Lily—though they were born abroad—St. Ives was, for the present, home.

I would often see Hugh when I went out early in the morning. A camera around his neck. "The morning light is soft," he said. "It's good to take pictures in." Or else his voice would show excitement. "You can't miss. The landscape does most of it for you."

One morning, before six, I saw him walking along the front. We were the only ones out. I said, "You're up early."

"The goldfish woke me up," he said and smiled. "It was the sound they made opening and closing their mouths. I thought at first that there was a leak of some kind in the room."

I would also see him, with a pair of binoculars, birdwatching on the Island. "It's the best place before a storm. They all fly by." Or birdwatching at the estuary, at Lelant, when the tide was out. Or else I would see him and Lily, on Saturday afternoons, on the island flying kites of large painted butterflies with their two small daughters.

People danced and drank and talked and some gambled at the gramophone. And there was a sprinkling of new faces in evening dress who had come in from the paying-guests' ballroom. Baby Bunting was on the swaying couch with a handsome blond boy, not a line in the young tanned face. The boy was talking about gliding.

". . . and then you release. And for about ten or fifteen seconds there is a moment of utter silence."

Baby Bunting was too moved to say anything.

"—but it doesn't last very long."

He put his hand around the boy's shoulder, leaned over, and kissed the boy's cheek.

A woman whose prettiness had not long faded, flushed with drink and sad at being thirty-five, went over, unsteadily, to a man sitting on the floor in a corner talking to some people. She stood behind the man and lifted her dress then lowered it over the man's head, hiding his face and shoulders. "Woo-woo," she said with a short laugh at the others. "Woo-woo." Then she lifted her dress off the surprised man and went across the floor, back to the bar.

A middle-aged couple in evening dress who had wandered in from the paying-guests' ballroom decided at half past one that they had had enough. While the band was playing "I Only Have Eyes for You," they began to walk off the floor, the man visibly disgusted: ". . . people who live off milking other people, like seaside towns, are corrupt anyway—"

As they went out of the ballroom they passed a couple who had also stopped dancing. They seemed totally absorbed in each other. They looked into each other's face, made telescopes out of their hands, put them around their eyes, touched hands, and said "Woo-woo, woo-woo," like a pair of owls. It obviously meant something to them, but not to anyone else.

Around two Abe decided to go out for some fresh air. He opened the glass doors and went onto the balcony. A warm summer night. He could hear the three musicians playing "Kiss Me, Honey, Honey, Kiss Me," and saw the lights and reflections of the French crabbers, the thin blue light at the end of the pier, the lighthouse flashing every fifteen seconds, the moon, the stars. How quiet it all is, he thought. A small beach was just below him, as if some large shovel pushed hard into the land and scooped out from the rocks and earth an opening. Two lights were still on in the terraces. And he watched a car move along the dark front, its headlights raking and reflecting in the passing windows; then it went up the slope from the slipway and disappeared. The musicians had stopped. And only the surf came quietly across. What a pretty place it is, he thought. And he knew he would never leave it.

A girl came out and joined him.
"Hello."
"Tired of inside."
"A bit. It's nice out here."
A record was now playing "Mack the Knife." The music came out to them and the lights from the crabbers moved gently up and down.
"Where are you staying?"
"In Academy Steps."
"My studio is not far from there—right at the top of the steps—"
One of the lights from the terrace went out and the strip of black of the land became thin like a cardboard cut-out.
"Isn't the water beautiful," she said.
They watched the exhausted waves sliding over the sand of the small beach below them.

"Do you feel like a swim?" Abe said.

"You mean now—"

"Why not."

He suddenly realized that she was only around seventeen or eighteen. Pretty, with black hair. Her eyes were bright, big, clear, and wet.

"Let's go tomorrow morning instead," she said.

"OK."

"I bet you won't come," she said.

"I will," Abe said, "if I say I will. I'll leave the door of the studio unlocked. Come and wake me up—"

"I'll surprise you," she said mischievously. "I'll be there at six."

They went back inside. Had a couple of dances. Then someone else took her away from him.

He was awakened next morning by shaking and an eager young face, that he did not at first recognize, only inches away.

"What time is it," Abe asked.

"Five past six. You coming for the swim?"

"Sure." He hesitated. "Sure."

He put on his blue trunks under his jeans, a dark blue sport shirt, and they went out armed with large striped towels. Fore Street was empty. Garbage was stacked outside the small stores. And in the Digey, outside the bed and breakfast places, bathing suits were hanging from half-open windows. An elderly woman was energetically washing her stone steps, and a smell of disinfectant came from her doorstep and the gutter. Gulls made a terrible noise. One flew low, wings outstretched, nearly touching both sides of the street.

"I'm not very good at remembering names," said Abe.

"Sylvia."

"Mine's Abe—"

"I know," she said. "The Canadian painter. What part of Canada?"

"Winnipeg."

"I'm from Reading. I go to college there."

"I once taught at a college in Canada," Abe said proudly. "I expect to be coming up to London later this month. Maybe we could take in a show or something—"

"I'd like that," she said, "very much." And gave him a shy smile, inviting him to talk.

They came to the long beach. It was empty. A few gulls were standing above the tideline. Where they walked they left small anchors on the washed surface of the sand. The water was halfway in, on an outgoing tide. And with each breaking wave it churned and pushed up sand and small pebbles. And as the water was sucked back it left some of the pebbles embedded in the sand with a small sharp V in front of each pebble.

Excitedly she ran in. He followed her. They swam beside each other, both doing the crawl, parallel to the beach. He turned around and she overtook him. He didn't stay in very long. She remained a few minutes longer, floating on her back. Then ran back to him and the towels. They were both shivering.

"That was my last swim for the summer," she said. "I'm leaving on this morning's Riviera."

She put on a blue bathing robe and removed her wet bathing suit from beneath it, dried herself, then put on her coloured summer skirt and white blouse. While he did a quick change using a large towel.

"When do you think you'll come up?" she said, rubbing her hair with a towel.

"In two weeks' time," he said, knowing it was a lie.

She spread out the driest towel and they sat on the fine yellow sand in a slight dune and looked out across the empty beach and at the gulls facing the wind and watched the waves breaking and the water flattening rapidly on the sand then sliding back.

"What are you thinking?" she said.

"I just realized," he said, looking out to the miles of sea. "There's nothing in between us and North America." And as soon as he said it, he regretted it.

"It's something I would never have thought of," she said.

There were times Abe felt hopelessly alone, and then at some trivial sight—like looking at the horizon or seeing a second-rate Canadian film or running out into the streets at the first sight of snow—it touched him where he was most vulnerable.

"Do you think you'll go back?"

"I don't know," he said. "I'd like to think I still can," he added without conviction. "How about some coffee?"

"Fine," she said.

They smelled the wild garlic as they passed the cemetery. At the top the road turned and sloped steeply down, ending in the sea. They seemed to be walking right into the bay, the lighthouse, the colours of the far shore.

"I think you're very lucky to live down here," she said.

"I think so, too," said Abe, suddenly feeling refreshed and lightheaded.

The only place open on the front was Connie's and they went in and had two cups of coffee and smoked cigarettes and held hands while they both brought out their small accomplishments for each other's approval. She gave him her address and phone number.

"You will get in touch."

"Yes," he said. "I will."

He walked her slowly back to Academy Steps and said goodbye outside a yellow-painted door that had "Cat's Cradle" in black letters above the letter slot. And went back to his studio now feeling the lack of sleep. Why do I go and do things like this? He didn't think he would ever see her again. But he thought about her. And told this episode to several people. How a strange, seventeen- or eighteen-year-old girl—a child—that he didn't even make a pass at, had woken him up to go swimming at six. And he went. It was to become one of Abe's fondest memories.

III

The height of the season came in the middle of August. The single-line train went to St. Erth and filled up with weary tourists from the mainline station who had come with immense patience in crowded compartments all the way from London, Manchester, Birmingham, and Glasgow. The single-line train brought them around the estuary at Lelant. Past the mud flats cracked like a jigsaw puzzle with some of the pieces missing and the curlews, oyster-catchers, plovers, gulls. The shabby houseboats with bed and breakfast signs. The birchwatchers out with binoculars. Climbed by the golf course, sounding like a water pump. Past the Towans, the squat Cornish church, the caravan site. Stopped at Carbis Bay to let some off. Then down the slope to their first glimpse of the bay, the harbour, the front, and at the narrow siding, above Porthminster Beach, it stopped and emptied its thousands into the fresh and glittering air.

This week was "Swindon week," an entire factory came down for its annual holiday; next would be "Newcastle"; the week after, "polio victims"; then "the nuns." Local girls who worked during the day in the shops up Tregenna Hill and finished at six went home for tea then back to work at the bric-a-brac stores along the front until eleven at night. Ice cream lineups formed by the slipway at Harts and in the post office. And there were lineups for hot pasties and for fish and chips. Outside Connie's, a wooden stand had stale bread in brown paper bags, "Seagull Food 3d a Bag." Nothing was wasted. The man who swept the streets for the local council in the morning put on a black and gold cape, a cocked hat in the afternoon and, with a handbell and "God Save the Queen," became the town crier.

There was the season's drowning when the pale girls from the mattress factory came running like schoolgirls at an outing onto the long beach giggling with excitement. While the maroons cascaded into the bay after the explosion and the blue-painted lifeboat was pulled by its neat tractor along the length of the front—a practice run for the tourists' cameras. There was the morning's token fish auction at the slipway. A few congers, dogs, skates, rays, lay on the concrete; the wooden cart and horse backed through their slime. And as they went across the wet sand of the harbour to the beached boats for the next load the wind blew through the spokes of the large wheels, making from the slime fantastic balloon shapes.

Otherwise the holiday crowds smothered what signs there were that said a different kind of life was going on. People died and funeral cards appeared on the fishermen's shelters. But a local death in summer did not have the same dominant effect in the town as one in winter. There remained, however, a few gestures. Sunday. When nearly everything was closed and from the chapels and churches the hymns and organs boomed out into the warm streets. And afterwards the walks; by the cemetery, along the moors, or to Tregenna Woods. While the tourists headed for another day on the beaches. And met the locals around teatime at the slipway where the Salvation Army held its regular singsong. Thousands overflowed along the front, the harbour, their voices booming out—"This is my story. This is my song . . ." While cars in the narrow streets scraped the sides of cottages blotting out the light, and the surf between the piers churned up thousands of discarded crab legs. And on the magnificent beach the tide left behind dead seaweed and used contraceptives.

The only people in the place who did not look well were the Cornish housewives who took in bed and breakfast. You could recognize them by their tired, pale faces.

Also in August the season's parties were at their peak.

This Friday it was Hugh and Lily's turn for a party. Hugh's "Atlantic Waves" had a large bare room on the ground floor and French doors that led straight on to Porthgwidden Beach. A bonfire was burning on the sand and couples were sitting or standing around the fire having hot dogs and hamburgers and wandered back inside to fill up with more drink or to dance. That's how they all started. After the pubs closed; an easy, relaxed, gaiety . . .

But by 1:00 a.m. a man had a girl down on the slope of the stairs, his mouth fastened on hers, and she couldn't get up. Another had a girl in a corner; her dress was up above her knees. Two young effeminate boys were dancing together. There were several girls in long black stockings and loose sweaters. There were girls who were no longer young. There were mothers dancing with their sons by a former marriage. And all the time the record player played and things were happening in the dark corners. But like a damp firecracker they only fizzed and went out; rarely did they explode into life. As the night went on there was the invitation to come to the darkened kitchen. Or to one of the untidy bedrooms upstairs. Strangers came up to women and asked if they were lesbians. And strangers came up to young men and asked if they were queers. A young girl with a very long neck and a small snake head was dancing with a stocky middle-aged woman who had fuzzy black hair. Suddenly the fuzzy-haired woman forced the girl to the floor. The girl called out. Two men tried to pull the woman off the girl. But she held on, eyes closed, her mouth on the girl's long neck. Another man joined the two, and in the end the men had to drag both the girl and the woman by their legs across the floor, across the sand of the beach and into the shallows before they were separated. A tall, strikingly dark girl, with a long squarish face, dressed like a flapper of the twenties, began to sing.

My mummy told me
That she would buy me
A rubber dolly
If I was good.

A very thin young woman with short black hair and a sad, simple face came over to a man wearing a black shirt. "Hello, Patrick. Have fun in Tangier?" she said in an accent that had in it a trace of cockney.

"Just as much fun as anyone has running away from things," the man in the black shirt said, and offered her a cigarette.

But when I told her
I kissed a soldier
She would not buy me
That rubber dolly ...

"I was in Penzance yesterday." A neat small man with fine features (slowly undermined by the extra fat) was talking, in broken English, to a young girl with glasses. "And a priest came along Market Jew Street. He was walking in the middle of the road. No one gave him any attention. About ten seconds behind him came a huge workman carrying a large TV aerial straight up, holding the stem by his belly, like people do with a cross. Immediately people stopped on both sides of the street and watched the man holding the TV aerial pass. That's all you would need to make your point. It's a wonderful opening shot."

The man's name was Oscar. He was referred to as the Polish Count and he had made films in Vienna before the war. Now he had the very English surname of Preston and taught French and German in the local grammar school. He was full of "opening shots" of films he would never make ...

Hugh and Lily's party ended in a fight, a swinging match, because someone was out too long on the sands with someone else's wife. The party didn't actually end; a few remained to finish off the rum punch, the bottles of cheap wine, and what remained in the beer barrel.

If anyone had been out shortly after three that night they would have seen a fairly tall man walking unsteadily along the front, going from side to side. He saw himself in the plate-glass window of the Shore Café and began to walk on tiptoes, then bowed to his reflection, and did a little dance. Then he went to the harbour rails, leaned over, and gestured, encouragingly, with his hand to the clear water as it slid up and down the granite steps. Then, pulling himself together and with great dignity, he did a low bow to the empty front. And quickly walked up the alley of cobblestones, between Woolworth's and Stevens Tours, and came out in Fore Street. As he started to walk down Fore Street he slipped and fell. He tried to raise himself but couldn't. Beside him was a puddle. He began to shout. "Ferryman. Take me across. I want to go home. Ferryman. Take me across—"

The man lying on the damp street was Abe Gin.

IV

I didn't worry very much about the book I wasn't writing. Getting through the day was quite easy. I would sleep late in my darkened room, drop in to Connie's for a coffee and later to the Celebrity for lunch. After lunch I would go to the beach, perhaps surf, and then join the others on the sand and soak in the sun. We were all a nice brown. The afternoons were pretty lethargic. In the evenings we came to life ...

We were lying on the beach on this hot, still, late August afternoon. Hugh and Lily Wood, Nat Bubis, the blond girl Thelma Eskin, who was posing for Nat—her eight-year-old daughter was happily playing by herself in the wet sand—

myself, Helen Greenway, and a happy, sensual little man, Peter Kroll, who owned a smart restaurant in London and had appeared at Hugh's party. Peter Kroll had an inexhaustible curiosity about Canada and Helen Greenway. She was lying beside him in a white bathing suit, very white against the colour of her body. Helen Greenway at thirty-four was a spidery kind of woman with an anxious voice, a largish head, and a nervousness that made her physically exciting. She gave the impression of a tense, playful kitten, wearing an old face, and being very brittle. She had a neat, whitewashed cottage along the front that she inherited from her mother, who had come down here to retire and to paint. I also knew, from gossip, that Helen was a small-time actress, divorced twice. I could see Peter Kroll pretend to look sideways, but it was to admire her figure. Helen Greenway kept it that way by going out after a heavy meal and being sick in the toilet.

"If you make people do routine jobs," Nat Bubis was saying, "fifty weeks in the year, then give them two weeks' holiday, they don't know how to enjoy themselves. They don't know what to do on holiday except go back to those days before they started to work. So they come here and undress and behave like children, chasing a ball and splashing each other in the water..."

Gulls wheeled over. Their shadows skimming across the dry white-yellow sand. From somewhere came a train's whistle and further away a church bell clanged twice. And the surf continued to break, carrying the bathers with their boards into the beach.

"I guess you're right," Hugh answered Nat, because no one else had bothered. "Did you know that Elizabeth is pregnant?"

Hugh was lying on his back, slightly propped up in a sand hole, wearing light tan shorts.

"Is she going to keep this one," Nat said, "or go to see Gurland in Penzance?"

"I think she'll go to Gurland," Hugh said.

"I bet Gurland's fixed just about every woman down here," Peter Kroll said. "Why doesn't he charge—?"

"Because he doesn't believe in unwanted children," Helen said. "He's a socialist."

"He sure is," Lily said with scorn. "He takes his time, keeps you coming to see him for weeks, and has his kind of fun—I had to threaten I'd report him if he didn't leave me alone."

"Did you hear what happened to Maria? Shall I tell . . ." Hugh appealed timidly to Lily, wanting her approval.

"You will anyway," Lily said.

"You know Maria, the Swedish girl," Hugh said. "She was having an affair with Baby Bunting's Tommy—she's pregnant."

No one seemed very concerned. And how could we be, for we vaguely saw Maria at one of the parties. The sun was hot. Helen turned over on her stomach and Thelma Eskin sat up to see where her daughter was. Her eyes finally found her by the shallows watching a lifesaver ride the waves on a board-like boat, legs in stirrups, leaning back, and overturning in the shallows. It was very hot and still and we all felt lazy and apathetic.

"I thought I knew this place," Hugh said slowly to no one in particular. "But our black kitten, after we let it out for the night, didn't come back. So I got up early in the morning and went out to look for it. It would be hungry then. And looking for the kitten—I began to see all sorts of things I hadn't seen before. The streets seemed to be full of stray dogs. I found alleyways, waste-grounds, passages that I didn't know existed."

"Did you find the kitten?" Nat Bubis interrupted.

"No."

Again we were silent.

I watched a blue and white French crabber come gracefully across the front of the beach, its mizzen the colour of dried blood.

"This is really a Chekhov situation," Helen said. "All we do here is talk. Nothing happens."

"I'll write a Chekhov story for you," Hugh said, "about this place."

"You," Lily said grimly. "You may have been able to fly airplanes once, but when it comes to people they're nothing but pieces of cardboard shit. What a shit you are."

Nobody said anything.

Hugh looked embarrassed.

"I thought we agreed to forget it."

"I can't forget it," Lily said. And stood up, took her clothes and towel, and walked briskly away.

"We had another row," Hugh said apologetically. "It was something at last night's party."

Nobody said anything. The strains of *Music While You Work* came from a portable to the left. And a white launch carrying passengers to Seal Island went smoothly through the sparkling blue water. From the wet sand a child was shouting "meanie Poosie, meanie Poosie" at a woman who had lifted the child out of a pool and carried it back to the dry sand. I watched a young girl, burned a deep brown, in a light blue bikini, walk slowly and sensually across the beach.

"Did you hear Oscar's latest opening shot?" I said by way of making conversation.

"The one with the priest and TV aerial, in Market Jew Street," Thelma said.

"No, this one has an Irish maid coming up the stairs of a cheap hotel in Paddington. In one hand she carries a breakfast tray with fruit juice, kippers on a plate, toast and coffee—in the other hand, a bed-pot."

No one thought it funny.

"Oscar's got a thing about pots," Thelma said. "The first time I met him we were at a Baby Bunting party and in the middle of conversation he interrupted himself to say he just thought up a wonderful opening shot. It's of a huge ballroom with grand dukes and grand ladies all dressed up with medals and ribbons and things. And they are dancing in this ballroom. The camera sort of weaves through them unpeeling one layer after another, getting closer to the very centre. Where, under a huge chandelier, in the middle of all these dressed-up people, is a small, nude child, sitting on a pot and straining—"

We thought that funny.

And Helen said, "I remember when Toby was three, running around in the morning in the nude. She couldn't talk very well. And as she ran around the house she kept on shouting, 'I'm in the mood, Mummy. I'm in the mood—'"

We laughed. And Thelma said, "When Betty was learning to write she began leaving me notes in all sorts of places. One of them was 'To Mummy with All My Hart.' I said to her, 'Betty, h-a-r-t doesn't spell heart. Try again.' She said, 'H-u-r-t, Mummy—'"

"She's a bright girl," Hugh said.

I watched the child. She had a long stick of bamboo and a small bit of white muslin at the end around a wire. And she was hunting imaginary fish in a pool.

"The best my kid's ever done," Nat said, "is sing 'Old Man Reefer. That Old Man Reefer.'"

"He don't plant taters," Peter Kroll sang on, imitating a Southern voice. "He don't plant cotton. And them that plants 'em are soon forgotten..."

But there was no direction to the conversation. And again we lay silent, soaking in the late afternoon sun. I watched a cormorant fly low across the water, its black neck stretched full out, and two narrow grey specks on the horizon, French crabbers coming in for the night.

"I couldn't get to sleep last night," Nat Bubis said. "And lying awake in bed I thought how it will be a hundred years from now. The beaches, the bay, the far shore fields—they will be the same. But in little churchyards around here, there will be our names on stones. And no one will know anything about us, or the kind of life we lived."

No one spoke. "Rain will spread from the west," came from the portable to the left.

"Have you seen Nancy lately?" Helen asked Thelma Eskin. "You remember how pretty she was? Now her face has gone fat—she must have put on half a stone. She said hello to me in the street—for a minute I thought it was Rosalie."

"Maybe she's unhappy so she eats," Nat said.

"I don't know why she and Abe keep on like this," Thelma said. "It'd be better if they lived apart—"

"Abe tried it," Hugh said, "but he came back. He said he couldn't stand being alone."

"Who is Rosalie?" I asked.

"Rosalie—" Hugh began, and doodled in the sand, "—is a collector. She collects people."

As usual, Hugh was only partly right. Rosalie Grass did not collect people exactly, but painters. She was living with Starkie in the finest house I had seen in St. Ives, called "Driftwood Heights." It was on the outskirts, on the high ground. A square stone manor house with lots of narrow windows, on a plateau. I could see it from the harbour—like a monument—above and a little removed from the town. A small wood and farmers' fields were behind it. Then the moorland with the gorse, heather, and granite boulders. In front, a long gravel drive came from the main road. Various trees lined one side of the drive. On the other, sloping well-cut lawns with flower beds. Then the continual slope down to St. Ives. And a marvellous view—especially at sunrise—of the bay, the harbour, the cottages with their numerous chimney pots; the railway line, above the beach, with the cut-granite station building.

When one first looked at Rosalie Grass—tall, with an attractive face, pale skin, a long neck, light blue eyes, long light-red hair, a pleasant smile—one thought of something English. But it was an England of the flat in South Kensington, of dogs and the country house, and frequent travels abroad.

And Jimmy Stark was a smallish energetic man, with cropped brown hair, very blue eyes, and a hooked nose that was somewhat pointed. He was the only Cornishman in the group I met down here. He rented the North Star Garage along the front. At thirty-six he was six years older than Rosalie. They teamed up, according to Hugh, not long after Rosalie had come for a holiday from Southern Rhodesia. She would not accept the limitations of camp life in a mining town of the bush, nor those of her engineering husband. Starkie had also come back restless. He had been a commando in the war and having been away he could not return to the cottage in the Back Road, the Methodist chapel, and a simple, doting Cornish girl who took in bed-and-breakfast visitors in the season.

When I first met him I thought he was the most volatile person I had ever seen. A bundle of energy that was rarely still. And his enthusiasms were infectious—words just seemed to flow out of him once he started to talk. And he could mimic almost anyone he wanted to.

During the day they seemed incongruous. Rosalie on the beach, in her green bathing suit, smoking cigarettes out of a gold cigarette holder, reading a book, surrounded by young men. While Starkie never turned up on the beach. Even on the hottest day I would see him in his garage, in light blue overalls, working at the open end of a car, or underneath it, calling out to some local person who was passing by, or running into the office to answer the telephone. In the evening he appeared with Rosalie at the Sloop, dressed neatly in a dark blue sport shirt, light trousers, sports jacket; buying other people drinks until closing time. Then back to Driftwood Heights.

It was the best place for parties. It was free of Wesleyan or Methodist neighbours, and therefore free of having a policeman come to the door and ask the party to quiet down—as had happened several times at Hugh and Lily's and Abe and Nancy's. Driftwood Heights wasn't all theirs. They had only one large wing of it. The house belonged to Sir Edward Lolli, an international banker who bought it for his boyfriend, Garry Diamond, a pleasant, shy young man of twenty-seven who wanted to be a painter. The banker installed Garry at Driftwood Heights and only turned up at Christmas, Easter, and for a few weeks during the summer. So when Rosalie and Starkie asked about renting a wing, the banker agreed. And they did it up wonderfully well. Starkie was very excited about the new place, the modern furniture, but mostly, I suspect, about him living in the manor house of the town.

V

The first formal party Bill Stringer attended at Driftwood Heights was a hat party on September the first. Rosalie wore a lampshade held by a ribbon under her chin. Red Cutler, a young man with canary-coloured hair (a discard of Baby Bunting's of two seasons, who was now staying with Garry Diamond), had an elaborate Edwardian hat with large feathers and flowers in tiers and lots of veil hung in front and tied under his chin. When he danced he had to without moving his head. Starkie wore a Victorian kind of nightcap, or perhaps it was a baby's bonnet—a piece of linen that came around his head and ears and tied under his chin by a white string. A small man in a beard had on a large sombrero. Most of the girls wore trilbies. Bill Stringer came in a ski cap.

"You know what I liked about you on the beach," Rosalie said to Bill Stringer as they were dancing. "The flatness of your belly." She pressed her belly against his. He didn't move away.

"Are you happy?" Bill Stringer said.

"Belly happy," Rosalie said and chuckled.

Ella Fitzgerald was singing "Moonlight in Vermont" and they went around the floor in confined spaces. Their bellies were against one another but their faces were apart. Rosalie smiled. Bill Stringer saw Starkie and steered Rosalie towards him. The music stopped and they released and went over to where Starkie was selecting a new lot of records to go on. "Boy, it's warm here," Stringer said. Starkie said yes, but he and Rosalie did not say much. Stringer left them and went over to the bar in the hallway and helped himself to some whisky, which was in a sherry bottle. A few minutes later Starkie came up to him. "Go over to Rosalie, Bill—we've just had a row." He found Rosalie sitting by the window looking dejected but she brightened up as he approached. Dance? She smiled and got up and again they were dancing. He suddenly didn't want to sleep with her—not like this. They danced and she kept close to him. Then by the door he stopped and opened it and, holding hands, they went out.

The fine rain had almost stopped and they stood against a tree. They could hear from behind the closed door the record player going—another song being played. The door opening and closing. And another couple somewhere to their right. He kissed her. But she wasn't going to let it go like that. Where can we go, she said. Where could they go. It was wet. Upstairs didn't make sense. She was ready anywhere. Against a tree? So they went behind the tree. There was a nursing sister he remembered, against a post, but she was smaller and lighter and he was nineteen then. It was over in a couple of minutes. She straightened her clothes and they had returned to the small corridor where the bar was when they saw Albert Rivers and Nat Bubis slugging it out. Stringer went in with a few others to separate them. But two businessmen in berets picked up Albert Rivers by the scruff of his jacket and forcibly began to carry him out, his legs thrashing in the air. As he was dragged by the door he kicked against the glazed door, breaking the glass into pieces.

Starkie quickly pulled the plug out of the record player.

"Who's going to pay for that door?" he said, red in the face.

An awkward silence was in the room.

"Nobody leaves here until I know who is going to pay for that door. It cost me seventy-five pounds."

Rosalie went over to him, with an anxious smile, and tried to talk to him, but he pushed her away.

"—we feed these people, we give them drink, and look what they do."

"Now, Jimmy, take it easy."

Starkie slapped her face. "You and your artist bums."

Although he was furious he looked very funny with the baby's bonnet on his head tied under his chin, his long thin nose sticking out of a red face. He hurried out of the room and up the stairs.

The guests left in twos and threes—Rosalie at the broken door, apologizing—into the rain, like cats being put outside for the night.

That night Rosalie slept in the other wing of Driftwood Heights, the one occupied by Garry Diamond and Red Cutler.

VI

I first met Garry Diamond and Red Cutler lying on the beach around Rosalie.

"You know who you remind me of?" Red Cutler said.

"I've been mistaken for a lot of people," I said.

"Joan Fontaine."

I thought it was funny.

I saw them again a couple of days later on the front. A frigate had come into the bay for a courtesy call. It was in the local paper that the navy would be guests of the town for the weekend. The frigate was outlined in lights. It looked like one of those pictures people made from using the Xs on a typewriter. Garry and Red were promenading along the front with everyone else. Red was wearing a black silk cape that was crimson on the inside. They said they had prepared a meal back at Driftwood Heights and they were going to pick up some sailors and bring them back. They were as excited as any child with the thought of adventure.

I had to go and see them on the Monday morning. They sometimes let out rooms and I had received a letter from a college friend who was thinking of coming down with his wife and children.

I walked up the gravel path. The large white front door was open and Wagner was booming out. Garry wasn't in, but Red was sitting beside a considerable mahogany table, smoking from a cigarette holder, in a dark green silk dressing gown. He was writing a letter.

"Sorry to interrupt," I said.

"No interruption at all, my dear Bill."

"Would you have room to put up a friend of mine and his family at the end of September?"

"I don't think so. In fact I'm sure Sir Edward Lolli is coming down at the end of September—I'll ask Garry when he comes back—isn't Wagner marvellous?"

Red Cutler was a plump, bouncy boy of twenty-five. When he walked in town he had a trick of putting his hands in the side trouser pockets and pushing the pockets further to the front, so that the trousers were tight at the back. His clothes consisted of tangerine bathing trunks, pink and blue cashmere sweaters, and very light-coloured sports shirts and flannels. He spoke in a rich, nervous voice. Gossip had it that he lived in a fantasy world. That he lied. And helped himself to other people's change when nobody was around. He showed me the letter he was writing. It was on stationery that said *Dorchester Hotel, London, W.1.* It was addressed to *Ludwig Jones,* and he signed himself, in an elaborate script, *Wolfgang.*

"Isn't it a glorious morning?" Red Cutler said, and put his cigarette holder back in his mouth and watched me go out, down the gravel path, by the lawn that the gardener was mowing, the large cactus, the goldfish pond, the borders of subtropical flowers, and the tall hedgerows enclosing everything inside.

There was a Dutch journalist. He had been in St. Ives four days and had already been to three parties. He was travelling around England sending back articles for a newspaper syndicate in Holland and they appeared in hundreds of small papers. He would remain in St. Ives until his cheque for his last article caught up with him, then he would move on. He had found out from Nancy that the painter to interview down here was Carl Darch, who lived in a cottage at Zennor.

The Dutch journalist took a green double-decker bus out of St. Ives and onto the Land's End road. He had never heard of the painter but had, with experience, been able to ferret out those people, in various places, who could put him on the right track. In any case he was well equipped. Like the bogus street photographer, he could pretend he had a film in his camera when he hadn't. And to make the other person feel good, click away, and then say he would send him a copy when it appeared in some paper.

The journalist got off at Eagle's Nest and walked down the highway. Large haunches of moorland were on the left of the highway with the gorse and bracken beginning to turn to their autumnal colours. And on the right, small neat fields with stone fences and hedges sloped to the sea. He went down a rough winding path off the highway to the right and found the painter in having tea.

Carl Darch was a stocky medium-sized man with china-blue eyes and a curious voice. He had what appeared a large face, but it was mainly because of the large jowls. He lived in this two-roomed cottage with Aladdin lamps, a bare table, bookshelves on either side of a fireplace, filled with paperbacks. The kitchen was the far end of the room, and its window faced the farmers' fields. Narrow steps led upstairs to a bedroom.

The journalist began by flattering Darch. But soon got down to the business side.

"Why don't you live in St. Ives?" he asked.

"I don't like St. Ives very much."

"But it seems to me such a lovely place," the journalist said.

"It is a nice-looking place," Darch said, "but don't you think it odd that these beautiful seaside resorts are just rest homes, where people with money come to die."

The Dutch journalist wrote this into his notebook. "How do you feel about death?"

"For me death is the end," Darch said, "and there is really such a short time when one is capable of living that one ought to have some moments of happiness."

The Dutch journalist continued to write quickly, and then said, "What's your politics?"

"I'm a reactionary in politics," Darch said, "but at least I feel at home with working-class people. Not like some left-wing people I know who love the lush life—large houses, good trimmings. If you bring a working-class person into their house—they can't stand them."

"What is your philosophy of life."

"I love life very much," the painter said, "and I just want to record it. I went on a bus yesterday to Penzance. And riding in it—I was alone on the top—I suddenly felt so much wanting to love someone—I suddenly felt so full of loving- Do you know what I mean?"

The journalist nodded his head.

"—So that if a person came along who wanted it I'd be only too ready to give."

The journalist began to feel embarrassed. He hoped the painter was not leading up to a point of intimacy when he would ask him for some money.

Darch took the journalist next door to his studio. It was another cottage, smaller than the first, and bare. A window overlooked the farmers' fields. In his notebook the journalist wrote:

> There were canvases facing the walls, with chunks cut out if them. He paints on the wrong side of the canvas, usually one colour, the ones he had on easels were all painted a dull green, and on them was one, a portrait of a woman, a rather ugly woman done in pinks, blacks, and whites, she was stretched out in the nude, but he was going to cut her just at the head, it was a distortion, but it looked like a person, and there was another of a rather long face, with the buttocks exposed to you and a long arm and a long leg, but he wanted to have the body, like a map if the human, he said, as if a person was squeezed flat, all of himself against the painting. There was another of a head showing a man shouting. And then he showed me a photograph of the Petersburg revolution with people running, people ducking, people falling, a cow fallen—that was one if his favourites, there was one of Rembrandt, several of Rembrandts, and he was enthusiastic about those—"frying pan makes good palette"—there were things cut out of magazines, "I like distortions," the people, portraits, often the mouth is open with the small teeth caught in the middle of a scream.

They went back to the cottage and Darch went into the kitchen side and came back with two glasses and a half-bottle of gin and poured some in each glass.

"You seem to be the only non-abstract painter down here," the Dutch journalist said. "—Don't you like abstract?"

"You have to make something particular when you paint. Things that have mattered in your life. A particular person. A particular bird. And not be too much concerned with fashion."

The journalist wrote this down, took a sip of neat gin from his glass, and looked around the small bare room contemptuously.

"I suppose I could be better known," Darch said. "*Time* did an interview with me when I had a retrospective show at the Whitechapel Gallery. It was a very long and exhausting interview—they even wanted to know what brand of toothpaste I used. The first week it was supposed to come out, it didn't— Castro made his revolution that week. They said they needed the space. It was rescheduled for the following week. I remember how that week all I could think of was whether the piece was going to come off or not. In Penzance I had to use the public telephone in a kiosk by Morrab Gardens. And I found someone had left four pennies in the box. I didn't take them, even though I was hard up. For some reason I felt I was being tested—that there was a connection between the pennies being there—whether I took them—and whether the piece was going to appear. Then, walking along Market Jew Street, by the station, I saw sixpence on the pavement by the man who sells the *Evening Standard*—I didn't pick that up either as I would have any other time. I felt this was still another test—"

"Did the piece come out?" the journalist said impatiently.

"No." And Darch gave an ironic smile. "That week the Russians launched a sputnik. The story was killed. 'Pill' is how the telegram said. I have it here." The painter went to the bookcase and from a cupboard pulled out a thick book, it looked like a Bible, and took from it, carefully, a thin telegram that was pressed like a leaf. The journalist read it and returned it. He saw the interview as a complete waste. And decided to leave as quickly as he could.

"Aren't you lonely out here," he said, putting away his ballpoint pen and notebook.

"No," said Darch. "Most winters I spend in London ... I like the corruption that you can only find in large cities." And smiled as he said this.

The journalist got up to go.

"In summer tourists come down here to get souvenirs," Darch said as they were walking to the door. "Lawrence lived in this cottage—"

"D. H. Lawrence?" the journalist said, and you could see him turn his interest on and off, just like a light switch.

"He lived here with his wife," Darch said. "Middleton Murry and Katherine Mansfield lived in that cottage," he pointed through the open window to the next group of cottages across the yard. "People come from all over, especially America. I've had one couple this August. She taught art in a school. They wanted to rent the cottage for a month—"

"That's very interesting," the journalist said. And he took out his notebook and ballpoint pen again. "Can you tell me more about Lawrence while he was here ..."

And the painter did. The journalist made notes. Then took some pictures of the cottage, the door, the lane, the view of the fields, the moors. Thanked the painter—he said he would send him a copy with his piece in it—and walked back along the rough path, noticing for the first time the bushes with blackberries on either side, the rocks, the dips in the earth, the gorse, the bracken. It wasn't a waste after all. He lit a Senior Service, noticed that the back of the matchbox he had bought in the Sloop had a joke. He made a note of this—*matchboxes with jokes*—he would have to get several others. Along with the exact wording on the plaque to Wesley, the exact number of Wesleyan and Methodist chapels and churches, and the number of urinals. It was details like this that had made his name in Holland.

Back in the cottage the painter was angry with himself for having talked too much.

By the middle of September the season was over. The sun still shone brightly but there was little warmth in it. You could walk comfortably in the streets and along the front. Although there were a few isolated, wealthier groups, with nannies, on the now deserted beaches, the summer haul was over. And those who lived here had replenished themselves to last through another winter.

Every day saw another hotel, café close; the chairs stacked upside-down on the tables and, in the window, guttered candles with the wax of the season run down and hardened. "Bed and breakfast" cards were put away in drawers. And those who lived on the moors lost their summer jobs and were back to their winter inertia and romantic helplessness. A few old men and women went along the tideline and gathered bits of damp wood that they brought back to their small cottages, dried them on top of the stove, and watched them burn with a salt-green flame. While the unemployed, with hands in pockets, stood outside Barclay's Bank watching the empty main street. 403

By October the place was desolate. Cold winds swept the deserted beaches and lifted the loose sand down the empty streets. At high tide the water in the harbour crashed over the seawall, hit the side of shuttered cottages, went over their roofs and landed with a *wump* in the next street. Few people walked the streets, even at noon. Signs creaked by the shut bric-a-brac shops. Gulls tacked across the bay. A whole white flotilla under a grey sky, their wings trembling in the wind to keep into their bank as they crabbed and fought their way towards the rocks. And one gull, caught in between the electric wires, hung head down, the neck arching with the wind like the neck of a kettle. Black-backs appeared in the harbour, and they were hungry. On a sloped street a boy kicked a soccer ball up, waited for it to roll down to him, then he kicked it up again. He played by himself this way for hours. The bell in the church tower sounded very clear and melancholy. The light faded early. By tea time smoke almost hid the place as fires were lit in front rooms and the white-green glare of the TV filled the windows.

There was a stir of life on November the fifth. Bonfires on the beaches, and the rockets and stars arched across the harbour, cascaded above the town, and into the bay. Things livened up even more at the start of December. The coloured lights—with shades of Little Boy Blue, Humpty Dumpty, Little Red Riding Hood—hanging on an overhead wire, in the middle of Fore Street, were lit again. And old fishermen went around the streets pushing old prams filled with Christmas parcels to deliver for the post office. While the unemployed stood grimly and watched.

Connie's opened for Christmas week. And decorations appeared in shop windows. Driftwood Heights had a tall evergreen in front of the lawn with lots of coloured electric lights. Rosalie Grass had turned her house into a "salon" for the painters. To many of them Driftwood, in winter, was home. They came in from the moors, or from the studios facing the beach. And when they came it was to play the part expected of them. In return, they would be flattered by the kind of subservience that Rosalie had to anyone who was pronounced "creative"; besides, there were also the comfortable chairs, the warm fire, the drinks, the food, the manor house.

Also in winter a different kind of sponger came down. They were quite unlike the people who arrived in the summer months. The ones now looked more like businessmen. They were very serious and they talked a lot about art and literature and values and integrity. They had, compared to the people down here, a purpose in life.

"Oh Rosalie, darling," said one of these, a very short nervous man in glasses, with a neat grey suit, and lips like a fish, and slightly bald, "may I use your phone? I must make a few calls to London to friends to send down some money. There's been a mix-up at the bank and my cheques are all bouncing…"

Rosalie said, of course; while Starkie, back for lunch, ate in silence for several minutes. Finally he got angry.

"He's been on that phone for twenty-three minutes talking about Van Guff—why doesn't he get down to it and ask the woman for money?"

Two minutes later an agitated Starkie stepped into the other room.

"Look, boy, I'm the Joe who has to pay the phone bill when it comes, not you. So get on with it or hang up—"

And Starkie remained there while the man on the telephone became flustered.

". . . I wouldn't have worried you," he spoke rapidly into the phone in a high-pitched voice, "but I've been going on by borrowing half-crowns and five bobs, I'll have plenty of cash coming in, so could you lend me six quid? That's sweet of you. I wouldn't have worried you if I wasn't so desperate, nobody is sending me any letters. That is sweet of you. And I'm stuck in this God-forsaken place. Absolutely cut off—"

The man hung up, thanked Rosalie graciously, and looked at Starkie as if he was a new form of peasant.

As soon as the man closed their front door, Rosalie said, "You didn't have to talk to him that way. Think how it must be for a grown man to have to humiliate himself in this way."

"I bet that bum—I've already lent him five pounds—goes around telling those other bums that I won't let him use the phone."

Rosalie was silent.

"I've also lent him some money, Jimmy," she said quietly.

They looked at each other. And Starkie went over, put his arms around her. They kissed. And made telescopes out of their hands, put them on their eyes, touched hands, and said "Woo-woo, woo-woo," like a pair of owls.

"That's something that is our own," Rosalie said. "No one can take that from us." And she touched his hair.

But the truce didn't last. A few days later Starkie came back early from the garage and found Rosalie with three young men sitting around a large open fire, drinking, and playing a game. In one corner was a drawn curtain and one of the young men was behind the curtain. He was the oracle. "Oracle. Oracle. How—shall I—my true—love know . . . ," a young man with a faint Irish in his voice chanted melodiously.

Starkie was furious. He told them all to get out. Smashed a nearly full bottle of rum that was on the table. And he and Rosalie had another quarrel. That night she slept in the other part of Driftwood Heights. By noon they had made up again. Starkie said he was sorry.

"We can't go on like this," Rosalie said. "What do you think —"

Four days after Christmas Starkie received three letters. One was from his bank manager saying that he had gone 200 pounds over the agreed limit of the overdraft and that he was not prepared to meet any further cheques. There was a registered letter from his petrol company saying that he owed 162 pounds, and since he hadn't replied to their last two letters they had placed the matter in the hands of their solicitors. The third letter was a Christmas card from a girl he met last summer, that he had forgotten.

On New Year's Eve, Abe and Nancy gave the last party of the year. Their cottage was really three cottages knocked into one. The ground floor of two formed the Celebrity, the third cottage and the top floors of the others their living quarters. Fifty people could get in, quite easily, but it made the room warm.

For some reason no one seemed to be having the party spirit. Perhaps because people were getting ready to go away. On Monday, Helen Greenway and Peter Kroll and Nat Bubis were off to Spain. On Wednesday, Garry Diamond and Red Cutler were going to Rome to meet up with Garry's banker. On Friday, Hugh and Lily were leaving for a month's holiday in Paris. The season's fun was over.

However, by eleven o'clock it livened up a bit. Abe had made a strong punch, more people began to dance, put on coloured paper hats, and more guests kept coming in. Around twenty to twelve, Rosalie came in with Garry Diamond and Red Cutler.

"Where's Starkie?" Nancy said.

"I don't know where he is," she said, "and I don't care."

She stuck a new cigarette into her holder, inhaled, then blew the smoke out through her nostrils. "We just had to take a taxi all the way from St. Agnes—the middle of nowhere."

Bill Stringer brought her a whisky. Her eyes were moving everywhere. After another neat whisky, she said to Nancy and Bill Stringer:

"We decided to go to the Metropole in Truro—it's a new place started by an ex-chef of the Savoy. We went in Jimmy's car. Jimmy drove. Everything at first seemed to be fine. We had a delicious coq au vin, wine, liqueurs, coffee, cigars. Then we got the bill. It came to just under eighteen pounds. Garry said to Jimmy that they should split the bill. And Jimmy just blew up. 'You want nine pounds for this when I don't know how I'm going to pay my mechanic this week—' Luckily Garry had a cheque book, and they took it. So we all got in the car and Jimmy started to drive back. Just after St. Agnes he went berserk. In the middle of nowhere he slammed on the brakes, opened the doors, and told us to get out. And drove off. Red walked until he found a kiosk and called a taxi. And we came straight here."

Abe came up looking a bit drunk.

"Hello, Rosalie—where's Starkie?"

"I don't care where the bugger is."

The *Light Programme* of the BBC was on the radio, and the crowds at Piccadilly, the notes of Big Ben striking midnight, filled the cottage. Those inside had formed a tight circle, crossed hands, sang "Auld Lang Syne," wished each other a happy New Year, kissed and drank each other's health.

By 2:00 a.m. it had thinned out. Some had disappeared upstairs to the bedrooms. Some went home. A few couples were dancing to the record player. And others stood around, or sat in the corners, drinking and talking.

VII

I felt very drunk and unsteady and decided to go up to one of the bedrooms. The first two rooms had their doors locked but the third was open and a couple were on a bed on the far side. I went to sleep on the small bed by the wall nearest the door. I remember a girl coming up in the middle of the night lying down beside me saying, I don't like sleeping alone ... and then being woken up by Nancy saying, Are you a vegetarian. No, I said. And then it was morning, and Nancy was asking me, "Are you a vegetarian?"

"No," I said.

"Would you like bacon and eggs for breakfast?"

"Fine," I said, "and some black coffee."

She went away. A tight feeling of pressure in my head. I did not want to close my eyes. When I did I felt everything turning. I put on my shoes and went to the sink and threw warm water on my face, combed my hair, but it didn't help much.

Downstairs, I saw Garry and Red, Hugh and Lily, Nat Bubis and Thelma Eskin. The room had the disorder of after a party and the smell of spilled beer and wine. Abe was the only one looking quite spry. I went over to help him collect the empty bottles and stack them in one corner. But from a few feet there was sleep in the inside corners of his eyes, he hadn't shaved either, and there was the indelible imprint of failure in that large, sad face. Then the doorbell went. No one made a move. So I went and opened it. There were two smooth-shaven, cheerful young men in trench coats and trilbies. One was carrying a brown leather briefcase.

"Good morning, sir," the one with the briefcase said, "would you like to discuss the importance of prayer?"

"I—" and mumbled something. "—Could you come back later. We're having breakfast."

They were reluctant to leave. And I wished I hadn't encouraged them. But in the end they did go and said they would come back later in the morning. It was now 10:36.

"Who was that?" Nancy asked from beside the gas stove.

"A couple of Jehovah's Witnesses," I said. "They wanted to discuss the importance of prayer."

"What did you tell them?"

"That we're having breakfast. To come back later."

We were on our coffees and smoking cigarettes and trying occasionally to say something intelligent when the doorbell rang.

"I'll go," said Abe. "I'm just in the mood to discuss prayer—"

He was back sooner than I expected. "Starkie's dead," he said in a flat voice. "He gassed himself in the garage. His mechanic found him."

There is always a little excitement after a death, especially a violent one. And for the next few days people talked and discussed Starkie. Some said it was his financial position, that he couldn't keep up Rosalie's "salon" and the manor house. Others said he really wanted to be a painter; that he was becoming homosexual; that he realized how corrupt he had become. Others said he wasn't intelligent enough to become corrupt. And in the Back streets Cornish parents used Starkie's death as a warning to their restless children to "keep away from them artists."

Over the next couple of days I was able to piece together what happened to Starkie when he left the others. He drove back to St. Ives around midnight, tried several houses, found no one in.

"I think, had he met anyone that night when he was wandering around," the local doctor said to me, "he would still be alive."

I walked around the empty front, the piers, the deserted Back streets, and thought of the utter loneliness of Starkie wandering around that night in this place, knocking on doors, while we were at Abe and Nancy's party. For some reason it brought back, very clearly, my first month here.

We didn't know whether or not to go to Starkie's funeral. Nancy took charge. "I don't think the Cornish would like a lot of us around at a time like this."

I went to Drew's to send a small spray. There were wreaths and sprays there from Baby Bunting, Abe and Nancy, Garry Diamond and Red Cutler, Hugh and Lily, Nat Bubis, Oscar Preston, and Rosalie. I wrote my name on a card and gave it to the boy.

"Do you want it sent to the death house?" he said.

I went out of Drew's wondering about the Cornish acceptance of death and their insatiable curiosity with all its details. Starkie's funeral card appeared on the shelters, in the grocery store windows, the butcher shops; like that of everyone who died, who belonged here. The North Star Garage closed its doors. And on the day of the funeral the unemployed dressed up and went en masse to the cemetery. In the end none of us did go. And Starkie was buried in unconsecrated ground overlooking the long beach and the Atlantic breakers.

I left St. Ives after Twelfth Night. Of those that were still here, no one came to see me off. I waited in the train's empty compartment, by the siding above the beach, and looked out of the lowered window. The sky was full of clouds.

Then the sun came through a break. It was like a spotlight, bringing out the pastel colours of the far shore fields, the magnificent ice-blue of the cliffs, the deeper blue of the bay, and the white of the lighthouse. "Such a nice-looking place." And I was back, I thought, where I started, with my immediate response to the physical sense of this place. But that wasn't quite right. I could never return here without bringing back these people and the events that went to mark a certain time in one's life. "That's what was made out of this stop." And as the train began to go up the gradient I watched the sun shine brilliantly on the discarded Christmas trees floating in the harbour to be swept out to sea. Perhaps it was a fitting end.

HELLO,
MRS. NEWMAN

WOULD see them in the street and we would say hello. And walk on. The men wearing suits and sometimes carrying shopping bags. The women well-dressed, well preserved. Sometimes as I saw them I would think—he used to be in charge of the waterways in Thailand, or, he was a bank manager in India, or, he was in control of a territory in Africa almost as large as Wales. Now they were walking in the streets of this small seaside town carrying their wives' shopping bags. The women were more friendly. I remember Mrs. Holland scrubbing her front door steps and calling out to me.

"If my servants could see me now."

They looked ten to fifteen years younger than they were. The sea air, the mild climate, and money helped to preserve them. The men played golf, the women bridge. And they lived in the large houses on the heights and on the outskirts.

One of the finest houses was owned by the Newmans. I got to know them not long after I came to England in the summer of 1949. I arrived in London towards the end of June. And as it was hot I thought I would go down to this small seaside town on the south coast.

On the second day I was having a drink in the saloon bar
of the Antelope, standing beside Mr. and Mrs. Newman and
their only son, Tom. We got to talking. Tom was leaving for
Canada—going to Vancouver. I told them a bit about Vancouver. And they invited me back for a drink. I gave Tom some
names and addresses. And in return they let me rent a wing of
their house.

I had never lived in anything like this before. Not so much
the house but the setting. I used to borrow Tom's bicycle and
ride up and down the long gravel drive just to look at the view
and see how it changed.

Along one side of the drive was an avenue of large pines.
And on the other—sloping well-cut lawns that ended with a
border of flowers and shrubs. And past the flowers and shrubs,
a few small trees. Then the side of a cliff with more pines going
down. And below that a beach with fine yellow sand and the
sound of a gentle surf. Further out was the water of the bay
and the far shore fields. When the tide was out you could see
the light blue of an estuary with yellow sand on either side.
And I have seen sunsets when the far shore fields appeared to
be lit up by a pink spotlight.

Whoever laid out the grounds had an eye for light and dark.
For at the very end of the garden—pulling the dark green from
the old pines along one side of the drive and the lighter green
of the grass lawns from the other—were two large golden elms.
A splash of light yellow that held the whole thing together.

For the first few weeks I just enjoyed being in these
grounds. There was so much to see. And it was quiet. There
were butterflies and bees. And sometimes a gull flew over and
a jackdaw. And several magpies came down onto the lawns.
There was so much space. And, at dusk, the smell in the air
of different flowers. This, I thought, is what money can buy—
quiet and space. And—in a place by the sea that is almost all
stone—trees and large well-kept lawns.

In the mornings Mrs. Newman brought me wicker baskets of fresh vegetables from her garden—lettuces, sweet tomatoes that had a nice smell, large eating-gooseberries that had a bit of pink in them, and apples and pears that had fallen from the trees. And Mr. Newman asked me into the house one evening. And on the white wall of the sitting room he screened home movies that he had taken in Africa. They showed flickering images of Mrs. Newman with her servants, Mrs. Newman playing tennis, Mrs. Newman out riding, Mrs. Newman at the club, at a summer house, on a boat—always immaculately dressed. And Mrs. Newman told me proudly about the princes she knew and showed me the jewellery they gave her.

They brought something of their life away from England back with them—the stuffed animal heads on the walls, the large teak gates at the entrance of the drive, the drinks outside on the stone veranda.

Sometimes I used to tease Mrs. Newman without meaning to. I don't know why. I think I wanted to go deeper than what I could see. When she was showing me the large rooms in their house I blurted out, "What a nice place to have an affair." I meant a wedding or a party. But then I said, "Have you had any affairs lately, Mrs. Newman?"

The expression on her face didn't change at all.

She was in her early forties but she looked ten years younger. Slim, dark hair with dark eyes, a small mouth. She seemed a determined woman and self-contained. Mr. Newman was in his middle fifties. He was short and thin. He had fine grey hair combed neatly back. He had a largish nose and his long face usually had a flush about it—the legacy of malaria that he got while in Africa. He looked a dour man who smoked one cigarette after another, wore silk scarves at his throat and colourful summer shirts. He didn't speak for very long. He let Mrs. Newman do most of the talking.

And Mrs. Newman had this voice. And people, as I discovered, can be put off by a voice. It was high-pitched. It sounded affected and unreal. Mrs. Newman's parents were a gentle couple, now retired, who once had a small fruit and vegetable store in the town. Mr. Newman came from the North of England. His people, I heard, made their money from wool. He had come here on one of his leaves. They met, married, and he brought her out to Africa and to the sort of life that white people lived in the colonies.

But the Empire was coming to an end. They had to leave. And she came back home with this voice and with a manner that indicated she was used to having other people do things for her. This didn't go down very well with those in the town who knew her before she left. "She's Elizabeth Green," said the middle-aged woman serving me in the tobacconist. "We went to school together. Now she doesn't know me—"

And a quiet man, a bachelor, who looked seedy, said he knew Mrs. Newman before she married. He told me that in the late 1920s there was a naval establishment near here. "Mrs. Newman," he said softly, "used to go after the officers. In the mess she was known as the guinea girl."

Whether this was true or not I don't know. I know that whenever I was with Mrs. Newman in the street and she saw this man she walked by him as if he didn't exist.

I was working then as a travel writer for a Montreal paper. And like all journalists I got things wrong. The slight exaggeration, the wrong phrase. I was at that time writing about things I didn't know much about. I would go to a nearby town, spend a few days in it, then write an article about the place for the Montreal paper. Perhaps that's why I got on with the Newmans. Casual friendships—when young—are pleasant. We made little demands on one another. And there were always the drinks on the stone veranda. The lawns, the trees, the splendid views of the bay. And an air of easy living, of idleness.

Mr. Newman spent most of the mornings in the greenhouse. And read two novels a week that Mrs. Newman brought back for him from W. H. Smith's lending library. Then, instead of the club, it was the noonday drink in the saloon bar of the Antelope.

The only thing that I saw Mr. Newman show enthusiasm for was a large cactus, about eight feet high, that he had by the side of the house.

"It flowers only once in fourteen years," he told me. "I've had it for almost five. And the person before me had it for nine. I keep looking. But I can't see any signs that it is going to flower."

That's all that really happened that summer.

I left in the middle of September feeling fit and brown. And I didn't return to this seaside town for five years. In that time I had a first novel published, married, and when I returned I brought my wife with me.

On the third day I walked over to the Newmans' place. It looked much the same, though some of the trees were cut down and the lawns had roses growing in them. Then I saw the cactus. It was like a huge green banana with several skins peeled back and the centre part forced out like a telegraph pole for about twenty feet in the air. And there, on top, was a bright red flower.

I rang the bell.

A woman I had not seen before came to the door.

"Is Mr. or Mrs. Newman in?"

"They don't live here," the woman said.

She was joined by a small white yapping dog.

"I'm a friend," I said. "Can you tell me where they live?"

"Mr. Newman died. And Mrs. Newman lives in town—in one of the terraces."

I did see her next morning, in the street, by the post office.

"Hello, Mrs. Newman."

She smiled and came close. Her legs slightly apart. She always stood like that. She looked pleased to see me.

"I went to call on you yesterday—"

"I don't live there—not since Jack died. The place was too big and expensive for one person. I'm in the end house. At the foot of Windsor Hill. Come and see me."

She hadn't changed. The pastel silk scarf tied sideways on the neck, the new beige suit, the makeup, the hair. To look at her, I thought, you would think nothing had changed in her life.

"How's Tom?"

"He's in Vancouver. He's had another promotion. He likes Canada. He married a general's daughter. She comes from an old Canadian family. The family have a building named after them in Vancouver. I'm going out to see Tom and his wife next month."

Next time I saw Mrs. Newman I was with my wife. I introduced them and hoped they would get on.

They did at the start.

Mrs. Newman would bring flowers, boxes of chocolates. And when I told her that my wife was pregnant, her immediate reaction was: "If you don't want it, I have some pills—"

Three months went by.

We were still in this seaside town. I was trying to write my second novel. And it took longer than I thought it would.

I saw Mrs. Newman not long after she came back from Vancouver.

"How did you like Canada?"

"It was very pleasant. But it's not home."

Then my wife began to talk differently about Mrs. Newman. She now found her voice irritating. And she complained about her behaviour.

"She sees me in the street and tells me all about herself. Where she has been. What ailments she has. Then, when she is finished, and I want to tell her about myself, she suddenly remembers that she has somewhere to go. And she's off."

Another time my wife came back from the library.

"I saw Mrs. Newman. The way she's turned out—she makes me feel like a hippie."

A couple of days later she came back angry.

"She's so boring," she said putting down her shopping bags. "I met her in the street and we talked about nothing. Perhaps if you talk about nothing then nothing shows. The clothes, the makeup, the hair—it's a gloss. A carefully prepared cover. It's as if she believes that when others see you *nothing* must be shown or given away."

"Aren't you hard on her? It can't be much fun living on your own, in a terraced house, after the life she had."

"There are people a lot worse off than that," my wife said.

Whenever I went out I now also saw Mrs. Newman, in different parts of the town, but always by herself.

One afternoon I saw her in a café, sitting by a table, having a coffee and looking anxiously at the door.

She saw me and smiled.

She looked stunning. If you didn't know—you would think she was dressed for some occasion.

I went in.

"Hello, Mrs. Newman."

"Come and sit down," she said. "Have a coffee and a cake."

And she told me about a trip. She had just cóme back from Scotland, touring with Tom and his wife. And I heard nothing about the scenery or where they went or what they saw. But it was an account of missed connections and other people's human errors. Then she told me how to save money on British Rail by buying certain tickets at certain times.

"I don't know why I stay here," she said during a momentary silence. "I have friends near London. I could move up there."

"Why don't you, Mrs. Newman?"

"I may," she said. "Shall we have another cup?"

While the waitress poured the coffee Mrs. Newman said, "Did you know there are a lot of three-legged dogs in this town?"

"No," I said. And we both laughed. Something we didn't often do together.

I went back with her to the end house of a street of terraced houses. The kind of house she grew up in. And where her parents lived out their lives. It was a long way from the surroundings of that first summer. An entire street of joined houses and every house the same. Some had a few yards of grass in front. Otherwise it was all stone. No trees.

And inside—the rooms were small and over-furnished.

She offered me a drink.

"Won't you join me?"

"I'm not supposed to," she said. "I haven't been able to sleep—not since Jack died. I have to take sleeping pills every night or else I don't sleep."

She looked nervous. I thought, for a moment, she was going to cry. But she made a visible effort and pulled herself together.

"Would you like to see the tennis at Wimbledon?" And quickly walked over to switch on the colour TV set. "It's the semi-finals today."

A few days later I saw her, by herself, standing outside a newsagent's.

"Hello, Mrs. Newman," I called out as I walked over.

Tears were in her eyes.

"I'm sorry," she said. "I was thinking of my mother. I miss her."

January is a depressing time here. Rain. The place is empty. And the emptiness is heightened by the large empty sand beaches, the sea, and the sky. They built the streets small and the houses small. And the effect of these small turning streets and small houses is to try to give—to those who live here—some feeling of importance against all the emptiness.

In February for two weeks it drizzled every day. And it was during this time that I heard, on the local news, that Mrs.

Newman's body was found in the sea washed up by the far shore fields. No one knew what had happened.

The funeral was in a small plain chapel in the cemetery. It was attended by about thirty people—most of the diminishing colony of ex-Empire builders who lived here. The men had put on weight, their hair was turning grey. Though the wives still looked attractive and well turned out. The few local people I talked to didn't have anything nice to say about her.

But I liked Mrs. Newman. I don't know why. All the social things that seemed important to her don't matter to me now. But then perhaps in the end they didn't matter to her either. Perhaps I liked her because we were both reminders of a time that was gone. Perhaps because we were both displaced people. And it was harder for her—this was her town. And I liked her for the way she put on a performance whenever she went outside.

Tom had come over. Though he was a Canadian citizen he looked and behaved like a conventional Englishman. Standing outside the chapel—shaking hands with each one of us as we came out.

"It was good of you to come," he repeated.

I walked with Mrs. Holland, all in black, to the car park and to her car.

"She and I were to play bridge on Wednesday. We arranged that weeks ago," she said. "She was also planning another trip to Canada. But we don't know people. Do we?"

And in the narrow main street of the town I met the sturdy widow of a former bank manager in Pakistan. I thought she may not have heard. So I told her about Mrs. Newman either walking or falling into the sea.

"What a sensible thing to do," she said briskly and went on.

And later, along the front, I saw Mrs. Miller, the wife of a former judge in Burma. We walked for a while in silence. Then she said,

"If only she could have held on until the spring."

A TRUE STORY

GOT INTO RIVERSIDE as the first grey light of the dawn came. It was too early to go to the address I had. So I walked around the place trying to find somewhere open for a cup of coffee. There was nothing. Just this river that went through the place with sloping muddy banks. You could smell the mud. And empty streets with lovely names like Gay and Joy.

Shortly after eight a small café opened in the town square and I went in. A woman was on her hands and knees washing the floor. She went behind the counter and from a steaming urn gave me some weak coffee in a glass. I sat by the wall radiator with my hands around the glass of coffee and tried to get some warmth into me.

At nine I took a taxi across the bridge and up a hill to what looked like a suburb. But it was deceptive. For the suburb extended only to the depth of one street. Behind it lay fields, as far as the horizon. The taxi driver found the address and I went down a country road to a wooden detached house that had its top overhanging the bottom.

Within minutes of meeting my landlady—a tiny woman but bright, like a bird—she told me she was a widow ("not bad for fifty-four"), that her relations were in Australia and she was thinking of going there herself.

I had a small kitchen, a bedroom, and a sitting room above her. It all looked new, especially the floors, which were highly polished.

Outside the window there was a nice-looking tree with yellow-green leaves, a field with apple trees. And on the road that I had come on I saw a girl in a light raincoat; a whippet was beside her. I watched until the road turned and the girl and the dog disappeared. Then I began to unpack.

The widow said she was pleased that I was a schoolmaster. They thought a great deal of the man I was replacing. She began to tell me useful tips about Riverside: how to get to the post office, the school, the Palace Hotel . . .

I went out hoping to see the girl with the whippet.

I didn't see her until the weekend when I was out walking on the country road. We both had a good look at each other. She was tall, around five foot eight, with short blond hair, a broad face, but it looked very white. I thought she had anaemia.

On Monday I got up early and walked into Riverside. I hadn't realized how wealthy it was. Street after street of large wooden houses, painted mostly white. Squirrels on the lawns, the sidewalks, the trees. I came to one of the two main streets. The stores were still closed. Only by the drugstore was a neon sign working, telling the time and the temperature. I went through an empty park with flower beds and children's swings. And past the park was the school. A brick building with white windows. It stood on high ground and on its side were fields that went down to the river.

In the staff room I was introduced to the other masters. All were wearing black academic gowns except myself and the new biology master, a New Zealander, who was also starting this term. He was soft-spoken, wore glasses, and kept to himself. But once when he had a free period and we were alone in the staff room he told me that he believed in reincarnation. He was sure he was going to come back in some other form.

I had the first and the last years in English. The older ones were already set in their ways. I don't think it mattered who was there in front of them. But the young ones were different. I set them an essay to write. When I got their books back I was surprised to see how very old-fashioned was their use of language. They spoke like boys of their age. But they wrote in such an archaic way that anyone would think they were brought up on bad Victorian novels. I decided to try and break this. For their next essay I told them to walk outside where they lived, with a watch, and write down what they saw and when they saw it.

The change in their writing was dramatic. Even if all it had at the start was "5:10 p.m. A herd of Jersey cows come down the road. The farmer is at the back. There are sixteen cows. A crow flies over them." Another had: "I went fishing after school by the river. The river is at the bottom of our farm. I got a bite at 4:42. It was a large pike."

School stopped at four but I never got back to the widow's house until after five, when it was too late to see her walking on the road. Only on weekends when I went out in the afternoon would I meet her. We now said hello and a few words about the weather. She spoke English with a French accent. But she gave me no further encouragement.

My stay with the widow was temporary—the headmaster had sent me her address as a place to stay until I could find something for myself. At the beginning of November I moved to a farm in the country. It was owned by the Browns. They let a small wing of their farmhouse in the summer to tourists. I took it until June. The place was six miles from Riverside but as Mrs. Brown drove in every morning to bring her son to the school she would take me as well. And I would take the bus back.

The farm was in a valley in the richest farming country I had ever seen. Low hills all around, cows and horses on the slopes and in the lush grass at the bottom. There were also apple orchards and countless rabbits. And at dusk I would watch a pair of buzzards working their territory. The Browns were Anglo-Irish. And what they were doing out here seemed ridiculous. You expected them to live somewhere like Surrey, Sussex, or Bucks. To go to Henley and Wimbledon, read the *Tatler*. But I have, since, come across others like the Browns, who have come from sophisticated societies in Europe, and have chosen to live out their lives in obscure provincial Canadian towns. Mrs. Brown looked like a tall Girl Guide with a ruddy complexion and loose curly brown hair. Although she was in her forties she thought she was still a girl and I would sometimes see her skipping with a rope and breathlessly calling out children's rhymes. She named all their cows after flowers. And every morning, as I had breakfast, I would watch Daisy, Rose, Lily, Buttercup, going by the door. Mr. Brown was an ex-colonel. A very tall thin man with a moustache and a porkpie hat that he wore with the brim down. He spoke of *gels* for girls. And looked more at home with horses than anything else. Although Mrs. Brown would tell me on Saturday mornings he was still in bed lying with their youngest daughter. They had been farming here only a few years. And I heard that none of the local farmers gave them more than another three. But they were wrong. They didn't know how tough this breed was. Although going by appearances their farm looked hopeless. Everything inside their house was in a continual state of untidiness. Mrs. Brown had her mother down for two weeks. And the old woman took a broom and began to go after the cobwebs while all around her was disorder.

Then things seemed to go wrong for the Browns. They had their own water supply but it often froze in winter. They had their own electricity, but the generator or pump went wrong and Brown couldn't fix it. He tried kicking the machinery, and sometimes that helped. Though often I made my meals by candlelight using a Primus. But the oddest sight was to see the

Browns deliver milk. They would load up the small Ford with milk bottles that he had filled up. And then the ex-colonel and the ex-Girl Guide Leader, both well over six feet, drove into Riverside and began to deliver small bottles of milk from door to door ...

Late one Friday afternoon I was waiting for the bus in the square to take me back to the farm when I saw the girl, but without the whippet.

"I thought you had gone," she said. "I haven't seen you. Have you been sick?"

I told her that I moved and suggested that we meet for a drink tomorrow in the Palace Hotel.

Next evening I came into the hotel a few minutes early but she was already there, sitting in the darkened lounge.

"Could we," she said, "have coffee instead of a drink?"

"Of course," I said.

We went into the coffee bar. And while we had coffee she told me her name was Marie Yuneau. I told her mine.

"The new teacher?"

"Yes," I said.

She told me that she had not long come out of a sanatorium and was living with her married sister.

I told her I came from Ottawa but I had never seen such rich farming country until I arrived here.

She said her sister's husband was out of work.

"It must be depressing," I said.

"I had a lovely dress," she said. "Blue and white. It was very gay. I liked it very much. Then I had to wear it every day and watch it get worn out and shabby."

I don't know what it was. Whether being in a sanatorium for so long or living in this backwater. But there was an awkwardness about her, something incomplete.

"I break things easily," she said. "I leave jam jars undone ... toothpaste tubes off ... My sister gets angry and follows me ... just doing up things I leave undone."

"Why do you do it?"

"I don't know," she said.

We left the Palace Hotel and walked towards the other main street for a Chinese meal. There are five restaurants in Riverside, all run by Chinamen. I led her through a narrow connecting side street. It was very dark. I didn't want to bump into anyone from the school. I put my hand around her waist and drew her closer.

"I know what you want," she said.

Over the meal she said that she believed there was a one and only. And you knew when he came along. And that it wasn't right to go to bed until you were married.

I didn't say anything to that. She had guessed my intentions. But I expected even a refusal to be a bit more sophisticated than this.

Outside, after the meal, we walked towards the river. It was cold and clear. I watched the neon signs from the other side reflect in the water as long bands of red, green, and the moving white of car lights. Neither of us had spoken for some time. Then she said, "I'm sorry."

"For what?"

"I don't know . . . I don't seem to know how to behave with other people . . . They see me once . . . but they don't see me again . . . I don't have friends . . . I don't seem able to give enough . . ."

I took her hand. We stopped walking. I saw she was crying. I kissed her. But she was moving her head. It felt awkward, as if I was off-balance. I tried again.

"I must go home," she said immediately after we had separated. "I'll miss the last bus."

"I'll get you a taxi."

"I'd better come back by bus or else my sister will think something was wrong."

"Can't you tell her you were out having a drink?"

She became evasive. "She wouldn't like it."

We walked to the bus station. She put her arm through mine. And there was a small green bus by the side of the building.

"Will I see you again?" she said.

"Of course," I said.

I watched her get on the bus. Then went and got a taxi that brought me back to the farm.

Next day the first snow fell, then frost. And getting into Riverside became difficult. I came in on Friday night—when all the stores were open and the farmers were in for their shopping—looking for her. I tried again the next week.

Then I had to spend Christmas and New Year with my parents in Ottawa. And it was after I was back and school had restarted that I read the notice of her death in the local weekly paper.

I went to see the headmaster.

"I'd like to take the rest of the morning off."

"Yes," he said. "Is it a relative?"

"No, a friend."

The crematorium was some distance away from Riverside and the taxi took twenty minutes to get there. I had never been to a funeral before. When I arrived there were only empty cars and trucks outside in the snow.

As I entered the chapel I saw, on the right-hand side of the aisle, four people dressed in black with heads slightly bowed, sitting together. I instinctively joined them. On the other side of the aisle there were about twenty to thirty people—entire families with children—all with bibles, dressed in their everyday clothes. There was nothing sad about them at all. They looked lively and curious at the few of us in black.

A cheerful man in a light grey suit took the service. And it was obvious that he belonged to the other side of the aisle. He quoted a lot from the Bible. And gave references to look up. And those on the other side did. They seemed to know

WELL TOO ANYONE KNOW TO WANT T'NOD I

the Bible well. I guess she belonged to them. And I wondered what it was that made her lose the certainty that they had. Sometimes the man in the light grey suit referred to "Sister Yuneau ... this was not the end, it was only the first step." And there was an occasional sob from one of the women from our little group in black.

Half an hour later I was walking up to the entrance of the school. The New Zealander joined me.

"Isn't it a glorious day," he said.

"It is," I said.

The sun was shining. The snow on the ground and on the trees glistened.

We could see our breath in the cold still air.

MY WIFE
HAS LEFT ME

I N 1953 I was living in a small seaside town in South Devon. I had come here to write a book. But the book took longer than I expected and what I thought would be one year went on for two.

I rented the end house of a row of Victorian terraced houses. It was very pleasant. The Devon winter, compared to Canada, was mild, no sign of snow. I worked in a top room where the window looked out to the bay. Sometimes I would go and stand by the window and watch the slow freighters, the gulls, the colours of the sea.

After the first couple of weeks of becoming familiar with the streets, the shops, the beaches, I settled down to a routine. It began in the morning, waiting for the mail to come. I got to know the three different postmen. One was slow. A bald-ish man with a fine moustache, waxed ends. When he was on, the mail reached the house around ten. The other two were fast. A tall young man with a dark crewcut and sharp features. And a stocky middle-aged man who didn't waste time talking. When they were on, the mail came around eight thirty.

After breakfast—and reading the letters and circulars—I walked down the road to the paper place on the front and picked up my papers. That's how I met Brennan. He also came down for his papers.

Brennan was a watch-repairer in his late sixties. He had a cautious sort of walk, as if he was on a boat at sea.

"I don't have a good sense of balance," he said.

His wife was a short woman, in her early forties. She gave piano lessons. They worked from different rooms in the house.

The first time I went in to see him was about getting a new strap for my watch. While he put it on I looked around the room: the strong light over his desk, the small vice, the neat tweezers. Instead of children there was a framed coloured photograph of a red setter.

"After Tommy died," Brennan said, "I wouldn't have another. We used to talk to him. He talked to us. I still put flowers on his grave."

I heard his wife walk by the partly open door and shout: "First call for lunch."

"It's all right," Brennan assured me. "We still have five minutes."

We could have been on board an ocean liner.

I began to see Brennan in the street regularly after that. He stopped to talk to a lot of people.

To me he always told jokes. "Here's another new one," he said. "It will give you a laugh. The little boy looked through the bedroom keyhole. When his Daddy came out he said, 'Daddy, what were you doing to Mummy?'

"'I was putting a tiger in her tank,' Daddy said.

"'I hope they don't fight,' the little boy said.

"'Why?' said Daddy.

"'Because this morning I saw the milkman. And he put a tiger into Mummy's tank.'"

And Brennan laughed.

Brennan also had strong hates. He was against the royal family, the church, all politicians, and especially the rich. Once he had just finished telling me a joke when he saw a plumber across the road going off to work. "Hullo," he called out, "just off to play polo?" Another time to another workman: "Just going down to see the yacht?"

He told me that he had gone to India as a young man to work in a bank. "When it was hot they would send the women away up to the hills. The women were bored with nothing to do. And there were these soldier stations up in the hills. We called them passion stations." He also told me that, besides the bank, he did a bit of amateur dramatics. He had a spot on a local radio station commenting on current affairs and telling jokes. "I'd listen to the Overseas Service of the BBC, take down their jokes, then broadcast them in Calcutta. I was known as the Voice of Calcutta."

He told me that he had been a bookie, that he had run a restaurant. He said he still had clippings of the time he did some amateur singing. "You can write about me," he said. "I had a very interesting life."

I never saw the Brennans in the street together. Occasionally I saw Mrs. Brennan out shopping.

"I must do something," she said. "I feel I'm just letting life go by. Jerome doesn't want to do anything in the evening except watch television. I've started to take night classes in French..."

And Brennan said, "I had the life early on. I'm nearly seventy, old boy. I don't want any excitement."

One morning I was late going down for the papers—the slow postman was on—when I saw Brennan on his way back.

"Tell me something that will make me laugh," I said lightly.

"I'm serious," he said. "Colette has gone into hospital. She has something wrong with her shoulder—arthritis, I think."

"When did she go in?"

"On Monday. She just threw in the piano lessons. And went off to hospital."

A couple of days later I saw him again.

"How is Colette?"

"You'll soon get to hear it. I might as well tell you. Come inside, old boy."

We went inside the house.

"Sit down. Have a sherry. I can't because of my heart." He made a fluttering movement with his hand. "I get them now."

He poured a nearly full glass of sherry.

"She's left me," he said.

"When?"

"It was Sunday. We were having chicken, as we always do, and I said, 'What's left over will make a nice curry.' And she said, 'Yes, we'll have curry tomorrow.' Three hours later she was gone. I have a nap every afternoon. And as I was going up I put my hand in my pocket and saw she had mended the hole. So I came back and kissed her. Thanked her for doing the pocket. An hour later she was gone. When I came down I saw the envelope. It was a long six-page letter. But I could only read the first two paragraphs. All the time we were eating and talking and kissing. She had her bags packed. I even heard her put out the milk bottles."

"Where is she?" I said.

"I don't know. I've just come back from the bank. They have her address. I write her name, Mrs. Brennan, on the envelope and give it to the assistant manager and they fill in her address that she gave them and send it off. I even sent her flowers. But this morning—"

I thought, how can he go to the assistant manager at the bank and say, "Can you tell me where my wife is?"

"—they wouldn't take my letter. They said they had no address. I don't know where she is. She might be in Glasgow, Dublin, on the Continent, even in Canada."

"Did you know she was going to leave you?" I said.

"I had no idea. I love her. I kissed her, as I do every night before we go to sleep. I kissed her for the meal. I kissed her for mending the hole in my trouser pocket. I gave her a thousand pounds. She was waiting for that. And now I've got this heart business. I get these flutters. I went to the doctor. He told me paroxysms. They're nothing to do with Colette going."

"Look after yourself," I said. "You must eat regularly."

"I do that," he said. "Don't go to the Star Supermarket. Their ham is no good. It's dry. Go to the Dominion. The ham—the girl there cut off a new slice for me—delicious. Not stale at all. But what am I to do?"

"Any idea why she left?"

"It's the change of life, old boy. I'm not dealing with a sane rational person. Do you know Cook—the builder up the hill?"

"No," I said.

"When his wife had the menopause—she was in touch with God. Some go through it easier than others. I read about it in the *Reader's Digest*."

"So you have no idea why she's gone?"

"No," he said. "I gave her a thousand pounds."

"That wasn't wise."

"She's very mercenary," he said. "She was waiting for that. She said she earned it. And as soon as it came through—she's off. Then there was her French lessons. As soon as they finished she left. The first time she came back from a French lesson her face was flushed. 'Why are you so red?' I asked her. 'It was hot in there,' she said. Next time her face was also flushed. She said she ran to come back here. Excitement, old boy. Excitement. The lessons were given by a young pretty woman. I'm not saying Colette is a lesbian. But you read about it all the time in the *News of the World*. One woman in twenty-five is a lesbian. I'm not saying Colette is. But in her letter she said, 'I haven't gone off with any man.' She didn't say 'any woman.' Have a little more sherry."

He filled the glass.

"I don't think she'll be away for too long. Her mother is up at the old people's home here. And she likes her mother. But I don't think she'll come back to me. She knows about my heart. Happens about once a month, when I eat."

A week later he phoned me while I was eating lunch.

"Can you come over right away? I can't tell you over the phone. I need your help."

I left lunch and came over.

"Colette has got in touch," he said. "I've just got her letter. She's going to see her mother and wants me to go up there at two. She wrote me a letter listing two pages of conditions for her to come back. She wanted it drawn up in front of a lawyer. But we don't need a lawyer. We had a lawyer last time."

"When was that?"

"About ten years ago. She left me then. But she only stayed away a week. I got her back. We'll talk at her mother's."

"Can't you see her alone?"

"There's no room at the old people's home. There's only the old lady's room and the lounge where others will be. So I'll have to see her with her mother present. She's very fond of her mother. I've got her a box of chocolates. I've got a bottle of sherry. Shall I kiss her when I see her?" he asked.

"She's left you—no, you don't kiss her. And you don't bring the box of chocolates either or the bottle of sherry. Just listen to what she has to say."

"That's very good," he said. "Yes, of course, you're right. Let her talk it out. The trouble with Colette is, she doesn't know how to say 'I'm sorry.' I learnt that from *How to Win Friends and Influence People*. Always say 'I'm sorry.' It helps. But Colette doesn't know how to say that. The first thing she'll say is, 'I want half of the house.' What shall I do?"

"Don't agree to that," I said. "You haven't any guarantee that she won't leave you after she has got that."

"Well, she'll say, 'I want half of the house in my name.'"

"Don't answer that. Just ask her what are her other demands."

'"Why don't you agree to that first,' she'll say. I know her."

"You ask her what her other demands are."

"That's very good. Let her talk. Let her get it all out. It's an old trick. Let's have a dummy run. I'll be her. You ask me questions and I'll give you the kind of answers she would give."

"Before we begin," I said, "just tell me. Do you want her back?"

"I love her, old boy. She's the only woman I have ever loved," he said. "I'm nearly seventy. I've left everything to her. She knows she'll have it. But I'm not dealing with a well person. It's the change of life. I've seen her sit at the table and stare at a thing on the tablecloth for minutes. I wave my hand before her eyes. No reaction. One time she came out of the kitchen with a saucepan and threw it down so hard on the floor, it dented."

"Why did she do that?"

"The change of life. I told you about this woman who thought she was in touch with God. Some women go through it easy. With Colette it's dragging on. Before leaving she remembered to put out the milk bottles for the milkman. Now why do a thing like that?"

"There was a woman," I said, "who set the table for breakfast before committing suicide."

"Let's go through this again," he said. "Let me take things down. The first thing she'll want to know is, 'What about half of the house?' What shall I say?"

"What are your other conditions?"

"But she'll say, 'Let's settle the house first.'"

"Don't agree to that. But find out the other demands. Tell her whether she comes back or not shouldn't depend on money."

"That's very good," he said. "Let me write it down. But she's very money-minded. I gave her a thousand pounds. Then she left me. I thought of taking that box of chocolates."

"No," I said.

"Shall I kiss her when I see her?"

"No," I said. "She's left you. Go up there and see why she left you."

"Of course, you're perfectly right, old boy. Now let's go over it again. When I go up there I let her talk. Let her get it all out."

"Yes."

"You be me. Tell me what I must say. And I'll be her and tell you her reactions. I'll start: 'I want half of the house . . .'"

He asked me questions. I gave him answers. I felt sorry for him. Nearly seventy. But all the time we were play-acting I found myself on her side. I thought, Good for you, Colette. It was a brave thing to do. I was hoping that, whatever it was that made her do it, she stuck to it. That she wouldn't come back.

I finished the sherry. And he put on a seedy raincoat. He came to the door. "Thanks very much," he said. He looked helpless. "I'm just going up there. Wish me luck. I'll ring and let you know how I make out."

Next day at lunchtime the phone rang.

"The saga of Mr. and Mrs. Brennan is over," he said. "She's coming back tonight. She was staying in a hotel in Torquay. Everything is all right. I didn't have to give in to her."

On the following Monday the doorbell went. It was the young postman with the dark crewcut. He had a registered parcel, a book. As it was raining I asked him to come in while I signed the piece of paper. I had gone out fishing, once, with his father (a retired fisherman) during the early weeks when I came here. And just to make conversation I asked after his father.

"He's in bed," he said.

"Anything serious?"

"No," he said. "He's getting on."

"I'll always remember going out with him," I said.

"I'll never forget July the seventh as long as I live," he said.

"Why?" I asked.

"My wife left me," he said. "I was working late that night and when I came back, there were the kids crying and hungry. No note. Nothing. She hasn't been in touch since."

And as he was talking, telling me about their lives ("We went through the usual things of not having enough money. The children came quicker than we wanted"), I remembered this blond girl in the ice-cream place along the front in the summer with the young children playing on the sand. She was very pretty, in her early twenties. I guessed what could have happened. A seaside town in summer. A lot of strangers passing through. People on holiday. People with money and cars. Perhaps it didn't happen that way at all.

"I thought we had gone through the hard times," he said, "and we were all right. But she left. No note. No reason. Nothing. It's eleven months now and not a word. I don't know where she is. Whether she's living or not. I tried to find out. But it's as if she disappeared into the air."

When I saw Colette in the street a couple of days later, I felt awkward.

"How are you?" I said.

"I was at a health hydro. I had arthritis. It's cured me. I should have done it long ago. I came back too soon. I can't wait to get away again."

She seemed very defiant.

I pass the young postman in the street.

He says, "Hello."

And I say, "Hello."

Then we both walk on as we always did.

FEAST DAYS
AND OTHERS

BECAUSE we were poor we lived in a semi-detached cottage in the country. Our neighbours were the Briggs. Mrs. Briggs ran the village grocery store. She was a plump woman, in her middle forties, with brown reddish hair that was permed in neat little waves. Sometimes I used to see her with a net over them. She had thin legs. In winter when she put on her coat and hat, the legs looked quite incapable of supporting the weight above them. She also had very white false teeth and a pink complexion that made her look freshly washed and blushing. She laughed at anything, whether it was funny or not. And said yes a lot of times, and nodded her head when people spoke to her. And she would say things like "As long as you're happy that's the main thing" or "It can't last forever—"

I would go get messages for my mother and take along my younger sister Kate because Mrs. Briggs always gave us a toffee each. When I opened her door the bell above it jangled loud enough for Mrs. Briggs to come from inside the house at the back of the store, and even from the back garden.

Their back garden was neat. Mr. Briggs worked in the Heatherbell Nurseries two miles away. He would go off in the morning on an old bicycle and come back around half past five. In summer he worked in his garden before he left for the nurseries, and again in the evenings. In winter, only on Sundays, and then mainly in the greenhouse that he built himself. On Saturdays he delivered weekend grocery orders with Kenny in their shiny black Austin.

Kenny was their only child. He used to go shooting in the fields and among the trees by the river. He would take his terrier, his air rifle, and go after rabbits, pheasants, pigeons, magpies. Sometimes I saw him come back with something.

They had an older daughter. She was killed by a car while riding her bicycle on the road in front of the store. That was before my time. I only knew that every Saturday—when Mrs. Briggs locked up and Mr. Briggs and Kenny finished delivering orders—the three of them would go off in the car with flowers from their back garden to place on the grave. The cemetery was in the village at the top of a hill, a mile away, and known locally as "the beauty spot." From there they would go on to Horsham or Cranleigh, to see a film. We knew when they had gone because they left the terrier tied up in the kitchen. And the walls were thin.

Father was doing book reviewing for a London paper. He read the books and wrote his reviews at night in his room. In the morning he left the cottage after the postman had gone by. Sometimes he disappeared all morning and returned just before noon with a loaf of bread, perhaps some cheese and eggs, or minced meat, which Mother made into hamburgers, and which we all loved. He tried to arrange it so that we had the hamburgers on Sundays.

When the review copies began to pile up on his desk he put them into a shopping bag and went to London to sell them. Mother allowed us to wait up for him. When he returned that night—the shopping bag filled with all kinds of delicious food—we had a feast. Usually the next day as well.

When Father was not out getting food he fixed things around the cottage. The sink in the kitchen kept getting blocked. I would go into the shed, get the bundle of long rods—like those a chimney sweep uses—and screw them in, one to another, until they formed a long sagging bamboo pole. Father held one end, I the other, as we walked to the cesspool.

It was in the back, dividing our land from the Briggs', and covered with thick rotten planks. Father lifted the planks aside, then manoeuvred the sagging pole into the grey, greasy water, jabbed until he found an opening. Then pushed and pulled. He spent a long time doing this and emptying the lavatory bucket. He emptied the pail in the back garden among the nasturtiums that grew wild. He dug a hole, tipped the pail in it, then covered the hole with earth. The garden was stained with these mounds.

The last thing I watched him do at night was set the mousetrap. It was a small one. It had "The Little Nipper" printed on it and was stained with blood that had soaked into the wood. I would come down early next day to see what it had caught. There was a mouse every morning. Caught behind the head. Twisting the head and making the eyes wet slits. One of the ears was filled with blood and the delicate hind legs were also dipped in blood. My father took the trap outside to release the mouse in the garbage pail by the shed. But when he lifted the steel, the mouse remained stuck to the wood. So he turned the trap upside down. Two small drops—the size of its eyes, of a brilliant golden green-yellow—hung like dewdrops under the stomach. Father shook the trap, banged it against the side of the garbage can, until the mouse fell in.

After seven or eight mornings it seemed that my father was catching the same mouse over and over again.

On a Saturday afternoon in August there was a storm. It passed very quickly. One moment a low cloud, almost like a fog, swept across the fields, by the river. Then the hail began.

We were all up in the back bedroom watching the hail turn the cricket field white. The house shook and hail cracked the windows. We huddled together and watched the pavilion tumble, then be blown like a piece of newspaper across the field.

I went down with Father to the kitchen. The door had blown open, and hailstones swept in as if the coalman had dumped several bags. Before Father could shovel them out enough had melted to flood the kitchen. Then it was over. And there was a stillness, just like it was before it began.

We went out to see the damage. The nasturtiums were flat, exposing the massive network of roots and stalks. Mr. Briggs's greenhouse had all its glass broken. Under the apple tree the ground was thick with wet leaves and apples. Mr. Briggs's plum tree was split in half. His beans, his celery, his lettuce, his flowers were a sodden tangle on the ground.

Mr. and Mrs. Briggs, Kenny, and the terrier were also out inspecting damage.

"I can't find the garbage can," Father said.

"The last time I saw mine," Mr. Briggs said, "they just took off."

Mrs. Briggs laughed at this, and for some reason we all found it amusing.

I looked at the shambles of our garden, and the smashed gardens on either side of us. It was the only time I've seen our garden looking no different than the others.

Then it began to rain. The river flowed over and swept down to the crossroads. The manhole by the pub was blocked and Ketchum, the village policeman, stood in high rubber boots directing traffic. The cars came through, one at a time, the water reaching over the running boards.

By now nearly everyone was outside. Going from cottage to cottage. Finding out how many windows each had broken, and what details they remembered of the storm. Rumours spread. One man was supposed to have been killed by a falling tree. A bus collided head-on with a truck, killing both drivers. And in the middle of all this a strange excitement, almost of gaiety.

The coalman's son went around repeating to everyone, "This will make the nationals, just watch—it'll be in all the nationals—"

Mr. Pike, who owned the Shell garage up the road, darted about in rubber boots, carrying his pot-belly and wizened arm. "I've lived twelve years in South America. I've never seen such a storm."

Miss Honey, the retired schoolmistress, was taking pictures with an old box camera.

And someone said, "It's an act of God."

Towards evening, traffic increased. There was a line of thirty to forty cars, on either side, waiting to go through the water. The electricity had been knocked out, and the cottages were looking very pretty with candles in every window.

No one wanted to go inside.

Mrs. Briggs, her hair in curlers, had her head out of the top window, and watched the cars. We stood by the front gate. Father saw Mrs. Briggs and called out, "Some pile-up."

She drew the top of the dressing gown closer to her neck.

"It's just like London," she said.

The storm was a local one. The cars coming into Bogtown were not prepared for it. As they waited their turn they looked at the candlelit cottages, the people standing outside, and asked, "What happened here? Anything serious—?"

Three weeks before Christmas Mrs. Briggs decorated her window with a small Christmas tree, electric coloured lights, artificial snow, crackers in boxes, and large boxes of chocolates showing winter scenes on their covers.

A week later Mother decorated the living room of the cottage. She hung coloured paper chains from the ceiling and blew up balloons and hung those from the ends of the paper chains. Father cut a small Christmas tree from the wood, put it in a large biscuit tin, filled the tin with earth, and placed it on an overturned tea chest by the window.

We looked forward to Christmas. Mother was evacuated to Cornwall during the war and lived with a childless couple on their farm. Since her marriage the farmer sent her a goose for Christmas. So that we were certain not only of eating that day, but of having goose.

Then a week before Christmas odd things began to happen.

There was this new policeman, Ketchum. I don't think Father or Mother liked him or his missus very much, mainly because they were snooty. And he worked under the handicap that we liked his predecessor, Mr. Turbot.

"I can't see Mr. Turbot arresting anybody," Mrs. Briggs said when someone had broken into the Shell garage.

And she was perfectly right. Mr. Turbot ought to have been a schoolmaster instead of a policeman. He rode his motorbike gently up and down the main road. He directed traffic at school time, and gave the smallest kids candies. Mrs. Turbot sometimes met Mother on walks and she would hurry over to tell her secret.

"I've got another heavy puriod," she said in a Yorkshire accent.

But Ketchum and his wife kept to themselves. Mrs. Ketchum was a small mousy woman who dyed her hair various shades of blond and rarely said anything more than hello. But rumour had it that someone had seen her in front of her bedroom window with a pair of castanets doing a sexy Spanish dance.

Five days before Christmas, Mr. Ketchum knocked on the front door and when Father opened it, Mr. Ketchum had a bundle of things in a shopping bag.

"Someone left this on the bus—it's perishable stuff—I thought you might be able to use it."

There was cream, grapes, eggs, bacon, and a small roast. We had a feast that day.

But by next morning Mother began to worry about the goose. Father asked the postman, and the postmistress at the sub–post office, who also had a tea shop at the crossroads. He walked to the main post office by the church at the top of the hill. It hadn't arrived.

However things worked out all right. For on Christmas Eve, my mother's father and Mother came down from London to spend Christmas with us. And they brought with them a duck, Christmas pudding, enough coal for both fireplaces, lots of fruit and pressed meat, nuts, and presents. Grandad had asthma for as long as I can remember. He found it very difficult to breathe, nor could he walk very far, but had to stop and take out an atomizer and spray some stuff inside his mouth. They often came down unexpectedly—usually on a Sunday—bringing with them food and coal. And after dinner Grandad would wander around the cottage fixing things. Like Father he was good at fixing things with his hands: the bad wiring in the cottage; Mother's second-hand iron; or some toy that had got broken. When he and Gran left they always gave Mother a few pounds.

That night I stayed awake. From the partly open window I couldn't see the trees that bordered the field across the road, but I could hear the dripping. Everything seemed to be dripping outside. A vixen barked from somewhere near the pub up the road, but closer were the soft clicks of the dripping leaves.

Next morning Kate and I went downstairs early—Father hadn't set the mousetrap—and began to open the presents. Kate had a top that spun all sorts of bright-coloured sparks. I had a book and a pen. The baby had a rattle, building blocks, and a tambourine. Mother got a box of Mrs. Briggs's chocolates and smelly soap, and Father some cigars. We wished each other happy Christmas. We had the duck and Christmas pudding with the brandy burning over it, tangerines, chocolates, and nuts. Then we sang carols and went for a walk. The dew clung to the bushes and leaves. And you could see the spiders' webs, for they were outlined by small drops of rain.

In the afternoon Grandad fell asleep in a chair. And when he woke we posed for photographs that he took in the back garden. They played with Kate and the baby. And after tea we played Scrabble. By eight o'clock it was time for them to go back. They left some money with Mother and I walked them down the dark road, past the police station, the pub, and up from the crossroads to the slope that led to the railway station. Grandad had to stop and struggle for breath every few yards, and use his atomizer. Gran was healthy and walked a bit ahead. We weren't sure what time the train came, but there was only this one back at night.

We walked up, slowly, through the mist. I now could see the light from the bridge.

"I don't remember going over a bridge," Grandad said.

"It isn't a bridge," I said. "It's just the part over the railway tracks."

Then he had to stop again and rest.

"I'll run ahead," I said, "and see when the train's supposed to come in."

On the damp platform there was a couple seeing someone off. A baby in the man's arms, and a young woman with a pram. The clock said eight thirty. There was still another seven minutes. I started back. As I came near the slope I saw a waving flashlight.

Gran was running down the slope with the flashlight and crying.

"What's happened?"

"Oh, Nick, it's Charlie. He couldn't help it."

"What happened?"

"He had to take his pants off at the bridge."

She started to weep again. "He said to me, 'Susie, you go ahead, don't wait for me.'"

I ran back to the bridge; Grandad was standing there breathing heavily. His coat, his scarf, his jacket, were on the ground, and his trousers were open at the top.

"You've got another seven minutes," I said. "Lots of time."

Gran came running back. We put his clothes back on and I took him under one arm and she under the other and we started to walk carefully down the slope. In between wheezes he said, "I stink."

"You couldn't help it," Gran said.

"I did it in my trousers and I've got them back on."

There was still no sign of the train by the time we arrived at the platform. Grandad went into the dark lavatory. "He couldn't help it," Gran said to me. "He's helpless. He couldn't help it."

She had given him a suitcase and told him to take out a sheet.

He came out of the lavatory, beads of sweat on his face, and puffing. Sounding as if a child was somewhere inside his chest, and crying. Gran kissed him.

"You couldn't help it."

"What a stinking grandfather I am," he said.

And we all laughed.

When the train came they found an empty compartment. He had taken one sock off and threw it away in the lavatory.

"Have I another sock, Susie?"

"In the case, dear."

Gran said she loved him, and kissed him again. And they forgot that I was on the platform as the train began to move and disappeared quickly into the mist.

Two weeks later, on a Wednesday afternoon, the postman rode up on his bicycle. On the carrier, over the back wheel, was strapped a badly wrapped brown-paper parcel. He brought it in, holding it well in front of him, and gave it to Father.

"You better bury this soon," he said in disgust.

It was our goose. Wrongly addressed, it had gone to a village in Surrey instead of Sussex.

Father and Mother and myself carefully inspected it. It

was a large bird, quite blue and shrivelled, and it smelled up the kitchen.

"What do you think?" Mother said.

Father walked away without replying.

We had an onion and some stale bread and jam for tea. Mother cut the onion in slices and fried it, and shared it out. Father climbed the apple tree and got the last two apples at the top that the storm had not knocked down.

After tea Father took the goose in the brown paper and a shovel and dug a deep hole in the back garden between two mounds where he had emptied the bucket. We stood silent, and watched him bury it. Mother held the baby in her arms and Kate stood beside me, holding my hand. Then we went back.

In the cottage Mother put the baby down. The sun was across the river, and there were low broken clouds pushed across the sky by the wind. The sun entered the cottage through the window of the living room. The baby began to chase it. "La la," she said and chased it on the wall. Mother said, "Here." And the baby turned. "La la. La la." She ran up to the wall again touching the sun.

LMF

During the Second World War one way of leaving the Forces was to be discharged LMF. LMF stood for "Lack of Moral Fibre."

A WARM spring morning. From the glass wall of the apartment I watched two firemen in blue shirts outside the fire station rolling out water hoses until they lay flat. Then, carefully, rolling them up. And carrying them inside. On top of the fire station the four-sided clock said 9:26. I shaved, poured another coffee, lit another cigarillo. I still had a half-hour. The television station at Bloor and Yonge was only a few minutes away. My Canadian publisher had brought out two of my books and I was expected to promote them. The program, I was told, would be taped in front of a small audience at eleven in the morning and broadcast a few hours later.

In the little waiting room a plump man in a dark blue wrinkled suit was sitting in a chair and looking through a flat attaché case. He looked to be in his thirties. A broad face, a wide mouth, prominent teeth, black wavy hair. As I came in he smiled.

I sat down against the wall opposite him.

He looked friendly and anxious to please.

I asked him when he was going on.

"I'm Bruce Grace's secretary," he said. And smiled again. "He's here for a concert. It's sold out. We've been to Ottawa, Hamilton, Windsor. They were all sold out."

I didn't know who Bruce Grace was.

Because he spoke with an accent I asked him where he was from.

"New Zealand. Have you been there?"

"No," I said.

A tall man came in carrying a book. He had a look of the outdoors about him. He was smiling.

"Have you read this book?" he asked me.

"What is it called?"

"*The Way to Happiness.*"

"No," I said.

"You must read it," he said enthusiastically. "It will change your life. I feel a different person since I've read it."

He looked confident and at ease. A small face with glasses, straight, slightly reddish hair parted on a side, a short neat beard. He wore a light brown safari jacket and light brown boots with high heels.

He sat in a chair against one wall. His secretary against another. And I against another. The small room seemed to be getting smaller.

"Could you sign a record for the host?" the secretary said and brought out a record from the attaché case. Then handed him a pen after he removed the top. Bruce Grace signed the record that had his name and photograph on it.

"You know," he said to me and continued to smile, "when I go onto the stage—I can feel the love that is coming from the audience. And when I sing—I give it back to them."

"I have only heard bad politicians talk that way," I said.

Bruce Grace stopped smiling.

His secretary began to look uneasy.

"What do you do?" Bruce Grace asked.

"I'm a writer."

"Then you must have had many disappointments."

After that we didn't speak freely.

A pretty woman came in, about five foot five. She walked slowly and looked around a bit suspiciously. She was middle-aged but well preserved. She had a slightly puzzled, slightly impish, expression in her face. Finally she sat down in the chair next to me.

"Is this for the talk show?" she said in a quiet but distinct voice that had something of Europe in it.

"Yes," I said.

Bruce Grace gave her a smile. So did the secretary.

She looked around the room hardly turning her head. Her face was continually changing expression but the changes were barely noticeable.

"Why are you all dressed in black?" I asked her.

"Because I am in mourning for my life."

"Chekhov."

"Yes," she said, "*The Seagull.* Act I."

"You must be an actress."

"Yes," she said and whispered her name. All I heard was her first name, Lydia.

"I'm sorry," I said. "I have been living in England for most of the last thirty years."

"I live some of the year in Paris," she said. "Some of the year in New York, and in Hollywood. I am in Toronto for a short time doing a play. The director told me to go on this show. He said it will help make people come to see the play."

The last person to arrive walked in quickly and sat in the chair beside me on the other side. He was a tall distinguished-looking man in a dark pinstriped single-breasted suit with vest and a watch-chain . . . a red silk tie, a white shirt. He had blue eyes and glasses and brown curly hair. We got to talking. He said he was a psychic. I said nothing. "I earn two thousand dollars a week," he went on. "No one knows where I live. I have a farm, a wife, and a daughter of fourteen. She likes horses. We have horses. But no one knows where I live. People come to see me from all over the world. They are screened first. Well-known people ... actors ... heads of government ... only rich people."

"What do they come to see you for?"

"About making money. Whether they should go ahead with some project. And when they are going to die."

Lydia interrupted timidly. "When will this program be shown?"

"Today," I said, "at 1:00 p.m."

She looked slightly surprised.

"I thought it was next week," she said slowly. "I must let someone know."

"Tell me the phone number," the secretary said. "I'll do it for you."

Lydia hesitated. "I don't know the number."

"Where do they live?"

Again she hesitated. Then, reluctantly, said,

"In Willowdale."

"That isn't enough," the secretary said, raising his voice. "What's the street?"

"I'm not sure."

"Can you tell me the name of the person?"

She hesitated and lowered her head.

"It's my husband."

The first to go on was Bruce Grace. A girl assistant came in and led him away. We all watched the small TV monitor in the room, tilted down from the ceiling. As Bruce Grace walked in there was applause from the audience. He smiled easily. He talked easily. He talked about his wife, his children, his home in Switzerland. How he loved them all. How he made these tours every two years. How he flew his airplane. And told a story of flying through a thunderstorm just before landing in Germany. He said he liked singing because it made people happy and he felt happy doing it. And he liked being in Canada . . . He came across as a likeable, open person. It was an excellent performance.

I was next. And I don't know whether it was the encounters with the others in the small room or my nervousness. Probably both. But while the commercial was on and before we began . . . I kept thinking . . . what am I doing here? This was show business. What did this have to do with writing? And though something in me wanted to do it well, there was also something in me that disliked the thought that I might be good at it.

After the opening biographical questions it stopped being a conversation and became a monologue. "I notice," I said, "that writers in the newspapers here write about how words are misused. But no one has pointed out something more damaging. The way people exaggerate when they use language."

"I went to a supermarket," I continued, "to get some eggs. I went to the section that was marked extra large eggs. I opened a carton of a dozen eggs. They were a dull white and small. An elderly woman beside me, seeing my surprise, said, 'If you go to those labelled large you would think sparrows have laid them.'

"Then when I wanted to take a bus to Ottawa. 'You can go super express or express,' the person behind the counter told me. 'What's the difference?' 'Super express doesn't stop.'

"I heard kids coming back from school talking about their exams. They didn't say 'I passed' or 'I failed.' But said 'I aced,' 'I creamed,' 'I bombed.' It was the language of show business. It's fine in show business. But anywhere else exaggeration is a form of lying."

The host didn't like the way the conversation was going. He looked worried. He had lines in his forehead. He was scowling.

I knew I should be talking lightheartedly—not like this. He suddenly changed the subject and asked me something about fishing off the Pacific coast. What fish did I like?

"Potatoes," I said.

The audience laughed. So did the host. And on this happy note he wound up my portion of the program by saying what fine books the two were and he repeated the titles and my name. And I walked off.

I just wanted to get away. I knew I had done badly. As I approached Lydia, waiting in the wings to come on, she gave me a look. It was the kind of look a professional gives to an amateur.

Instead of walking straight out of the building, I stopped in the next room where the program was being put out and saw Lydia on several monitors. Her face was in close-up. And, on the screen, she just seemed to grow. All those slight expressions, which I barely noticed when she was sitting beside me, were now registering strongly. She had presence. She had personality—as did Bruce Grace. They both looked much more substantial on the screen than the person I talked to.

Outside the sun was shining. I walked along the street wondering why I go and do these things. Passing a delicatessen I went in to have a smoked meat sandwich. The large room was almost empty. A short man, in his fifties, in glasses and with neat grey waves in his hair, was standing by the cash register. He showed me to a table in the centre of the room.

Halfway through the sandwich the man in the grey suit came over.

"Last week Richard Burton sat in the chair you are sitting in," he said. "The week before that, Sir Ralph Richardson."

I couldn't get away from it.

Back in the apartment, I took off my jacket and tie, undid the collar—made myself a cup of coffee. No, I thought, I'm not going to see the program.

But at one o'clock I walked over and switched on the TV set. Instead of seeing Bruce Grace, the station was showing a debate from the House of Commons in Ottawa . . . A Member of Parliament was standing up and talking. I wondered what was going on. Then a voice said that because of the Quebec referendum the talk show would not be seen.

I wanted to laugh. I felt relieved, lighthearted. I remember the psychic telling me about life. "Of course it's meaningless, but if you have no money you're in trouble." Then he told me how he believed in destiny. Was this destiny?

Quebec voted not to separate from Canada and I quickly forgot what happened on the talk show.

Until two days later.

The phone rang.

And someone working on the program said a man in British Columbia saw me on the show and phoned up.

"He would like you to call him back—collect."

And she gave me the number.

"But it wasn't shown," I said.

"It was blacked out in Ontario and Quebec because of the referendum. But it was shown everywhere else . . . He said he was with you and your wife in Minneapolis."

Now I knew this wasn't right. For my wife had never been to North America.

"Did he give his name?"

"Orville," she said.

I didn't know anyone called Orville.

But for the rest of the week it bothered me. It was the part about Minneapolis. For I had been, for a brief visit, to Minneapolis—or was it St. Paul? It was during the war. While I was training to fly in the West. Disjointed bits and pieces kept coming back. Then I remembered. It could only be Bell—was his first name Orville? I had forgotten. In any case no one called him that. He was always called Bell.

It was 1943, the late summer. I had just finished a course on a flying station in southern Alberta and along with the entire class was posted to an advanced flying station in Manitoba, near Winnipeg. We had five days' leave before reporting to Winnipeg. Those who came from this part of the country went home. But there was Harris from Toronto, Bell from British Columbia, and I from Ottawa.

I am remembering a time thirty-seven years ago, when Bell and Harris were in their mid-twenties and I was nineteen.

Bell was around five foot ten, well built. He had a clean-cut look: a fine nose, grey eyes deep set, and lots of straight black hair that he combed back. But there was something awkward about him. I don't mean it in any noticeable way. He smiled, he laughed, he talked well. But sometimes Bell just stared—not for long, but enough to tell me that there was something about Bell I didn't know.

Harris was a bit shorter than Bell. When he talked he nearly always seemed to get a laugh out of things. Though he was around twenty-five or twenty-six he looked older. His brown hair had started to recede. He was dapper. He always looked well groomed in the uniform and smelled of after-shave. He wore his forage cap tilted at more of an angle than regulations allowed. He had a pencil moustache above his top lip, kept very thin and neatly trimmed. And he chuckled a lot.

Where Harris was bubbly, Bell was restrained. He was married less than a year. And though he didn't talk much about his young wife, he wrote her a letter every day. Harris was married longer but he was on the lookout for girls.

We came together because we were stuck for five days, far from home, without money, and we didn't want to hang around the station.

It was Bell who suggested we go to the States by riding a freight car. Harris and I had not done this before. Bell said he had. So had his father before him. There were freight trains, he said, leaving Winnipeg regularly for Minneapolis. All we had to do was get on. Bell said it would be easy if we just followed him.

At dusk he led us past the railway yards, a bit into the country. It would still be going slow here, he said. Then we waited for it to get dark. I could hear the lovely sound of a train whistle coming out of nowhere—those two deep notes—and somewhere else it was answered.

The first freight train was going too fast. Bell said to let it go. But when he saw the second one he shouted, "This is it." And he ran fast alongside the moving freight cars. So did Harris and I. Bell, on the run, got hold of the iron ladder on the side of a moving freight car and quickly climbed several rungs. I got on behind him. Harris followed. Then Bell climbed up to the end of the iron ladder and, half crouching, he walked along the top of the freight car. I walked after him, on the narrow plank of wood that was on top of the freight car. I saw Bell lie down on his back, fully stretched out. I did the same. He indicated to put my feet on either side of his head and body. He held onto my feet. I had Harris's feet come down on either side of my head and body. And I held on to his. And in this way we travelled in the dark. There was a wind . . . the stars were out . . . the freight cars shook . . . and we didn't stop.

I don't remember if I slept that night or not but some time in the early morning the freight train stopped. Bell told us to follow him. "We'll find a nice-smelling empty grain car." He climbed down the iron ladder. Then ran alongside the motionless freight train. Bell found one that was empty and clean. We pushed the heavy doors apart. Then hopped in.

The train started to move again. Bell suggested we take our black issue boots and socks off. So we did. And there we were, the three of us . . . sitting at the open edge of the freight car . . . bare feet dangling over the side . . . and watching fields of wheat and buttercups go by.

After that I don't remember details. But we did get off when the train slowed down on the outskirts. We had a shower in the YMCA and something to eat. Then, feeling much better, we walked in the wide main streets of Minneapolis. Because of our uniform—blue with white flashes in our forage caps—we kept getting looks from passersby.

Then a car stopped. And two attractive blond girls of about nineteen or twenty were in the front seats. The one driving put her head out; her cheeks were slightly flushed. She said to me,

"Are you Andy Smith?"

"No," I said.

"But you look just like him."

I could see Harris giving me all kinds of signals that I didn't understand.

The girls kept saying how much I looked like Andy Smith and I kept telling them that unfortunately I wasn't.

They drove off laughing.

Harris was angry. "Couldn't you see what they wanted? They wanted to pick us up. You must be an idiot. We could have slept the night with them."

Bell was laughing at all this.

We slept the night at the Y and over breakfast Bell suggested that we go to the British consul in Minneapolis and tell him who we are and that we have no money and see if he would lend us some to get back to the station. He didn't lend us money but he gave us bus tickets to Winnipeg and showed us, proudly, aerial photographs taken of the Mohne and Eder dams, in the Ruhr, after they were breached by Lancasters.

Two months later we graduated from Winnipeg as pilot officers. And separated when we were posted overseas to different parts of England and Scotland.

I don't know what happened to Harris. But some time in the spring of 1945, Bell turned up on the same squadron that I had not long joined. The war in Europe was nearly over and the trips into Germany were getting longer. We were given pills to take with us to keep us awake. While over the target there was more danger of bumping into another Lancaster than of being shot down.

When I came into the crowded briefing room I saw, by the stretched red ribbon on the flat map of Europe, that it was going to be another long trip.

Briefing had started. The intelligence officer was in front telling us why it was necessary to go and bomb the railway yards just outside Leipzig . . . when I saw Bell stand up, by one of the small wooden tables, about fifteen feet away.

The intelligence officer also saw him.

He stopped what he was saying and said to Bell, "Have you a question?"

And Bell quietly said,

"I want to kill Hitler."

I could see he was tense. And he began to tremble as he repeated, "I want to kill Hitler. I want to kill Hitler . . ."

Then he began to shout it out.

Two service police, standing by the wall, quickly came over and forcefully bundled him out of the room.

We were all relieved when the trip to Leipzig was cancelled.

After that Bell disappeared from the station.

I heard he was shipped off to Florida. And a joke was going around the mess that he was spending his days lying on a Florida beach recuperating. While gossip had it that it was because of his wife—she was having a baby. Then I was told he was discharged LMF. And I heard nothing more—until this phone call to the television station.

I did hear Bruce Grace. I was flying, as a passenger, to England. And somewhere over the Atlantic, in the dark, I plugged the headphones into the armrest. And, on one of the channels, he was singing how marvellous it was to wake up in the morning and to see the start of a new day.

I saw Lydia more recently. When I returned to Toronto I went to see a film in Cumberland Street, not far from where the talk show took place. She was playing the part of a middle-aged woman who has cancer. But, according to the film, she didn't know it. Her husband was taking her on a trip across the country ... seeing relatives, friends, and going to different places. There was one scene ... they had come to a deserted beach in California. And Lydia, on an impulse, took off her shoes and stockings and ran along the white-yellow sand to the tideline. Then she began to do a slow circular dance ... her hands above her head ... her head tilted up. She looked like a young girl just enjoying being alive.

CONTINUITY

I

WHEN I was eleven my parents arranged for me to spend the summer holidays on a farm a few miles out of Ottawa. I was a city kid. But that summer I learned how to smoke by packing the dry hairs from the end of a cob of corn into a clay pipe. I was taught how to pitch horseshoes at a steel stake driven in the ground. I rode a farm horse bareback and was shown how to lasso a fence post. On hot dusty days I drank cold water out of a tin ladle like the film cowboys (Ken Maynard, Buck Jones, Hoot Gibson) that I saw in the Français. And, at night, I sat on the wooden veranda and listened to the cowboy records being played inside: "I Have No Use for the Women"; "Strawberry Roan."

The farm is no longer there—it is part of Uplands Airport. But when I was growing up in Ottawa it was owned and farmed by Mr. Marcovitch and his four sons. They grew sweet corn in the summer. And I helped by going beside the horse and the high cart (with the two wooden wheels) pulling the ripe cobs from the stalks, throwing them into the cart and later counting them into sacks for the Ottawa market.

Mr. Marcovitch—a short lean man with a black moustache and reddish face—had come to Ottawa from Europe, as had most of the small Jewish community. He had been farming here for almost twenty years. There were a few other farms around. Poitvin was the nearest. But the territory hadn't been farmed very long. The cemetery was a small green field with three headstones.

I didn't forget that summer. Because next year when I decided to run away from home, one Saturday morning, I hitchhiked to Marcovitch's farm. They let me stay the weekend. Then talked me into going back.

Thirteen years later I got further away when I sailed for England with the manuscript of a first novel in a black Gladstone bag. It was 1949. And because of the wartime interest in reading it was still comparatively easy to find a publisher. When the novel was accepted I lived a kind of bohemian life with other hopefuls. We were mostly in our twenties, with little money. But we thought of ourselves as writers and painters.

When the novel came out it earned me fifty pounds. And as I had got married I took a job—head of the English department—at a boys' grammar school in North Devon. And again lived on a farm.

Unlike Marcovitch's farm, this one had red soil, lush vegetation, and thick hedgerows. It was also quite isolated. Just two farmhouses not too far apart. There were the Sweets—we rented the house from them. And further down were the Whites—he was something like Governor of Gibraltar or Malta or Cyprus before the last war. He brought us holly at Christmas from their trees. The postman came from Barnstaple. He came, once a day, on an old bicycle, when he picked up our letters and put them inside his cap. He couldn't pronounce our name and called my wife "Mrs. Leaving." Later, I would see him in Barnstaple on a corner selling newspapers. If the papers were not being bought fast enough he would make up headlines: "Nude Girl in Street," he shouted. "Girl in the Nude—"

At breakfast I would watch cows go by the front door on their way to the fields. And there were always ducks around. And more by the small river. And lots of daffodils that my wife used to pick. And guinea fowls in the field across the road between the apple trees. And there were horses and rabbits and foxes. And badger hunts. And ferreting on Saturdays. It was all very green and luxurious and relaxed. Rolling hills everywhere.

At Christmas the boys in the class brought butter, eggs, chickens, for the masters. And I was invited to their homes. The large hams hanging from the ceiling, the highly polished saddles. They showed me the work they had to do on the farm. School, I realized, was for them only a small part of their lives.

Before the year was up the headmaster (he also had a farm) asked me to stay on. But I was restless, and I wanted to write, not teach.

When we were leaving my wife said,

"I'm glad we are going. Everything here is so rich—it makes you feel poor."

We left Devon. And for a while moved around. In London. In Brighton. Before coming to rest in this seaside town in Cornwall. But I haven't forgotten that time in the country. Living by the sea with all this grey stone (and the colourful sunrises and sunsets over the bay, the fine sand beaches, the gulls) I find I miss trees, green fields, and things growing.

Then this summer.

The front doorbell rang. And our eldest daughter, now twenty, called out, "Dad, there is someone at the door who says you taught him English."

I came down and saw this tall man in a white shirt. He was smiling. He had rosy cheeks with black straight hair thinning on the top.

"Yes," he said after hesitating a bit and still smiling. "Yes."

"Hello," I said shaking his hand and not knowing who he was.

"I'm John Barrett," he said. "You taught me in 4A. I'm here on holiday. I was here last year. I tried to see you but you were away."

"John Barrett," I said.

"You taught us *The Mayor of Casterbridge*."

"Yes," I said.

"I don't read much," he said. "But I have read that book four times since."

I introduced my wife.

We sat in the front room. My wife brought in coffee. He told us that he was farming. That he had five hundred cows, eight hundred sheep, and two trout streams. That he sang in the local choir. That he played cricket for the local team. And rugby for the local club. That he hadn't been away from home for the first thirteen years of working on the farm. "I didn't sleep one night away from my bed." And that he hadn't forgotten those days when I taught him.

All the time he was talking I tried to remember who he was. But couldn't.

"What happened," I said, "to the postman who sold papers in Barnstaple?"

"Gerald."

"Yes, what happened to Gerald?"

"He died last year. Thousands came to his funeral."

"He used to call my wife Mrs. Leaving."

"Do you remember Watson?" he said. "He came from Scotland."

And I remembered a thirteen-year-old in short trousers, brown blazer, and cap. A toothy smile, well-mannered, anxious to please. I had to set him an essay to write to see if he was good enough to go to the school.

"He joined the Air Force," Barrett said, "and was killed just after he soloed in a jet—Remember Shepherd?"

I didn't say anything.

"He's playing cricket for one of the counties."

"The fat little boy in the second form that no one could bowl out?"

"That's him."

He kept telling me names that I tried to fit faces to. Now and then I did. They were all doing well, he said. So I finally asked him.

"Anyone not do well?"

"No," he said hesitantly. "I can't think of anyone."

I thought I'd show him where I work. And led him up the stairs to this large attic room. He looked at the wooden desk, the papers, the books, the magazines, the proofs. Then he walked over to the window and looked out to the bay.

"You've got a nice view. But do you have enough work to keep you busy?"

"Yes," I said. "I wonder, sometimes, what I would do if I had nothing to write about."

He didn't understand. For he repeated, "But you have enough work to keep you going?"

"Yes."

"And you're doing all right?"

"A lot better than ten years ago."

We went back downstairs.

I asked him how long the farm had been in his family.

He said he was farming the same land that his father did, and his grandfather, and great-grandfather. That a builder had offered him 175,000 pounds for it. But he wouldn't sell.

I told him that I didn't even know my grandfather. The furthest I could go back was to my father.

Again he looked bewildered.

So I said, "There are some people who belong to the place they live in. There are others who don't. They just pass through."

It was the only time I felt I was still his teacher.

He replied by saying that he liked meeting people. And liked to keep in touch with those that meant something to him when he was growing up. Then he told me of what he did on the farm. How the work was never finished.

I have met so many amateurs in my line of work that it was nice to hear a professional talking.

"We have a house with over twenty rooms," he said. "If you're ever in North Devon, let me know. I'll come and get you. And you can stay with us."

We had talked for over two hours. And I didn't know who he was.

Then, at lunch, while he was sitting opposite me at the table, I said, "You sat in the middle of the class."

"Yes."

"You were a bit fatter then."

"Yes."

"You used to wear a lot of green—and you had a bit more hair and it was straight and black."

He grinned.

"Yes," I said. "I remember you."

After that things went even better.

On impulse I decided to give him something to take back. I left him with my wife in the front room while I went upstairs to see what I could find. While I was looking I heard singing. It was coming, very clearly, from downstairs.

I went quietly down the stairs. And saw him standing by the piano. His feet were apart and he was swaying a bit as he sang.

Where my caravan has rested
Flowers I leave you in the grass.
All the flowers of love and friendship
You will see them when you pass.

He looked to me a happy man. And when he left I felt regret.

II

In 1964, at the end of August, a friend of mine, a painter, died from a gliding accident. A week later, another friend, a poet, died from a heart attack. The painter was forty-six. The poet was thirty-six. The painter was a Cornishman. And he was buried not far from where he was born and where he had lived and worked all his life. The poet was born in New York, brought to Scotland as a child, moved to London during the war, then to Cambridge. And he died while in Plymouth. His ashes were scattered on the sea outside Plymouth.

It was not long after this that I went into Penzance to see if I could find the old Jewish cemetery that I had read was there.

I kept asking old people in Market Jew Street. But they didn't know. A schoolboy told me to go up a side street from the railway station, then by a narrow dirt lane, beside the backs of terraced houses.

From the outside it didn't look like a cemetery, but a small backyard that had been walled up. There was an old green door in the front wall, with a new bolt and lock. And on the door it gave the name of the caretaker and where he lived. Nothing to say or suggest what was inside.

I tried to look over by climbing. But there was nothing to get hold of. Finally, I went to the address that was painted on the green door and an elderly man came out with a key.

It looked even smaller inside. There were old gravestones close together. "In memory of Lemon Woolf, aged 65 years." I couldn't read the Hebrew, only the English. "Sacred to the Memory of Jacob James Hart Esq., late her Britannic Majesty's Consul for the Kingdom of Saxony and a native of this town."

I looked around this walled backyard with its slate and granite stones. What did this have to do with me? I wondered how I would behave if there was still a Jewish community in Penzance. I know I would have bought the bread, the salami, the hot dogs. Gone to a Jewish restaurant, if there was one. But anything more than that?

Over the next year I tried to find out what I could about the extinct Jewish community of Penzance. I asked the public librarian. He didn't have much information.

"The Jewish community," he said, "lived in Penzance from the middle of the eighteenth century to 1913, when the last Jew moved away. The small cemetery is all that is left."

Then my wife came across references. In a specialized book on British clockmakers of the eighteenth and nineteenth centuries there were several clockmakers in Penzance. And some had Jewish names. She looked through old copies of local papers for anything she could find. It was becoming more like a detective story. But we had few clues. And after a while I began to lose interest. And I didn't think about it.

Until this April when the phone rang. And a young man's voice said that he was speaking from Penzance. That he heard from the Penzance librarian that I was interested in the old Jewish cemetery. So was he. Could he come and see me.

"Of course," I said.

He arrived in a white sports car. He stood at the door carrying a folder with papers. And he had an easy smile.

"My name is Jonathon Singer," he said.

I asked him in and introduced my wife.

Jonathon Singer was thirty. And he looked as if he was used to the good life. He had a lively, intelligent face, brown eyes, brown wavy hair. He smiled often, showing good teeth. He had on a flowery shirt with a light orange kerchief at his throat. And he wore casually a well-cut grey suit.

"Have you come far?" my wife asked.

"I go all over the country," he said. "I've seen old Jewish cemeteries in parts of Scotland, at King's Lynn, at Yarmouth. I'm now doing the West Country. I thought I would start at the end of the line, Penzance, and work backwards. From here I'll go to Plymouth, then Bath, Gloucester, Cheltenham."

I had a fire going in the grate. He sat in a chair on one side warming his hands. I was in the other. My wife brought coffee. And we all had hot coffee and biscuits.

"What do you actually do?" my wife asked.

"I'm a professor of Hebrew at Cambridge," he said. "I give courses in medieval poetry. But I'm doing this for the Jewish Board of Deputies in London. I go to places where there once were tiny communities. I go to the cemetery. And note down every stone. What condition it is in. Whether it is granite, marble, or slate."

"Which lasts longer?" I interrupted.

"Slate," he said. "I note down whether the stone is flat or upright. And what it says on it."

"In Penzance," I said, "I could only read the English."

"The Hebrew," Jonathon said, "is much more interesting."

"There is a stone there to the father of Lemon Hart," I said. "He had the rum concession for the British Navy."

Jonathon looked eagerly through his folder and picked out a single sheet of paper. "I'll translate by sight—

"Here lies a faithful man, President of the Congregation, who walked in the ways of the good, righteous and upright, bold as a lion and fleet as a deer to the voice of Torah and prayer, evening and morning his house was open wide, he gave of his bread to the hungry, his body dwells among the holy ones who are in the ground, but his soul is in the Garden of Eden: the President (of the Congregation) Rabbi Asher, son of the President Rabbi Hayyim died 9th Adar II, buried the 10th, in the year 5608 AM, may his soul be bound up in the bundle of life.

"And in English it has, 'In memory of Lemon Woolf, aged 65 years.' The year 5608 would be 1848."

He turned over a few more loose pages in his folder. "Probably there was a learned man in the community who would know how to phrase these things. People would come to him. Listen to this—

"And Jacob's days came close to death and he called to his friend and said, I shall sleep with my fathers, bury me in their grave, give thirty pounds to my sister: the grave of Jacob son of R. Solomon the Levite, who died on the eve of the holy Sabbath, 24th Shebat, buried on Thursday the first day of the New Moon of Adar in the year AM 5606.

"Then in English it has, 'Sacred to the Memory of Jacob James Hart Esq., late her Britannic Majesty's Consul for the Kingdom of Saxony and a native of this town ...'"

"Are you doing this for a book?" I asked him.

"No," he said. "Other people will come after me, and make something from this information. But it's important to have it. And to have it recorded accurately. It is also something I enjoy. When I am in one of the cemeteries, I feel a sense of continuity. These are my people."

I opened a bottle of red wine. And my wife went to the kitchen to prepare lunch.

"Your wife isn't Jewish?"

"No," I said. "And I'm not a believer."

"Christianity and Islam," he said, "put great emphasis on belief. You can be a Jew without believing."

"But it's impossible to be a Jew by yourself," I said. "You need a whole life-supporting system around you. Sometimes in the past, here, I would see in the diary that tomorrow was Yom Kippur or Rosh Hoshannah. And I would get all dressed up in a new white shirt and tie, put on a new suit. And when my wife and kids said, 'Why are you all dressed up, Dad?' I would say, 'Today is Yom Kippur' or 'Today is Rosh Hoshannah.' But where could I go? There's no synagogue in Cornwall. And if there was one, I doubt if I would go in. So I'd go for a walk. And remember my childhood in Ottawa."

"I can go back several generations in England," Jonathon said. "My great-great-grandfather was chief rabbi."

"My parents came to Ottawa from Europe in the early 1920s."

"You have an immigrant's past," he said. "It brings problems."

"What sort of problems?"

"Insecurity," he said.

"At one time I wanted to go to Poland," I said, "to see where my parents came from. But my mother told me it wasn't a good idea. In any case, she was certain that the town she came from was wiped out by the Germans."

"Is your father alive?"

"No," I said. "The biggest stone in Ottawa's Jewish cemetery is his. My mother put it up with the insurance money. She bought a double grave."

"My grandmother did the same thing in London when my grandfather died," Jonathon said. "She bought a double grave. Two years later she married again. Now she doesn't know what to do."

I filled our glasses with more wine.

And Jonathon said, "I'm also a rabbi. I didn't have any vocation for it. I just thought it was something I'd like to be."

"Have you married and buried people?"

"Yes," he said.

"I read something by Graham Greene. He was writing about Norman Douglas. He said that there are some rabbis who perform circumcision with their thumbnail so rapidly and painlessly that the child never cries."

"No," Jonathon said. "They wouldn't be allowed to do it that way. They have to use an instrument."

My wife came in and asked us to go into the kitchen. The table was laid out. She said to Jonathon, "It's just eggs, cheese, and a salad."

"It's just what I wanted," he said. "I'm a vegetarian."

While we were eating he told us, with enthusiasm, how Jewish peddlers used to work the West Country. "There was a man called Zender from Falmouth. About 1750. He hired peddlers to go around Cornwall on pack horses. And there were certain inns they would make for. The landlord had a key to a cupboard for the cooked things. And on the frying pan there would be the person's name, who last used it, the date, and the appropriate quote of the day from the Torah. And when the peddler was ready to leave he would wash up, put his name in chalk on the bottom of the frying pan, the date, and a quote from the Torah. So whoever came after would know it was all right."

"It's fascinating," my wife said. "You make it all come to life. Shall we go in the front room for the coffee? It's much warmer there."

I stayed to give her a hand in the kitchen.

"Who does he remind you of?" she asked me, as she put cups on the tray.

I didn't know.

"Those early photographs of your father."

I hadn't thought of it. But now that she said it I saw the resemblance. The brown wavy hair, the full lips, the manner.

"He looks so secure," she said, "so happy in what he is doing, in knowing where he belongs."

"He is secure," I said. "He told me he has his job at Cambridge for life. He can't be fired."

Later, in the front room, Jonathon became impatient. He suggested that I go with him, in his car, for part of the trip to Plymouth. And he would leave me off at a railway station on the way so I could go back.

Soon we were in the country. How marvellous the orange-yellow gorse looks, the bluebells and campion in the grass on the sides.

Suddenly it began to snow.

"This is the first snow we've had this year," I said. "And it has to come in April."

"I knew it would snow," Jonathon said. "It was so cold in the cemetery, I had to wear gloves while I was writing."

We passed small fields with their hedges. And in the valleys, light green and dark green trees and here and there a copper beech. I've seen this landscape often. But either I keep forgetting or else it changes. Because every time I see it I think, how beautiful.

And just as quickly the snow stopped. The sun came out.

"This has been a very lazy day for me," Jonathon said as he drove into Bodmin Road Station. A quiet country station. "I don't have time to be sidetracked."

The only other person at the station was a farmer, by the side of his car, releasing some pigeons. A sudden *whirr*. The pigeons rose, flew one way, turned, they seemed confused, before they all turned west and disappeared.

"They have to line up with the sun," the farmer told us, "to find their direction."

Jonathon looked at his watch. "You have another seven minutes to wait. Do you think you'll stay down here much longer?"

"No," I said.

After he drove away, I walked slowly up and down the long platform. I listened to the birds. Looked at the surrounding farming country. How full of colour. The upward-sloping grass fields, the trees—the sun shining on them. Until the train appeared on the curve of track.

GIFTS

L ATE NOVEMBER 1979 I flew to Canada to give three lectures and readings. In Toronto and Montreal I would talk at universities. In Ottawa—where I was to start—I would give a reading to the blind. A light snow was falling as the taxi went through heavy afternoon traffic to the Château Laurier. I was shown into a large, comfortable room on the second floor, newly furnished, with a double bed, easy chairs, a writing desk, telephone, colour television. From the window I could see the Peace Tower, not far away, hear the chimes on the quarter-hour. In the other room, bright from the fluorescent lights, the bath was long with no taps, just a metal wheel that I could turn for hot or cold. I flicked a switch by the television; soft music came in both rooms.

After the bath I felt refreshed. I rang an old girlfriend. She wasn't in. I rang my mother.

"Where are you?"

"At the Château Laurier."

"What are you doing in the Château Laurier?"

"They have put me up here."

"How much is the room?"

"I don't know—I'm not paying. See you in half an hour."

"Yes," she said. "When you come you'll have something to eat."

No matter how many times I have told my mother that I now earn a living from my work and I can travel where I want to, whenever I'm in Ottawa and go to see her, she is convinced that I have no money and that I'm hungry.

I walked across Confederation Square in the fading light feeling cheerful. In the window of Books Canada there was a poster about the reading to the blind. I went down Elgin to Laurier, crossed the canal by the bridge, down Nicholas to Rideau . . . and realized I was following the route my father used to take with the horse and wagon.

There were now, of course, no horses and wagons. And there were other changes. But the slowness, the small-town atmosphere of this part, was the same.

I took a shortcut by Rideau Flowers and came out, opposite the little park, to the senior citizen building. I rang the bell, the downstairs door buzzed. She was waiting at the open door of her apartment.

"You look well," I said and kissed her.

"I feel much better than a couple of months ago."

The small apartment was very warm. The table in the living room was set with all the courses laid out for me: orange juice, salad, marinated herring, gefilte fish, chicken with potatoes and carrots, and apple compote.

"Sit down," she said. "You eat—I'll talk.

"I went to see the doctor last week for a checkup. He tells me I'm in good condition. Good condition. 'How can I be in good condition, Doctor, when I've had seven operations?'

"'For a woman your age you are in good condition.' Then he says, 'I'm not saying tomorrow or next week, but did you think of going into a nursing home?' This upset me. 'Doctor,' I told him, 'as long as I don't burn my dinner and I don't have to run with my water to the bathroom every few minutes—why should I go to a nursing home?'

"'That's the time to go to a nursing home,' he said, 'when you can enjoy it. There is no shopping, no cooking, no cleaning. You come and go as you like.'

"He made going into a nursing home sound like going to Florida. The gefilte fish—"

"It's delicious," I said.

"—I no longer make it. It's from a tin. Do you want another piece?"

"I don't know if I can eat all this."

She had lost weight since my last visit. It suited her. The flesh on the underpart of the arms was hanging loose. But the alert expression in her pale face, the large blue eyes, were the same.

"In the last war," she said, "you were in the Air Force. If you were in the last war then the government will give you a job here."

"Doing what?"

"Being a commissionaire at one of the government buildings."

I thought I might as well go along with her.

"But there must be a lot of people still alive from the last war," I said. "How can the government give every one a job as a commissionaire?"

"They work shifts," she said.

She went to the kitchen and came back with a large cup of hot coffee. I listened as she told me how they put the pacemaker in: "It saved my life." How she fell and broke some ribs: "That was a killer." All the while she talked about her ailments, I thought how independent she was and spirited and self-contained.

"When I'm in hospital I try to get on my legs. And I walk up and down in the room. Then I get better."

She caught sight of herself in the wall mirror and, a bit of vanity, casually smoothed her thinning white hair.

"No one in my family has lived this long."

"Do you see many people?"

"When I go for a walk...or in the park. I don't have people come here any more. It means I've got to cook. And the talking wears me out. I watch television, I read the paper, and I have the telephone. Sometimes I get lonesome—and feel sorry for myself. Then I take a bus to a shopping centre. Not to get anything. Just to see people enjoying themselves...buying things, looking at the merchandise, the money changing hands. I like all this. Years ago, Pa and I should have got a little business. I know I would have made a success—"

I looked at my watch. I had to go back to the Château for an interview. A reporter from the *Citizen* was going to be there in fifteen minutes. I told this to my mother.

"I enjoyed this visit," I said. "Thanks for the meal." And stood up to put on my coat.

"It's a pleasure to talk to someone you know."

She tried to give me a five-dollar bill.

"Mother, I should be giving you money."

At the door she opened her purse and took out a handful of change and insisted that I take it. "You can always use a few quarters and dimes."

When I came out of the building I looked back. She was at the window waving.

A young man with pink cheeks and a black straggly beard was sitting at a table by the wall drinking a cup of coffee. He had two of my books beside him.

"I'm sorry I'm late."

While I was answering his questions and he was writing in my notebook I noticed two young men and a girl sitting at the table opposite. They were finishing their supper. They kept glancing in my direction. After the reporter left, and I was on my second cup of coffee and a cigarillo, one of the young men walked over. He said my name.

"Yes," I said.

"We like your stories. May we come and join you?"

"Of course," I said. "Are you staying at the Château?"

"We're on the third floor."

"I'm on the second. Where are you from?"

"Toronto."

"I'm going there the day after tomorrow."

They were youthfully attractive. And appeared uneasy . . . perhaps they were shy. The girl was called Julie. She was very compact in her smallness—alert dark eyes, dark hair, small nose, small mouth. She had a look of slight surprise on her face. She told me she wrote poetry and had some poems in the *Canadian Forum*. The taller of the two men, with a head of dark wavy hair, was called Frank. He had conventional good looks and wore white corduroy trousers and a black roll-neck sweater. The stockier one, Jim, had brown curly hair, a wide face, was in jeans and denim windbreaker over a blue T-shirt. They were students.

"I read in the paper," Frank said, "that you are coming back to live here."

"Yes, in the spring."

He looked disappointed.

"After what you wrote, I didn't think you would want to come back."

"Circumstances change," I said.

"But what made you leave is still here," Jim insisted. "If anything it has got worse."

I listened while they told me how provincial the life still was . . . that the centre of a community was the supermarket . . . that people's attitudes were "there must be something in it for me." And that the country remained on the edge of the map—"Things happen somewhere else."

"It just isn't good enough," Jim said.

"It's a lot better than it was," I said.

"Maybe. But it still isn't good enough. We only have one life and I don't see why we have to live it out here."

They didn't look like social misfits. And I could tell they came from people with money. They had another year at university but they couldn't wait to get away.

"What do you need a university education for?" Julie asked.

"For when you're in solitary," I replied.

By the time I finished another cup of coffee, I realized that Julie was with Frank, and Jim was a friend. And the sort of society they wanted was something between socialism and utopia.

Changing the subject, Julie said, "I have only read a few of your stories in magazines. I like the way you describe the small details of everyday life. But if I may make one criticism—you don't make use of fantasy. If you could have fantasy in your stories then you would reach a wider audience."

I wasn't going to try and explain the complicated way I go about writing anything.

"You may be right," I said.

"Look at Isaac Bashevis Singer," she said. "He believes in the afterlife, in demons, goblins—God."

"I'm not a believer," I said. I suddenly felt tired.

"If you will excuse me, I have to get up early for an interview."

"Perhaps we will see you at breakfast," Julie said and smiled.

"Yes," I said.

They were not there for breakfast. But I didn't linger, as I had to go to the sixth floor to the radio studios. And from there a car was waiting to take me to the outskirts of Ottawa for a TV interview. I came back after lunch to the room to go over the parts I would read from my books. At three-thirty, as I still had a half-hour, I thought I would walk to the institute. It was a cold, bright, sunny day. As I came near the place, in a residential area, I could see men and women in winter coats walking in the same direction and could hear the tapping of the white sticks.

The lounge, where I was to read, was full of light. A table, at the far wall, had coffee on a burner. There were white cups standing in saucers and some biscuits and a cake. People kept coming in; some had dark glasses. They stood, quietly, against the walls. Others felt their way to the chairs that were in irregular semicircles. The sun was coming through the windows and onto the sides of some of the faces but they didn't seem to be aware of this. A middle-aged attractive woman came in, elegantly dressed in a red suit. She stood by the table at the back and smiled in my direction.

There was no introduction. I began by saying that I grew up in Ottawa, in Lower Town. And this was the Ottawa I grew up in ...

Not a sound, all the time I read. And when I finished there was silence.

I continued by saying I went to university in Montreal, to McGill, and read them a bit about that.

Still no sound.

I noticed that some had their clothes on awkwardly. I could see the white bloomers of an elderly lady. She was sitting beside an elderly man. They were holding hands.

I asked if anyone had questions.

No one spoke.

I told them that after McGill I left Canada and went to live in England. And read descriptions of St. Ives: the bay in summer and during a storm ... seeing rainbows ... the white-yellow sand beaches ... how it looked when the tide was in and what you could see when the tide was out ... the harbour with Cornish and French fishing boats and gulls ... the moors with gorse, bracken, and granite boulders. And the small green fields with hedgerows full of wildflowers.

I asked again if there were any questions.

A thin woman with glasses and white hair, sitting very erect, said quietly, "I like your descriptions."

A tall man with dark glasses, standing against the wall, said in a stronger voice, "We prefer when you describe things to dialogue."

I then read a description of the sun coming up on the prairies, of a snowstorm in downtown Montreal, of spiderwebs in a garden after a rain.

I had read for almost an hour. They still seemed reluctant to talk. I thought I would stop.

The attractive woman in the red suit thanked me for coming. And said John was now going to give me a cup of coffee.

A young man in a white shirt, a resident, left his chair and felt his way to the table at the back. I watched as he poured the coffee and began to walk slowly in my direction. I was talking louder than usual to someone near me (he said he had a tape recorder for Christmas and he had recorded my reading) when I saw John stumble and fall. He picked himself up, someone else picked up the cup and saucer, and went back to the table. I walked over; he poured coffee in again. I took it from him with a piece of cake and thanked him.

They began, quietly and hesitantly, to talk among themselves. Then they left their chairs, and the wall, and came up to me. A bald old man said, "I saw a rainbow once. I was on a lake, near Ottawa. I was ten." A plump, short lady dressed in green said she remembered Lower Town from what I read. She grew up on St. Patrick Street. Someone else said they remembered winter with icicles and being pulled in a sleigh by a dog. The attractive woman who thanked me moved closer. "I hope you don't get the wrong idea," she smiled. "But it is only when I stand this close that I can see you at all, and then only fuzzy." She hoped that now that I had come, perhaps other writers would come and read to them. And told me that most of the audience were people who lived at home—there weren't that many residents—and that not everyone was completely blind.

A young woman came up and asked if she could run her hands over my face.

When I came out I was glad to be outside. I walked very briskly a few blocks. Then stopped. And stood there. Staring at the sky, the bare trees—what lovely colours—a bird on a wire, a young grey cat on a veranda, a black squirrel crossing the road. I just stood there and looked and looked . . .

When I got back to the Château Laurier there was a note from Julie that said could I come up and see them in room 320.

I did go up. They were very relaxed, with two bottles of champagne on the desk and all kinds of delicatessen food around them. "Glad you could join us," Frank said. And Julie produced an extra glass. Frank had a copy of the *Citizen*.

"You're on page five—"

There was the interview, over two columns, with a photograph taken four years earlier.

"—and we're on page one."

I couldn't see anything that might refer to them. He pointed to a small notice—two sentences—a branch of the Bank of Montreal was robbed by a man and he got away with an undisclosed sum of money.

Nothing, I thought, surprises me any more.

"Why did you do it?" I asked.

"It's something we have been thinking about for a while. We wanted to see if we could do it. Jim worked in a bank—so he knew how—all he needed was a uniform and to go there before it opened."

"Did you have a gun?"

"Yes."

"Bullets?"

"Yes."

"Would you have used them?"

"I don't know," Jim said. "We didn't have to."

I thought, was this bravado or was there something unstable? And why did they tell me?

Julie poured more champagne and I had smoked meat and a pickle.

"What are you going to do with the money?"

Silence.

Frank finally said, "You are going to Toronto for your next lecture."

"Yes."

"So are we. It would be an honour if we could drive you there."

"Thanks," I said. "It's very good of you."

"Could you be in the lobby and ready to leave at three a.m.?"

"Are you going to rob another bank?"

They found that amusing.

They were waiting in the lobby with their luggage when I came down. Outside, in the dark, it was cold. I sat with Jim in the back. Frank was driving, Julie was beside him. They didn't appear tired. But I could hardly keep my eyes open. On the car radio a woman was singing "Weekend in Canada." The streets were empty and Frank was driving fast.

"You drive very well," I said.

"I thought at one time of being a racing driver. But I knew I didn't have the dedication."

When we got out of Ottawa they appeared even more at ease. Gone was that vague discontent that was there when I met them. They began to sing a mixture of revolutionary and popular songs: "Joe Hill," "John Brown's Body," "Ode to Joy," "Kevin Barry," as well as John Denver songs that I knew, and the Beatles. I didn't join in. Although I sing when I'm by myself, friends have told me I can't carry a tune. In any case I felt too warm even with the window open.

I DON'T WANT TO KNOW ANYONE TOO WELL

I must have fallen asleep because when I woke up the car had stopped. We were in a small town, or village, on the main street. Not a soul was outside.

"Where are we?"

"About halfway," Frank said. "Have a good sleep?"

"I think so."

"You were snoring," Julie said.

A light snow. I could see the flakes by the streetlight. Everything looked shut and quiet.

"Why have we stopped?"

"Would you like to help us?"

"What is it you want me to do?"

Jim took out a leather case and opened it. He handed four bundles of twenty-dollar bills to each of us. "You and Julie do the side streets on that side. We'll do the side streets on this. Then we'll both do the opposite sides of the main. Put two twenty-dollar bills in each door. Not the stores. Only the houses."

For the next fifteen minutes or so I walked briskly to the front doors of houses and pushed through the letter slots two twenty-dollar bills. I no longer felt tired or sleepy. At only one house was there a moment of anxiety when a small dog barked. But no lights came on and no one came to the door. Otherwise we moved from house to house, street to street . . . the snow falling . . . coming back for more bundles—until there were no more.

When it was over, and we all were in the car, there was a shared sense of excitement as if we had taken part in a for-bidden pleasure. Julie suddenly kissed the three of us. "Money makes a girl passionate."

Jim said, "I kept these back as souvenirs." And gave two twenty dollar bill to each of us, including himself. They were crisp notes and I put mine in my back buttoned-down pocket.

"I'd give anything," Frank said, "to see some of the faces when they go to the door this morning."

The ploughs, the small trucks, were attacking the fallen snow when we arrived in Toronto. It was like a small army. The university had reserved a room in the Windsor Arms. When we got there it was time to go our separate ways.

"You're famous," Julie said, looking affectionately into my eyes. "I thought famous people were different."

I shook hands with Frank and Jim.

Julie gave me a prolonged kiss.

"I'll read all your books," she said.

"And I'll look in the paper to see what banks have been robbed."

At the lecture I talked about the past confronting the present and what matters are moments. And gave examples from my stories. Afterwards there was a small party at a professor's house. I got back to the hotel after midnight.

Next morning I caught a taxi early as I had to get the morning train to Montreal. The taxi driver spoke English with a heavy accent. I asked him where he was from.

"Israel," he said.

Outside Union Station the driver brought my case from the back. I asked him how much. He said four dollars. I put my hand in my pocket and drew out one of the twenty-dollar bills.

"I can't change that," he said. "I have just started. Where would I get money to change that?"

"Make it ten dollars," I said.

He began, slowly, to take out crumpled one-dollar bills and crumpled two-dollar bills, from different pockets, and placed them into my open hand.

To pass the time, and to apologize for the much too large tip, I said, "It's only money."

He looked startled, then angry.

"What do you mean it's only money? Why do you think I get up when it is still dark and cold—to drive through these streets. Only money." He began to shout hysterically. "I have to work long hours, nights too, and weekends. For what am I doing this? Tell me."

I walked away ... aware that I'd stumbled on a simple truth, if there is such a thing. While he continued shouting and waving his hands so that people walking by looked in wonder as to what was wrong between us.

On another occasion, seventeen years earlier, in December 1962, when the children were still small (ten, eight, six), we were living in St. Ives, Cornwall, in a large old terraced house that I rented from a widow at twelve pounds a month. I only had a few books published then and was behind with the rent. I was writing mostly short stories as a way of earning money and at the same time trying to get on with a new novel. The weeks before Christmas were an anxious time. It seemed that I was always waiting for a cheque. This time was no exception. I had sent a new story to *Harper's Bazaar*. They had accepted it on December 7 for their top price of twenty-five guineas. And I was watching every postal delivery. Meanwhile I had to tell the milkman that he would be paid next week, the same with the baker, and the groceries from the co-op. As the days passed the children began to make decorations and paper chains and cards. But my wife began to worry, how were we going to get through with so little money. We got by with beans on toast, cheese on toast, and macaroni with cheese.

A week later I went, with the little change I had, to the public phone box at the top of the cemetery and called up *Harper's Bazaar* hoping I would get the literary editor. She assured me the cheque was on its way. And could I send her another story in the spring.

But three days later the cheque still hadn't arrived. I was up here, in the attic room, wondering what to do when Martha, our eldest, came running up the stairs shouting. "Dad. Dad. Look what the postman left—smoked salmon."

She gave me this long, neatly wrapped parcel with white stiff cardboard on the outside. In the top left-hand corner a label said "Nolan, fishmonger, Dublin." And there was my name and address and in large letters "Smoked Salmon—Perishable."

I quickly brought it down to the kitchen.

My wife and kids watched me unwrap it.

It was the largest smoked salmon I had seen.

"Who sent it?" my wife said happily.

I looked through the parcel.

"It doesn't say. They forgot to put it in."

I sliced large slices, very thin. And we ate them with brown bread, cut lemon, and pepper from the small pepper mill.

We had smoked salmon for lunch and smoked salmon for dinner and, next day, smoked salmon for breakfast.

It was too large for our small fridge so we kept it where it was cold—between the outside front door and the inner door. And had to take it away when the milkman called, the baker, and the grocer.

It seemed such a luxury (the whole family at the kitchen table, eating platefuls of smoked salmon) when there was hardly any food in the house.

At night in bed we couldn't sleep.

"Who do you think sent it?"

"I don't know."

"It's from Dublin—you don't think Edna?"

"No," I said.

"I hope not," my wife said.

"Perhaps it was Francis."

"I hope it's Francis," my wife said.

We went through the possibilities.

"Your stories are all about how we have no money. Some reader of *Vogue* or *Harper's* after reading one decided—"

"The fishmonger," I interrupted, "probably forgot to put the card in. Good night."

But it bothered us.

We had the O'Caseys in, Doreen and Breon, for a smoked salmon treat. They also had young children and money was tight. I did large slices cut thin with more lemon and brown bread and pepper. They said it was delicious and nothing like that had ever happened to them.

Then on December 22 the cheque came from *Harper's Bazaar.* And I felt like a new person. I gave my wife most of the money—paid the milkman and part of the bill we owed at the co-op. We got the last tree from the greengrocer. And the children and my wife suddenly got into the swing of things. I went out and got some greenery to put up around the rooms near the ceiling. They put up decorations . . . small presents began to appear under the tree, neatly wrapped up. The schoolkids, when they knocked on the front door after singing a carol, now got a few pennies. And later, at night, in a light rain, there was the massed choir in the street, men and women dressed all in black singing "While Shepherds Watched Their Flocks by Night" unaccompanied. They held flashlights under their chins and umbrellas above them . . . beautiful sound . . . their voices clear. Then they walked up the slope, in the dark, regrouped . . . and sang some more . . . the flashlights lighting up their faces.

Next day there was a letter from Canada, from my mother, with a twenty-five-pound money order for the children. And in the evening Morley and Florrie came. (He was a farmer near Truro and ran a butcher shop and she had the postal sub-station—my wife was evacuated there during the war.) They came with their day's takings in a carrier bag and gave us a goose and a chicken. I cut some of the smoked salmon while my wife told them what happened.

"Well, I never—" Florrie said.

"It's very good," Morley said.

Next morning before seven I was at St. Erth station waiting for the train to come. I was there to meet my wife's mother, who had recently become a widow and was coming on the overnight train from London. I walked up and down the open platform to try and keep warm. Over to the west the clouds were low and grey. And one cloud, like a smudge, detached itself and was moving closer. I watched it. Suddenly I realized it wasn't a cloud but starlings. They came just over my head—and above and below, on either side of the tracks. Thousands of them. It felt as if I was in a black snowstorm. And the continual sound of their wings.

Then just as suddenly it went quiet. The train arrived, no one got out. A porter ran up to me. "Are you waiting for a lady?"

"Yes."

"I can't wake her up."

It was my mother-in-law having difficulty keeping her eyes open. I put on her sheepskin jacket, took her case, and the porter and I got her into a taxi. Her chin was on her chest.

I managed to wake her up on the drive back.

"What happened?"

"I took some drink on the train—to help me sleep—then a sleeping pill—"

"How many pills did you take?"

"One—two—"

Her head went down again.

When I got her into the house I told my wife what happened and to make a large jug of coffee. We forced her to drink. Then held her up, one on each side, and began to walk up and down the room and in the hallway, her feet dragging, I slapped her face when she closed her eyes, gave her more coffee, and continued walking. We did that for over an hour until she could stand by herself.

"I'm all right now," she said. She looked worn out. "I'll go upstairs and lie down and have a rest." She slept right through until next morning.

In the morning I made a fire in the front room. The pile of presents under the tree had grown almost overnight. Then, when we were all down, we sat on chairs, the children on the floor. My wife brought in a pot of hot coffee. And after we had coffee I started to give out the presents. One for each, and I would wait until the person opened it. Then I'd go to the next. The children saved their wrapping paper ... the pile of presents by them.

And later we went into the next room and sat around the large dining room table, dressed in the new sweater, the new shirt. A fire was going in the fireplace. The kids' paper chains were crisscrossing from the ceiling. And I had tacked some branches of ivy on the top of the walls as well.

We began with the last of the smoked salmon. Then the goose was brought in ... and the vegetables ... I poured brandy on the pudding and lit it ... And it burned with a blue flame.

We had finished the pudding and sat around the table with paper hats on our heads, when Martha had to go upstairs. When she came back she said, "Dad, there's a goat on the front steps by the door nibbling at the tree."

We went to the front room, to the window. And there was a dirty billy goat with part of an old torn rope hanging from its neck dragging on the ground. It was on the front granite steps nibbling at the pittosporum.

And we all laughed. It was so dirty and bedraggled and it didn't look domestic at all. It was black with some hairs that might have been white but were now dirty grey. The hairs were matted together and of different lengths. When it went down the slope, to the next house, I opened the front door and we went out. And watched it go, slowly, down the street. Stopping at the front gardens, the front steps, or staying on the sidewalk, then standing in the middle of the road. It looked so out of place in this suburban street of terraced houses.

Then I saw that the whole street was now out ... in small groups ... in front of their doors ... or on their steps. Some, like us, with paper hats still on their heads. And everyone was laughing or smiling and talking ... and looking at the goat.

Someone must have called the police. For later I heard they brought the goat back to the farmer, a few miles from here, who reported it missing.

On December 28, I couldn't put it off any longer. I wrote to the fishmonger whose address was on the label. Two and a half weeks later a letter arrived. In large, almost childish, writing it said:

Dublin, 4 January

Dear Sir, I am pleased you enjoyed the salmon. We received a money order for same with instructions to send to you. It was signed, "anonymous gift."

Yours truly

P.J. Nolan

A MARITIME STORY

WHEN I THINK of Max Bleenden I see him driving a 481
long red car in Fredericton, dressed in grey flannels,
a navy blue blazer, or (if it was warm) a light purple
shirt, and smoking a Gauloise. He looks solid. Broad shoulders, a strong neck, a wide face. His dark wavy hair is brushed
back and receding. There is a slightly crooked smile. He wears
glasses. The eyes are brown. In public he has the air of a celebrity. People look pleased when they say, "Hello, Dr. Bleenden."
I can hear him come up the worn steps of the George Hotel,
knock on the grey-painted door of my rented rooms. When I
open the door he speaks in a rough, low voice that has something of Europe in it.

"Can you lend me five dollars? I forgot to go to the bank.
I have the gardener coming this morning. And I need to buy
some tea and eggs. It's a tradition. I always make breakfast for
the gardener."

I would give him the money then make some coffee while
he looked around at the way I was living in this hotel with the
second-hand furniture, the worn linoleum.

"I envy you," he said. "You live such a simple life. Mine is
complicated."

Later, leaving Fredericton, he was driving me to the airport. We were silent. Suddenly he said, "You're going away . . . that's awful . . . I won't have anyone to talk to. There's no one down here."

I came to the Maritimes in 1965 because of Max Bleenden. He had written to me in England. He said he liked my short stories. Would I like to come to Fredericton and be resident writer. And because we needed the money I said yes. I owed rent for two years. Had a lawyer's letter threatening action from the landlady's son. The landlady was a nice old lady who apologized for this. It only came out when she was sick. Her son happened to see what I owed.

I left wife and children behind—I had no intention of settling in the Maritimes—and flew over at the end of August.

Max Bleenden was to meet me in the lobby of the Beaverbrook Hotel. As he came in he looked around expectantly. But as soon as he saw me he looked disappointed.

"I didn't think you would be so short."

Max was several inches shorter. He drove me to his house—a solid greystone facing the river with a gravel drive, grass on either side, and a heavy wooden front door. Behind the house were tall trees and large gardens of fruit, vegetables, and flowers. Inside, the rooms were high, painted white, and lightly furnished with antique wooden furniture and blue carpets. On the walls were abstract oil paintings, and a photograph of a serious young girl. There were irises, roses, gladioli, in different colours, in glass vases and earthenware pots. There was a glass bowl full of fruit.

.   His wife came in. She was a bit taller than Max. Thin and shy with red hair. When she smiled she looked like a pretty Tallulah Bankhead. She hardly spoke. If I spoke to her, she smiled back. We sat in the comfortable chairs, in one of the front rooms, looking out at the river, and had tea.

A large elderly woman in grey walked in with sandwiches on a tray. As she went out Max said, "She is here to look after my mother. My mother's name is Nettie. I want you to meet her."

He led me up the stairs, past three rooms, to a bare white room where a small elderly woman sat in a high-backed chair. Her hands were clutching the armrests. Her feet were not touching the ground. She was dressed in a purple blouse, a black skirt. Around her neck a light silk lemon scarf was tied loosely. Her grey hair was cut short and permed and I could see the pink scalp between curls. She sat by a window and beside a fish tank that had three small fish swimming in it. Max introduced me.

"Who are you?" his mother said in a flat voice.

"I'm Max's friend."

"Do you live here?"

"Yes."

She looked out of the window at the road, the river, the far shore, the sky.

"I write to Max every week," she said. "Did you know I'm going to Canada?"

She left us again. Went back to the window.

She had an interesting but worn-out face. She must have been pretty, for the structure was still there with the prominent cheekbones, the small mouth with the noticeable front teeth as if a smile was never far away.

"I hate this house," she said. "It goes quiet. I don't know where everyone is."

She looked at the tank.

"They are trying to fob me off with fish. I don't want fish. I want people."

She looked at me.

"Suddenly it's quiet," she said. "They don't explain things. I don't know where they are. I don't know when they are coming back. They don't ask me if I want to go. They just go away …

"Did you know I'm going to Canada? To the Maritimes. I have a son in the Maritimes."

Max began to walk impatiently up and down. She followed his movements. When he stopped near her she said, "How long am I going to stay here?"

"How long would you like to stay, mother?" Max said. "Forever?"

"That's not very long," she said.

As I was leaving, Max said he and his wife were driving to Boston tomorrow for a short holiday before the academic year started. Would I like to come?

When we got to Boston all Max wanted to see were films. We saw six films in three days. He also wanted to go to a striptease. We went into a dark place where a young girl with long legs performed on a small stage, in the centre of the room, while the customers stood around and watched. A cigarette girl, not young, came by. Max picked up a small cigar from her tray, and took out a coin from his pocket.

"Can I put a quarter in your box?" he asked with a grin.

"Don't be an asshole," the cigarette girl said. "You can't get into my box for a quarter."

She couldn't have known that she was talking to the dean of a university.

On the drive back from Boston, with his wife asleep, Max told me about himself. He was born in Hamburg. "Both my parents spoke Yiddish. I also spoke Yiddish. But I have long forgotten it." His father was a publisher. They had a comfortable life. When he was thirteen—it was 1933—his mother brought him to London. They didn't see his father again. He went to an English grammar school, then London University. They had little money. His mother did a variety of jobs, whatever she could get. It was while he was at university that his poems began to appear in the little magazines. His reviews in the weeklies. And talks on the BBC. That's when I first heard of him. But we never met. Although I used to go to the same Soho clubs, the same pubs: the French, Joe Lyons, the Mandrake. Max said he played the piano, for a while, at the Colony. And we talked about Muriel Belcher and Francis Bacon. After the war ("My father was a conscientious objector . . . his father was a conscientious objector . . . so I was a conscientious objector. I was sent to work on the land. I was digging ditches. And all I wanted to do was fly a Spitfire.") he came to Canada to lecture at a small college in Nova Scotia where he met his wife, the daughter of a general. She inherited money. They moved to Fredericton. "After I married, the writing stopped. The instinct for it had gone. And I haven't written anything since. But I can tell the real thing when I see it. And, boychick," he slapped my knee, "you have it."

But despite this friendliness I was uncomfortable with Max.

In the first week of term he asked me to meet his creative writing class. There were about twenty students, mostly girls. "Here is our resident writer," Max began. "He writes short stories. They are mostly stories about being hard-up. But look the way he is dressed. He is wearing an expensive English suit, expensive English shoes, an expensive shirt and tie."

I didn't know where to look.

(The thin light grey suit I bought in a discount house in Truro, Cornwall, for nine pounds. It was made in Bulgaria. My shoes, also cheap, I bought in Exeter. They were made in Romania.)

I also disliked the way he took it for granted that I would just fall in with his plans. He never asked. He just said, "Let's go—" or "I'll pick you up for a football game at—"

My reaction to this was immediate.

When I was supposed to be at the president's reception to introduce new members I was in the Riverside Room of the Beaverbrook Hotel drinking a beer and reading a thriller.

Next morning he came to my office, three doors away from his. A hurt expression on his face.

"Why weren't you at the president's reception?"

"When was it?"

"Yesterday. I made a speech telling all about you. People clapped. We waited for you to step forward. Nothing happened."

I turned down all invitations.

Max would walk briskly into my office and say, "I just had a phone call from the Rotarians. They have a monthly meeting. The food is very good. They would like you to be their next speaker—"

"I'm busy," I said. "Working."

I wasn't working. I was moving. From the Beaverbrook, that he put me in, to the George, which was less than half the price. I was also getting to know Fredericton. The long residential streets with the front lawns and the large wooden houses with verandas and trees. The short business streets, by the river, with the small stores and Chinese restaurants. But it didn't take long to walk through it. And I had a feeling of isolation, of being cut off.

One morning I walked to the supermarket by the river to get some groceries. When I came out a mild man in glasses, dressed like a farmer, came up to me.

"Have you got education?"

I didn't know what to say.

"Have you got education?"

I thought this was a new way of asking for money.

"Yes," I said hesitantly.

"What is eight at fifty dollars each?"

"Four hundred dollars."

"Four hundred," he said loudly. And repeated it as if he didn't believe it. He walked away delighted.

Another day I went to the legislative building. I was listening to a debate on fishing from the public gallery when an usher came up to me and whispered, "Sir, you can't sit like that."

I had my legs crossed.

"Why not?"

"The members below—they can see."

"I'm wearing trousers."

"It's a rule sir . . . because of the ladies. They'd come here . . . sit like you . . . and from below, with some, you could see the time of day."

On Armistice Day I went to the cenotaph. A service of remembrance was going on. Names of local people killed in the Second World War were being read over a loudspeaker. The voice said:

Graham Budd, Royal Canadian Air Force.

487

Robert Pichette, Royal Canadian Corps of Signals.

Jim Smith, Royal Canadian Air Force.

Brought to you by Frank's Fast Foods . . .

Tommy Symons, Royal Canadian Navy.

Fred Towers, Royal Canadian Engineers.

Brought to you by Dominion Supermarket . . .

I wasn't sleeping well. At first light I'd walk to the river to see the trees in their autumn colours, the solitary white house on the far shore, reflected in the water. After breakfast, I'd go out again, buy a paper. Then to the post office to see if there were any letters from my wife. I wrote three times, sometimes more, a week (as she did) telling her I missed her. That I disliked being here. And couldn't wait to get back. Meanwhile I was going to earn as much money as I could.

With this in mind I walked to the newspaper building in the square. And was shown into the owner's empty office. The owner walked in. Small stubby brown shoes with thick heels and thick soles and rounded tops. A black eye patch over his right eye. He was about five foot ten. He had a small moustache, thin dark hair, and spoke in a clipped English voice. He was referred to as the Brigadier. And told me he was a friend of Beaverbrook, knew the Duke and Duchess of Windsor, and, for my benefit, he talked about Arnold Bennett. He said that when Arnold Bennett reviewed a book in the *Evening Standard* the book would sell out. He would give me a page in his monthly magazine for the Maritimes, and he expected me to do the same as Arnold Bennett.

But the books I wanted were published in London. And often they didn't want to send review copies to a Maritime monthly they hadn't heard of. The Brigadier was furious. I saw him pick up the phone, in a rage, and shout to the London publisher demanding a copy. Sometimes it worked.

I did articles on an anthology of short stories, a novel by Graham Greene, books on Hemingway, Babel, Chekhov, and an anthology of the Second World War. I also had some of my stories reprinted. From this I earned an extra five hundred dollars a month.

It was by doing this work that I met the journalists who worked for the Brigadier. They were young Englishmen, from English public schools, that the Brigadier brought over. Their calling cards said "Gentlemen of the Farm." They lived in a run-down rented farm across the river. In the city they wore suits, ties, clean shirts. I expected a rolled umbrella, a bowler hat. And when they played cricket or soccer, against the university or the army camp, their sports clothes were immaculate. But on the farm—they only had chickens—they wore worn-out shabby clothes. They went around unshaven, uncombed. The rooms had disorder and chicken shit. The kitchen looked as if no one had washed up for months or put the garbage out . . .

When I went for my early evening drink to the Beaverbrook, I would join these neatly dressed journalists and listen as they joked, discussed life and the world situation.

With them, sometimes, was Marcel, a French Canadian from Moncton. He was in computers. He drove a green MG. He was convinced that I was getting the wrong impression of the Maritimes by mixing too much with intellectuals and people with money. So he took me to various beer parlours. Then, to the outskirts, off the highway, and onto a dirt road, to a string of unpainted wooden shacks spaced far apart. Smoke came from a tin chimney. No one was outside.

Marcel then drove to an Indian reservation. The same signs of poverty and hopelessness. As if everyone inside was lying fully dressed on a bed, not sleeping, in the middle of the afternoon.

"I don't read books," Marcel said on the drive back, "but I'll read one of yours. If I like it—I'll buy it."

Max came to the George.

"Have you been avoiding me? It's over two weeks since I've seen you."

"I haven't," I said.

"Come for a ride."

Then he said, "Let's go back to my place for a drink. I'm depressed."

When we got out of the car, instead of going into the house he went around it. We cast long shadows on the grass. He led me to the trees. And, among them, to a wooden hut. He unlocked the door.

Inside it was Spartan. A plain wooden table. An ordinary wooden chair. Used books on planks of wood held up by bricks. An open fireplace with sawn wood stacked beside it. There were picture postcards stuck on the walls of paintings by Rembrandt, Monet, Pissarro, Chagall, Bonnard. A small sink, a single tap, an electric kettle. Empty jars of instant coffee, packs of Gauloises and matches. A bottle of Remy Martin was by a small radio. A used upright piano by a wall. Beside another, a couch was made up as a bed.

"I feel at home here," Max said. "The house . . . that's my wife's place. This is mine." He indicated the books, the faded poster of *The Threepenny Opera* on a wall, the faded magazines.

I looked at the books. I knew them. They were English books of the late 1940s and 1950s. He showed me magazines with his poems, his reviews.

"That was my time," Max said. "Who knows what I would have done had I stayed in Europe. But I'm here. And, boychick, most of the time I like it."

He showed me letters he had from T. S. Eliot, Picasso. And, from another folder, he brought out obituaries that he had cut from the *Times*. They were of writers, painters, editors of little magazines, who were known just after the war and who died young. They were people I also knew.

"That's why we get on," Max said. "We have the same references."

The only sign of luxury was a large window looking out to the trees and gardens. "I come here when I can," Max said. "In the morning the dew is on the grass . . . the birds have started . . . the flowers are at their best . . . I read, I smoke, I have a drink. I listen to the BBC Overseas Service for the news . . . I play the piano . . . I daydream. It's my bolthole. Then I go to work."

He poured Remy Martin into the cracked cups. He sat on the couch. I, on the wooden chair. He lit up a Gauloise.

"I read the same books again and again," Max said. "Now that I don't write—I copy out things that I like." He opened a thick notebook, turned some pages, and read aloud.

"'The heart—it's worth less than people think. It's quite accommodating, it accepts anything. It's not particular. But the body—that's different—it has a cultivated taste—it knows what it wants.'

"You know who said that?"

"No."

"Colette." He turned more pages. Read out, "To exist is enough." Then turned to the last page of the notebook, showed it to me. The only thing on it was, "The final unimportance of human life."

"Who said that?"

"I don't know," Max said. "I didn't. But when I read it—I don't feel so bad."

He put out a Gauloise, lit another.

"I'll miss Fredericton—"

"When are you leaving?"

"When I'm sixty-five, I'll retire to England. Somewhere in the country. Not too far from London."

"And your wife?"

"She won't want to come. But when the time comes she'll go. As you see, my wife and I don't talk much. Not now. We keep certain thoughts to ourselves."

We finished the brandy in the cups. He locked the door. We were walking to the house when his wife came quickly towards us.

"Nettie's escaped."

"When?"

"I don't know. I went into her room. And she wasn't there."

"I'll use the car," Max said. "You," he said to his wife, "look in the restaurants, the library, the stores."

"I'll look for her," I said.

"Fine. Do the side streets and by the river."

"What was she wearing?"

"A pink sweater," his wife said, "grey skirt, and slippers."

I walked and looked for over an hour and a half. No sign of Nettie. I phoned up Max, from a call box, wondering if she was still alive.

"The police have her," he said calmly. "I'm going just now to the station to pick her up. She was trying to get on a bus. She had no money. She told them she was going to Canada."

"Has this happened before?"

"Yes," he said.

Two weeks later it was a different Max who came to the George. He had come back from a three-day conference in Calgary. And he talked nonstop about women. "It's all in the angle of penetration . . . If they have large bums . . . it's better to use a pillow. I picked up a professor at the hotel bar about thirty-five or thirty-six . . . a medievalist . . . I asked her to spend the night with me. She said she would if I promised I wouldn't do anything."

"What happened?"

He looked surprised. "Nothing happened. I gave her my word."

That night he picked me up for the annual party of his creative writing class. The parents, he said, were away. "We'll enjoy ourselves." There were drinks, music, food. Max was the first one to start dancing. Then spent the rest of the evening, in a dark corner, with the girl who was giving the party. When he drove me back to the George he was like an adolescent. "Now you see why I have these creative writing classes."

"Better wipe the lipstick off before you go in the house."

Next morning he walked into my office. He was excited.

"I needed a new secretary," he said. "They sent me one. But I'll have to let her go. I couldn't work with her."

"Why not?"

"Too sexy. Come, I'll show you."

He led me down the corridor to the main office. And introduced me to this young tall girl who was smiling. She looked like girls I saw in the street. Blond short hair, healthy, outdoor type, in a tight sweater and a tight skirt.

"Turn around," Max said.

And she did, as if she were a fashion model, still smiling.

"How could I work standing close to her?"

"She probably needs the job," I said.

"She'll go back to the typing pool. Alone with her . . . I wouldn't trust myself."

I liked Max better when the macho side of him was absent. One afternoon he picked me up and drove by the river into the country for about an hour. "I make this trip about once every six or seven weeks," he said. "My wife goes more often. We have a daughter. She lives by herself, a solitary. She's a lovely girl, twenty-four, you'll see."

We went down a dirt track. There was a wooden shack with asbestos on the outside and on the roof. In a clearing, a small vegetable garden and some flowers. A brown dog came out and a black and ginger kitten. The dog barked. A voice said, "What is it, Fred?"

Then Max's daughter came out of the shack. She was tall and slim and she looked like one of those pre-Raphaelite paintings. She ran over and kissed Max.

"Hello, Dad."

He introduced me. She looked a bit shy. She spoke softly. She brought us inside, made some coffee.

There were different herbs . . . books to do with the psyche . . . Buddhism . . . happiness . . . there were plants growing in small pots . . . lots of paperback books . . . and postcards put up . . .

I went out to leave them alone.

We stayed about an hour.

Max didn't talk much on the drive back. "Every time I come back from seeing her I feel sad. And there is nothing I can do."

Before driving to the airport, I went with Max to see Nettie in her room. I told her I was leaving. But she took no notice. Max had bought her a colour television for her seventieth birthday. She was watching a train going across the country from the Atlantic to the Pacific. It was a travelogue showing the different provinces in the autumn.

When it was over Nettie was silent.

Then she said to Max, "Why did you keep that country all to yourself?"

I returned to England, to my wife and kids, paid off the debts. Had a three-week holiday with the family in London. And there was enough money left for the next nine months. I began to write.

All the time I was in Fredericton, I thought I hated it. But bits and pieces began to appear in my next novel and in several short stories.

Max and I wrote regularly. He always included small details that I suspect he thought I might be able to use.

> ... *On a freezing night our mayor was pushed out of a moving car on the main street at three in the morning. He was pushed out by a lady who wasn't his wife. He was in the nude ....They tried to burn the George down twice since you left ... both times the fire engines arrived too soon . . . . The Brigadier died while on holiday in the Bahamas . . . . The Gentlemen of the Farm gave a farewell party ... they are leaving for British Columbia. Sometime after midnight we went out of the farmhouse and there was a large wooden cross burning fiercely. Someone said, "Ku Klux Klan." Someone else said, "This is New Brunswick."*

At Christmas he sent five pounds to each of our daughters.

The following summer he and his wife came to see us. They were travelling through the southwest in a rented car. In St. Ives they stayed in the best hotel, the Tregenna Castle. Max took us there for a meal. As we entered and saw the glass chandeliers, he said, "Ribbentrop was promised this hotel for his residence by Hitler after he conquered England."

Next day it rained. They stayed with us in the house. Max

played ping-pong with the children. Then records. *Hair* was in fashion. Max played it over and over. He twisted to the music, he sang the songs, he liked the naughty words ("Mummy, Mummy, what is fellatio?"). He tried to get my wife to dance on the table.

That is how I remembered him on that cool September morning when I heard that he and his wife were killed when their car went off the highway.

Later that day I wrote his obituary for the *Times*.

I came again to Fredericton, eighteen years later, this summer, to give a lecture. I stayed at the Beaverbrook. After a good breakfast, by a window facing the river, I went for a walk. I walked along the main street and to the side street where the George was. It was burned out . . . gutted. Planks of charred wood were hanging precariously. And where I had my rooms I could see blue sky.

Wherever I walked I kept remembering Max. And things that happened. But for some reason I couldn't find my way to the university. I asked a woman on the opposite side of the street. She said she was going part of the way. She told me she came from Ontario, from Hamilton. And couldn't wait to get back. They had another year here—until their only daughter finished school.

"This is failure city," she said.

I walked up the slope, by the trees and the grass of the university. They named a new building after him—Max Bleenden Hall—a girls' residence. And on the quarter-hour the clock, above its entrance, has a delicate chime.

TRICKS

I N THE LATE SPRING I received an invitation to tutor, for four days, a class of teachers in their final year of training. On a bright morning I set off for an estate in West Cornwall. I took the train to Penzance. Then a green country bus. It went slowly up a steep road. At the top it levelled out. We were on an open moor. It was exhilarating. I could see for miles. A brilliant blue sky. Haunches of earth with gorse and bracken and scattered granite boulders. The only sign that said people were about—a row of wooden telegraph poles, by the road, carrying a single wire.

I got off the bus on a plateau, and walked with my bag along a rough dirt road. It brought me still higher onto the moor. A cool breeze. A smell of coconuts came from the gorse beside me. I watched three gulls fly over. They appeared to fly in slow motion. There were no sounds. Not a car, not a person.

When I saw the estate I didn't expect anything as isolated to be so grand. From the moor it was almost hidden by trees and a few granite boulders. And the boulders, made smooth by the centuries, were taller than the trees.

I swung open a heavy white gate and walked along a pebble drive. On either side—behind tall, trimmed green bushes—

were thick subtropical gardens with flowers whose names I didn't know. Bright pinks, whites, orange, yellow, light and dark purples and blues. A gap . . . a low stone wall . . . and behind it a fruit garden. Another stone wall . . . and behind that a vegetable garden with a greenhouse.

The drive ended at the side of a large house with tall windows. A bus ("Hereford Education Authority" on its door) was parked by a used truck that had gardening tools. A path to the left of the house. Another to the right. I walked to the left, under a granite arch. And past the arch a sunken grass lawn neatly cut. The sunken grass lawn, with steep grass slopes, was sheltered on three sides by bushes, trees, and the front of the granite house. The wide other side was open. To the left, the upward-sloping moor, and the road across it the bus had taken. While in front, and to the right, tall grass with campion and foxgloves. Then a sharp drop of bracken and gorse. Several hundred feet further down the bracken and the gorse levelled out to a patchwork of cultivated small green fields with hedgerows for fences and cows around an isolated farm. The small fields went right up to steep cliffs. And past the cliffs, to the horizon, was the sea.

Looking at all this, I didn't notice a tall man with a stick (who must have come from the house) walking towards me. His feet kicked out—slightly ahead and to the side—while he held his head and shoulders back, as if to balance his walk. It gave him a slightly arrogant presence, even when he smiled. Fine features in a longish heavy face, a strong jaw, thinning white hair combed back. He was neatly dressed in grey flannels, a light grey tweed jacket, a red-checked shirt, a dark blue tie. He looked English and vaguely familiar. He also looked out of place here. But so did the sunken lawn, the sub-tropical gardens, the large house.

"You a student?"

"No, a tutor."

"You must be the other one."

It was then that I recognized him. Eric Symes, a singer in musicals, looking much older than the photographs I had seen in newspapers and magazines. But they belonged to the time he was well known. When I used to hear him on the radio and on records.

"You will have the goose-house," he indicated with his stick. "Past those trees. His is further along. After you leave your things, go to the other side of the house to the kitchen. Meet your students. They arrived earlier. If there is anything you want—ask Connie."

We stood looking at the view, in silence, for several minutes.

"It's beautiful," I said.

"Yes," he said. "I have to fight to keep it this way. It's Bronze Age."

He began to walk . . . stiff and erect, using the stick, while his feet kicked out—I guess he had a stroke—along the top of the grass slope . . . by the sunken lawn . . . towards an opening . . .

"Come and see me," he called back. "I'll show you the house and the gardens."

A half-hour later I was in a warm kitchen, by a scrubbed wooden table, having a coffee (a red enamel pot was kept warm on the Aga), looking, from a wide window, at the moor, the sea, the sky, and talking with some of the students.

When a taxi drove up, a tired-looking man of average height appeared. He wore a mustard military-cut overcoat and a black fedora. When he came in, carrying a green canvas bag, everyone stopped talking.

"I'm Adolphe Cayley," he said in a nervous voice.

He looked uncomfortable.

One of the girls said, "Like a coffee?"

"Thank you."

"Milk and sugar?"

"No. Black."

He had a few sips. Then walked over and asked if I was the other tutor. We shook hands formally. Coming closer he said, "Your first time, isn't it? Don't worry. I have done this many times. They usually send me to break someone in."

I had heard of Adolphe Cayley in much the same way as I had heard of Eric Symes. And in both cases I met them too late. Adolphe Cayley was known because of a short poem he had written some forty years earlier. It was used in an understated English war film. I can't remember the lines. But it was how ordinary life, during a war, goes on. And will continue to go on after the war is over.

He took his glasses off. He had light grey eyes. And, with the other hand, rubbed them. He put the glasses back on and asked if I was Canadian. He said he had been in Canada as part of the Commonwealth Air Training Plan.

"Did you fly?"

"No, I wrote propaganda."

He had a sister, he said, in Toronto that he visited.

I asked if he liked Toronto.

"It is very clean."

He kept wearing the black fedora. I thought he was bald. But later when he took it off, his short straight hair was black, not a grey hair anywhere. And I knew he had to be in his sixties.

I also assumed he was English. But it was evident he was something else. When I finally asked him, he said, "I'm not thoroughbred. My mother is from France. When I'm introduced, if people look surprised, I tell them—like Hitler but with an e." He smiled. "Any of your books in print?"

Surprised by this directness, I said, "No."

"Neither are mine. So we both know why we are here."

The white shirt was frayed at the neck. There was a stain on his tie. His brown shoes had the leather split on top. And the heels were worn right down. Yet despite his awkwardness and the outward appearance the impression I had was of someone with an inner dignity.

And the awkwardness also seemed to disappear when he took charge. He told two students that their jobs would be to go out every day and bring back dead wood for the fireplace. He picked two others, told them to see Connie in the office. She would give them money and a list of food to buy in Penzance for the rest of the week.

"We have to look after ourselves," he said.

On a sheet of paper he drew columns for the days we would be here. And asked the students to write their names for specific jobs.

"Every day two people will prepare lunch and dinner. Two others will wash and clean up. At breakfast we fend for ourselves. The best cooks will be on the last night, when the final meal will be something special with wine."

That evening we had supper in the dining room. Bare timbers across the ceiling. A bright fire in the large fireplace. We sat on fixed wooden benches by wooden tables. While we were having coffee, Adolphe stood up. "I thought," he said, "I would say a few words before we begin.

"Tomorrow morning, at eight, we start to work. I'll have seven—Peter will have seven. I'll pass around these two pieces of paper. They are marked for every half-hour of the morning with a five-minute break. Put your name down for the time you want to come. We will see you in that order. We'll talk, give you assignments and, when you write them, go over them. The rest of the time you are free to do what you like. There is a small library. There are rooms to be by yourself—though everything in them is faintly damp. There are good walks. This extraordinary landscape. And no distractions. No radio, no television, no newspapers. We are cut off—"

He drank some coffee.

"One of the things you need is a good pair of eyes. I was in Paris last summer. Walking in a street. When I saw, on the pavement, outside a shop, cages with small animals inside. In one cage were pigeons. They were pecking at the grain on the bottom of their cage . . . sending some of the grains outside. A lone pigeon came flying along the street. It landed beside the cage. It began to peck at the outside grains. Then at grains it could reach between the bars. Someone came from the shop, clapped her hands, "*Va t' en.*" The pigeon flew away. Those inside the cage went on pecking at the grain."

The students were making notes.

"Take things from life," Adolphe said. "Bad experience is better than no experience. Invent as little as possible. You are inventing the piece the way you use words and the way you are telling it. Wherever you go you will notice things.

"After Paris I went to a small provincial town. It was the end of July. All day Christmas carols were being played on loudspeakers in the streets. I got to know a teacher in this provincial town. Her name was Natalie. She had taught French in a London school and had come back to where she was born because her marriage broke up. Her parents bought her a wool shop. And they kept an eye on her. Natalie and I were having dinner in a restaurant—it was nine thirty—and there was her mother and father standing outside the restaurant window, smiling at us, and pointing to the time. Next morning we were having a coffee in the wool shop and talking about Richard Burton . . . his death was announced . . . when Natalie said, 'A young boy, from across the street, was killed last night in a car accident. He would always wave to me when he went by. I won't see him again . . . We can't talk about him.' She said angrily, 'But we can talk about Richard Burton and neither of us knew him.'"

Adolphe waited for this to sink in.

"Sometimes when you see something it will suggest something else. On the train coming down I saw two magpies. I remembered the rhyme:

One for sorrow
Two for joy
Three for a letter
Four for something better.

"And made up this scene. There is this young family in a train. Mother, father, young daughter. They have just left their older son in a mental hospital. Mother and father are tense. The young daughter—standing at the window looking at the passing fields—sees two magpies. She calls out excitedly.
"'We going to have joy. We going to have joy.'"
He hesitated.
"Of course if you have two magpies in a country cemetery. With one bird on a gravestone and the other on the earth beside it—you have other possibilities.
"And if you are in this country cemetery. And see a man, as I did, bringing flowers to the grave of his wife. In the next scene you have that man carrying flowers as he goes courting his new lady friend.
"Any questions?"
There were none.
"To end this evening," Adolphe said, "Peter and I will read you something we have written—so you can see our credentials."
Adolphe read an amusing account about his experiences with a dating service. "All the women they sent were handicapped."
And I read a ten-minute story.
That night, in the goose-house, I went to bed with the samples of writing my lot had brought with them. I looked forward to reading their work. When I finished, I thought, What

am I doing here? The writing was amateurish. The prose flat, lifeless, and going all over the place. It was as if they wanted to write and didn't know what to write about.

We began at eight next morning. A student would knock on the door of the goose-house. It was Spartan but clean. I would have them sit opposite at the scrubbed wooden table. Someone had put primroses and violets in a glass. I asked them, why did they want to write? And they talked. One student (a heavy handsome woman from Birmingham), the oldest on the course, said she was married with two small children and her husband was unemployed. Another, a small lively girl from a northern provincial town, said she was having an affair with her husband's closest friend ("He and his wife are constantly in and out of our house") and things were getting difficult. They also told me that their teachers' training college was closing at the end of the year. They were the last course. And none had jobs to go to when they graduated.

"Our tutor has started to write a novel."

"What will you do?"

They didn't know.

I went over their work. I showed them how to cut unnecessary words. And not to explain too much. After a few minutes they were able to do the revising themselves. I said their only responsibility—to discover their material. And gave them their first assignment. "Go outside. Describe something. So I can see it."

The last of the seven to come to the goose-house was also the youngest on the course, Sally. A small cheerful blond girl with a lovely smile. She had a habit of pushing her long hair away from her face. She wasn't as bad as the others but she still had some way to go. And I told her this.

"What does it matter," she said, "if someone is writing without a view of getting published. I get pleasure out of writing. I like doing it. I just want to get better. That's why I came."

I didn't understand this. I assumed that everyone who writes wants to get published. But here was someone realistic enough, at so young an age. Yet she couldn't stop. And neither, as I found out, could the others.

Walking to lunch Adolphe caught up with me.

"End of our surgeries for the day," he said, a little out of breath. "I've been going non-stop. How did yours go?"

"All right," I said, without his enthusiasm. And told him about Sally.

He smiled. "What makes people interesting is their dedication."

Tomorrow morning. It was Sally who came to the goose-house at eight. (The last person yesterday was the first person the next.) And as it was a warm sunny morning I suggested we have the lesson outside.

We were sitting, quite near, at right angles. Sally was facing the gardens. I was facing the moor. Close by, the tall grass and bracken. Then the distances. Areas of water, earth, sky. How timeless and quiet. I told her that I liked her descriptions, especially the way she described an outcrop of granite. "As if a giant toothpaste tube had been squeezed and the granite came out in layers, one on top of the other." For her next assignment, I said, I wanted her to try and trap an emotion. I was telling her how to go about doing this when I noticed a flash of light as the sun caught the windscreen of a car moving on the road across the moor. I turned my head towards Sally—her eyes were filled with tears. I went back to the moor—the car, like a toy, was now against the light green then the dark green—and talked as if nothing was happening. Sometimes I turned my head slightly—she was still crying—and continued to talk as I watched a kestrel hover, then glide, and turn into the wind and hover again, beating its wings without moving—in the wind—and not moving—then still. I cut the half-hour short, said I would see her tomorrow.

The next to come onto the grass was the married woman, Mrs. Goodhand, from Birmingham. I was more upset than I realized, for I told her what happened.

"I was sitting like this looking at the moor and talking about writing. When, for no reason, Sally started to cry."

I turned to look at Mrs. Goodhand. There were tears coming down her cheeks.

"Why are you crying?"

She lowered her head and said quietly,

"Because of you."

I didn't understand. And must have shown it. For she said, "You're on the page."

When I saw Adolphe I told him what happened. He wasn't surprised.

"They are reminding us we are writers."

Adolphe was taking me on one of his favourite walks. We passed four students playing croquet on the sunken lawn and I could hear the sound of wood on wood as we went down a rough path between the bracken and the gorse. Then the small fields. Butterflies were flitting around. Small light blue ones that I hadn't seen before. A light blue sea, in front, to the horizon. This immense sky. And, behind, the haunch of the moor. We walked along the curving side of a small potato field. Then another small field where the grass was high, the hedgerows full of campion, brambles, foxgloves, and primroses. We sat by a hedgerow, took our shirts off, lay on the grass facing the sun.

"You know what writers have in common?" Adolphe asked.

I didn't answer.

"A lack of confidence."

Was this true? I didn't think so. Not when I'm writing. It's when I finish something that the doubts set in.

"There are times," I said, "when I think the whole business is a confidence trick. The last time I walked into a public library it was like going into a cemetery. All those lives. All those ambitions. What does it come down to? A few books on a shelf."

I could hear a rooster crowing from the farm. And further, towards the cliffs, a working tractor.

"What else is there to do?" Adolphe said, his eyes shut. "You married?"

"Yes."

"I was. For twenty-seven years. We were married in a thunderstorm ... just after the war ... seems like yesterday. She now lives with someone in television. She likes celebrities. People she doesn't know. I have a housekeeper. She comes twice or three times a week. Stays the night. It's the best tonic I know."

Again we were silent.

I thought, he makes too much of being a writer. Perhaps I did too, once. But I had learned since not to make too much of anything.

"I'm a little to the left," Adolphe said. "In the thirties I was staying with an uncle in London. I went to dances. Sometimes two or three dances a night. I would pick at a lobster, a chicken done in something. Then, in the morning, walking to my uncle's house, I saw men sleeping on park benches with newspapers around their feet. I thought something wasn't right."

The sun was warm.

"Isn't this marvellous," Adolphe said, sitting up, looking at the silent view. I watched the shadow of a cloud going across the moor. As the cloud moved the light green slowly became dark green, then light green. Close to the cliffs a small fishing boat, its mizzen up. The water white in front and behind. Seagulls low over it and around its sides.

"I have led a futile life," Adolphe said. "Perhaps futile is not the right word. But it's days like the days here ... They are nothing in themselves ... but they help to give stability. I always come away from here feeling refreshed."

After another silence I asked him what happened after his poem was in that film.

"A lot of people came into my life. They said they wanted to look after my interests, to promote me. The phone kept ringing. I was going out to lunches, to dinners. I put on weight. I read the poem throughout the country, in town halls, in churches. It was taught in schools. I travelled. In the South of France I took a villa and stocked it with drink and food. For a while I had an enormous amount of friends.

"A few years later I wasn't news any more. When the money ran out I did whatever I could get. Then five years ago the poetry started again. It started after a woman I loved was killed in a car crash. I kept writing. All the time waiting for it to dry up. But it wouldn't let go. I sent the poems to the magazines who published me. But that was over twenty years ago. There were new editors. They sent them back. Sometimes they came back so fast I don't think they read them. They just looked at the name. I was old hat.

"For a while I did nothing. When you live alone—there are days when you do nothing. Then I decided to send them out under another name. They were accepted. I've been doing that since. I don't write as many as I used to. Two or three a year at the most. But they get published."

"What name do you use?"

"My secret. When I have enough for a book I'll write an article for a national paper and expose it all."

The sun no longer warm. We put on our shirts and started to walk back. The estate, from below, looked like a fairy-tale castle. And what we were doing here also seemed make-believe. The students treated us as distinguished writers. They didn't know about the little articles in the provincial papers, the radio scripts, the translations. And what, I wondered, did Adolphe do for a living?

As if guessing my thoughts he said, "You know how we're going to end up. Don't you?" He was laughing. "On the street. Like those men with the newspapers." But he wasn't laughing when he said in a flat voice, "I will probably end my days alone in a rented room."

Early on the third morning the light woke me. I got up and went onto the road. It was quiet. The smell from the wildflowers. And in this light all the colours looked freshly washed. I was singing. Sometimes the road went down to a narrow valley with the earth high on either side. And sometimes the road was at the very top. And I could see for miles. Crows, rooks, gulls flew slowly over. And the occasional rabbit in the bracken.

I wasn't the only one out. I saw students, in different parts of the moor, doing the same thing.

The morning surgeries also went well. Perhaps Adolphe was right about futile days. I was becoming impatient to get back to my wife and to a short story I had been trying to write for over a year.

In the afternoon I went to see Eric Symes. He led me into a large room, spotlessly clean. High ceiling, a wall-to-wall purple carpet, a piano ... the wood shining, a comfortable settee and chairs, white walls—paintings on them. It looked like an art gallery. I recognized a Soutine, a Terry Frost, a Peter Lanyon, Bryan Wynter, Patrick Heron, Alan Lowndes.

"I bought them, very cheaply, after the war. Afraid I'll have to sell some this year."

There were large painted dishes, with gold on the edges, propped up on the ledge above the fireplace.

"People have been very kind."

While Eric Symes was showing me around (and asked how I liked it here, and how the course was going) I could hear soft music. A pleasant woman's voice was slowly singing

I'll close my eyes
And make believe it's you ....

He walked stiffly on shaky legs, leaning on his cane, into the hall. And asked if I wanted to see upstairs. More paintings above the stairs. And, in another high room, another piano with black and white photographs propped up of a young Eric Symes. With Ivor Novello ... with Noel Coward ... with others, who looked vaguely familiar, in double-breasted suits and with cigarettes in long cigarette holders. There were photographs of him in the costume of an Arab sheik, a hussar, and a Foreign Legionnaire.

I'll close my eyes
And make believe it's you ...

He led me along the hall into another large and high white room. A low bed, neatly made up, books on wooden shelves, paintings unframed on the walls. A window looked to the moor and the sea.

"Haile Selassie slept here," Eric Symes said. "He had a daughter at a school in Penzance. Before my time."

Then he led me outside. I could smell the flowers before we entered the gardens. And hear the wind. A narrow path. On either side walls of green. The path kept turning. Blue flowers, purple and white foxgloves, birds singing, slabs of granite covered in a green moss, fallen flowers on the path as well as on the trees. Clusters of red hanging, bushes of them. Some hung down from stalks, most pushed up. Delicate white-pink flowers, light purple flowers, splashes of yellow on the green.

"I won't go through," Eric Symes said, out of breath. "Follow the path. I'll see you when you come out."

The path was overhung in places by shrubs and branches of trees. I had to bend to go under. Some branches had broken and were on the ground, a light green lichen on them.

As I continued to walk, on both sides, all kinds of exotic flowers and moss and lichen. The sound of flying insects. And fallen petals, fallen flowers, decaying leaves.

When I came out Eric Symes said there were seventy-three azaleas, sixty-five different camellias, ninety-three kinds of rhododendrons. And they came from Chile, New Zealand, and other far countries.

We went back the way we came and stopped in front of the sunken lawn. There wasn't a sound. The drop of bracken and gorse; the wooden poles going down with the single cable to the small green fields, the farm, and past the farm more small fields to the cliffs. Then sea and horizon. It looked so calm.

"There's always some battle going on," Eric Symes said. "Others want to change it. I'm fighting to keep it the same. So far I've won. But they don't give up. I had to fight developers who want to build hotels. I had to fight the war ministry. I covenanted the land to the National Trust. But I don't trust them. All it needs is some small war somewhere, with British interests, and they will have soldiers and helicopters all over the place. Sometimes there is a drought. I have to get water from the fire department. And there is always something going wrong … pipes, roofs, ceilings, windows, pumps. A bit of money comes from these courses. And I let it out in the summer. But not everyone likes it. They like the scenery. They can't stand the quiet or being cut off."

"What's going to happen when you're no longer here?"

"I don't know. I don't have children. I don't have family."

The effort of walking and talking had exhausted him. I thought I would leave.

"I read a lot," he said. "Send me one of your books."

On the last morning and afternoon both groups were together in the dining room. The students read out their assignments. The others commented on them. Everyone was saying nice things. My lot wrote mostly about the different views. Adolphe's wrote about railway journeys and funerals.

In the evening there was a sense of occasion. We all washed, dressed in clean clothes. (We had caught the sun.)

Adolphe looked ten years younger. The best cooks were on. Avocados with a French dressing. Roast chickens, roast potatoes, a salad. Apple pie with ice cream. And bottles of an inexpensive red wine. Everyone seemed to be in a light-hearted mood (telling us how much we had helped them, how much they got out of the course) so I thought of nothing when Adolphe came up to me with his coffee and casually said, "When I walk out of the room, the last person talking—that's the one you select."

Minutes later he called for everybody's attention.

"We have been together for four days cut off from all the things we are used to. We have got to know each other. And we have got on well. What I'm going to do is something of an experiment. I have tried it before. Sometimes it works. Sometimes it doesn't. It depends entirely on us ... I'm going to go out of the room. You select someone. Then I come back. And we'll see what happens."

There was some excitement. People were talking. I listened. As Adolphe went out it was Sally whose voice I heard.

"Let's pick Sally," I said.

Another student called Adolphe back.

He stood in front of us.

"The brain is a generator," he said. "It gives off electric waves. We can pick up these waves if we concentrate. Now close your eyes. And concentrate on this one person. Put everything out of your mind—just concentrate on this one person. Say that person's name in your mind. Don't think of anything else. Just concentrate ... Concentration is what writing is all about ... Put everything out of your mind. Just think of that one person."

I looked. They all had their eyes closed and their heads down as if in prayer. It was quiet.

"Someone is not concentrating," Adolphe said, his eyes shut. I closed my eyes. "That's better," he said. Another long silence. "It's getting ... better. Yes. Yes. I'm getting something ...

it's coming through ... it's becoming clear ... it's Sally."

They opened their eyes. And looked surprised, pleased, excited. Adolphe was smiling.

"Shall we do it again?"

This time I picked Jimmy—a Scottish boy who was in Adolphe's class. Jimmy was sitting beside his friend Christopher.

Adolphe went through the same routine. And when he finally said Jimmy they were again surprised.

The third time he went out I said we will have Mrs. Goodhand.

A student said, "You always do the picking. Why don't we pick someone?"

"It doesn't matter who does the picking," I said calmly, and asked a student to call Adolphe.

After Adolphe said Mrs. Goodhand the surprise was still there, though several looked puzzled and some suspicious.

We had a break to fill up with wine or coffee. The students were around Adolphe. I finally got him alone. "They're on to us," I said. "They want to pick the next one."

"Leave it to me." And walked away.

"As it is working so well," Adolphe said to everyone and smiled, "I'm going to ask Peter to go out and see if it will work with him."

I went out of the room and came back. Following Adolphe, I said, "Everyone concentrate." And I saw them close their eyes and their heads went down. The room was silent. I waited. "I'm not getting anything," I said. "Some are not concentrating." And waited for as long as I could. Then, quietly, said, "Something is starting." And waited. "Yes. Something is starting to come through ... I can't tell if it is a man or a woman ..."

I saw Christopher getting red in the face.

I quickly said, "It's becoming clear. It's Christopher."

Again the mixture of surprise and puzzlement. Except for Jimmy and Christopher, who looked sideways at one another.

Next morning we were outside. (Connie had called a taxi the night before to take us to Penzance station at nine.) Adolphe was in his element. He went around in his black fedora and mustard military coat saying, "Everything ends too soon." Some of the girls were visibly emotional. He gave them his address. (Only Mrs. Goodhand and Sally asked for mine.) He went off with one girl—when they came back they were holding hands.

The taxi came. We were getting in when Eric Symes appeared, walking as fast as he could.

"The phone has been cut off."

"Why would they do that?" a student asked.

"Because I didn't pay the bill. I forgot. I forget a lot of things. Could you," he asked Adolphe, "go to Penzance post office and put it right?" And Eric Symes gave Adolphe the bill and a cheque. "It's kind of you—without the phone—"

The taxi began to move along the drive. Adolphe was smiling and waving. So were the students. "Goodbye," he called. "Goodbye...Goodbye..."

As soon as the taxi turned onto the road Adolphe withdrew into his corner. We drove in silence and looked out at the landscape.

Some miles later we were passing a granite outcrop. It went up in horizontal layers. I could hear Adolphe muttering to himself. "Things have to last, to endure." About a mile later we were driving with the road on top. The moor on both sides of the road. And further down, to the right, the sea and the horizon. "Once we're gone we will be forgotten," he said. "It will be as if we have never lived."

Then, half turning to me, "Why do we go on?"

Not waiting for a reply. "Because I have to go and see about that telephone. You have to get back to your wife. And who knows what we will have to do tomorrow—"

A few miles further, with St. Just in the distance, he took out a folded piece of paper from his coat pocket. "A sentimental girl. I gave her my address. She gave me this." He passed the paper to me without turning his head. It was a short poem called "Volcanoes" by one of his students. Under the title she had written. "For Adolphe—who made things happen."

Outside Penzance station the taxi stopped. I got out of the car with my bag and went around to the window where he was sitting. He looked different from the person on the moor. A shabby elderly man, older than his years, with bags under his eyes.

"Now that you know my tricks the next one you'll be able to do yourself."

"Yes," I said.

He stared back at me. It became awkward. We didn't know how to say goodbye.

"The most terrible thing that can happen to a writer is success," he said in his flat voice. Then he started to smile, his face changed. "Expect a cheque in three or four weeks." He waved as the taxi drove away.

I walked into Penzance station. And the noise . . . of the trains . . . people moving . . . the clatter in the small café . . . Even the advertisements seemed an intrusion.

THE MAN WITH
THE NOTEBOOK

I F YOU SAW HIM by himself, sitting in the park or in the corner of a pub, you would have noticed the clerical appearance of his face, the soft eyes, the grey straight hair, and the glasses. About his features there was an overall mildness. You felt certain that he had never raised his voice, no matter what the occasion, and that he would be prompt to apologize if he so much as brushed against another person.

He lived by himself in a room in Bayswater. Every morning he would wash, dress, go down to the first step, and pick up his morning paper. Then come back and prepare breakfast in the kitchen at the end of the passage. He would have a raw orange, bacon, two cups of black coffee. After reading the paper he would wash the dishes, make the bed, clean the room. Then pick up a small inexpensive dark green notebook from his desk and go out.

His favourite walk was to Kensington Gardens. In the early morning he would walk past the deserted playground, watch the birds—the fat wood pigeons with their small heads—avoid the water that lay in the hollows of the path, until he reached Round Pond. Here he would sit on one of the benches, take out his notebook, and write at the top of a clean page: *Day cloudy. Wind moderate.* Then he would put the note-book down, smoke his pipe, and watch.

He came to the Gardens to observe people. The nannies, in grey uniforms with white collars, pushing expensive prams. The well-dressed men and women taking their dogs for their morning walk. The businessmen going through the park to work. But if, like today, he came early and few people were about he would take his notebook and write of the landscape around him. *Trees without leaves. Sun getting warm. Water in pond, green, blue, grey. Groups of young birds at edge preen-ing themselves. Ducks asleep. Flycatchers on a wire fence—sun catches the weeds in front of them and reflects the green to the underneath part of their bodies.* And he tried even with this warming-up exercise to see in the familiar landscape some-thing fresh—like this morning's flycatchers.

From the Gardens he walked to Hyde Park and got on a bus that took him to Piccadilly, Trafalgar Square, the East End, or to one of the railway stations, a street market, or along the embankment—a choice that followed a list drawn up every month. And once there he would mix with people, go into a café, a pub, watch and listen. And write down what he saw and heard.

In the late afternoon he would return to his room and type out what he had written that day. And from these notes, over the next three days, he would put together a sketch built around a particular person in each of these places. On Thurs-day night he would type out the 1,500 words and send them to a weekly journal. On the following Saturday he received a copy of the sketch as it had appeared and a cheque for thirty guineas. The editor of the journal, not long out of university, was a firm believer in taking things "directly from life." When he had read two of the early sketches, sent in by chance, he accepted them. And, after he had published five more, con-tracted the old man to send a sketch a week. This arrangement had now gone on for over two years. The old man was always punctual with his story. And the weekly cheque removed the financial insecurity he had experienced before.

He saved all his clippings, pasting them neatly in large leather-bound volumes. And in the evenings he often would sit and read about the different people he had written. Occasionally he wondered where some of them might be. For though his livelihood depended on being with people, watching them, listening to what they said—he had few friends.

This uneventful life would have continued had not the government requisitioned the site where he lived for the construction of an office building. He disliked not so much the idea of leaving his room, or that part of London, but the fact that his routine would be upset. When his editor suggested that he move to a cottage, in a small fishing village in Cornwall, that he knew to be vacant, he was glad that the decision was made by somebody else.

From his window he could look out at a kind of valley with a lot of narrow streets and stone cottages with chimneys belching out smoke around tea time. And though the cottage was small and damp it was much better than his room in Bayswater. He could now work in one room, sleep in another, and eat in still another. And the longer he lived in the village the more he grew to like it.

He liked the way people recognized him when he walked in the streets, said good morning, or spoke about the weather. He liked it even more when they began to tell him the local gossip. He became a familiar sight along the front, the High Street, in the pubs. People referred to him as the man with the notebook. And after he had been there six months accepted him into their communal life. The editor continued to be satisfied with his writing.

He had lived in Cornwall seven months and his morning began with the usual walk down the slope to get his paper, then to the fishmonger by the front. The fishmonger, a small ex-sailor, knew what his customers wanted. Their conversation, apart from fish, was negligible. The fishmonger selected a long thin mackerel from a wicker basket, cut and flicked off the head to the pail below. The fishmonger said, "Did you know Bill Stevens is dead?"

"No," the old man said. "No, I didn't."

It was by the bandstand on the front that he first saw him. A row of chairs was placed near the band for the feeble-minded who came to hear the music. And Bill Stevens stood by the rails beside them. Otherwise he spent all his time walking. He was ninety-three. A small neat man in a grey double-breasted suit, very light blue eyes, always wearing a fedora, carrying a cane, and walking out his days.

He came across Stevens often when he was out. And they always stopped and talked. Stevens told him what this place was like when he was a boy. When winter was the busy time, not summer. And the visitor such a rare thing that, if one came, it was news and his name and where he was staying appeared in the local paper. Fishermen, at the start of the season, were blessed at the slipway. And coffins were carried through the streets. When the pallbearers tired, they stopped, and small stools would be placed on the road. The coffin put on the stools. And everyone rested.

The old man put it all in, in his sketch of "Mister Bill," as he called it. He had liked Stevens. He had written about him. Now he was dead. As he drank his second cup of black coffee he went to his book of clippings and reread "Mister Bill." He wondered if in his way he had made Bill Stevens alive for thousands of people who had never seen him.

In a couple of weeks' time he had forgotten about the funeral. Though it was only the start of February—snow-drops were out and the crocuses beginning—the place was getting ready for the summer season. The harbour rails were repainted silver; the summer cafés and restaurants redeco-rated; the holes in the streets repaired. The sand that the winter tides had swept up to the walls was bulldozed back into the sea. And the few remaining fishermen were repainting their boats and bringing out the mended gear from storage.

The old man enjoyed this activity and recorded it in his notebook.

But this sensation of feeling part of this village changed abruptly when he realized, with the death of the pier car park attendant, that all the funerals since he arrived in this village were the funerals of people he had written about.

Most of the early sketches from Cornwall were descriptions of the sea, the village, the harbour. He had written about few people: "The Town Crier"; "The Man with the Heavy Eyelids"; "Jack the Fisherman"; "Mister Bill"; "The Pier Car Park Attendant." But all these people, soon after he had written about them, died.

At first he thought it was coincidence. After all, he wrote mainly about old people.

He went to the notebook, read over the beginning of the week's sketch that he was working on.

The bell was tolling at ten on the Monday morning and I knew that someone was being buried. This was Mister R.'s daughter. Our landlady said that when she was being born he told the hospital to ring him up. If it was a boy, they were to say "strawberries," if it was a girl, to say "peaches." He came running down the hill to tell the landlady. "It's peaches," he said. "It's peaches."

That was as far as he had gone with it and he knew he would go no further.

For the next two days he was depressed. *I am reluctant to leave this cottage and be seen in the streets,* he wrote in his notebook. *Therefore I wake up just before six. Then I go out for my walk and get to see what the place is like. I do some window shopping. Walk around the front. Along the pier. Watch the gulls, the black-backs, the sparrows. And I am back to the cottage by seven.*

The next day, because a gale was blowing, he felt safe enough to go out at noon.

There are five French crabbers in the Bay, he wrote in his notebook, *facing the land, anchored and swaying violently. In front of them about a dozen gannets are diving for sand eels. They rarely go higher than the masts of the crabbers. I watch, from a shelter by the ladies' lavatory. They come low across the water, turn into the wind, climb sharply, drift across, then plummet down, entering with a splash.*

But these were the reflexes of a writing animal. The human was no longer observed or noted down.

After another day of trying to come to terms with himself he decided to satisfy his conscience by deliberately writing about someone young and healthy for his next sketch.

He chose his next-door neighbour's son. A young man in his twenties. He worked in the post office by the Methodist chapel. It seemed odd to see him—looking like something from a physical fitness poster—sit on a high stool and give out stamps in the small post office. His girlfriend was a waitress in a café along the front during the summer and a telephone operator in the winter.

The old man went to the post office with his notebook. It was not an easy job. For not only was he under a strain, but the young seemed to wear a mask for him. His first draft of "Hal," as he named him for the sketch, was not of a young man, but that of an old person. He tried again. Not knowing what he was after he wrote too much. Besides describing the restless eyes, the trace of boredom already showing in the mouth, the power of the body; he noted down every poster, every announcement and warning that was on the walls. He decided that he would write "Hal" as a paradox: the young man, full of vitality—and the drabness of his surrounding and lightness of work.

He sent off the sketch on the Thursday night. He did not return to the cottage but walked aimlessly by the harbour in the light rain. He was not certain whether he believed that there was a link between the recent deaths and his writing—or whether, getting old, he wanted to give his work some kind of recognition.

They found his neighbour's son on Monday morning. He was lying at the bottom of the courtyard. Apparently he visited his girlfriend by scaling the side of the house, going across the gable roof, and then entered her room through the bedroom window, which she left open. The policeman thought he probably lost his footing and fell some thirty feet onto concrete. The scandal that this accident revealed helped to talk out the tragedy. But to the old man Hal's death was no accident. And neither were the others.

He spent Monday and Tuesday by himself. He ate sparingly and didn't bother to wash up or tidy the room. In the evenings he took down his leather-bound books.

His first sketch was of "Konrad." A Polish actor he met by chance in Soho. They spent the afternoon drinking and "Konrad" told him how he was liberated.

One night British come in farmyard. Next night SS. I stay with the cows. I have big P on left breast. I saw British soldier come. I could cry I was so happy.

Young blond with dictionary in hand.

Wer sind Sie?

I am a Pole.

Do you speak English.

A little.

Sind Sie ein Pole?

Ya.

Wohnen Sie in Warsaw?

Yes.

Come in.

Everybody was drunk singing "Hurrah Konrad." I meet my best friend. You need suit. What do you need? Here drink, and took from his blouse a bottle. Ah Konrad, freedom. Drink. Let's

get drunk. British soldiers give whisky, cigarettes, everybody
drinking, kissing, eating, all cans of petrol filled with spirits.
Sometimes German planes come and machine gun. All women
drunk. All suits given away free. Fifteen nationalities in camp.
No organization. Everybody drinking, dancing.

"Who is drunk can't leave camp."

Good, now I'm imprisoned by the British. That is fine. Das ist
liberation. Good. Let's drink. Germans in barns. DPs in house.
Germans cook for us. All DP camps drunk. Fifteen nationalities,
fifteen camp leaders, fifteen committees. Loudspeakers going all
day from five until twelve at night.

Viva holiday.

We have revolvers. We shoot. Ping. A place is cleared. We
throw grenades. Give prizes.

He liked the "Konrad" sketch and the other early ones.
"Jerome," the debt collector who looked like a professor. He
met him in Lyons in the Strand. He worked for a firm that
bought up old debts at a discount then employed "Jerome"
to collect them. The third sketch was "Doris." He met her at
Waterloo Station. She was pushing a tea trolley. She told him
how she made her money by bringing her own packages of tea
and putting these into the tea urn and selling them, instead of
British Rail ...

"Obituary notices," he said to himself. "That's what I was
writing."

He knew he would not have a sketch ready that week. The
editor said nothing, and reprinted an early one. But after it
happened twice he received a telegram asking if he was ill. He
replied that he was but he would try to send him something
soon.

Weeks passed. The cheques stopped arriving. He tried to write
of places he had never seen. But he knew that they were not
right. He had always used the notebook and these attempts
to write imaginative pieces, he knew, were lifeless. When,

in desperation, he sent one of these off, the editor promptly returned it, at the same time reminding him that he was one of the best writers "in the naturalistic tradition," and that was what he wanted.

He believed it would be more humane if he went to people who were already dying. He visited the small hospital. There was one old woman. The doctor told him that she was dying. He looked at her. Her teeth had fallen underneath the bed. She asked him to pick them up for her ...

Summer passed. He would lie in his bed during the day, not wanting to get up. Sometimes at night he went out and wandered in the back streets worrying what he could possibly write about to bring in some money. He felt certain that what he had done, especially in the village, was wrong. But he did not know why. He wanted to write but not to harm anyone.

I am reluctant to leave my cottage, he wrote on New Year's Day in the notebook. *When I do, I'm afraid of running into someone I know. He will show surprise and say, I thought you were away. And I say, Yes. It stops a lot of questions. I keep away from certain streets because I owe money to two grocers, the paper place, the tobacconist, the butcher, the milkman, the coal merchant. On Christmas Day, as a gesture, I went by the side streets and alleys to the old pier and sat down on the bench by a couple. They must have been in their fifties or sixties. They were on holiday. She took hold of the man's hand and began clumsily to stroke it. She had a small fattish hand. And there is something desperate about her action. They talk about the far shore fields, of travelling in a car there some time ago.*

"What's the time?" the man says suddenly.

She leaves go the man's hand to look at her wrist.

"Nearly two."

"Why is it so early?" he says. "It's been early all day."

I get up and quickly walk away from them. I can't use them, I can't use them, I can't use them ... And I realize I am walking through the streets talking to myself ...

Late in January, on a particularly cold night, weak from hunger and cold, the old man died. And when they found him, he had burned the leather-bound books in an attempt to keep warm.

IN LOWER TOWN

WHEN I was a kid we lived in Lower Town, Ottawa. The first house was on Guigues Street. It was a brick house on a corner. On one side was King Edward Avenue with its boulevard of tall elms, their roots above the ground. And on the other, our neighbour Nadolny. Mr. Nadolny, a nice-looking man in glasses, had been something different in Europe. Here in Ottawa he was, like my father, a fruit peddler. The rest of Guigues Street was French Canadian.

It was a large three-storey house and to help things out, my mother took in boarders. All of them were recent immigrants from Europe.

There was Isaac and his wife, Ethel. He looked like a professor with his monocle, and worked in a jewellery store, uptown, doing watch repairs. She stayed home, as she was pregnant. She looked a bit scatty with her blond fuzzy hair that she had difficulty in combing and her large pale eyes. She also couldn't speak English. When she started to have labour pains, she called out to me.

"Me hoits. Me hoits."

They soon left Ottawa for California.

And there was Bobeh and Zaydeh Saslove. They were brought over by their sons when they were in their late sixties. He was short and quiet and had a long beard and not much to do except go to the synagogue. In Poland, when he was younger, he was something in wood. Here he would go to the market and buy, in summer, the wood we needed for the winter. I'd see him come back with the horse and wagon and blocks of wood piled high in the back. He made several trips. Then he spent days building the blocks of wood carefully together along the back fence near where the wild cucumbers were growing. He took care and had the wood meshed evenly—like I tried to do on the table with matches. After he had stacked the couple of cords he would ask us to come out and see how it looked. We all said it looked very nice. A couple of days later he would knock it all down flat. And then start to build it up again, very neatly.

Both he and his wife spoke in whispers. And they ate their meals together out of the same bowl.

My father only knew a few words of English and a few words of French. When I was twelve—and we moved from Guigues to Murray Street, where just about everyone was either a fruit- or a rag-peddler—I decided to help my father with the peddling. When school finished at the end of June, I left the house early in the morning and walked to the market and helped him load the wagon with the fruit and vegetables that he bought from the farmers and the wholesale stores. Then we went out—the white horse pulling the high red wagon over Rideau, along Nicholas Street, by the jail, over Laurier Bridge and across the Rideau Canal, to the first street with my father's customers—Gloucester.

It was a quiet street with lots of trees and squirrels on the grass lawns and wooden houses with verandas painted green or brown. In the middle of the block there was a greystone convent where someone was always practising the piano.

It was a humid day and our shirts were damp when my father asked me to come along to his first customer—to help break me in.

We walked around the back of the house to the kitchen. He knocked on the screen door. A pretty woman in a black slip appeared. She was in her thirties. She began to ask questions as to the price of the corn, bananas, tomatoes, cucumbers, potatoes—and she started to squeeze the peach I had, as a sample, in my wicker basket.

"*Kvetch, kvetch.*" My father began to talk in Yiddish. "I bet you know how to squeeze in bed."

I looked at the woman's face, trying to pretend I didn't hear what my father was saying.

"How much are the spring onions?" she asked.

"Three bunches for twenty cents," I said.

"Look at the prostitute," my father said in Yiddish. (The word he used was *curveh*, which is much more evocative.) "You can see she's got nothing on underneath."

"How much are the cherries?" the woman asked with a nice smile.

"Twenty-five cents a box," I said, looking at her brown eyes, the dark hair cut short, the even teeth.

I tried to keep a straight face while she gave me her order and my father went on in Yiddish about her likely performance in bed.

As we walked back to the wagon to get her order made up, I felt embarrassed and pleased. I had never heard my father say anything like this before. Without turning my head, I glanced at his face. He was grinning like a kid.

That evening, after he had put the horse in the stable and had his supper, he came outside to sit with my mother and sister on the veranda. He was the same self I had known before, in his chair, in the corner, by the hanging morning glory, drinking Kik. And looking at the families sitting outside on the other verandas doing much the same.

I thought it was only my father who behaved differently away from Lower Town until I happened to be in one of the wealthier west-end streets a couple of days later. By now I knew the route as well as the horse. And I used to go well ahead of the horse and wagon so I could sit on a veranda, in the shade, and rest a bit, while my father served his customers.

I was sitting like this when I saw old man Pleet—our neighbour on one side in Murray Street. He had a broken-down horse pulling a shabby wagon with old mattresses, old bedsprings, bottles, and sacks. But instead of calling out "Rags, rags for sale," which he did in Lower Town, here he was saying, in a slight singsong, the evening service of the synagogue. He didn't see me. As the horse and wagon went by I looked at his face. Mr. Pleet was miles and miles away.

Another time, also in a wealthier street, in Rockcliffe, I saw Mr. Slack, another rag-peddler from Murray Street. He too was going through with his horse and wagon, very slowly, on this hot summer's day, junk piled behind him. And calling out sadly in Yiddish.

"Thieves. Thieves. Nothing but a bunch of thieves live here."

I guess they knew that once away from Lower Town they might as well have been in a foreign country. And they also knew that they could never become part of it.

But I would.

At school I played not only with the other Lower Town kids but also with kids whose parents only spoke English. Had nice jobs in the government. Some of these kids asked me back to their houses. (It was a very democratic place.) Large houses with maids and with trees and bushes and lots of grass. I remember being asked back by a classmate whose father was an aide-de-camp to the Governor General. And when I arrived there was a garden party on the lawn. Another time a doctor's son asked me. And after we had nice things to eat in a large gloomy house we went in their white boat along the Rideau Canal. Another time a blond girl in the class asked me back for her birthday party—it was to a large house off the Driveway. We had to take our shoes off because the floors were new.

I couldn't invite them back to the house in Murray Street. They had made me ashamed of where I lived, of the house that smelled of the stable, and of parents who couldn't speak English.

I used to go to school daydreaming that I had other parents, pretending I lived somewhere else. And wondering when I could get away from here.

I did get away when I was eighteen and a half. The war was on. I joined up, went overseas. And after the war I went away to university in Montreal. Then moved over to England and thought I had put all this very far behind me.

But what happened.

Now that most of the fruit and rag peddlers are dead and Lower Town has changed—I find I am unable to stay away from it. It's become like a magnet. Whenever I can, I return.

The last time was this summer. I was supposed to go to Montreal and Toronto. But I only spent a short time in those places. I wanted to be in Ottawa. And though I stayed in a hotel with everything modern and neat, I kept on walking through the streets of Lower Town.

On Rideau, I went into Nate's Delicatessen. And saw some of the kids I grew up with—children of those men who used to go out with a horse and wagon.

"You've really made it," Moe Slack said, shaking my hand. "Both the *Citizen* and the *Journal* gave you a full page. My wife bought your last book when it came out. I tried to read it but gave up halfway. Why don't you write dirty books? That's what people want to read."

Harvey Reinhardt came in. He was the same size as me but had put on more weight.

"How are you?" I asked after he sat down.

"I'm impotent," he said.

(Except he pronounced it important.)

"Ten years ago I had five dames going at the same time—"

"What do you mean?"

"I had five mistresses," he said. "My mother caught me with one at home. She said, If you don't get that woman out of the house, I'll cut my throat right here. Do me a favour, I said, go out on the lawn. You'll spoil the carpet. I was a real bastard," he said with a grin.

We were sitting around a table in the back of Nate's. Moe Slack and I were having smoked meat sandwiches and coffee and there was a blown-up informal photograph of Trudeau on the wall. We were now about the same age as those fruit and rag peddlers.

Harvey Reinhardt ordered a kipper.

"I like an English breakfast," he said. "The English girls— do they like to screw? What is it?" he asked me.

"It must be the damp climate," I said.

"You think so."

The kipper came.

"Have you ever gone to these group things?" Harvey Reinhardt said.

"No," I said eager to hear more.

"Very high-class people," said Harvey. "They only let you come with your wife or your girlfriend. It starts off like a real party. They give you a drink. Then you start dancing. And you go off to a room. I had this beautiful twenty-five-year-old. And I couldn't do a thing."

"Didn't she know what to do, to help things along?" I asked.

"She knew what to do," Harvey said. "But it was no good. She said she worked at some agricultural place with boars. And when some boars overdid it they were no good after that. I think this has happened to me. Later I saw her go off with some other fellow into a bedroom. I don't think I'll go again. There's no fun in it for me."

"You're a millionaire—I hear," Moe said to Harvey.
Harvey took out a cigar and winced. "Who knows," he said.

I left them at Nate's, remembering when they were younger and I was younger, remembering their mothers and fathers, their sisters and brothers. And crossed into Lower Town.

The streets were being altered, the wooden houses demolished, and other houses had doors and windows boarded up waiting to be pulled down.

I walked along York, Clarence, Murray, St. Patrick, Rose, McGee—

Here my father's horse got loose from the stable and came out into the street one summer evening. And then the whole street came out to watch the men coax him back.

In this courtyard I saw a wedding where the young red-haired bridegroom broke the glass on the ground under the held canopy. And the white bits of fluff from the dandelions, or the trees, were blown across by the summer wind so that it looked like falling snow.

Here in winter we hired two horses and a long sleigh without sides. About ten boys and ten girls. We rode at night to the sound of bells on the harness. The overhead street light showed the hard-packed snow. And in the shadows, on either side, the wooden houses moved slowly by. We pushed one another into the snowbanks, then ran to get back onto the sleigh ...

I came to the small park at the end of King Edward Avenue, sat on a green bench, and felt strangely timeless. The white Minto bridges across the hardly moving Rideau River, the swans, the blackbird in the tall grass seemed—like the streets—to be frozen like a photograph. And in an extraordinary stillness.

I went to see my mother.

"Where have you been?" she asked.

"I walked along Murray Street and St. Patrick Street and down to King Edward Park."

"I haven't been there for over ten years," she said.

"They're knocking the wooden houses down," I said. "And changing the streets. Soon there will be nothing left of the place the way it was."

"You'll see how nice they'll make it," she said. "All those wooden houses—that's past. We need high-rises, motorways. It will be a lot better. You can write about that," she said. "Tell how nice everything is here. Look at that high-rise across the park. At night, when the apartments put on their lights, it looks like a ship . . . You won't write any more about fruit and rag peddlers?"

"No," I said.

"That's the old life—it's finished."

She fussed over me, giving me things to eat. And as soon as I finished something on a plate she quickly took the plate away and I could hear her washing it up in the kitchen. Her whole flat was spotless, everything in place. After a while, all this neatness was getting me down. Until I went to look in the drawer of a dresser in the living room for the old photographs. And saw, to my relief, that the neatness, everything in its place, was only on the surface. That in the drawers, in the dresser, things were still jumbled up.

I looked at the faces of people in the Lower Town of not so long ago. There was a photograph of my mother in her early twenties with two friends . . . my father on the veranda . . . a family picture in front of the house . . . a photograph of my sister and me by a large elm on King Edward Avenue when I was five and she was three . . . a gathering at someone's wedding . . .

My mother watched me. "When I'm gone," she said, indicating the photographs with her hand and then sweeping her hand downwards. "*In* the garbage! *All* in the garbage. You'll see."

She said it almost defiantly.

On the day I arrived for this visit men in yellow machines were busy knocking down the large convent on Rideau Street.

I asked Harvey Reinhardt why were they knocking down a perfectly good convent?

"You can't make a buck out of a convent on Rideau Street," he said.

A few weeks later all that was still standing was part of the chapel. I could see a large painting painted on one wall of the chapel. It showed a young nun in a black and sky-blue habit. And coming down from the top left of the picture, down to the upturned eyes of the nun, was a wide ray of sunshine. Several cherubim were in this ray of the sun. They had curly blond hair and wings.

On the day I left Ottawa the chapel had also been knocked down, the rubble cleared. It was all very tidy. Nothing to show that there ever had been a convent there at all.

THE ABILITY
TO FORGET

I WAS in a small town in southwest France teaching English to adults when I decided to go to England. To the northeast, where, in the last months of the war, I was with a Canadian Lancaster squadron. I stayed in Barnard Castle, a place I hadn't heard of but I liked the name. And it was near enough to the places I wanted to see again.

I rented the end part of a large stone house by a river. It went up three floors. The best and largest room, where I spent most of my time, was at the top. It looked onto the river. And to upward-sloping green fields with trees on the far side. When I opened a window the continual sound of water as it went over rocks. And on a still morning I watched from this window a man, on a flat rock in the middle of the river, fly fishing.

After I settled in I went to the places I had known some fifty years earlier: Leeming, Dishforth, Northallerton, Topcliffe, Ripon, York, Harrogate, Scarborough, Thirsk. And it was as if I was seeing them for the first time. The only thing I remembered was their names. So I decided, for the rest of my time in the northeast, to get to know something of Barnard Castle.

It is a small market town on a plateau. The ruins of a medieval castle overlook a fast-flowing river, the Tees. A stone

Elizabethan bridge, humped above two large arches, goes across the river by the castle. And not far is a large château-like building, the Bowes Museum. All its elongated windows have rounded tops. In front, a sunken French formal garden. And lawns and acres of grounds with different trees on the sides and behind. But when I went out and walked through the streets, I wondered what was I doing here? No one said hello, or good morning, or even looked at you in passing. Then I saw the plaques. By the church.

*Richard III
And later King of England
Was Lord of Barnard Castle
From 1474 until his death in 1485
He made improvements to the Castle
Took a close interest in the Town
And was a great benefactor
Of its church.*

And on a large stone house.

*Formerly
The residence of
Sir Roderick Murchison
Twice President of the Royal
Geographical Society. He died
in 1571 . Age 79. A Great
Geologist and Explorer. A Town
in New Zealand. Falls on the Nile,
A mountain Range and River in
Australia and a Sound in
Greenland are all named
After him.*

On another stone house with nine large windows.

> *This house is the birthplace*
> *(30 July 1909)*
> *of*
> *Cyril Northcote Parkinson*
> *Author*
> *Professor of Various Universities*
> *And Discoverer of*
> *Parkinson's Law—Which reads*
> *"Work Expands so as*
> *To Fill The Time Available*
> *For its completion."*

And there were others. In the small library I read, in an old book, that Barnard Castle was a place known for its gossip.

Because I felt so out of place, I went for walks in the near countryside. I walked through fields. Dogs came up. I spoke French to them. And they were friendly.

I was wondering how much longer to stay when I walked up a slope, the Bank, and turned into a narrow street with small houses on one side. This short street led to a large open grass area. A sign said "The Demesnes." The left side went up a steep grass slope. And, at the top, it levelled out to an upper field. I walked along this field. Suddenly there, close, was the Bowes Museum. And when I looked down the slope to the right, across the large flat-level of grass, it went to the river with trees on the bank. And, on the far side of the river, upward-sloping light green fields with dark green trees, and sheep at the top. And here and there a large stone house. An old church with a tall spire, and a small cemetery.

This became my daily walk. Others came here to walk their dogs.

One afternoon, when I turned into the narrow street to go to the Demesnes, I saw a man in the middle of the street star-

ing at me. He was neatly dressed—white shirt, dark blue tie—
stocky, and a few years older. As I came near he said, "Were
you in the war?"

"Yes."

"What were you in?"

"The Air Force."

The expression on his face changed.

"Come in and have a drink."

It was a small house, a few small rooms, hardly any furniture. On the walls, large picture frames with photographs
under the glass. There was one of him with his wife at their
wedding. She was in white. He in Air Force uniform. All the
other picture frames had, under the glass, photographs of him
in uniform in warm and cold countries.

"I was a squadron leader," he said, "a wireless operator."

I never met a wireless operator who was a squadron leader.

"I was acting wing commander," he said. "I went to Cranwell."

Cranwell, I thought, may explain the squadron eader. But I
didn't believe the acting wing commander.

"What did you do?" he said.

"Drop bombs."

He poured more whisky.

"Where were you before coming here?"

"In France," I said. "In the southwest."

"We flew to an airfield outside Paris near the start of the
war. Once we had Churchill on board. Another time the Duke
of Windsor."

Again, I didn't know whether to believe him.

"I was told to go into cafés, restaurants, railway stations,
and listen. Never let on that I knew French. Then, back in England, I had to report to Intelligence."

"How was it in Paris before the Germans came?"

"Panic. Everyone was trying to get out. Those with money
did. They went south. Those who didn't have money had to stay."

For the next half-hour, probably more, he never stopped talking about the war. Finally, I interrupted.

"The English had a good war. The French didn't."

He looked puzzled.

"In my English class, I asked Madame Larrere. Give me a sentence using the word *tenderly*. And Madame Larrere slowly said, 'When my husband came back from Buchenwald I kissed him tenderly.'

"Another student, an attractive widow of a doctor, told me when we were having dinner that when she was a young girl her mother cooked a piece of meat, strapped it to her body, then put on her dress. Then she went to see her father in jail—he had been a collaborator—so he could have something good to eat."

He still looked puzzled.

"In France, I sometimes have an evening meal in a restaurant near where I live. And because it was summer people ate on tables outside the restaurant. A new waitress was on. She was older than the usual one. And if you saw her in the street you wouldn't have noticed. A new and expensive German car drove up and a young man and woman, both tall and tanned, stepped out and sat at the next table. They were obviously German. The waitress brought food to the other tables. And took orders from others. But did not go near the table where the healthy-looking young man and woman were. Everyone knew what was going on. No one said anything.

"After about half an hour the couple got up, walked to their car, and drove away. The waitress continued as if nothing had happened."

He still looked puzzled, as if he didn't understand why I was telling him this.

"In France," I said, "I live beside a boulevard. In the early morning I take the dog out for her walk. We go down this long boulevard. There are plum trees in the middle, then plane trees. And the sun on the Bassin d' Arcachon. At the end of the boulevard I turn to the right and walk by the water. After a while I retrace my steps.

"This morning, when I came back to go up the boulevard, I saw a woman on a bicycle. She was watching the sun on the water. One foot was on the ground, the other on a pedal. When she saw me she stared.

"She was not young. There were lines in her face. Her lipstick was put on badly. Her brown-reddish hair was dyed.

"'Do you live here?' she said in French.

"'Yes.'

"'Where?'

"'Up the boulevard.'

"'Are you alone?'

"'No,' I said.

"Again we were silent.

"She continued to look at the sun and the water on the Bassin. After a while I said, 'Do you live near here?'

"She was silent, sitting on her bicycle, looking at the Bassin. And remained silent. Then turned her face towards me.

"'I loved a German soldier.'"

Suddenly he left the room. And came back with his logbook and gave it to me. I wasn't interested in his logbook. And no one had done this to me before.

"Take it," he said.

And I did.

When I came back to the large top room of the house by the river, I looked through his logbook. It was so remote. What did interest me was that he had cut out part of a faded page from the *Daily Telegraph*. And glued it to the inside back cover of his logbook. It had the "Anniversaries (Births and Deaths)" for November 22. And it listed George Gissing, Charles de Gaulle, Benjamin Britten, Aldous Huxley. And two small black and white photographs of Mae West and John F. Kennedy.

Below them, he had written in ink, "Squadron Leader Albert Richardson."

Next day, when I went to return his logbook, I couldn't remember which house he was in. They all looked the same. So I went around to the backs of the houses. There was a drive area where cars could park and turn. And the far-end house had a conservatory. And, on the side of it and the house, a garden sloping upwards with a stone fence around it. And inside: flowers, vines, shrubs, and small trees. A woman was working in the garden. I asked her where did Albert Richardson live? She pointed to the back of a house. She had a pleasant and lively face.

The next time I saw her was in the main street. It was Wednesday, market day, and there were the stalls, and people walking by and buying things. We talked. And she invited me back for coffee.

Then she invited me for dinner. Ruth had been a farmer's wife. And we were on our own. When she realized that I didn't know this part of England, she said she would show it to me, starting with the North Yorkshire moors when the heather was out. Our favourite rivers were the Tees and the Wharfe. Her son had a farm about a half-hour's drive away from here. And when he had to be away for several days or more, we would go and stay on the farm and look after his sheep. It was very pleasant to walk in the country by a stream and see the farms; some had sheep, others cows. And, in late afternoon, Canada geese flying low, in a line across, as they flew to the reservoirs for the night.

Our favourite place, close by, is the reservoirs. Except they don't look like reservoirs. More like a series of small lakes—elongated in places, with the land coming into the water with grass and trees on the bottom slopes and sheep towards the top. And it is always still and quiet.

Ruth is the most generous person I have known. She buys me things that she thinks I need. And continues to take me to places that she thinks I should see. And does all kinds of things for other people. She is also a good cook. And we started to have our evening meals together. And morning coffee on Sunday. The one thing that upsets her is when someone tells her a lie.

Albert also has a lady friend. I saw them walking up the Bank, holding hands, tightly clenched, arms bent upwards at the elbow, the tops of their bodies leaning forward as if they were walking into a gale. Her name is Nellie, in her early eighties. She is small and delicate and always elegantly dressed. She invited me into her house. (It is near where I live. The back of her house also faces the Tees River.) The house is neat, spotless, and nicely furnished. But it was the watercolours on the walls that I noticed. They were of narrow streets in an old city, of parks, gardens, and by the sea. And portraits of people. I thought they were very good.

"Who did them?" I asked.

"I did. I went to the art school in York. I wanted to be an artist."

Next time I saw Albert on the Demesnes, he said, "Someone has a key to my front door. My clothes get stolen."

And I didn't believe him.

But a few days later, I found that three of my shirts that I bought in France were missing, also two sweaters. And when I was walking on the Demesnes, a woman walking her dog came towards me. She looked angry.

"I saw you talking to the wing commander. He came up to me and said, 'If it wasn't for people like me—you wouldn't be living in freedom.'"

I saw Albert on November 12. I was coming up the Bank and he was going down. He was wearing his Air Force uniform and cap and his greatcoat on top.

"I've just come back from London. I was at the Cenotaph. There are only three of us left. I won't go again."

A few weeks later, Sunday morning, I was having a coffee with Ruth, when we saw Albert at the back door. He was dressed in his officer's cap, his officer's tunic, shirt and tie. And he had his squadron leader's greatcoat on top. The only thing that was not part of the uniform was his trousers; they were civilian brown.

He sat in a chair. Ruth gave him some coffee. After a few minutes he said, "I've been asked to lead the parade."

I waited a while then said, "Where is the parade?"

He looked uncomfortable and mumbled. "In the south. It is in the south."

We didn't know what to say.

So we were all silent.

"I'll be in front," he said. "They will all have to follow me."

Again silence.

Then, brightening up, he said, "I'll probably get a gong for this."

He didn't stay long.

As soon as he left, Ruth and I decided to go to see his daughter. She runs a hotel in the country about a half-hour's drive away.

When we got there it was lunchtime. His daughter was busy in the kitchen. We talked to her husband. He went to see her. And when he came back he told us, "She arranged for a doctor to see him tomorrow morning."

I did see Nellie, several days later, walking up the Bank. "I put a get-well card through his door every day, but I don't have a reply. I went to the post office and posted one there so they would send it on."

"Do you know where his bank is?"

"No, I don't."

"Who is his best friend here?"

"You are."

Later a *For Sale* sign appeared by his house. Then the *Sold* sign. People disappear. And that's that.

KADDISH

(A Sketch towards a Portrait of Norman Levine)

"John...? Hello...?"

A voice familiar.

"Is that ..."

"It's Norman."

"Christ, Norman!"

Peering at the pulsing numerals.

"It's 4:13, Norman. It's dark."

"I'm in the Bassan."

"The *what*?"

"It's my mother's unveiling."

"*What*! What do you mean *Bassan*? What do you mean '*unveiling*'?"

"Well, that's it, you see ... And I was wondering ..."

* * *

Such tentative, wistful probes in other years came from Toronto, then France, then Yorkshire; a couple of weeks later Norman was ensconced with us in Ottawa as he usually was when visiting his mother. The "Bassan"—though why he couldn't have just named the town in the "Bassan" that he was calling from, I'd have recognized Andernos-les-Bains from our letters—

4:13 a.m.

The "Bassan" turned out to be the Bassin d'Arachon, the bay on the Garonne to the south of Bordeaux.

The mysterious "unveiling" turned out to be the central reason for his visit.

It is the Ashkenazi custom after a burial and the erection of a tombstone that there is held within a year a service of commemoration, a formal dedication, as it were, of the grave. The unveiling, often an "unveiling" merely symbolic, is the removal of a veil, cloth, or even a handkerchief from the tombstone by a designated family member.

The service itself is conducted by a rabbi and a cantor. It involves first the recitation of Psalms, most commonly chosen from among Psalms 1, 23, 24, and 103:

Blessed is the man that walketh not in the counsel of the ungodly, nor standeth in the way of sinners, nor sitteth in the seat of the scornful . . .

The Lord is my shepherd; I shall not want. He maketh me to lie down in green pastures; he leadeth me beside the still waters . . .

Who shall ascend into the hill of the Lord? or who shall stand in his holy place? He that hath clean hands, and a pure heart . . .

Bless the Lord, O my soul: and all that is within me, bless his holy name . . .

The Psalms are followed by the eulogy which is delivered by the rabbi. The veil is then removed. The cantor then sings the prayer *El Malei rachamim . . .*

God, full of compassion . . .

The service culminates in the Jewish mourners' prayer *Kaddish.*

Pressured and most probably harassed by an emotional and recriminatory sister and an even more outspoken niece (a prickly and tenuous relationship I avoided in conversation, a relationship soured, so I gathered, by the shame of Norman's lack of religious observance), suffering possibly from twinges of vestigial and filial guilt, suffering under the expectations of nephews, nieces, and cousins, from the assumptions of friends and acquaintances of his mother—and, as it later turned out, from sometime neighbours from Guigues Street, old school friends he scarcely remembered, members of the Golden Age Club, a doddery tailor from the Market and a seamed acquaintance from the Rideau Bakery, a cutter from Dworkin Furs, aged people unknown, pressured by the sheer *machinery* of the Jewish Community, Norman had returned to Ottawa to say *Kaddish*.

This observance, this prayer, this ritual unveiling, was fraught also with emotions unmentioned. I had gathered over the years that some part of the motivation for Norman's residence in England was a flight from his mother's dominance, a dominance that he felt threatened his sexual ability with women, his sexual being. The story "A Father" suggests that Norman feared becoming his father, the nebbish whose role was to fetch soft drinks and make sandwiches for the players, the card-players with money, the players with power, his wife among them.

"Let's hear you, then," said Myrna as we were sitting in the kitchen that first evening.

She passed him a prayer book.

Without looking at it, Norman briskly declaimed.

התכלמ דילמיו .התוערכ ארב־יד אמלעב אבר המש שדקתיו לדגתי
.ןמא ורמאו .בירק ןמזבו אלגעב לארשי תיב־לכד ייחבו ןוכימויבו ןוכייחב

Glorified and sanctified be God's great name throughout the world which He has created according to His will.

May he establish His Kingdom in your lifetime and during your days, and within the life of the entire House of Israel, speedily and soon; and say, Amen.

"Go on," she said.

Norman frowned at the page.

"Um …" he said.

* * *

Norman was telling me an anecdote typically full of relentless digression. I wasn't following closely. Smoke from his cigarillo as he gestured. He raised his scotch.

"This is very nice," he said.

"It's only *Ballantine's*," I said.

"No. I meant the glass. I like the weight of it."

What I was really thinking about was his boots. Not ankle boots but short or half-boots. Polished leather. In good repair. I was thinking how much "Englishness" he'd absorbed in his years there. He was always neatly dressed, dapper, formal almost. I was thinking that in England, still, shoes were perhaps *the* class indicator. A grubby suit or trousers held up with an old tie told little but shoes told nearly everything.

When Norman became a pilot officer he was sent to Quebec City to take what he used to call "gentleman lessons." In the short story "In Quebec City" he wrote: "We were instructed how to use knives and forks. How to make a toast. How to eat and drink properly. It was like going to finishing school."

(One cannot usually read fiction with any assumption that it is autobiographical. Norman's stories, however, are unusual in that invention is not his real interest; a little judicious rearrangement is often as far as he's prepared to go. Michael Winter told Natalee Caple in *The Notebooks* interview: "I asked Norman Levine this question. About why his protagonists are always writers. And he said he's not interested in making things up. I feel the same."

Norman was a man of contradictions. He certainly never repudiated his Jewish identity but at the same time he resented some of the circumstances of his life. In the story "A Father" he describes a photo of his father taken in Warsaw.

"There is a picture of my father that is still around the house in Ottawa. It shows a youngish, handsome man with a magnificent moustache, waxed ends; a fine head with black wavy hair and eyes that I know to be brown. That picture was taken in Warsaw. And to it belong the anecdotes: 'Man about Town'; 'Friend of writers and painters' ('Yes, I knew writers. I used to buy them meals.'); Owner of a shoe concern ('You can always tell if the leather's good by the way it creases.'); and 'Smuggler'—I'd like to think it was of diamonds.

I never knew that man.

The person I got to know in Ottawa was in his early forties, a fruit peddler. Slightly built, bald, with a sardonic face."

A fruit peddler with "a heavy white horse with nicotine-coloured tufts, and a delicate slow walk."

James Atlas wrote in *Bellow: A Biography*:

"For immigrant Jews, life in America, especially in the early years of their transplantation, was difficult, perplexing, even shameful. Aran [Saul Bellow's father] was a proud man who—in his own estimation—had lost status. In Russia, he had considered himself a gentleman; in America, he was a labourer. Like his wife, he felt he'd come down in the world."

Norman felt much the same way and often talked about the French Canadians they lived amongst and did business with in the Market in those days. They were generally considered by the Jews, he used to say, as bumpkins, hopeless rubes.

He concludes *Canada Made Me* with these words:

"I wondered why I felt so bitter about Canada. After all, it was all part of a dream, an experiment that could not come off. It was foolish to believe that you can take the throwouts, the rejects, the human kickabouts from Europe and tell them: Here you have a second chance. Here you can start a new life. But no one ever mentioned the price one had to pay; how much of oneself you had to betray."

These words cost him dearly. McClelland and Stewart had taken 500 copies of the British edition published by Putnam.

Jack McClelland, however, refused to put his name on the book, refused to issue the book under the McClelland and Stewart imprint. The 500 copies quickly sold out but Jack McClelland refused to import more.

After the 500 copies were gone, Levine said, "I realized that Canadian publishing was closed to me." He remained unpublished in Canada for the next seventeen years.

* * *

While he never wished to repudiate his Jewish identity—after all, it formed the subject matter of his life's work—he was at times ambivalent. England, the RCAF, and officer status in the most glamorous branch of the Armed Forces offered him a more sophisticated and expansive life than the house on Guigues Street with a stable off the kitchen for Jim, the horse with "nicotine-coloured tufts." For while Norman was the son of a rather ineffectual fruit peddler, a man whom life had brought low, he was also a pilot/navigator flying Lancasters out of Yorkshire over Germany, one of those the British affectionately and gratefully had called "the Brylcreem Boys."

After the war he entered McGill taking a B.A. in 1948 and an M.A. in 1949. He then returned to England where he dithered for a while at Kings College of London University beginning to write on Ezra Pound. (He once said to me that after hearing recordings of what Pound had been spewing he had no more stomach for the man. He did finish the thesis, however, and submitted it to T.S. Eliot at Faber and Faber. He showed me Eliot's courteous letter of rejection; Eliot observed that academic theses always seemed have trouble evolving into books of general interest.)

That Levine had chosen Pound is of considerable significance given his subsequent intentions and inventions and the progression of his artistic career.

Norman married a Gentile, lived in St. Ives for forty years, and had little contact with Jewish life or belief. In St. Ives, dependent on magazine payments, the vagaries of royalties, occasional school-mastering, Norman was chronically short of money and sometimes applied to Mordecai Richler in London for loans. Mordecai at the time was writing film scripts and was reasonably flush. He told me that Norman would request loans of such sums as £53, 3s., 3d.—the exact food or heating bills he owed—and that these loans were always repaid.

Other friends, too, used to worry about his financial straits. The painter Francis Bacon sometimes took care-packages down to St. Ives, food hampers and treats for the children. Once while Norman was thanking him profusely, Bacon, probably embarrassed by the gratitude, interrupted him saying, "I don't come down here to see *you*. I come to fuck sailors."

But impoverished or not, Norman was fastidious about what he would or would not write. In Ottawa, years earlier, I was chatting to someone after a reading while waiting for Norman to finish up. He was talking to a man in a dark suit.

"Who was that?"

"It was the son—I think he said Bertram—the oldest son—do you know Loeb's grocery store downtown?—he's the son of Moses Loeb."

"A fan?"

"Do you know," said Norman in scandalized tone, "what he said to me? He wanted me to write the history of the store and the biography of the family."

"*Hoo-hooo!*" I said. "Pots of money there, Norman. You could set yourself up for ages."

For Norman, being an artist was a priestly vocation. His face took on an expression of pain and distaste as if he'd been accosted in a public lavatory.

I winced inwardly.

"So what did you say?"

In a low voice, he said, "I told him that that isn't the sort of writing I do."

Myrna was becoming frustrated by our sitting around drinking scotch and smoking cigarillos and yakking. Myrna wanted to get him *organized*. As a boy in Ottawa, Norman would probably have spoken English mainly, perhaps a few words of Polish. What Hebrew he would have learned for his bar mitzvah would have been learned by rote and doubtless swiftly forgotten.

(He claimed that, growing up, his main language had been Yiddish. In Robert H. Michel's excellent *CNQ* article, Levine is credited with claiming that "Until school, his first language had been Yiddish." What is meant by the word "school"? He left school at sixteen and worked as a clerk in a government office so he must have been working in English as his French, to the best of my knowledge, was non-existent. "School," therefore, must mean primary school and the years at home subsequent to that. "Until school" seems to imply up to the age of Grade One—five or six years old. Yet when Myrna spoke to him using words and phrases of "kitchen" Yiddish it was obvious he had no idea of what she was saying.

Another odd contradiction.

(There is much about Norman that suggests there were several of him, that "Norman Levine" was a shifting invention.)

Myrna was still trying to get him through the first line of the second verse, the response of the congregation.

:אימלע ימלעלו סלעל ךרבמ אבר המש אהי

May His great Name be blessed for ever and ever.

"Now, Norman," she said. "The first part—*May His great Name*—sounds like this:
Y'hei sh'mei rabbaw . . .
Now, can you repeat that?"

"*Y'hei* ..." he said.

"*sh'mei rabbaw*," she repeated.

Norman was not an apt pupil.

"Again."

The unveiling was but three days away.

*   *   *

I am not at my best before or during breakfast. I am civil and dutiful but not exactly affable. After sleep, I like to re-enter the world quietly and in silence, preferably while reading the newspaper in which I have no particular interest. These days I find myself doing little more than mentally copy-editing it and supplying for the words which spell-checking had accepted the words actually intended.

Norman, on the other hand, chattered; sometimes positively gibbered. The phrase "stream of consciousness" might have been invented to describe his unending flow. He was inexhaustible with tiny enthusiasms. The tartness of home-made marmalade, that Apostle spoon beside the dish of marmalade, hallmarks on silver, hallmarks in general, "*there has to be a leopard's head on it*," bread in France, Poilâne bread, croissants, "*you must have French butter in the croissants because it has a higher fat content*," the patina on the pewter wine-measure on the mantelpiece, the thumb-piece on the wine-measure handle and lid a pair of acorns, acorns as feed for pigs that produced an extra-delicious ham that Anne bought in Andernos-les-Bains, "*It comes from Spain.*"

Moira Dale, companion of his last years, said to me in Yorkshire years later, "Everything's a little excitement to him. He's like a child."

On the third day of his visit, I got up early, went out and bought croissants for breakfast on Elgin Street—not Parisian, unfortunately, but Japanese from Boko Bakery. Then I bought two copies of the *Globe and Mail*.

Andernos-les-Bloody Bains, I thought, *in the bloody Bassan*.

When Norman came downstairs, I said, "Thought you'd like the paper," and returned to reading mine.

Moments later, in a move I had not foreseen, he started to read from his *aloud*.

There was in those days a small column headed *Nota Bene*. After some rustling, he suddenly said, "Not a beeny! What does *that* mean!"

I glanced up to see if he were attempting ponderous humour.

It seemed he wasn't.

I was astounded.

Although Norman had two degrees in English and then had done further degree work at Kings College, he never made any reference to matters which such an academic background would have made entirely familiar, the daily furniture of the mind. Not only that, I cannot remember his ever talking about books at all. He never asked me about my own writing, never chatted about any of the young writers I was publishing at the Porcupine's Quill.

Thinking of this, I realized that he had probably never read such writers as Anthony Powell, Kingsley Amis, Beryl Bainbridge, Muriel Spark, and such . . . and almost certainly not Eudora Welty, Richard Yates, Raymond Carver, and, say, Ann Beattie.

(The only literary comment I recall his ever making concerned Mordecai Richler's comment on Margaret Laurence. When she was living near London and beginning to publish—*This Side Jordan*, *The Tomorrow-Tamer*, *The Stone Angel*—Norman asked Mordecai what this new writer was like. Replied Mordecai, "An innocent.")

In contradiction to the Norman Levine who chattered was the *very* unchildlike Norman Levine who spoke not at all. When I began to think about *Nota Bene* and his literary absence, as it were, I came to the conclusion that he had cut himself off from contemporary literature in a quite deliberate way. He lived in St. Ives, a remote and difficult part of England to get to. Mordecai Richler had chosen London (and, earlier, Paris), London and casual journalism, and film scripts. Norman had turned his back on such worldly frivolity. He had lived—*implacably* was the only word—to create, at whatever cost, what he was creating. This endeavour consumed him. He did not concern himself with the artistic aspirations and achievements of others. What mattered to him was to perfect—*implacably*—his version of high modernism.

* * *

Myrna was losing patience.

"But Norman," she said, "when you arrived you rattled off the opening without even looking at the book."

"I got it from a book that had that verse in Roman alphabet ..."

"Well, I'm going to have to do the same thing," she said. "There's simply no time. Transliterate, I mean."

"My sister sent it," he said. "*Judaism in Family Life* it was called."

"Hardly kosher, is it?" I said. "Transliterating."

She gave me a look.

"But actually he's got a point, Norman. The rabbi's ultra orthodox."

"Severe," I said. "Intolerant. Suits in need of dry cleaning. Unwordly."

"Be," said Myrna, "*ultra* discreet."

"Cunning," I said. "*Monstrous* secrecy!"

"Roger!" said Norman.

That evening she rummaged in the junk drawer at the end of the bookcase and found her silver propelling pencil and a Staedtler eraser and settled to work. I watched her. Half-listening to Norman's account of a dinner party in Toronto at which

Elizabeth Smart appeared with a shopping bag containing full bottles of gin, scotch and vodka in case the hostess's provision proved meagre and some sad detail about her offering later in the shared taxi to suck Norman's thumb, I watched the fall of Myrna's hair, watched light glinting on the silver pencil.

We had bought the pencil at Antiques on High, an arcade of tiny boutiques in a building on The High in Oxford. I had bought myself a silver letter opener. The pencil was Edwardian from the look of it, very slim, elegant, at a guess originally nestled next to the spine of a leather-bound diary or address book. The knob at the end was *quatrefoil*; it was always the archaic usage *knop* that came to mind. At my brother's house we'd polished the pencil and letter opener with Goddard's Silver Polish.

Short weeks later after we'd returned to Canada, my mother died; she had been nearing one hundred and five. That morning of the pencil-buying we had been to see her in the nursing home.

Her hands gripped the arms of the wheelchair.

With eyes rendered sightless by macular degeneration she gazed down the bedroom's length.

Tapping the back of her hand, the orderly said, "Here your son."

I stooped towards the useless hearing aid.

"John? Is that you, John?"

I squeezed her hand.

"I have bad news," she said. "Your brother is a wanted man."

"Really?"

"He is being hunted by the police. He beat Dorothy for her behaviour. On her posterior. When she visited me, she was unable to sit down."

"Really!"

"I am sorry to tell you that Dorothy gave birth last night to a child not your brother's."

"Good heavens!"

My brother is an internationally famous numismatist and historian of matters medieval with vast expertise also in Anglo-Saxon and Viking coinage and trade routes. His most recent work had been three volumes on the White Bezants and Deniers of the Frankish Kingdom of Guy de Lusignan in Cyprus. Now retired, he had been for many years the Keeper of the Heberden Coin Room of the Ashmolean museum. He and Dorothy were in their seventies.

"And now both are dead."

"*Surely not!*"

"She was walking along the verge on that M-road with the baby in her arms when they were struck by a lorry. I washed the bodies, of course, and laid them out in Lime Street Methodist Church and sat in vigil all night. But your *poor* brother!"

The story as it progressed grew more vivid. I was becoming hoarse with shouting denials into her hearing aid. Filipino staff were gawking through the open doorway. Myrna was pulling faces. A soul some doors away was wailing repeatedly: *I wish to go home! Summon a taxi! Summon a taxi!*

"This afternoon," I bellowed, "we're going to walk in the grounds at Blenheim. You know! Capability Brown and ... oh, *fuck!*"

"John!" said Myrna.

"A sandwich?" said my mother.

She lifted her face in the vague direction of mine.

"Well, I *am* surprised!"

In The White Horse I sat in silence drinking a double gin and tonic and watching a man playing a slot machine. Light flickered through decorative numbers on the machine's plastic body. On a central boss:

CASH

£70.00

CASH

Into the wooden trough the occasional PLUNK PLUNK of one-pound coins.

Suddenly a burst of lights.

A trumpet fanfare.

A robotic voice.

WIN WIN WIN

* * *

When he returned from his sister's the next afternoon, he was uncharacteristically agitated.

"She gave them to the Salvation Army," he said coming in.

"Pardon?"

"My mother. Two Bernard Leach mugs I sent her. My sister says she gave them to the Salvation Army! And *she* drove her there!"

"Well, perhaps," I said, "she—they—didn't know, you know. What they were."

"His early stoneware," he said.

"Oh, dear ..."

"Have you *been*," he said, "to this Kanata?"

I nodded.

"The Salvation Army!"

Later, when he'd calmed down a bit, he said, "But at least I've saved these."

"Who is it?"

"Well it's not Alfred Wallis but it's another St. Ives—how would you say—a naïf ..."

He passed me the two small framed paintings from the carrier bag. They were behind dusty glass, about thirteen and a half inches by ten, thereabouts.

"My sister had put them in the cupboard under the sink in the kitchen."

Ships, a harbour, a breakwater. The other a clipper under full sail.

I looked at them and then tilted the glass. They were on paper. On pimpled paper something like wallpaper. Crude reproductions.

"I *think*, Norman, I *think* these are possibly reproductions."

"*What!*"

"Maybe cut from a magazine or ..."

He took it from my hands.

He stared at it.

I said, "It's maybe—difficult to see—some sort of photogravure."

"But I was sure ..."

"Well, there's a framer down on Elgin. He'll take the back off for you. Tell him you're staying with me."

I watched him walking across the park with the carrier bag.

Another odd contradiction.

Norman had spent all those years in St. Ives living among the painters there—painters in their early years largely unappreciated, in their later years honoured and shown internationally, their importance eventually given national and international imprimatur in the form of a St. Ives gallery of their work in the Tate Britain.

Norman was in and out of the studios looking at the work of Peter Lanyon, Terry Frost, Patrick Heron, Bryan Wynter, and Roger Hilton and on some evenings, a beer or two and conversation in The Sloop.

(Few people in Canada know that Levine arranged the tour in Canada in 1955-56 of the exhibition *Six Painters from Cornwall* and wrote the accompanying catalogue.)

In certain ways, if we don't push the analogy too far, Levine was the literary counterpart of the painters. His mature work is marked by its fragmentation, unorthodox grammar, and denial of cadence, Pound's influence reverberating on and on.

* * *

The front doorbell rang.

Norman handed me the carrier bag.

In the kitchen, I held up a glass.

He nodded.

"You were right," he said.

Was it on this Unveiling visit or an earlier one? Certainly while he was living in France. In my unreliable memory for dates, it was an earlier visit. His marriage to Anne Sarginson was unravelling. He talked rather haltingly about the situation; Norman never wore his heart upon his sleeve.

He had showed me then two Peter Lanyon sketches, pencil, a few strokes in India ink, a dash of watercolour. They'd been torn from a wirebound pad. He was going to try to sell them in London on his way back to France. Lanyon had given them to him in the late fifties.

"When you know the paintings," I said, "*these*, well if you know *Cross Country* or *Offshore*, say, or *Silent Coast* ..."

"She used to be proud of being married to a Jew," he said. "Once we were on a train and she was talking to the conductor and she said, 'Nous sommes juifs.'"

I nodded.

"She thought it was romantic being a writer, being a Jew, being married to a writer," he said, "but there was only the pension ..."

I nodded again.

"Now she holds it against me. The money."

I sighed.

He fell silent.

"So now she's denied me ..."

He made a sudden dismissive gesture; the confidences had ended; the silence grew uncomfortable.

"So," he said, sliding the sketches back into the manila envelope. "This is what I'm forced to."

Years later than these events Myrna and I were pottering about in London near where Clifford Street meets New

Bond Street. We'd just bought a Liberian Dan-N'gere Poro Society mask from the Gordon Reece Gallery. Further down Clifford Street I saw a gallery with a Peter Lanyon painting in the window.

Behind a black glass desk sat a young woman with haughty tits.

"The Lanyon?" she repeated.

She consulted a Lucite binder.

"Fifty-four thousand pounds," she said.

"Good Lord!"

"Plus," she said, "VAT."

*   *   *

"Just put everything in this garbage bag," said Myrna. "I'll sort 589 it out later. No, not the maps. We're bound to get lost."

MapArt's *Ontario Road Atlas*. Rand McNally Canada Inc's *Ottawa Hull*.

Norman stood keeping the spare tire balanced upright with his right-hand fingertips.

"Do you want the vacuum cleaner?"

"No. Get the vacuum-gun-thing. That'll do."

Myrna's plan was to turn in the old car and pick up the newly leased one before the ceremony. She'd completed all the forms and credit-check bumph days before.

The dealership was glass and chrome and brushed steel. On the forecourt on an inclined plinth shaped like a wing or a spearhead they'd posed a glittering car. Myrna was talking to a generic golf-player in an Italian-cut suit. I riffled through a display of fat brochures. Over at the counter, smiles, ballpoint pens. I'd never learned to drive, never gave any thought to cars. Air freshener permeated. Myrna rummaging in her purse. I found myself wondering how much the colour separations for the brochure would have cost. Thought of telling Norman the Frankie Howerd monologue line about visiting a pneumatic travel agent *I've come to look at your brochures—* pause—*yer tours,* but humour often seemed to pass Norman by.

The only funny story of Norman's I could think of, and that not exactly a thigh-slapper, was "My Karsh Picture." And following from this somehow, I found myself thinking about Norman's poetry collections, *Myssium, The Tight-Rope Walker, I walk by the harbour* and how generally awful they were. As was the poetry of Katherine Mansfield; as was the poetry of Ernest Hemingway; as was the poetry of James Joyce—four stellar prose writers who simply couldn't write a line that lived.

Odd.

"Pardon?"

"He's just changing over the plates," said Myrna, leading us onto the forecourt.

"Oh, smell the smell," said Norman, "the new-leather smell."

"They spray it on," said Myrna.

"Does it handle differently?" I asked.

"Heavier," she said.

She was finicking with the rearview mirror.

"We're far too early," she said. "Let's loop round and take Norman to Cedarview."

"Oh, look, Norman! Canada geese! Hundreds of the buggers."

Picking and gleaning in the stubble.

"The yellow corn stalks and then the black. Their necks," he said. "The black. It's just like those flowers, isn't it? And their heads."

"Pardon?"

"The geese are like the black bit in the middle."

"Ahhh ..."

"Do you know the ones I mean?"

"Well, I'm not *entirely* ..."

"Anne," he said, "now Anne knows the names of all the flowers and all the trees and even the birds in the Bassan but it's the *people*. I'm more interested in the people. There was an old waitress ..."

"Here we are," said Myrna. "Now cast your eye over this lot, Norman."

Cedarview was like a park-cum-golf course, an enclave giving the impression of "gated community" though there were no gates. It was a bloated subdivision studded with grossly vulgar travesties of architecture. Monster Homes on Mown Monster Lots. Spire, turret, widow's walk, portico, pilaster, Corinthian capital-crowned-column, entablature and architrave, protruding air-conditioning units, lead-latticed windows, integral four-car garages beside the front doors.

"But this is *awful*!" said Norman.

"Oh, sod it!" said Myrna as the car lurched through a water-filled pothole.

"But funny," I said.

"Bloody mud on my car!" said Myrna.

"You know," I said, "it was Betjeman who was the first ..."

"Do you know what Betjeman's famous for?" said Norman. "His teeth. His teeth were *green*."

"*I* was going to say," I said, "that Betjeman was the first to find bad buildings funny."

*   *   *

The car wash was a sway-back clapboard structure listing under the Scotch pines at the end of the disintegrating concrete pad. A sandwich board on the edge of the ditch bore an arrow pointing inwards and the words OPEN and McLEODS FRIES.

"It'll only take a minute or two," said Myrna.

She read the instructions and pressed the green button.

Advertisements on tin for Coca-Cola.

"Collectibles."

I was just pointing out Millais' rusting *Bubbles* on an advertisement for Pears Soap when the car checked and rending metal screamed. Her side-view mirror had somehow engaged with projecting angle iron. She turned the ignition on again and lowered the window; the mirror dangled on wires. She tried to close the window but something had buckled leaving a three-inch gap along the top.

As the brushes spun nearer, I said, "Cover the gap! Use the Rand McNally! *Now!* Open it to the middle and jam it ..."

"There's no need to shout."

"I am NOT shouting!"

"I don't know what's got into you!"

I was trying to read through the steam.

I shoved her over towards the window, pointing to the small uncovered gap.

"USE THE OTHER MAP AS WELL!"

"*Rude!*"

Rivulets of water, drops, chasing up and off the windscreen.

I tried not to think of mirror on threads as eyeball on cheek.

Ignoring her "finer-feelings-offended" face.

Jab-jabbing with my forefinger towards the notice.

"*Hotfuckingwax!*"

*   *   *

"Are you my Uncle Norman?"

"No," I said, "that's Norman over there talking to that lady."

"I've got new gloves."

He held out both fists. Difficult to tell how old he was. What, eighteen, maybe twenty? He'd been dollied up in a suit and a floral tie and a three-quarter-length dressy overcoat.

"And there's a secret. Inside they're stuffed with rabbit."

He turned back the wrists to show me. I stroked the fur lining with a fingertip.

"*Very* nice," I said. "That makes them *very* special."

A solemn nodding.

A to-do amongst the ladies around Norman's sister. We drifted over.

"*Are* you his uncle?"

Norman shook his head ... His mouth shaped words but no sound came out. Shook his head again and spread his hands in a denial of responsibility, culpability, connection to this cemetery, these people.

"So what's going on?"

"It's the grave," said Norman. "No one can remember where it was."

"...definitely this row."

"...in line with that tree ..."

"...more with that gate. That's what *I* remember."

"I know!" said Norman. "Perhaps she's buried under Gurwitz. Annie Gurwitz!"

"All these years, said one of the ladies, "I thought it was spelled 'Gur-evich.' Shows you what *I* know!""You'd *know* it was Levine," said Norman's niece, "If you'd made the effort to attend."

"It wasn't a question of effort," said Norman. "I was in France and ..."

"Or contributed," she added, "to the cost of the stone."

"I was in France," said Norman, "and I hadn't the wherewithal to come to Canada."

"'Wherewithal," sneered his niece.

I touched Myrna's arm and we moved away.

Norman's sister was holding at her thigh a loosely-gathered blue and white homemade banner-thing emblazoned with the Star of David. Satiny-looking. It hung by big wooden curtain rings along a gold-painted rod. For the unveiling, I assumed. She was holding it by the rod. That, and the angle against her thigh, I thought for a second of a *muleta*.

A crow raucous on a dead branch. I stood looking at the top edges of tombstones. Many were crowded with pebbles. This, too, was an Ashkenazi folk-custom. It was a sight that always moved me, a custom simple and heartfelt and un-undertakerly.

Myrna started humming the tune.

"*Please,* Myrna."

It was *Shir Ha-Palmach*, one of the Palmach marching songs.

From Mettulah to the Negev
From the sea to the desert
All young men to arms ...

Once she'd started, the tune, half-sensed, would be there all day like the linger of spearmint on the air or Juicy Fruit; intermittently the *words* would erupt.

"*Please.*"

People visiting graves—wives, husbands, children, friends— left the pebbles, pebbles picked up from the walkways.

The pebbles say
I hold you in my mind always
Do you remember ...
I love you

I looked up at the commotion as the mourners fanned out along the gravel paths in search of the grave.

Weiman	Michaels	Federman
Kaell	Weiss	Charney
Fishman	Perel	Wise
Miller	Katzman	Kaplan
Stein	Zichermann	Lipshitz

"Do you want to help, Robert?" said one of the ladies. "Help find Annie's headstone?"

He nodded and trailed behind them.

We trailed behind the three of them.

People began hurrying from headstone to headstone. Mild hysteria seemed to be setting in. Robert started scurrying along the paths, stooped at random headstones, pumped his arm in the air in the manner of athletes on TV.

"Go, Annie!" he shouted. "Annie, go!"

Each of his discoveries proved a disappointment.

"Robert!" called one of the ladies. "This is a cemetery. You have to show some respect!"

His face turned bright red.

He stopped and deliberately hung back, then with his coat sleeve swept the pebbles from the top of the headstone.

"Fuckin' A," shouted Robert sweeping off other pebbles.

575

Hochberg   Rosenfeld
Jacobson   Passman

"Bernice! *Bernice!*"

Stopped sweeping with his filthy sleeve.

Stood weighing a pebble.

"*Bernice!* He's swearing and throwing stones at us!"

Bernice—his mother? Surely too old?—hurried over. Robert retreated behind a headstone.

"Here!" said Bernice, pointing at the path at her feet.

The smack across his face sounded vicious.

He sat on the path moaning and weeping.

"Annie," he sobbed, "Annie."

He pulled at the knot of his tie.

"Over here," waved an old man with a walker. "Right the way down here!"

An immediate drift began.

"There's rabbi," someone said.

The cantor, I assumed, and the rabbi, *tzitzis*, a sweat-stained fedora.

Robert sat on the path and cried more or less silently and continued burying his floral tie with gravel.

* * *

The rabbi flanked by Norman on one side and the cantor on the other faced the semi-circle of mourners.

"It's Psalm 24," whispered Myrna.

The Star of David banner-thing stirred in the breeze.

The *yarmulke* was causing me great anxiety; the bloody thing was always sliding off the back of my head and I cursed myself for forgetting to bring hairgrips.

Hairgrips. I found myself thinking that the words I inhabit, that inhabit me, would be unknown now to the young. *Kirby grips* they'd been called in my boyhood and youth, bronze-coloured, six on a card, and in America, *bobby pins* . . .

"Now it's Psalm 103."

The rabbi then delivered a lame eulogy mentioning Annie Gurwitz's activities and many friends at the Golden Age Club, her knitting, her green thumb, her renown at euchre and casino, her kindness to fellow-residents at the Retirement Home—

Who among us having partaken of her bounty will ever forget her cholent, her brisket like a dream . . .

Then the contentious niece unveiled the headstone, wrinkling upwards the banner-thing.

Following *this,* the cantor sang *El Malei Rachamim*
God, full of compassion
The Moorish cadences plangent.

It was with the recitation of *Kaddish* that the day became indelible in memory. Only film could have captured the full pleasures of the proceedings. And perhaps only one actor/director could have created the flow of movements and moods. The film is black and white. The actor/director (d. 1982) is

Jacques Tati. The template for my film is that homage to Buster Keaton, Tati's *Monsieur Hulot's Holiday* (1953).

The scene from *Les Vacances de Monsieur Hulot* that Norman's unveiling brought to mind was Monsieur Hulot changing a tire. His car has stopped beside a cemetery where a funeral is taking place. Monsieur Hulot's inner tube bowls away from him, he madly chasing. The tube, picking up sticky leaves as it goes, wheels into the funeral proceedings. An officious mourner, thinking it a wreath, hangs it on the cross above the grave where, hissing audibly during the obsequies, it steadily deflates.

My inadequate film would open with a high dolly shot—the grave, the semicircle of mourners—tracking down onto the cantor, Norman, the rabbi...

The cantor fell silent.

The rabbi looked up at the gravel sounds as the mourners grouped themselves more closely. He raised his prayer book an inch or so above his waist like a baton, turned slightly and inclined his head towards Norman. Then rabbi, Norman, cantor, and the mourners launched into *Kaddish*.

Norman's voice was distinct because halting and humdrum; he had no knowledge of cadence, modulation, inflection, the musical pleasures I thought of as "the twiddly bits." I resolved to look up—what would you call it? *Prosody? psalmody?*

"...and say, Amen," proclaimed Norman belatedly.

Myrna squeezed my hand making her *"Ere-we-go!* face" as they moved into the next line.

The rabbi was looking at Norman.

Pecking glances.

Muffled mercifully somewhat by the staggered recitations of the doddery mourners, Norman stumbled on.

rhubarb rhubarb rhubarb

Then the rabbi—puzzled? unhappy?—moved closer and was blatantly trying to look over Norman's shoulder at Norman's prayer book; Norman shielded it with humped shoulder and edged away. The rabbi followed. The cantor followed the rabbi. With each of the trio's advances, the mourners drew away, giving them space.

I found the morning's events deliciously funny and satisfying but had Jacques Tati been filming, the sequence would have had exquisite pacing and the inevitability of a piece of extremely expensive machinery at work and would have been inbued with feelings that would have haunted one for years.

Tati made only five feature films in his career. Following *Jour de fête* came the three great "Hulot" films, *Les Vacances, Mon Oncle,* and *Trafic.* The *Oxford Dictionary of Biography* refers to Tati as "internationally known as a comic actor"; the *Penguin Encyclopedia* describes him as "the greatest film comedian of the post-war period" while the *Concord Encyclopdia* describes the "Hulot" films as "comic film masterpieces"; producers and investors came to hate him for his money-squandering pursuit of perfection.

I imagined Tati filming the unveiling as a kind of dance, a dance with the formality—albeit a somewhat grubby formality—of a *pavane.* That sweat-stained fedora! The horrid beard! With the mourners something like a chorus of urban Jewish versions of Silence, Shallow, Shadow, Doll, and Feeble.

Unfocussed thoughts of *Henry V* and *Under Milk Wood.*
rhubarb rhubarb rhubarb
At last, *at last,* it came to an end.
"…and say, Amen."
Cantor, Norman, and rabbi had performed more than half a circuit of the grave.

* * *

Har gow!
Shu mai!
Ginger squid!
The girls pushed the carts of *dim sum* along the aisles; we'd caught the tail end of lunch at the *Yangtze*.

The waitress clunked down three bottles of *Tsingtao*.

"It's pronounced something like 'Ching-dow.'"

"It smells," said Norman, "just like apples!"

"It's Chinese but the brewmasters are German."

"Oh, *then*," said Norman, "*Prosit!*"

Fry noodles!
Sticky rice!
The sticky-rice packages always gave me a quiet pleasure, the colour of the leaves, the fact that they *were* leaves— banana?—the yellow raffia that tied the solidity of the green packages.

"The yellow with the black in the middle," said Norman, "there's a song …"

"Pardon?"

I glanced at Myrna.

Perhaps catching the glance, he said, "The Canada geese."

"What do you mean?"

"It has a banjo in it."

Chopsticks and shrimp arrested mid-air, I stared.

"You mean," said Myrna, "that the Canada geese in the corn field remind you of a flower that's yellow with a black centre and there's a song with the name of the flower in it— and a banjo."

Norman nodded encouragingly as she made each point.

Setting down her glass of *Tsingtao*, she sang,
Oh, Susannah,
Oh don't you cry for me
For I come from Alabama
With a banjo on my knee.

"How do you know that!"

"We used to sing it at camp when we were kids."

"Black-eyed Susans," I said.

"Rudbeckia," said Myrna.

Norman beamed.

"Isn't it all," spreading his arms expansively, "isn't it all *jolly.*"

John Metcalf
Ottawa 2017